Tara: Legend of the Earth
Book One

By Taya Raine

First Edition 2022
Published by
Tara Teachings Publishing
Hawaii, USA

By Taya Raine
tayaraine.com

Original Cover Art, Illustrations
& Design by Kai Wilder ©
www.kaiwilder.com & @kaiwilderart

First Edition
First Printing, 2022

ISBN: 978-1-0879-5444-8

TABLE of CONTENTS

To my beloved children: Kumara, Naia, Yama and
Yamuna… and my twin flame…
love you forever and ever.

Tara: Legend of the Earth
Book One

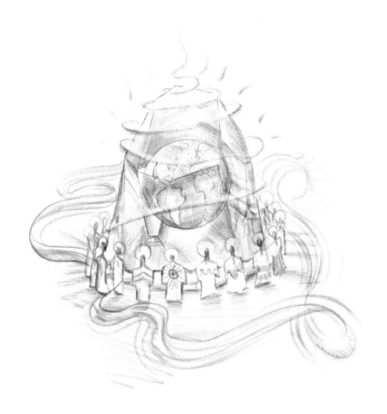

CHAPTER ONE

Not Alone

At ease in the passenger seat of my best-friend's little blue sports-car, I reclined my seat, smiling, as I absorbed the lush beauty of the forest canopy above; grateful for the warmth of spring and the little convertible that had taken us on so many adventures. Julia sped along the familiar back-county roads and winding coastal passes toward Stinson beach, (an hour from our hometown Santa Rosa, not far from San Francisco), her beautiful long curly red hair blowing in the wind. In the back seat our dear friend Alexis held her arms up, dancing with the wind as she sang along with Bob Marley's 'No Woman No Cry'.

Julia tapped her fingers lightly on the steering wheel. I laughed out loud, so happy to be with my two dearest friends. There was something so harmonious about our time together, as though we floated in a place just outside of 'reality'.

As we pulled into the parking lot, I gazed contentedly at Stinson's endless golden sandy beach, feeling a sense of freedom that expanse always brought and a tug of excitement.

As she pulled the car to a stop; we smiled at each other, excited for the adventure ahead. Hopping out of the car I stretched my arms, breathing in the fresh, salty air.

Julia hopped out and tied a sweater around her waist asking,

"Anyone hungry yet?"

I shrugged, "I could wait."

"Let's walk first," Alexis offered, crawling out of the back seat.

We linked arms, walking in unison along the shore; headed towards the towards a section of beach towards the far end, where massive rocks jutted skyward. Allowing the waves to wash over our bare feet, each of us grinning ear to ear with sheer pleasure. The late morning sun felt so good on my skin, and the way it sparkled on the crashing waves filled me with aliveness.

The morning crowd had already filled in the beach. Many staring eyes on us was so common, we paid it no mind. We three born with beauty, whose young adult vitality drew much attention. We drew more attention when together; yet it was so much more comfortable then being watched on my own. There was some kind of empowerment that came from being with two beautiful friends, a support in the knowing that being watched was something we are all used to. I loved that for me there was no thrill in being so admired or probed as it were by onlookers. Knowing that my friends held the same kind of humility not always present with model perfect women, was deeply comforting to me.

Minutes later we arrived at the massive rocks. We stood unlinking arms. I stretched my arms, gazing up at the huge rock in front of us. We had daringly climbed just about every rock in sight over the past year, always set on reaching the top only to gaze out towards the horizon feeling the thrill of victory.

Alexis pointed up at the looming cliffs that lead to the winding coastal highway above the long stretch of beach.

"We've never climbed those." Alexis offered suggestively, already breaking into a run.

I smiled at Julia knowingly, excitement building within me. Ahead, Alexis was already beginning to climb. Moving quickly, focused on whatever goal she had already set her mind to. I laughed; running after her thinking the way Alexis climbed was just the way she approached everything, determined, and extremely willful. I turned to look back at Julia who was grinning knowingly. Julia had become the easy-going one; always relaxed, just going along for the experience.

I turned to the massively tall and steep cliff, accessing a path upward as I stretched my hamstrings, still sore from last night's work out, but grateful for the strength they provided for climbing. Pulling my hair up into a tight bun I began my ascent up its near to vertical face, moving from one handhold to another, placing my feet carefully on the dry sandstone as I went. My petite and agile body moved swiftly, all the years of dance and gymnastics had lent me a grace and mobility that made me feel invincible with things like this. There was something so gratifying about climbing, concentrating on where the next best step was, what vines looked strong enough to hold my weight.

Suddenly a troubled cry from Alexis interrupted my concentration. My heart skipped a beat as I quickly froze in-step. Looking up I could see Alexis struggling for a foothold knocking loose material onto me.

Alexis' eyes gave away her fear. "Look out! It's not safe! Everything is falling away. I have to keep going up but there's nothing left behind me to hold onto! Tell Julia!"

∞

Her frantic voice trailed away leaving me to watch helplessly as my friend scrambled up the cliff. With each hurried movement the dirt and gravel beneath her gave way and tumbled to the jagged rocks below. She disappeared out of sight around a curve in the cliff-face.

I quickly turned my head downward to look down at Julia, hardly having a moment to process the startling news and concern for Alexis. Julia was at least twenty feet below.

I yelled. "Go back, Jewels. Alexis says it's not safe!"

Julia stopped, the smile disappearing from her face. "OK!" she yelled, focusing on making her way back down one careful step at a time.

I watched her descent without moving myself, not wanting to send any debris down. Careful as I was, I still felt the dirt beneath my own feet shifting and slipping away. Quickly I reached for the next handhold, a single small vine on the cliff face. My feet moved to the place my hands had last been, two tiny crevices four feet apart. The only way I could get a purchase on the rock was to rotate both feet completely outward, as in an exaggerated ballet plié, my hands firmly gripped the vine.

I quickly looked for another handhold. Looking up all I could see was loose dirt. To either side the cliff was barren. There was not a rock or plant closer than ten feet in any direction. I couldn't see a safe way to get back down. Given that rocks I had last held onto had fallen away as soon as I moved upward. My mind reeled as my body broke into a sweat and I hoped fervently that the vine would hold, that my feet would not slip from the tiny crevices where they were jammed against the dirt. I stole a glance at the giant boulders bordering the foot of the cliff below trying to breathe through the panic that was welling up in me. A fall would mean instant death.

My knees were still uncomfortably turned out; legs bent halfway, pressing against the cliff. Within minutes my leg muscles began to burn. My knees trembled and I willed them to be steady. I could not afford that movement. The burning intensified. My arms also began to burn, as I forced them to hold their positions, trying not to place more weight from my upper body on the vine.

Every second stretched into an eternity. I felt certain I was going to die. I was only 17 and my life was about to end. What would the point have been, all the agony I had endured, all the goals I was striving for, all to end in this one careless act of stupidity? I saw myself falling backwards, arms flailing, toward a very certain death on the rocks below. All I could do was hope that this little vine would hold me up long enough to…what?

To cherish each moment I had left, to remember my life as it was and to say good-bye to it, to all those I loved and would never see again. "Oh, little vine, I know you are small, but you are so strong. Please, please hold me up! Keep me with you!"

Life began to pass by just like people said it did in moments before death, my mind reeling with memories: both good and bad.

I had to think of something, I couldn't just wait for death. When I was little 'Mother Earth' had been a magical protector, I had forgotten that, put it aside because it wasn't 'cool' enough for the world around me.

Squeezing my eyes tight, I prayed, it was the first time I had ever done so. "Mother Earth, please keep this vine strong! Please, I don't want to die!"

My life seemed to be coming in waves, memories, feeling flooding my bloodstream relentlessly.

Oh how desperately I wanted to live, like never before! How much time I had wasted being angry at the injustices of life. What was the use, when you could die any moment? Why had I never realized how much I was wasting life! What had I lost, missed out on? Was it innocence, trust? It was something else; something more. Most of my time had been spent either dwelling in the heartache of a broken childhood, being a 'model', posing, being beautiful, dressing up, putting on make-up…dancing, just being pretty, caught up in a life of vanity, living in the California dream, suddenly it all seemed such a grand waste of precious life.

I had lost faith or any connection to God a long time ago, probably when I was just seven and childhood quickly slipped away, replaced by adult things no child should know about. Where was God in all that hurt and pain, all the hurt and pain I saw around me, a world of such suffering? But here on this cliff, about to die, I wanted nothing more than to give up all the anger, guilt and shame, and just be. I just wanted to be alive! I wanted the chance to embrace life, to live, really live, and to remember what I had lost. I wanted to never forget it again, not for one moment.

I found myself beginning to plead with God for my life, promising to be a good person, to do anything it would take for my life to be saved by some miraculous act.

With each passing moment the burning of my legs intensified, a burn like nothing I had ever felt before, wanting to give way, bringing me to that certain death. How long could I keep myself up like this?

With that thought, everything became still, like time had stopped.

Three beautiful white birds flew by me in slow, unified movement. In that stillness, that timeless moment, a voice lifted me up as it spoke to me, seemingly from everywhere at once. "Everyone fears death Luna, which keeps people from living. You will never die. Not truly, not ever. Your physical body will not die until your time has come, and that is not now. Hold on, help is coming."

I stared wide-eyed looking out at the serene figures

floating effortlessly in the sky, at once unreal and yet more real than anything I had ever seen. The voice seemed to be coming from the birds, yet at the same time it was everywhere. I felt more, than heard the truth of what I was being told. There was something greater than just the vine holding me up on that barren cliff: something spiritual. Not just Mother Earth, but more.

I was not alone! There was nothing to fear, and if I didn't fear death, I could live, truly live! This knowing was so different than belief or faith. It was unshakable, and nothing could ever change it.

The birds flew toward the horizon in silence. The eternal voice resounding in my mind, "You will never, ever die; the soul lives forever Luna, never forget this."

I was alive as never before. The sweat pouring down my face tasted salty, and I was glad for it. That and the trembling, awesome burn in my legs proved I was alive.

I felt like something else had happened, something huge, something I would never fully be able to give words to. I remembered some other part of me long forgotten, a part of me that was not just the self I thought I was... my name, my job, my past... it felt as though these communications and the feelings I was having stemmed from some inner part of me, an inner-self I had all but forgotten. This was the most important thing of all.

I also felt that if I was going to live there were things I would have to give-up. God wasn't going to let me off easy, I just knew it, but it was more than that. Suddenly I wanted to let go of everything that didn't matter; modeling, dance, ambitious desires for fame and glory, the thrill of being in the spotlight. Worse, I would have to let go of Tommy, (my boyfriend since 15) he wasn't good for me, but I had been holding myself back, imprisoning myself, unable to release the ideal of what we were together and the love I felt for him.

Looking down at the jagged unwelcoming fate I thought, how had it come to this? I resolved that I would let Tommy go, so that I could live. I knew without a doubt, he would destroy me if I didn't.

Suddenly I became aware of voices above, not the voice of God, but human voices, male voices. Lifting my gaze up slowly I saw two rescue crewmen descending the cliff with ropes. I was being saved! In seconds the two men were directly above me.

A man's voice yelled out. "It's okay. You're going to be okay, just keep holding on."

One man descended twenty feet away on my left. The other was about ten feet up. The nearer rescue man seemed to assess the situation. Calling out to his partner he said, "I'm going to head in below and lock her in."

"Don't move." He called to me.

My heart leapt for joy, but I held still. It was nearly unbelievable; God had sent a rescue crew! I could hear him adjusting straps and there was the sound of metal on metal. Then he called up to his partner, "All right come on down."

I watched as the second man slowly came toward me, adjusting his rope with each careful step downward. Soon he was just inches above. With one swift movement he carefully jumped back from the cliff face and landed directly behind me. I could feel his very real, warm human body as he wrapped his arms around me, and quickly buckled my body against his own. I began to sob uncontrollably as my exhausted body collapsed, shaking violently.

Squeezing my shoulder gently this heroic man said. "I've got you."

I continued to heave with great sobs while the rescue man laughed gently. It was clear that he could feel my relief and gratitude.

"I'm going to lower us down now. All I need you to do is hold on to this rope and jump your feet with me. I know you are exhausted; can feel your legs trembling. You don't need to have strength, just move your step with me so we won't crash into the wall."

I nodded through hot tears, forcing myself to concentrate. The process seemed to happen so quickly. We took tiny leaps down the mountain, the other rescuer leading the way. The moment of crisis ended; we were on the ground.

I looked around and saw a crowd of twenty or more people cheering. At that moment the rescue man unlatched me from his harness. My knees buckled and I almost fell, too weak to stand.

The man held me up. "Steady now."

I could see my dearest friends running toward me from the corner of my eye (thank goodness Alexis was okay!).

The next moment the three of us stood hugging as though

there was no ground beneath us, only love holding us together. Time stood still and I was oblivious to the crowd around us and the cameras flashing as people tried to capture this rescue mission on film. The next day I would read the paper in fascination, knowing it would be the last time I posed for the camera, that life was behind me, just like that, complete change in one instant of time.

I would passionately seek the source of God, not through religion or beliefs, but through the direct connection I felt in my heart, and any knowledge I could find to help me recognize that connection. It was one of pure love, bliss, and an indescribable connectedness to all things. Nothing would ever be the same, I just didn't know how much would change, how much I would change.

CHAPTER TWO

Listen To Your Dreams

I sat cross-legged on the floor of my room wearing my favorite turquoise dress, covered in little red beads with tiny white feathers hanging from the loose-fitting sleeves. It was just the style a Native American woman would have worn long ago. I loved the way the soft little feathers felt on my arms when I moved.

My room was a silent haven, soundless, save for the soft drumming that floated quietly from my stereo, blocking the static noise of my stepfather watching TV in the next room. I felt as though a barrier of light surrounded my room. In fact, I often visualized a giant golden bubble protected my little sanctuary. I had come to understand that no matter where I was in the world: I could create my own safe cocoon.

Candlelight danced on the walls, along with the smoke of the lavender incense I burned. Together they brought to life the large painted words of my prayer on the ceiling- "Great Spirit, Teach me to Heal, Show Me The Way, I am here to serve, I am here, here to serve." I whispered the words aloud with earnest prayer. Prayer had become so deep, so real to me, that I was moved to tears, and felt my soul alive. Even if all I had was prayer, I wanted to be alive for that alone, it was my greatest joy to be that prayer.

Gazing at my beautiful altar with a luminous smile. I thought (tomorrow was the big day), I would be on an Airporter at 5:00 a.m. My backpack was ready to go. I reviewed once more all that it held, everything I needed for the journey that had no chosen end - sleeping bag, clothing, bathing suit, toothbrush, hairbrush and sunscreen. I didn't know when or if I would return to Northern California. After Hawaii - my life might bring me anywhere in the world. I was wide-open, like a vast blue sky. I had no obligations, no bills to pay, no one to answer to. There was just a dream to follow, one in which magical dolphins mysteriously beaconed me to Hawaii with an urgent message that time was running out. I wondered, time for what?

The items on my little altar, stones collected from special places, a small carven angel, pinecones, crystals and a stick of desert sage filled me with intention and hopes. The crystals shot rays of light on the hardwood flooring at my bent knees. I stared above the altar at the picture of the dolphins swimming that I had found in a National Geographic magazine. I imagined I could feel them swimming there in the warm tropical water, so peaceful, so serene. I shuddered, thinking about how that would soon be reality. I had saved up a little over three thousand dollars, to someone else it might not be much, but to me it was a fortune. I knew that if I was very careful, I could live off that for a year in Hawaii, maybe even more. Since my parents were so poor, I knew how to be frugal. It was no large task. In some sense, I felt having little made you feel more comfortable getting by. If I hitchhiked, ate sparingly, camped, and didn't do anything luxurious.

It had been just two years since that day on the cliff yet so much had happened; in some ways it was truly unbelievable how much had taken place. It was as though time was incredibly sped up, but at the same time each event of my life held so much power and amazing experience they seemed to be eternal.

I relived the night after my cliff experience; Tommy had mocked me for claiming I had 'discovered' God and that humankind was not alone. That day would be the fateful end to our relationship. I told him to leave, that I wanted never to see him again. It was the most heart-breaking thing I had ever done, and the most liberating. That wasn't the end to our story, but it was the turning point leading to a sad and painful parting for both of us.

That first night, and many more after, I sobbed myself to

sleep, letting go of my shattered heart, rebuilding a new one.
I would silently thank him for letting me go, for letting me live.

Now, I was more like I was as a little girl, rainbows woven
into my long hair, long skirts twirling freeing as I danced endlessly
through summers of bliss at reggae concerts, drum circles on the
beach, traveling across the states in a converted bus, chanting with
native Americans. Life had felt like one big ecstatic dream where
all I had to do was wish for something new and adventurous and it
would just appear, as though by magic.

I had so much passion to share, and I did so relentlessly,
especially with my dearest friends who seemed to be soaring at the
same speed. This sharing, caring, opening, growing; it was what I
had decided life was meant to be after that fateful day on the cliff.
If only everyone could learn to love life that way, I thought, and so
I tried to share that message with anyone I could.

There had been relationships, nearly too many to recall, but
there was not one I regretted, each one had held its own special
kind of magic, healing kind of magic, playful magic... deeply
touching magic. There was not one man I had found myself with
that was not in some way absolutely incredible, that had not in
some way become a part of who I was.

There was Billy, the reggae star whose sparkling green eyes
spoke of vision and revolution, sweeping me up with his music.
Then there was Christian, the actor, the high-profile model, dancer/
choreographer whose physical beauty was otherworldly; but it
was his boundless sense of humor, and high energy I had fallen in
love with. I thought back to our good-bye dinner last week, even
though we had not dated for over a year we had remained friends,
an astounding accomplishment for two such passionate souls.
Christian had asked me advice on whether or not he should move
to Hollywood to accept a leading role in a major film. I had smiled
thinking back to my own decision to pass up dreams of fame.
It was not difficult to imagine his charisma and stunning beauty
taking the screens by storm.

I smiled at him across the table. "Follow your heart, that is
the only true advice I can give you." He looked at me searchingly
then. "Follow my heart... I wouldn't have a clue how to do that."

I reached over and held his hand. "Go to your favorite place
out in the redwoods and listen, you will hear it... listen closely."

He had called hours ago exclaiming ecstatically that it had worked, he would not go to Hollywood after all, but would follow his life-long dream to help other people to make a new start. I felt so good knowing anything I had gone through could help anyone else. Was there more I could do? Our world was in so much pain, what could I do, one little person, to make any difference?

There had been other beautiful, amazing, wonderful men who taught me that men could be gentle, honest, loving, compassionate, others who were wounded and rough, but I had been able to share love with them. Yet I was not attached to any of them, each relationship seemed to have a timing of its own, a grace where both partners learned and grew and shared some tantalizing dance, and then it was time to move on.

The real passion I felt was the experience of my inner- self, this self that had long been lost to me. This inner-light, this magical being that loved to seek growth in all ways, loved to look into the darkest crevices and find life growing there, wishing to bring it out in the sunlight and celebrate its growth. I craved with every cell this magic being, who seemed to understand innately what life was really meant to be - a dance with creation, opening to the very source of the universe, pushing beyond all limitations and beliefs.

It was this 'self' that would challenge any fear my former self had, conquering it with love and strength that seemed to have no end. Could I claim this self to be my own? It was not the self I had been, afraid, angry, insecure despite it all, restless, and nervous. There truly was no me, there was no self to cling to for this was the unlimited self. Sometimes it truly felt like some other being had just simply stepped into my body and begun to reside there, filling me with faith and understanding beyond the reach of my years. Was it that, or had I really grown with the speed of light years?

My dog (Kahuna) barked outside the door, reminding me of the reality outside my little cave; I shivered lightly remembering the dark hallway, the smell of my stepfather's smoke from inside his bedroom and the dank smell of mold and dust. I felt a lump forming in my throat. Kahuna was so special to me and we were so close, leaving her was the hardest part of all.

My dad was proud of the little house, as it was a big step up from the small trailer, we had lived in for six years. For that I was grateful, to see him happy with himself was always a good thing.

Last night he had thrown a little going away party for me, the first party he had ever made effort to create for me. There was a bonfire, and he and my friends sat around drumming and singing, offering blessings and gifts for my journey to Hawaii.

It was a sad night for them all, especially for Alexis and Julia but they knew they would be with me again, in fact Alexis had already planned a trip to meet up with me in Hawaii; and to visit her latest 'bo' who lived in Hawaii part time.

There was such sweetness in seeing my dad's eyes light up as he led the circle. When he connected to his native roots, it was as though he set free some deeply hidden part of his soul, a place where the true sensitivity of his heart was unveiled, no longer masked by the grumpy bear. In those moments he was a sight to behold, strong and gentle, like a wise old chief from another time. There was sadness for me in leaving too. I was giving up everything I knew and loved everything I had ever identified with. But the elation I felt about my upcoming journey far surpassed the sadness.

I had through the past years began to live my life with the understanding that we truly never die, that the soul does exist, I could feel it. I knew that was who I truly was. I learned to live my life feeling that I was never alone; spirit was all around me and in all things. I had learned to follow my intuition and guidance and was living an amazing life filled with wonder, magic, and abundance. I had learned to follow my dreams, literally!

I closed my eyes, turning away from thoughts of the past, taking a deep cleansing breath, entering the meditative state that had become so familiar. Tomorrow my life would change once more as I embarked upon the next chapter of my journey, the path meant for my soul, just as all beings have a soul-path to follow.

Eager to rest well, I lay back on my pillow and fell into a deep sleep, not waking until the alarm clock went off.

CHAPTER THREE

Trust

The moment before boarding the plane, I took in one final gulp of brisk San Franciscan air. It was the last familiar thing I would take with me. I'm going to Hawaii! My excited mind sang to itself.

I found my seat toward the back of the plane and settled down with backpack, journal, and a book to pass the time. The bells around my neck jingled as I moved myself into a comfortable position. My hands naturally went to my heart to the collection of necklaces I wore, a dolphin wrapped around a quartz crystal, a small Native-American medicine bag filled with a variety of healing stones, and a pendant of Isis 'the Egyptian Goddess'. These small treasures helped me feel energized, as though they held a special magic.

Taking a deep breath, I opened my journal to review my list of intentions for the trip:

- Swim with dolphins
- Forgive my mother
- Let go of anger
- Discover life purpose
- Be Friends with men, just friends!

Although there were only five little items, in truth it was no small order! I did not know how long it would take to accomplish these goals, nor how it would happen, but I trusted the process of manifesting from intent.

Reading the list, I thought of my mother's fears for me, which was ironic because my mother had never protected me from dangers. I could still hear her worried words from the last dinner we had shared. "You can't just put on a backpack and go off to Hawaii, knowing no one, with a few thousand dollars to your name. You could get kidnapped, raped, or worse yet, killed!"

I had smiled, trying to convey the peace and assuredness I felt. "I know you just care about me. You all do. But I'm going to be fine. Don't worry!"

Inwardly I thought about how little my mother really knew of what was happening to me. If she had known the full truth… that not only, was I going to find my heart's calling: but that I had been dreaming of dolphins for the past six months, that they were calling me to Hawaii because they had a message for me. Well, if she had known all that, she would have found a way, somehow, to prevent me from going. I never did assuage my mother's concerns before leaving

As the plane readied for takeoff, my excitement mounted. In less than six hours I would arrive in paradise, a world away from the chilling winds and bleak cloudy skies I looked out on now.

The hours passed and I absorbed myself in my book, 'Call of the Dolphins'. I was fascinated to learn about people who swam with the dolphins and how the dolphins seemed to heal people of all kinds of things, from injuries to cancer.

When the captain announced our approaching arrival, I looked eagerly out the window squinting against the bright sky and my faint headache from the long journey. Beautiful blue sea soon gave way to fields of black lava. The striking landscape startled me. There was no soil or greenery in sight—just black lava fields as far as I could see up to the slope of a tall mountain, whose top was obscured by mist and clouds. I recalled reading about the Big Island's active volcano, which was said to be the home of Pele, the Goddess of Fire. The Hawaiian people paid homage to this ancient Goddess believing she had the power to destroy or heal. Soon a small airport came into view, standing alone in this black sea. I could soon see palm trees around the terminals; they looked so lush, surreal even.

As the plane landed a familiar feeling crept into my belly, like the nervous excitement of the first day at a new school. I hadn't made any plans, wanting to allow myself to be guided when I arrived. I was tired from the journey however, and quickly began to pray that I would find a safe place to stay.

I exited the plane with my small pack smiling excitedly and walked slowly to the baggage claim, savoring the warm balmy air filled with tropical fragrances, sweet and intoxicating, so different from the cold air I had left behind.

I had taken off my fleece jacket and wore only a green tank top and a long purple skirt that hung loosely around my ankles. As I stood looking for my larger backpack on the carousel, tucking my long sandy blond hair behind my ears, I began to look over the crowd. I needed to find the right person to ask for a ride to town; my time traveling around the US had given me experience in spotting the right type of person.

Most of the people looked like tourists eager to get on with their vacation, but across the carousel I spotted a young couple with a small boy at the next carousel, facing my direction. They were probably from the mainland but with deep, natural tans; both were smiling at me as though they knew me. Feeling the familiar sensation of soul recognition, I beamed a smile back. I had experienced that type of connection a lot over the years, as though I were part of a large group of souls that knew each other from some other world, or some other place and time. I smiled back and waved, just then glimpsing my pretty purple backpack passing by.

I quickly moved to my larger pack and swung it adeptly over my right shoulder, balancing my small pack on my other shoulder and walked quickly towards the young couple. The young woman held the hand of her little boy and stopped a few feet before me beaming a genuine smile.

Holding out her hand she offered, "Hey, I'm Sara." After hearing about my plans, or lack thereof, the couple offered me a ride to what they described as the perfect place to camp. Soon we were walking toward an old Volkswagen bus painted with bright yellow flowers. My smile grew even larger as I was reminded of my flower child past and all my journeys in converted school buses across the states. In the distance I could see an enormous mountain. I recognized it from my reading as Mauna Kea, the tallest mountain in the world from its base on the ocean floor. It looked mighty and surreal with its peaks floating in soft white clouds, such a stark contrast to the endless stretches of black lava sloping down the sides.

We stopped a little health food in the town of Kona. I shopped quickly, getting what I thought would last for the next few days and three gallons of water.

Along the way I learned that the family had moved to Hawaii from Washington. They had just returned from Oahu for shopping. They were caretakers on a coffee plantation where they picked coffee beans for $10 an hour and lived in a tiny shack, which allowed them to keep most of their time free for relaxing on the beach or surfing.

I was fascinated to learn about their carefree life. I had never even thought about where coffee came from and looked out the window eagerly as they pointed out farms covered with endless rows of low coffee trees, white flowers emerging between dense dark green leaves.

Sara's husband Jason explained, "This side of the island doesn't have a lot of sandy beaches, none where you can camp for free. The state charges for all the nice spots they own, and they don't want anyone camping at the rest. Not too many people camp at the fringe spots anyway so it's not a big deal here. Maui, now that's another story. That place is so overcrowded it might as well be the mainland, yeah? The place we are taking you is on a lava cliff, next to what we call Dolphin Bay."

Shivers moved through me. "Does that mean dolphins come there?"

Sara smiled over her shoulder. "Oh yeah, for sure!"

Jason continued. "There's a beautiful white sand beach just up the way from where you'll be. You can spend time in the day, you just can't camp 'as the locals don't like it."

Sara added as though reading my mind. "It's completely safe here. The locals are cool. You don't need to worry about anything. They just have their houses back from the beach. This part of the island is one of the last spots that's mostly Hawaiian owned."

We had begun to descend a long windy road lined with flowers and large, lush trees. Jason pointed, naming the fruit trees as we passed - banana, mango, papaya, something called passion fruit, and lots of coffee. He explained that long ago the Hawaiian people traded along this road. "Those that lived in the high lands traded wild boar. Those along the route traded fruit, taro, and sweet potato, and those along the sea traded fish."

When he was done describing everything I exclaimed. "It sounds so perfect! I'm amazed. It's so different from home!"

Jason nodded his head but then frowned. "Yea it's great, but there are problems. Life is great here on the Big I, but the other islands, Oahu, Kauai, Maui, they have all been taken over by people who want to live in paradise but bring all the mainland commercialism with them. Those islands are covered with billion-dollar houses, fast-food chains and a mass of stores and roads. Many Hawaiian families can hardly afford to live where they did and in the way they used to. Big houses cause land-taxes to go up for everyone. Those of us who live here with the land and respect the local culture don't want to see that happen here on our island."

Hearing all that made me realize I knew next to nothing about the islands. I had taken such a leap of faith! Suddenly I was here in Hawaii! I could hardly take everything in, it was like a dream but so vividly real. I would never forget those first moments, and the sweet little family that blessed my passageway.

There was a protective tone to his voice; he clearly cared about this land and its people. I offered my sympathy. "I can relate. I can remember when there were endless fields and little streams where I used to live in Northern California. Then almost overnight the suburban sprawl took over. Now there is very little left of nature… just malls, highways, and smog. It makes me really sad, and kind of angry too."

After that there were a few silent moments as the van made its way slowly over a very bumpy dirt road. Soon we were beside a lava cliff giving way to the calm turquoise sea. My eyes were wide with rapture as I took in the heavenly beauty. Everything sparkled, almost like it was brighter, and definitely cleaner, than nature back home. I could feel myself falling in love with this place.

They came to a stop and Jason hopped out. "Here's your stop!"

I was beaming as Sara turned from the steering wheel to bid me farewell. I squeezed her hand in gratitude. "Thank you. You have a beautiful family. Maybe we'll see each other again!"

Sara nodded eagerly agreeing. Jason had taken my backpack and large water container out of the van.

"Be safe and have fun!"

I smiled at both of them. "Thank you so much for bringing me. Peace and be well!"

I watched as the van pulled away and then turned toward the sea-cliffs. Grabbing my packs and bottle I walked out onto the rich, dark lava, magnetized by the sparkling sea. Resting my belongings against a tree, I removed my shoes and walked to the cliff's edge. Barefoot, I could feel the warmth and variations in the pure black lava stone; some spots were smooth as glass, others bumpy and rough. I could feel energy pulsing through the lava into my body. It almost felt as though it were still alive.

The sea stretched out forever, waves crashing gently on the base of the twenty-foot cliffs in front of me, and all along the wide expanse to either side. I looked down into the clear, deep waters where a coral reef displayed a dozen different bright shades. The sun was still pretty high, casting long golden rays on the glassy surface. I could see that I faced west, that meant I would witness my first ocean sunset!

Already the velvety smooth waters enticed me to take a plunge, but I saw no way into the water. Black lava cliffs lined the endless sea, none shorter than a 20-foot drop to the cool waters below. I had never seen or felt anything like this place; the black lava meeting the vast sea with the golden sun hovering in the distance, it was like landing on another planet. Behind me, majestic, lush mountains peaked toward the clear sky. The smell was mixtures of warm salt air and that intoxicating aroma of tropical fruits and flowers. I felt the soft warm air just wrap me up, penetrating my skin feeling clean and silky.

The sun's warmth filled my body with renewal, it felt so different from the more glaring California sun, softer somehow, and yet more vibrant at the same time. Behind me I took in the sound of unfamiliar birds. They sounded so peaceful, an integral part of this magical land.

Just as I was deciding that I could stay right here for all eternity with a blissful smile glued to my face, a human voice startled me. I spun around abruptly to see two men approaching, a younger good-looking boy, and an older man with long white hair. Both looked like they might have come from the mainland, but like Sara and Jason, they had the healthy golden-brown hues of those who had been living in Hawaii a long while.

The older of the two walked toward me and extended a hand, "Hey."

I shook his hand, smiling.

He glanced at my pack. "Did you just arrive on the island?"

I nodded, wrinkling my brow. "Is it that obvious?"

He laughed. "You look like a local really, except your skin hasn't been touched by Hawaii's sun or sea. You don't have any wrinkles."

I laughed. "Yeah, I am pretty white."

He responded unabashedly. "You are so stunning; you glow, like an angel."

He had this look I have seen in some wise people along the way, like he was peering into my soul. I gazed back transparently and curious. He spoke with a deep hypnotic tone. "I believe you must be Pele's long-lost daughter."

I could not have heard a more shocking statement. Chills ran up my spin as I stared back blankly. I stammered. "The fire goddess?"

"Yes," He smiled seeming to star right through me. "Indeed, there's a legend that Pele's lost child would return to reclaim these islands, helping them become what they once were, before white man came along."

I surely was not expected to believe this wild statement. Yet, he seemed to sure of himself. I didn't know what to make of it, but one thing was certain I was not likely to forget it. Trying to avert attention I turned my gaze to the younger one.

The boy reached out his hand and I noticed how his light blue eyes sparkled with life. He looked about sixteen.

"I'm Luna. And you?"

The boy smiled mysteriously. "I gave up my name. Call me as you will."

I smiled at this uniqueness asking as I looked from one to the other. "Are you camping too?"

He smiled casually. "Yeah, yeah; we came here all the time. Hardly anyone ever comes down here; it's a local secret. You know you're lucky to have found your way here. Where'd you come from anyway?"

I looked from son to father, feeling rather relieved that they were camping as well. "I literally, just got off the plane. A couple brought me here from the airport. I do feel very lucky!"

He reached into a cloth bag. "I'm Handel by the way. Can we offer you dinner?" He was already holding out the largest orange and avocado I had ever seen.

I looked up at his wise eyes and replied rather stunned, "For me?"

"Yeah, yeah," Handel replied, (I could already tell this expression was a local one), "and there are plenty more where those came from." He looked up at the mountains. "They grow abundantly here. We've got some friends that have a farm up that mountain."

I looked up at the beautifully lush mountain slope. It really was a big island. Reaching out my hands I exclaimed, "Oh my goodness, thank you!"

I thought my response may have seemed over-the-top to them, but I had never in my life been offered fresh fruit free of charge. Both men were smiling, and I could see that sharing was just as exciting to them as it was for me to receive. Spiritual people tended to be like that, as though they carried the understanding that to give was to receive, and vice versa.

The three of us sat down to 'peel' our dinners. I was amazed at the incredible juiciness of the fruit, so alive compared to those I'd bought at stores. The avocado was so rich and creamy. It was a meal within itself. Eating only raw and organic was what I wanted; so far, I was off to an amazing start!

The sun had begun to get lower on the horizon by that time and the three of us sat mesmerized in silence. My eyes were wide with wonder as the golden disc of the sun sank right into the sea. I imagined for a moment that this was true; every night it would rest gently beneath the surface of the water, welcoming the coolness. As the last golden rays faded, a slight breeze picked up. I felt its light touch on my checks, as a deep silence seemed to move over the land.

Handel interrupted the deep silence. "That's it for me. I'm going to go to sleep."

His son looked up with a warm smile. "Night, Pop."

I smiled up at Handel's sweet wrinkly face, exclaiming. "Thanks for everything. I feel so welcomed, and safe too!"

Reaching down, he squeezed my shoulder. "The island herself welcomes you, magic lady."

The boy spoke matter-of-factly. "I'm going to make a fire. If you want to stay, you're welcome to."

I responded eagerly. "I love fires. You know, I thought I would be completely exhausted. I guess the excitement has me all wound up."

For a while we sat quietly by the small fire the boy had made. I blurted out. "I know the perfect name for you!"

"Oh, yeah? What's that?"

"Blue - like your eyes and the beautiful sea which you seem so at ease with."

He laughed. "Sounds good!"

We talked for a while. I felt so comfortable with him; I realized I could already check one goal off my list: be friends with males... that had happened quickly I had this feeling that things were going to happen really quickly in Hawaii, as though the power made things manifest faster here than elsewhere. In the flames I felt the spirit of Pele and took time to offer gratitude for all that had taken place to bring me there. After a few moments of silence, Blue said goodnight and walked back to his camp.

Rolling out my sleeping bag I laid on top of my soft pink sheet, finding my mind drifting to thoughts of dolphins, hoping I would at least see some dolphins, if not swim with them myself soon. After all, they were the ones who had brought me to Hawaii. I listened to the pound of the surf as my mind neared sleep, and felt an ancient story there... a story hidden in the waves and the stone, that of love and envy between land and sea.

I wondered what this was, the energy I could feel pulsing here. I soon fell into a deep, peaceful sleep with a smile on my face. I was really in Hawaii!

I woke to the light of day dancing over my eyelids. Before opening my eyes, I took in the sounds around me, the gentle crash of waves, the sweet morning song of doves in the distance. The air was so fresh, so fragrant, like flowers and sea and sunlight all mixed together. I lay this way for several minutes, feeling so utterly content. The first rays of the sun touched my face as it raised over the mountain in the far distance, spreading golden rays across the verdant, misty hills. The air was warm, not too hot - just perfect, moist and so very gentle. I felt the sea calling me with its enticing salty smell and gentle lapping sounds. The morning water was as still as glass, dazzling in the sunlight.

Walking toward the cliff's edge drawn into that sparkling aqua beauty, I gazed out to the horizon: stretching my arms overhead with a big yawn. I never completed that yawn, however, as the most extraordinary thing occurred just then: I gasped, bringing my hands to my mouth. Out just two hundred yards or so from me a group of dolphins swam by like a flash of silvery light; their fins rose falling in unison. I couldn't believe it was really happening; the very moment I awoke, on the first day! Time stood still as I felt the dolphin mind reach out to me just like in my dreams; seeming to say, 'You see, we are here, just like we said we would be!'

Elated, breathless, and near to tears, I watched the pod quickly swim past in one smooth line. I knew this powerful first encounter was all that it needed to be: besides, they were way too far out to swim to. I couldn't have handled more, and definitely was not about to swim out to sea alone. That I would have to work up to!

In those moments I felt much like Dorothy in Oz, transported to a place where everything was ever so different, magical, and new.

I stood transfixed thinking (Wow, I did it! I had made it to Hawaii, and they were there just like that!) I was so excited I began to laugh out loud. And then an even more unbelievable moment occurred: just beyond where the dolphins had just swam by, disappearing as quickly as they had appeared; two massive sized whales breached at the same time. Their bodies simultaneously soared toward the sky and then splashing back into the water sending enormous plumes of water into the air. Again, and again, they breached and slapped their tails.

"I can't believe it, dolphins and whales!" I could barely contain myself. I laughed, crying at the same moment.

A pulse hit my third eye and I heard the dolphin mind again. "Prepare yourself in the presence of Hawaii. There is a journey here for you that will require great strength and courage.

Get ready to swim with us, the time will soon come."

I bowed my head in silent consent; guided by a power vastly beyond normal human comprehension. This presence, this guidance, was not something I could question, after all they had called me to Hawaii and here, they were. It was overwhelming, there was no doubt about that.

Not wanting to lose the depth of the moment I concentrated on the water, breathing deeply as I had been taught to do in yoga, intent on keeping these precious moments in my heart forever. There was nothing about this new place that wasn't incredibly powerful. Each aspect of nature surrounding me called me to see beyond the reality I had come from in California; it was raw power, and somehow so familiar, like a distant memory I was walking into, walking backwards in time. I felt like I was on an entirely different planet, a place where things stood outside of time, all inter-connected and smooth, like the glassy water that morning, perfection embodied.

The whales remained there in their powerful dance; and I sat for a long while completely in awe of their grandness, realizing on some level what this meant - I would not only swim with dolphins, but whales! What could be more overwhelmingly daunting, and what could possibly help me get ready for this huge leap, if anything?

I suddenly felt a pulse of light fill my entire body and I heard the voice that had been there on the cliff... the voice, I imagined, was Great Spirit's voice, "This is the place where light and dark meet, and the two become one." I had no idea what that meant, but I felt it, some truth beyond the realm of reason, that somehow this was true, (the place where light and dark meet and become one), those words were to be etched into my soul, and one day I would come to know, more than I could have imagined, just what that meant.

I spent the next three days exploring the nearby white sand beach uninhibited by anyone, save the occasional shell-collector strolling along the shore. I tried to not think about swimming out to sea alone, not here in this place, maybe there was another place where I wouldn't have to swim so far, and maybe just dolphins to start with. The idea of the whales was just too big. I often sat for hours simply absorbing the pristine beauty - the stark contrast of white sand against the black lava fields that stretched as far as the eye could see on either side. Clear, turquoise waters of the protected lagoon, sparkled endlessly in the summer sunlight. The long hours giving me so much time to soak it all in.

I felt my skin darkening, as it absorbed the healing rays. Everything about my awareness was so different from anything I'd been taught by "society". I had read, but also realized, that daily sun exposure without sunscreen was critical to being healthy. I chuckled to myself, thinking about how this fact among so many others stood in direct contrast to all the complete garbage the mainstream media filled peoples' minds with. Sure, moderation was important with all things, but to think that the sun's rays were actually bad for us was so sad to me, especially for children.

That night I lay on my sleeping bag looking up at the dark, sky filled with a million stars, so happy with all the day had been.

∞

The gentle breeze in the coconut fronds above coaxed me into deep relaxation, and I soon drifted into that special state between awake and asleep...

CHAPTER FOUR

Beyond Time and Space

The pounding surf lulled me even deeper as a tremendous energy took over my body: I felt as though I was spinning into confusion. I could no longer see the night sky, only bright colors - greens, purples, and shimmering golden light.

Every part of my body began to vibrate, filled with an ecstasy I had never before felt, yet was strangely familiar. The dancing lights blended, brightening into pure white, and then began to take shape. I could vaguely see an enormous figure above me: maybe twenty feet tall, enormous to be certain! It occurred to me to be afraid: yet I felt such a deep peace from the presence. I stared; in complete awe as the image sharpened. The figure, clad in a flowing white gown, flanked by large, iridescent wings stretching out behind her, seemed almost to smile. Her eyes caught the light of the aura that surrounded her, deep pools of golden, liquid life.

Not wanting to breathe or blink, for fear the angel, for surely was an angel, would disappear. Suddenly I had some sort of recognition, like a deep memory, so deep it sent an ache through the center of my heart. "You're here!" I whispered.

Her delicate, long arms extended down toward me "It is time."

The vibrating of my body increased as my surroundings

began to disappear rapidly. The next moment I found my spirit-body propelled through a tunnel of extremely vivid colors.
Tones: sweet and powerful began to ring all around me, but I was disappearing quickly. The experience was so tangible, so physical, but looking back I could see my body on the lava rock below; fading away until I could see it no more.

With a fearful jolt I asked myself disoriented, (Am I leaving my body?)

The angel's voice was there, answering my thoughts. "Your body will be safe: you will return to it. This is only a journey. Relax as well as you can."

Even as the words were spoken; the reality around me changed: we appeared to have left the tunnel. I struggled to orient myself. I was standing... no, rather hovering, above the ground. We seemed surely to be in a different realm or world altogether. The environment appeared physical but lighter, and much brighter, while softer at the same time. We hovered over a meadow covered with brilliant purple and pink flowers; through which a gentle stream wound its way through to a meandering valley beyond. It was by far the most extraordinarily beautiful place I had ever seen. Above me the sky glowed with an ethereal quality. Wispy clouds took on a magical luminescent quality as though filled with electricity. The air had a sweet vibrancy that made me want to never exhale, but how could I smell? How could I possibly take all this in, what was happening to me? The angel motioned for me to look toward the lush hills in the distance.

Wide-eyed I asked the angel. "How did I get here and how is that I still feel and breathe and smell?"

She answered. "Time and space don't really exist; we travel at the speed of light as you just did. You are in your spirit body now and it can feel and sense just as your physical form can, but with more sensitivity."

My mind whirled. Traveling at the speed of light, that was what that was, a tunnel of some sort of warped time... time.

She interrupted my thoughts. "Yes and you will do that again and again. There is no limit to what you can experience here."

Beyond the valley, just at the very top of a lushly covered till stood an enormous temple-like dome structure glistening in the soft rays of a subtle sun that lay just beyond. I felt a dawning remembrance again, not knowing if it was my own memory or the angel sending it to me somehow. I was like had come home and for a moment there was pain in this memory. I had forgotten for so long! My longing for this place was so deep I felt it would break my heart. This was my true home, much more so than Earth! Yet a part of my soul was still pulled to the Earth. I loved Earth, too. In this place of light, I knew that answers always came just as soon as questions formed in my mind.

Taking my hand, the angel lifted me once more into the air. We floated over the meadow and beyond the valley upwards to the dome. The effortless flight filled me with awe as I gazed down upon the quickly passing landscape. Soon the mighty temple stood before us and we gently descended near the entrance. I stared up at the immense golden doors of the temple expecting them to open at any moment. Enormous white pillars stood on either side; silently, the large doors did indeed open, seemingly of their own accord. The angel entered floating just feet above the smooth white- rose marble floor, motioning with a gesture of her hand for me to follow her down a long corridor. I heard melodious voices coming from down the corridor at the far end. A comforting light emanated from all directions. The end of the corridor opened into a large circular room that appeared to be made of pure glass, save for the side we had just entered, where the voices were.

Through the glass I took in an expansive view of the meadow and the glorious mountain peaks beyond.

Following the angel into the immense hall I couldn't believe what I saw: there, evenly spaced around the circumference of massive room were dozens of chairs, some ever so small, some enormous, in tiered rings, rising up to the walls on the far side of the hall, like an angelic amphitheater. All were perfectly smooth and glimmered with the silver light that permeated the entire temple. In the innermost ring of chairs sat ten of the most divine beings I could imagine, I hardly knew where to look. My eyes came to rest in the center; where something like a stage with two large chairs, or rather thrones, ornately carved in crystal. I had the same feeling of familiarity, yet overwhelm, all at once. What was normally found in the realm of dreams and imagination was now very real; with a light and power that was almost too much to take in.

The angel bent down; placing her hand reassuringly on my shoulder; motioning for me to move toward a smaller chair outside the inner circle. A profound silence came over the room and I cautiously sat down, looking to the angel. Just as I sat down the chair literally moved up the wall and stopped about 15 feet up, offering me a grand view of all before me. My petite body felt so small compared to the space around me. I gulped … or thought I gulped … could I gulp? This was immense, beyond anything I'd experienced and almost unbelievable, certainly shocking. How? Why was I here? What on earth was going on? But then... I wasn't even on earth!

With a graceful motion of her hand the angel indicated that I should wait and watch, directing my attention to the center of the room. I looked around the room at the beautiful beings gathered there, each of whom acknowledged my presence with loving and compassionate gazes as I struggled to maintain a sense of calm. I was struck by the awesome uniqueness of each being in the circle and the variations in physical appearance. They all seemed to be seated in pairs.

To the right of the circle there were two humanoid beings similar to humans but maybe fifteen feet tall with wide set eyes and long slender limbs. Their faces were pure, almost like porcelain dolls. Next to them were two little delicate beings about three feet tall with slight graceful features and long ears. Another pair was also short in stature but were rounder, with small, but muscular, arms and legs. Enormous blue eyes danced with merriment protruding slightly from their gentle faces. Both smiled at me and I stared openly in complete awe. Another couple had translucent blue bodies with faces like lions and the wings of eagles; they seemed very powerful and wise. Lastly there was another angel very similar to the one who had escorted me, only more masculine, with brilliant purple eyes.

Just then the angel communicated directly to my mind once again. "We are waiting for our leaders. These extraordinary beings before you come from the far corners of the galaxy to consider the possibilities for helping humankind. This council is comprised of those most closely related to the evolution of planet Earth. They are known as the 'Galactic Council'. You are here to serve as a messenger."

I was stunned. Had she really said that? Me, a messenger?
Somehow trying to 'think' anything back towards this great being,
with all these other very pure beings around me just didn't seem
appropriate.

They appeared as though they might be a great king and
queen or some such title of grandeur. They sat in silence seeming to
tune in with the group for a few minutes. Suddenly there was a soft
tone and the beings around the room opened their eyes and shifted
in their seats.

The male rose and Bowed to all. His eyes, unlike any I had
ever seen, were so mesmerizing; golden like the sun, burning almost
with fire.

His voice suddenly vibrated over the gathered crowd breaking
the powerful silence. "Beloved Ones," he began, "Blessed be this
most important council meeting." I'd the sense that I was the only
one hearing his voice in English, as though he could be translated
into my language and the one they all shared.

"We have reached a critical moment in the time/space
continuum of All That Is," he continued. "Let us reflect upon the
Law. All things are One. All life affects all else."

Tones of agreement moved throughout the room once more,
in acknowledgement.

Sunanda continued, looking directly at me with a piercing
gaze. "Those that rule your world are on a path of certain
destruction: if this is not reversed there will be little left of your
world that is worth saving. The way humans are treating their
bodies affects their offspring through damage done to the DNA.
But it is more than humans that have done this; it is time for your
to see the truth. In viewing the future potentials of your world, we
saw that there would be little left to salvage of the original DNA,
but the greatest danger lies in the nuclear power held by those who
do not have reverence for life. We will go more into that but for
now that I speedily move into your education." He paused there for
a moment and then carried on. "All humans are connected. Have
you have heard of the 100th Monkey Theory?"

I indicated I had not, shaking my head.

"Once a group of spider monkeys were observed by your
scientists", he offered, "then one day a female monkey decided to
wash her sweet potato in a river before eating it. Other monkeys

nearby looked on and suddenly started doing the same. Once a critical mass of approximately one hundred monkeys had adapted to this behavior, other monkeys who had no physical contact with the first group, who lived their entire lives on other islands, even, began to wash their sweet potatoes as well. Each species has what is called a 'consciousness grid.' It is an energy field that exists all around the planet like a golden sphere of light wrapping itself all the way around the globe. Each and every animal in the species is connected to their own specific grid. The information they hold; the way they live and the ways they evolve are seeded into this information matrix. Once a new realization is added to the consciousness grid by enough individual members experiencing that reality, all members of the species can easily access that new information and adapt to that new way of being."

Lord Sunanda paused again and then carried on with a stronger tone. "It is so for the human species as well. If enough of you remember who you really are and work hard enough to return to living in harmony and peace with each other and your world, then you make this possible for all others. But more than this, it is time for you to reclaim your world." His face suddenly looked sober. "You will come to feel more comfortable in our presence. Of course, it is not as simple as you just knowing truth, you must live it, breathe it, become it."

With that his introduction seemed complete. A three-dimensional screen appeared in the center of the room far above his head just at my eye level. I watched as a holographic image displayed planet Earth as seen from space. From this vantage point, the Earth looked so peaceful and quiet, a perfect sphere of life in the vastness of space.

Silently Lord Sunanda took his seat and the female who rose in his place. This exquisite being seemed the perfect embodiment of feminine grace and beauty. In that moment I knew her to be Lady Nada. She was also humanoid in nature: like the female counterpart to Lord Sananda. She stood about eight feet tall, much like him, with long elegant arms and delicate hands. I understood that they were equal not only here but equal in all ways: the embodiment of the divine couple that had reached complete wholeness within themselves and with each other. Their union was eternal and everlastingly devoted to serving the light. It was such an overwhelming feeling of love they held: I wanted to melt and stay in that feeling of perfection forever myself.

Her powerful, yet immensely sensual and soft, voice filled the room effortlessly. "Your planet's poles indeed have a scheduled date of reversal, as it has gone through in other cycles. It has been this way since the inception, you will understand soon enough why this is." She paused for a moment. "Yet something different has occurred this time."

She paused. "In 1972, the planet had reached a critical-mass. So much negativity and density were on the globe that the planet began to wobble sooner than expected, this happens when the delicate balance of life is too upset. It was seen that the population levels and the trend of living would one day destroy the preciousness of your world eco- systems, creating great suffering for all life. But worse, some of what we saw was so tragically impacting, it would spread beyond your atmosphere creating chaos for life beyond your world."

She continued. "The year 2012 is very important. There is a very specific alignment with Galactic Center, the alignment of the stars and an evolutionary leap in consciousness and the end of not only a 26,000 cycle the earth moves through, but also the end of all the past cycles of time as a whole. From the end of 2012 forward, there is a great acceleration of consciousness and energy such as your world has never known. In past times on your planet, the experiences of polar shifts time and time again have generated a new phase of existence, in many ways each cycle seeming disconnected from the past, as though you have all gone into amnesia. Were you as a species to still be in ignorance, not awake to who you really are, and not protected in anyway, most of you would die, and those that lived...? Well as we have seen from your records you would be sent back to the stone-ages, having lost all memory of who you were before the shift. You are connected to the earth's electro-magnetic field and when it reverses you have lost so much. If this happens again you would lose even the basic knowledge of how to start a fire, all the incredible information your species has come so far to embody, all that would be gone forever. Worse, those of the darkness who understand all of this would survive and take complete control, as they have time and time again."

I sat on the edge of my seat as the beautiful light-being continued. "We created a plan, after reviewing your world's records. We needed to awaken the memories of truth in your world. We saw a need for there to be humans that were once again awakened to the great truth of who you really are, so that by the time the poles shift a 'New Human Being' can rise, humans capable of greatness, as you will see from learning about your ancestors. We did the only thing we could. We seeded ourselves onto the planet, with a plan to activate the energy-fields of our human vessels and remain awake no matter what might come to pass. Even if there were no pole shift, Luna, it is crucial that you awaken as a species and do not destroy, not only your planet, but damage life beyond your world through the dangerous use of nuclear power."

She paused again, giving me a moment to assimilate this very shocking information. She seemed to peer into my very soul. "We sent parts of ourselves, seeded our consciousness if you will, into certain human lineages, most directly linked to your original human ancestors. We did this for a few reasons. With aspects of ourselves on the planet we would be capable of guiding ourselves Home, gaining information, and holding this light, re-awakening the New Being, with supreme Divine Intelligence and intact DNA. Over the years we maintained contact, building a structure in the DNA of our human vehicles, and therefore transforming the damaged DNA of the human-being, preserving the precious DNA of humankind so that all would not be lost forever."

I sat completely still trying to absorb this massive information.

She went on. "As humans we could choose through free-will to allow Divine Intervention, allowing our higher aspects to work with the planet doing all that we can to awaken and preserve truth. It remains up to the human race to create a life that is sustainable for the planet. You, our star-seed, are your planet's greatest hope."

This too was shocking: so that was why there had been cave people; a polar shift had caused the destruction of previous civilizations. Somehow this made perfect sense; I had always wondered about all of that and never seen any reasonable answer in our world, certainly not Darwin's theory. Amazed that I had never heard of any of this, but then again, she said those who had dark power were the only ones to remember anything, normal humans would have been so gullible to the ideas they suggested, as though there was no past.

As though to answer my thoughts Lady Nada explained. "You will see all of that and more as we view your records. You cannot forget, ever. It is crucial that you learn how to do something that will keep your memory intact as you learn and grow spiritually. We will teach you how to do that, how to achieve what was not in the past cycle - Divine Remembrance, and awakened DNA."

Lady Nada smiled softly. "Luna indeed you are one of us, one of our children, if you will. We like the term of endearment - 'Star Children' or 'Star Seed'. And one day you will come to know that you are even more."

My heart soared and plummeted at the same time. That was who I was. This was why I always felt so different! How could I take in all of this at once? I was not human, not really? I was a divine light being in human form with awakening DNA, on Earth. Wow, wow, wow. There was nothing else to say, nothing to think... But then a thought did come. There were others like me... these, these Star Children! Were my beloved sisters Julia and Alexis part of this? Was Blue? Who else? What would they do? What would life on Earth become? A wave of ecstatic joy moved through me, beyond exciting. It was glorious and daunting, awe- inspiring, and overpowering. There could be no larger purpose I could ever think of no greater truth to the reality of who I, and others, are! It was so much to take in, yet wasn't it something I had felt for the past two years? I had once told my mom after the day on the cliff that I thought I was from the Pleiades, had so quite matter-of-factly, I guess I knew what I was talking about then! But really, how as I to take this in, this deeply?

Nada interrupted. "This and more is who you are. You will remember, and you will grow more comfortable with this information. Give it time. And yes, there are others, and yes those you are thinking of are like you, born of the stars. One day soon through the work we do and the work you do, the opportunity will exist for all of humanity to become free."

She sat down, this beautiful poised being of pure grace, and Sunanda stood as she did. "The only chance for preventing complete destruction of your environment is for humans to realize how they are being controlled. They must realize not only how they are mistreating the planet but also how they are being misled about the way life can be lived. There is a history to your world that has been hidden. Those in power have made certain that most humans never know the truth about who they really are. In this way they control the secrets, the powers, and the keys to the ancient truth. They have told you that your history began 10,000 years ago or less. In truth, your history as a race and a planet extends for millions of years. In order to understand how and why you are controlled, and by whom, you will need to remember the true history. In order to remember, you must first be shown."

Sunanda continued "Luna you have been lied to since you were born. All of humanity has been lied to in this way."

He continued. "When someone is deceived and manipulated, when lies are bred into entire civilizations, you take for granted that what you are told is true. This in turn prevents you from remembering what is real. If you had not been lied to you would know the truth, because truth lives inside each and every being. Just as a mother lion knows how to care for her young because her very DNA holds the memories of all her ancestors, so too does your body hold memories of your ancestors. Once we remove the illusion of what you have been taught, you will begin to feel the truth of this in your own cells."

As though sensing my confusion he continued with his gentle way of speaking. "At this point the group calling themselves the 'New World Order' on earth continues to move forward with their plans to centralize all governmental control and military. They are making progress all too swiftly with their plans. They have manipulated many countries into giving up farming, enticing them with monetary loans they will never be able to pay off. Without realizing it these countries are selling themselves into mass slavery, causing their people to suffer and die from disease and famine. In so many other ways the masters of control influence entire populations through fear and manipulation. They also take many people underground, and even off planet, where they use the human-race for experimentation and as slaves."

This statement was also shocking, taking people off planet? What?

He continued. "There is so much more you must understand about who they are and what they are doing. But do not fear, for you and those of your kind, there is protection if you follow our guidance."

I nodded, understanding through the bewilderment. Hadn't I always known this truth somewhere inside? Wasn't this why I had always refused to say the Pledge of Allegiance in school, why I had rebelled in so many little ways against the norms of society? Had I not known this day would come, that I was born for this purpose they spoke of? I felt a shiver move up my spine and knew I indeed had.

He penetrated my thoughts. "All that we are going to share with you is real. You must be strong to handle all that you are to be shown. All that you have endured in your life has been a testimony to what you can handle. You have been prepared for everything you are about to go through. But that doesn't mean it will be easy. There will be times when you feel very alone, but remember we are always with you."

He sat down and traded places with Lady Nada who continued. "Shortly we will begin to review the planetary history and discover how things came to be the way they are now. You have a great responsibility here. You need to record everything that you see here in your mind, and within the very cells of your body. You must bring this story back to Earth."

Sananda's will pressed in on my mind like warm sunrays. "Remembering is one of your gifts. Control your emotions. Use your mind. Think back over your life. Realize that you have always remembered everything, recorded every detail of what was spoken and the exact events of all you have experienced in your mind. This is a gift. Allow it to be used."

Lady Nada hovered closer to me, motioning with her arms as she spoke. "You will see that time moved differently on your planet in the days long past. The higher the consciousness, the faster time moves. This difference is hard to convey through words so you must feel it. In a sense, life was timeless then... eternal. Love is what is eternal. If something is loved, cherished and honored, it lives forever."

I could well remember that feeling, the dread, the bored, and the cold isolation of it all.

She continued. "Think about moments when you have been in perfect bliss, how it lasted forever, yet your experience changed and grew."

"We will pass through many eons in what will seem the blink of an eye, but you will remember everything forevermore. We want you to write down a main lesson from each of these sessions. The essence of those will become a series of teachings. It will be the path for you and others to follow home to the light."

This was a giant step beyond all that had occurred in my life so far. Little did I know the end of the year I would see proof of every detail that the Council was to reveal with their guidance.

CHAPTER FIVE

We Are Divine Creation

The room was quiet, and I felt a white light envelop me as I reclined in my chair, following Lord Sananda's guidance to close my eyes and relax.

Suddenly I was called out of this state and sat upright once more. Nada smiled softly motioning for me to look to the hologram at the center of the hall.

Slowly the images before me began to change and I was brought back to the time before Earth's creation!

The holographic screen began to swirl with colors and light, it was soft and felt like I was inside of it, there was depth and realness to all I was seeing such that it felt like I was experiencing it, smelling, breathing it in, feeling it in my own body and mind. The screen zoomed in on what looked like a giant golden sphere encompassed by these dancing lights.

Lady Nada's narrated, seeming to feel the space around and within me, with words I will never forget...

"Beyond your time and space Creator Gods gathered in a capsule of light. It was time for these blessed 144 beings to create a planet through pure thought and feeling. This responsibility had been granted to these beings, known as the Children of One, by their beloved parents - Divine Mother and Father. It was them, that created this ethereal- realm of perfect light, a realm completely protected from all darkness in the universe, surrounded with the blessings of their love. This place of beauty and peace was all the Children of One had ever known, the soft embrace of their parents. Yet, as it is with all things, change was at hand. It was time for them to grow, to experience what life would be in physical matter. They rang with jubilation having waited a long time for this moment. Excitement filled their bubble of light as the moment approached... "

Lady Nada turned to me. "This is earth's true story of creation; it is one far different from any you have been told. Remember it, cherish it, and never forget it from this moment forward. Always remember... always remember, dear Luna."

The first image was of two magnificently radiant and compelling beings. Their bodies were light and so enormous I could not tell how big they really were as though they were infinitely large and could not be defined by boundaries. They hovered in what felt like an infinite space; I sat spellbound taking in their most beautiful features. Their faces looked not too unlike humans, though brilliantly pure and clear, they seemed to stare with deep emerald eyes right at me. One had masculine features, while the other was feminine; in this way they seemed similar to Lord Sananda and Lady Nada. Adorned with white silken robes, embroidered with what looked like gold and sapphire stones, their long slender bodies were nearly transparent, so bright they were nearly impossible to look at. My heart began to ache as though I knew these beings!

"Who are they?" My thoughts reached out to Lady Nada. "They are Divine Mother and Father, Io and Ama, the beloved parents of those who originally seeded your planet." The ache in my heart felt unbearable. I did know them! Divine Mother and Father! Suddenly I could feel them within every cell. I longed to be in their presence. How did I know them? My awareness returned to the screen where the image had changed and begun to move rapidly.

As the beautiful image of the Divine Parents rotated on the screen Lady Nada spoke again.

"Of Oneness, the source of All That Is, was born a Divine heritage – as it evolved and became familiar to itself, it would come to be known as 'Family of Light', a family that would remain linked together for all of eternity. Light is energy and information, and this is what they are, capable of existing in many dimensions of thought, vibration, sound, feeling, and existence. This vast network of beings spread out through the multiple universes, because they were born of primordial consciousness, they had a power to create through thought and feeling. They began to create and expand life that was full of goodness and love. What humans usually think of as love, is often not what love really is, but something else, either lust, desire, attachment or even fear. The beings you will encounter on this journey of remembrance are the very embodiment of love. They are the most-high beings in the universe created by the Highest Divine Creator."

Watching the images of Divine Mother and Father, I could tell just by looking at them and feeling the emotions that stirred in my heart, that they were pure love. There wasn't anything negative or tainted. They had no insecurities, no hidden motives. They were so very pure.

Lady Nada continued. "Divine Mother and Father birthed a set of ethereal-worlds, and later physical worlds. They nurtured and cared for the life they had brought forth and for their children who would one day obtain the role of Creator Gods themselves. Through time they learned and grew in many ways, becoming more and more wise and powerful. Of the divine light also were born the highest angels, now known as the Archangels, and their children, the Angels. These beings resided in the non-material realm but remained connected to the worlds of matter."

I watched great lights and geometries of energy patterns floating through the ethereal realms, witnessing beings of many vibrant colors flying on iridescent wings. Each being was unique, their translucent human-like faces filled with wonder and joy.

The images changed again and began to slow down. I sensed we were approaching the part of history that was Earth's heritage.

Io and Ama sat in midair as though on invisible thrones. A large group of very majestic looking beings floated around in the middle of a golden sphere of light, surrounded by a field of brilliant interwoven colors that seemed to pulse with a heartbeat of its own.

Lady Nada spoke again. "These were the original 144 perfect Creator Gods of your planetary world. They are the children of Io and Ama, ethereal-beings of light known as 'twin-flames', for each pair of beings you will see, one master soul was born, which then split into two counterparts: a female and male. They existed in the ethereal realms for what in your time would be hundreds of thousands of years. During that time, they perfected the mastery of creating in realms of light and of existing together in harmony and love. The scene you are about to enter was to be their first journey into physical matter. They were preparing to express their creative energy through the manifestation of a planet and of their own physical bodies."

My awareness was drawn to a smaller group of beings within the 144.

"These beings were so close in energy and expression they were known as the Children of the One; the oldest souls and the most evolved of all of them. They were in the truest sense the big brothers and sisters of the group. It was them that would create the planet, while the others would help and come along to inhabit the new world with them."

I was absolutely amazed at their perfect beauty, and this incredible concept of twin flames... it sounded so familiar.

Nada continued. "The Children of the One were eight in number, four female and four males, and in all ways did each child match his or her soul mate, or 'twin-flame'. In essence all that they thought, felt, and expressed was completely in harmony with one another. There was nothing that they felt or thought that was of anger, jealousy, greed, or any other limiting human emotion. They simply existed in a state of complete perfection, their masculine and feminine qualities balanced within each of them, they were able to exist together cooperatively without any sort of hierarchical domination. Each set of twins also embodied an element, water, air, fire, and earth. Therefore, they were also known as 'the elementals."

This journey, these images... they would take me home. Home was a feeling I longed for, a place where my soul felt at rest without all the density and struggle of Earth. There was no time to feel afraid of what that might mean, or what that would change for me; I focused on the story unfolding before me.

At that moment I felt the heart energy of Divine Father as he watched his children, joyfully dancing about in the capsule awaiting his word. He remembered the excitement of creating his first planet with his beloved Ama and their own brethren. Their journey had been filled with delightful experiences; what it felt like to breath air, to run, to drink water... to make love. There had also been the many lessons unobtainable without form; like patience with the body, how to control and direct its movements, and how to harness the energy of the mind to use thought while in a body.

Io shared in his children's joy, yet he was not without his concerns. Many new experiences might unfold for his precious children beyond the sanctuary of the ethereal- realm. A strong tugging in Io's heart made him wants to draw the Children close and never let them go, but he knew this would not be right. He understood that all of life must continue to change and grow.

With difficulty Io pulled his mind back to the present moment as he smiled upon his precious children.

Divine Father's noble voice rang out through the golden sphere of protection. "Children it is time for you to create your own physical bodies. They will be the likeness of all that you are here, although each will have its own unique expression."

The Children of Light moved further into their own group and began to focus their consciousness on an image before them. I watched as these magnificent beings offered their energies to the group creation one by one, and as I watched, I understood who each of the individual twins were.

Each pair hovered in the air near each other. The remaining siblings sat cross-legged in a mid-air circle around them. Each of them seemed to concentrate intently on the twins learning from what they were about to witness. Before each of them appeared an enormous three- dimensional star, larger than their ethereal-bodies, by at least three feet. Each star rotated quickly so that it appeared to me that the triangle pointing upward spun in one direction, and the one pointed downward spun in the opposite direction. Each was a vivid golden color on the outermost layer. Inside this layer were the most beautiful hues of all the other rainbow colors. I thought I could hear sounds, like high-pitched tones being produced by these spinning stars.

Curiously I turned my mind toward Lady Nada who instantly responded. "It is this shape that comes into existence before the human forms, they are the essence of who you truly are. Inside this shape, as you are about to see, the original humans placed all their information, higher energies, and all that was precious to them, and then created their physical bodies within them."

Her voice was suddenly laced with sadness. "Each human has one of these around them but the memory of it has been erased from your history and memories. It was through these vehicles of light that the twins traveled to your world, and it is how they remained conscious of who they truly were. This sacred geometry is also what allowed them to remain immortal and disease free."

I stared wide-eyed at the powerful images before me and tried to imagine that such a shape existed around my body, but I could feel nothing.

Lady Nada offered. "It is there Luna, you have this shape, and others around you. It just lies dormant; you could consider it a device that has not been activated by you but is there for you to use when you learn how to."

I felt a shiver move through me as I excitedly looked at the beautiful twins. Lady Nada responded to this wave of joy. "This device can also be activated by us for you, this is how we brought you here."

I exclaimed. "You mean that's what made me feel all that energy, that buzzing around me when the angel came?"

"Yes Luna, exactly."

"Are you saying this is a time-travel device, that we all have them around us, and could learn to travel through time and space?"

Lady Nada laughed. "Yes, you did just travel through time and space. You have this shape."

I stared in absolute awe as the Goddess of Water, named Summersara, began to create a ball of liquid-blue light in the golden star before her with mere thought and intention. I could feel this happening through her almost as though it were me, empathically! Her eyes seemed to swell with concentration, creating waves of pure spiritual emotion around the ball. Soon, a rotating sphere spun within the star. An image began to turn and grow inside the sphere changing with Summersara's every breath of beauty and grace. At last, in perfect calmness stood a woman of sensual strength and grace. Brilliant-blue eyes shone with the light of clear waters, expressing immense love. Long flowing golden hair gently swayed against her sides as though water moved through it.

A silk turquoise gown wrapped her petite, yet voluptuous body in serenity. She smiled, radiating the essence of purity as she delicately reached her milky-white hand toward her beloved twin, Sunta. I was astounded, how much time had passed I did not know, but it could not have been long. I had literally just witnessed a light-being create a perfect human being; with the most extraordinary beauty and poise, just like that. These were our ancestors; this was whom we really

are, not biology formed in the ocean evolving over millions of years!

The God of Water's new form stood in the center of his own golden star of creation; like his twin his sacred shape was also a sphere. I was already beginning to understand - each set of twins must have the same sacred shape. Long graceful hands reached toward his beloved, his eyes shining with wisdom, these deep-blue pools reflecting the ever- flowing movement of the sea. Curly-blond hair rested gently on his shoulders, draped with a beautiful blue and violet cloak; gemstones of sapphire blue and soft rose adorning his golden forehead and arms.

Summersara looked up and down his tall, graceful body and called out with a delighted giggle. "You are beautiful, my love! So very beautiful!"

Sunta responded melodiously, "And so are you, oh one of perfect beauty! What bliss we share!"

The Goddess and God of Water turned to watch their siblings in their own creation.

The Goddess of Air, An, called out to her twin in her mind, "It's happening. We are making human bodies!"

They shared in a moment of complete joy and a nearly overwhelming awareness of what this meant. These new aspects of themselves would be independent from the embrace of their parents and entirely responsible for a planetary system, though they would always remain connected,

Suddenly An longed to be held by her Mother's love. Her higher self - the self that was ethereal - would remain in the realm of pure light. Her new self (all their new selves) would be so very far away from Divine Mother and Father on their new planet.

An sent a silent thought of gratitude to her Mother. "The memories of your comforting embrace will be with me always."

Hearing her daughter's thought Ama turned to An, "My dear one, you will thrive in your new creation. There is so much responsibility in being a guardian to an entire planet. Learn well all that you can, and do not forget this responsibility as you play and dance with your brothers and sisters."

An bowed deeply, keeping her hands to her heart as though to keep the memory of her beloved mother close.

I felt there was nothing to compare their perfect bodies and crystal-clear minds within my world. It would take the most beautiful human features and the expressions of everything good and pure that had ever existed in every single person on Earth, without any defilement or imperfection, all blended together, to even come close.

Divine Mother and Father watched the continual creations of their children joyously. Ama exuded the pure joy of a mother watching her child doing something new for the first time. I shared in her children's delight, yet at the same time her heart ached for the metamorphosis that was taking place. No longer would her beloved ones be under her protective wing. She ached with a mother's protective concern for her young. She did have complete trust in their ability to care for themselves, but it was a vastly different realm they were entering.

Io smiled endearingly at all his beloved children. "It is amazing; each soul-group will be forming a new race in the universe."

Laughing, he pointed to one of the groups. "Look how beautifully the rainbow manifests its form. Here our children have created exquisite, pointed ears and delicate, yet tall bodies, and such a brilliant blue color skin." (I thought these gracious eight feet tall beings must have been elves or fairies).

Mother laughed, pointing out another group to their right. "How round they are, with such bright red hair, and eyes so filled with the spark of life, they are no more than three feet high!"

I thought these beings were indeed very short, and adorably stout. These must have been the gnomes and dwarf beings, known around the world by different names like 'Menehune or Leprechauns', those little beings that rarely showed themselves to humans. I wondered what had happened to make them hide away from those that were once their very own siblings.

Ama shook her head back and forth in amazement. "It is perfect the way that thought and emotion can create unique forms."

The Children of One were gathered in a circle while their parents and 136 siblings looked on with silent observation, all were wide-eyed and positive. Inside the spacious circle the Children focused their burning gaze; their arms swayed this way and that as though their fingers were brushes against an empty canvas, painting this invisible landscape that was to become 'Earth'.

I understood that the light-beings had been practicing their creations in the ethereal-realm for a long time. Much effort had been focused on forming unimaginable beauty. They had also named everything, imagining what it would feel like to have a body to interact with solid matter.

There was so much for me to take in and it all happened so fast. It was easy to see that each pair of twins embodied an element; they looked like images I had seen of the Goddess of Earth, with deep brown skin rising up from a fertile field, or a Goddess of Fire rising out of a volcano with fiery red hair. It was truly amazing how mythical they were. This made me realize that all earth myths were in some way real; here I was actually witnessing proof of the ancient myths and legends about divine beings and immortal Gods. It was so different then just reading a long-ago story where one wasn't sure if it was real or made up. It was more real than anything that had ever been!

The Goddess of Earth swirled her arms through the air, the movements smooth and graceful. A landmass began to form. First a great mountain, then several valleys, gorges… Her twin joined in with swirling motions. Trees began to grow in the heart of the forest, spreading far and wide. Flowers of every size and color - colors more vivid and diverse then anything I had ever seen - blossomed before my very eyes.

Ayia, God of Air, flew into the circle playing an emerald-colored glass flute and before long a bright blue sky filled in the space around the Earth. Gentle clouds began to dance in the air as the Goddess of Air flew through the atmosphere, spinning her body round and round. Finally, the two met, hovering above the sphere. With hands on hips, they seemed to inspect their creation, at last smiling at each other in satisfaction.

Delighted with her brother's creation Summersara soon joined in, gracefully waving her delicate hands back and forth smiling with complete satisfaction. Around the continent a beautiful blue-green ocean took shape. Her twin joined in sweeping his long arms from side to side. Stunning rivers emerged with huge waterfalls, lakes, and streams opened new spaces across the Earth, many of them racing with gold veins.

God and Goddess of Fire concentrated their intense gaze steadily on the land. The planet warmed and here and there volcanoes began to pour lava, creating before my eye's huger mountains and majestic cliffs.

Time truly stood still as they floated around the globe in silent concentration; yet on the surface of the new planet things were happening at super speed. Volcanic eruptions became mountains within minutes. Details filled the bubble of creation; curves in the land forming hills, caves and caverns filled with brilliant crystals and underground springs. Rapidly, magical animals like unicorns and Pegasus's, dragons, and enormous colorful birds appeared everywhere, galloping, grazing, resting, and sometimes taking to flight. The continent was enormous, filling over half the globe with its vastness.

Soon, the sphere was turning and ringing with a melody all its own. The images were now crystal clear. Beautiful valleys, spectacular meadows of gloriously colored flowers began to gain definition and crispness. Soft rays of a golden
sun brought further illumination to their world. To the left of the sun rested a blue moon, and to the right another moon: a soft pink. The Children closed their eyes, and I experienced their minds as they called forth their beloved friends, the cetaceans. The spirit-bodies of these magnificent, gentle beings quickly journeyed from other planets to meet in the capsule of creation.

Thousands of whales and dolphins sang as one with the Children of Light in celebration of the planetary creation. Families, with their babies, came leaping into the air, spinning joyously as their tails reached for the sky!

Summersara called out to her parents excitedly. "Isn't our world magnificent!"

Mother responded, "Indeed, my daughter, it is most splendid."

Sunta sang out with great joy. "Oh, Mother and Father, thank you so much for this gift!"

The children silently joined their thoughts together once

more.

After a moment Ayia spoke for them all. "We have decided to call her Tara, 'sacred land', and it shall be a jewel within our universe."

"It shall truly be that" replied Father happily.

They sat in this glorious silence for a long while, filled with excitement and joy, watching the blue and green planet from the space around her. Around the group delighted eyes took in the ineffable beauty of the newly created world.

Io paused turning his attention to Ama as he silently communicated. "I feel I must tell them."

Ama responded with thought. "Though you may warn them it is quite possible they will not understand."

He turned once again to the large group. "There is something I must warn you of." The children looked to him with innocent eyes, eager for his wisdom. He continued, "There is a creation that exists born of All That Is and yet very different from any that you have ever know; a creation separate from the Light."

Even in saying this, Io felt a shiver move through his body. It was best they do not dwell on the subject for long, for although darkness could not penetrate the realms of light, merely speaking the word could cause it to be attracted to the Children's new physical world outside of that immaculate protection. It was a risk he had to take, they had to know what was out there.

An spiraled high in the air giggling. "But what else could there be Father?"

Extending the seriousness of his knowing, Divine Father responded. "It is called - darkness!"

The Children called out in unison, darkness?"

The Children held no concept of what 'darkness' meant. Io knew he could not transfer the meaning directly, lest he contaminate the purity of their beloved children. He could not interfere with their free will and protect them. All he could do was warn them and then they had to decide for themselves.

He responded calmly, "Though you know not of this energy, it is possible that you will draw it to your new planet, if a source discovers your world sustains life."

The Children looked to him with puzzlement and curiosity.

He continued. "Light is energy, and light is information that creates, as you know. It always acts as one for the whole, and for the betterment of all. Darkness acts to defeat all of creation, destroying life. Although this is hard to understand from your perspective, know that light always seeks to evolve, while darkness seeks to control that evolution where and when it can."

Understanding that this was confusing to the Children he ended by saying, "Darkness came out of Oneness just as light did. It can serve the purpose of creating light through its reflection. It can even become light through your reflection, but you too can become lost in this darkness through absorption."

The Children placed their thoughts together pondering this new concept. It was clear that they could not imagine blocking any form of creation. Their way was to share with, and love, every aspect of life. After a few moments Rasha, God of Fire, sang out for the whole, "Father we shall welcome the dark!"

Around their floating circle the Children giggled nodding in agreement. This welcoming nature, this way of being one with everything around them, was all they had ever known.

Io wished once again that there were some ways, he could give the Children his own wisdom in this matter without contamination, but there simply wasn't. He would not hold back their growth and adventure by preventing them from growing and learning … that was not the way of light.

Ama sighed, knowing the inherent innocence of the Children.

Her voice rang out to the Children, "Dear ones, we cannot say more about what this energy is without calling it to you. You must please, if ever there is a need for your protection, let the angels come to do our bidding. If ever they call to you, you must do as they say. Can you understand this?"

After a moment Ayia spoke out for them all. "Yes Mother of course, we will do as you wish."

Divine Mother smiled compassionately at her beloved son. This was all that could be done. For several moments there was nothing but silence, as the enormous group sat mesmerized by their new creation.

The main continent was enormous, at least three times the size of all the Americas put together. Even if I could combine all my own memories of the most beautiful places on Earth; the vistas of the Grand Canyon, the enormous power of the Redwood forest, and the tranquil turquoise seas of the Cayman Islands, none of it could truly compare to the perfection of what the Children of Light had created.

It wasn't just that the great continent was larger than anything currently on Earth, or the mountains were taller, or the sea calmer. An inherent light moved in shimmering waves across the land. Enormous mountains of pure amethyst shone in purple glory. Rays of violet filtered down to the forest floors between great trees, the likes of which I had never seen. Some of the treetops were laden with fruits in shades of color that would have been unimaginable to me had I not seen them with my own eyes.

The entire sea around the vast continent was calm, yet it sparkled and pulsed with tremendous life force. Its energy was so magnetic, I felt I would never forget how beautiful it looked, as though I could just leap into it, and swim forever in its perfection.

I could also sense that there was nothing frightening or dangerous on this original earth. I recognized it as my own planet, but yet it was so very different. There were no poisonous snakes in the deep tropical jungles, and no man- eating sharks in the sea. Of course, this was how it would be, I realized. The Children of Light had created the planet in perfection, in pure joy and harmony. Everything they created was in their image, and they were the image of Divine Mother and Father. Ultimately, even they were but a part of a larger whole, their own Divine Creator.

A chill moved through me, as I realized this continent clearly no longer existed on earth, what had become of it? I wondered how frightening creatures had come to exist on Earth, and I shivered with a memory of a recurring dream, where strange monstrous beings swam in a murky ocean surrounded by lava and boiling pits that seemed to drop into forever. I shook myself out of the darkness. The dance of energy across the land and sea beckoned the Children to come and play. This first life was what life was truly meant to be; enjoyed in all its glory, an act of play and innocence, nothing more, and nothing less.

Compared to that first time, it was as though the current world had a gray haze over it. In my time everything was shadowed, so very imperfect. Hints of that original beauty were still present; in the grand forests of America, the Swiss Alps, the sacredness of

Hawaii, but even these places were now touched by pollution, if not environmental, then thought pollution, disease pollution...

The images on the screen slowly faded away. Around the room a soft murmur began. I blinked myself back to the reality around me, from the creation of my own planet by divine twins to the galactic council, equally as astounding, which now stared at me so lovingly. Lord Sananda rose from his seat, opening his arms lovingly toward me.

In that moment I had a sense of why I was seated so far from all of them; it was enough to be in their magnificent presence; being any closer would have been overwhelming. Maybe it was best for them too, so I didn't contaminate the purity of who they were.

Sananda spoke softly. "That is all for now. You will journey back through the tunnel of light into your physical body. Rest deeply and remember all that you have witnessed here."

With that my body began to shake and I felt myself being lifted into the tunnel, moving at a rapid speed back through the tunnel of light.

I heard Lady Nada's voice like an echo in my mind, following me all the way to my body. "This is the story of your creation, never forget, cherish it, and see it dancing in the light all around you, its song still being sung....".

CHAPTER SIX

Light In Everyone

I came back to my body feeling the deepest sense of peace I had ever known, albeit dazed and bewildered. The moon was no longer up, and the sky was quite dark, sparkling with starlight. I wondered for a moment where in the wide universe I had been, where was the galactic council and that perfect world? I also wondered if it had happened at all, though I lay there, knowing it had, and at the same time I was in disbelief that it had. There was just no way to integrate such a thing, such vastness, nothing to do other than accept it, fantastic as it was.

I stood up slowly, struggling for balance and walked to the nearest tree to relieve a very full bladder. The journey was still pulsing like waves of light in my mind. Not fully awake, I walked back to my sleeping bag and curling up on my side, fell into a deep, dreamless rest.

When I woke again the sun was already sitting high above the mountain, I was covered in sweat.

Sitting up, I realized I was dehydrated, so I reached for my water bottle and began drinking thirstily. Seeing that the water was almost gone, I understood, with some remorse, that I would have to leave my sanctuary for provisions.

I had to lie down again. It would take a lot to integrate that it had all really happened. Closing my eyes, hearing the sound of the surf, I felt the hard lava rock beneath my little sleeping pad. It reminded me of the Twins of Fire. I could still see them so vividly creating their bodies; I would never forget that, not ever!

It was real ... so real. There she was ... Fiona, Goddess of Fire, replaying her act of creation. More beautiful than anything I had ever seen, her deep emerald, green eyes shining as clear as crystal, suddenly seemed to stare into my soul. Long, curly, red hair fell over round shoulders, her smooth curves like those of flowing lava perfecting her milky-white body, adorned with a splendid emerald gown to match her eyes. The semi-translucent fabric seemed to flicker, changing form and movement like embers of a fire; the most beautiful clothing I had ever beheld.

Then there was her twin, creating his amazing body; his concentration the intensity of a thousand burning suns. Fiery red hair cascaded over his shoulders to meet a green silk gown, gently hugging his muscular body. His wide green eyes also seemed to stare out at me. I thought of the legend of Pele, the Goddess of Fire who created the Hawaiian Islands. Was this who they were? Was this what I was really being shown? The elements, me, everything on earth, created by these Creator Gods? It was all I could do to marvel at everything that had occurred, and just try my hardest to be surrendered to the startling new reality I had been brought into.

I spent most of the day in a daze. I tried writing it all down, hoping that would help me feel more settled, but even that was overwhelming. My emotions ran rampant; everything from joy and excitement about this incredible new, absolutely unbelievable experience, to weeping with a grief that I could not understand. At other points walking along the beach, I felt afraid, afraid of what I was becoming, this person no one on earth was going to relate to. I was definitely not going to tell anyone about it. Kicking the sand in frustration, I was startled by a voice.

"Hey there beautiful lady, what you are kicking' sand on us for."

I gasped. How had I not seen Handel and Blue lying just feet from me? Something about it struck me as funny; I was so caught up.

I laughed and tried to get the words out. "Sorry... I didn't see you there."

Blue stood up beaming a bright smile, laughing with me. "What's wrong? You looked so sad just then... not your usual self."

I shrugged my browned shoulders, so warm with the sun they were probably near to burnt. My gaze darted around almost nervously, and I felt I was in another world, unable to speak. There was nothing I could say, not yet; it was all just way too crazy to share!

Handel stood up opening his arms wide for a hug. I accepted, enjoying the human touch. It somehow helped me feel more real. "It's alright precious girl, Hawaii does that to all of us. Emotions come and go."

I pulled back thinking, if he only knew the half of it. I just wasn't remotely ready to share my story... not yet!

Taking the attention off my vulnerable emotions I blurted out "Hey, I've been thinking. It's time for me to head on. I don't really want to, but I need more water and some shade, and I feel ready to see another part of the island."

Blue looked down at the ground to conceal his sadness. "Yeah, my Dad and I were talking and it's time for us to go too. We need food, and we promised the people at the farm we would help out soon."

Our eyes met and held each other's gaze for a moment.

We had shared something neither would ever forget.

Breaking the contact, I turned to Handel. "Are there other places where I could get in the water with the dolphins? It's just way too far out for me here."

Handel smiled. "This island is full of magical places. For those called to her by spirit such as yourself, she leads you on a journey from one to the next. You will find the dolphins again. I'm not surprised you need to go. I have an idea though. Why don't you spend the night on the farm with us? I'm sure those folks would be happy to have you. That way
you can have a good dinner and a hot shower before you continue your journey."

I hadn't even thought about a shower. My skin had grown used to the stiff saltiness, and my feet were becoming nicely calloused by the rocks. But at the mention of it, I remembered how nice it would be to have that squeaky clean feeling I hadn't felt since I arrived in Hawaii.

"That sounds great. It will give me time to think about where I want to go."

Turning to Blue I smiled, "How about one more swim before we go?!"

We ran toward the water laughing excitedly. The play helped me empty my mind and was just what I needed.

I was torn about leaving the magic of this place, but I was ready for more, ready for change. The farm was about a twenty-minute drive up the steep mountain, overlooking the bay of dolphins from high above. I enjoyed seeing green again, and all the fruit literally hanging off trees. My stomach still turned with last night's journey. I needed simplicity; to try some other tropical fruits, and to touch base with some other humans.

Stepping out of Handel's little island rusty pickup, I was greeted by a completely different reality. The smell of earth and trees mingled with the scent of fragrant flowers drifting up on the moist breeze from the ocean. The air was cooler, though still pleasant. Handel motioned for me to follow them toward a small wooden house. The sounds of crowing roosters and chirping crickets felt welcoming, grounding. The grassy farmland was such a contrast to the rocky shore I had grown to love, but equally wonderful in its own way.

Handel called out as they opened the door, "Company's a-coming'! "

I entered the small, simple space and adjusted my eyes to the dim light. Blue followed behind.

A couple emerged from some back room. The large woman called out boisterously, "Welcome back, old friend! How was your journey?"

He hugged her back warmly. "Awesome as always, we caught a few huge Ahi and saw some amazing sunsets."

She didn't seem surprised to see me standing beside Handel and Blue. "Aw, I see you've brought a friend with you. Now, who might this be?"

Handel turned with pride. "This is Luna, a magical soul come to bring her blessings to Hawaii."

I smiled and reached for the woman's outstretched hand. "Welcome Luna, I'm Gracie, and this is my husband, Jake."

Jake peeked out from behind his wife and held out his hand.

"Nice to meet you."

I smiled back. Gracie motioned to the kitchen table, which was actually a picnic table, with a large basket of fruit on top. "Come sit. Let's 'talk story'."

She turned to Blue and embraced him. "How's my boy?"

Blue smiled brightly. "Couldn't be better. Only wish I wasn't going so soon."

I smiled at the closeness between them; there was a sense of family that was quite warming.

Gracie laughed intensely. "Don't blame you! Who would want to go back to that toxic waste dump they call the mainland?"

Everyone nodded and grumbled in agreement. Though the scene was warming, I also felt a bit strange being in this social realm of humanity after my celestial travels. Life held such diversity and that was the beauty of it, I reminded myself. These people were so welcoming, and the simple interaction was maybe just what I needed, so I wouldn't float away. Sitting down at the table I decided to become fully present with the situation.

Soon Grace had prepared a delicious-smelling dinner in the midst of hearing the adventures of Handel and Blue. I sat absorbing the simplicity of the surroundings. The house was unpainted, just rustic natural wood. On the wall hung a few paintings of tropical flowers. I had been camping for only a week, but I had grown so used to being outdoors that the enclosure around me felt foreign. In fact, I had spent most of the past year outside, so living indoors was a bit strange in general at this point, sterile and dark, but also in some way comforting.

Before eating, everyone held hands and closed eyes. Grace offered a prayer. "Great Spirit... Spirit of this sacred island, of sea and sky. Mother Pele, we give many thanks for the blessings of this abundant meal and the friends gathered here. May you hold them in your embrace and guide them in your way."

At that, we all squeezed hands and opened eyes with genuine smiles. I thought of my early childhood, when thirty or more people would gather around a huge table offering thanks before the evening meal. I smiled, feeling my heart warmed by the very real humans around me.

Gracie described the delicious food. "This is Taro, a root which is sacred to the Hawaiian people. It will give you grounding."

I smiled. "I could use that. Thank you so much for this meal."

Grace smiled effortlessly back. "It's our pleasure. Isn't that right Jake?" She nudged her husband.

Jake nodded through a mouthful of the white mash.

Grace continued. "These other purple things are sweet potato, also sacred to the Hawaiians. Not so long-ago Hawaiian people ate only from the land and sea. That was all there was. We try to follow in this example, taking most of what we need from our own land."

I looked around the table at the many bowls of food. Besides the abundant servings of taro and sweet potato, there was a large green salad, a bowl of tomatoes, and some stewed greens. "Did all this come from your farm?"

Grace responded, "It sure did. After dinner, Alex can show you around."

Blue smiled. That was the first time his 'real' name had been revealed to me.

I smiled back and commented, "I still think Blue suits you better."

The others seemed to notice the special bond between the two of us and smiled fondly as they continued to eat. I sure, hoped they weren't getting the wrong idea. To me, it was that Blue and I had such an amazing platonic friendship. I hoped the others could see this was all it was, after all he was only sixteen.

After dinner the sun was just beginning to set. In the dimming light Blue lead me around the farm. I pointed to a cluster of large trees. "What are those?"

Blue picked up a round, light brown nut from under one of the trees. "These are macadamia nuts. Want to try a few?"

We sat down and began cracking the nuts with large rocks. I was amazed at how rich the nut was, delicious and filling. Meanwhile, I asked about every tree I could see. There was a lipstick tree which had a pod on it filled with bright red squishy stuff. When I smeared it on my arm, I saw that it indeed painted on just like lipstick.

"What fun this would be for children!" I exclaimed. "Yeah." Blue responded smiling fondly at me. "I'm going to miss you so much. You are so different from most people, so curious about everything, almost like there's innocence about you. Most pretty girls just seem to care about being beautiful, but you don't even seem to care about it… even though you're the most beautiful girl I've ever seen."

"Blue," I reached out and held his hand. "You feel like a true brother to me. You have allowed me to feel free, to be myself, without wanting more of me."

He squeezed my hand. "People seem to think that's all there is, but they miss out on the magic of everything else. That's what has been so special about our time together."

I smiled. "You are special. I hope you always keep your innocence and get to spend a lot more time here."

Blue looked in the distance. "I hope my mom will let me."

I squatted down and touched the now cool earth. "Just think of it this way. Another year and a half and you'll be on your own, free to choose for yourself."

He smiled and seemed to return to the present moment. "Please promise me you'll always stay in touch."

I nodded, feeling certain that I would. We were silent for a few moments, enjoying the night air closing in around us. I blinked. Out of the darkness, a brilliant white mist was suddenly filling the space around us, until it was all we could see. Its touch was soft, refreshing, and mysterious. Somewhere across from me I heard Blue gasp. I wanted to stay very still, so that whatever it was wouldn't go away.

Blue whispered through the mist. "Doesn't it feel magical, almost unreal? The Hawaiians say that white mist is a blessing from the Aumakua, the Great Spirits."

I could only whisper. "Yes, it feels like a blessing." I felt the mist was speaking to us, blessing us with unspoken words. It seemed to be telling me that there was indeed a special connection the two of us had. I hoped we would stay in touch.

It was truly a perfect ending to our journey together. It would be sad to say good-bye though. We sat mesmerized for a long while as the mist floated about us and finally lifted, leaving no evidence that it had ever been there at all. Slowly, we walked back to the little house to say goodnight.

Gracie and Jake offered me a bed, but I graciously declined. "Thank you so much. You have been so generous, but if it is okay with you, I'm eager to set up my tent. I didn't even need it at the ocean!"

Gracie laughed, and hugged I tightly. "You do whatever you need. May we at least offer you a shower?"

I let out a sigh. "Now that would be great!"

I stood under the warm waters of the outdoor shower looking up at the stars. It was the best shower I had ever taken. I didn't know when I would see my next shower, and though this didn't bother me too much, I took the time to clean my body very thoroughly. I smiled to myself thinking about how amazing it all was. I was probably starting to accept the vast new reality I was in. The Children of Light were so amazing. I longed to know beings like that, so perfect and pure. But for now, things had to be okay. There was light in every person I met along the way. As long as humanity could realize what the Council needed them to do, before it was too late; then every single person could find that inner light and make it shine! I remembered in those moments what Lady Nada had said about writing everything down and finding the greatest lessons for each session.

CHAPTER SEVEN

Born To Create, Play and Love

I set up my tent just as the sun set, the sky turned pitch black quickly, stars glittering with the new moon. Lying on my back feeling deeply satisfied with the day and my beautiful little red tent, my mind began to empty as I took in the quiet sounds of the night. Crickets called out to each other through the warm night air and somewhere in the distance a dog barked. The intoxicating smell of night- blooming jasmine hung lightly in the air, drifting in through the tent screen.

Soon the sensation of spinning and ecstasy filled my body, and I found myself moving back through the tunnel of light. The angel wasn't there this time. I traveled with greater and greater speed until everything was a blur. On the other side I found myself immediately seated beneath the crystal-dome. The Council members were all there just as I had last seen them. The space was quiet, meditative. I shifted in my seat working hard to bring my awareness into the vastly different 'plane'. Surrounded by the grace and warmth of the council, after a few silent moments, I began to feel more at ease. In this reality there was no need for social niceties to make a new arrival feel welcome, rather they acknowledged my arrival by offering a welcoming and healing energy that any trusting soul would quickly absorb.

The screen in the center of the great room began to rotate. Once again, the 'golden sphere of creation' hovered in the center of a whirlwind of colors. I had no trouble recalling that the eight twins had just completed the act of creating their new forms.

Each new human being turned to admire all the others, showing their ecstatic appreciation with delightful laughter.

I found myself so blissfully immersed in the rapture of the dancing, twirling Children of Light that, for a second, I forgot things had ever changed, that humanity had fallen so far. What I saw displayed so vividly the great light, the perfect visions that were so vastly different than what humankind experienced in 'my' world of today.

Divine Father's voice filled the enormous capsule of light. "It is time for your new bodies to journey to your beautiful planet. For a time, they will remain in isolation capsules while the energies stabilize and coalesce."

He smiled peacefully at all his children in their ethereal-forms and continued, "You, my children, will always have a connection with these physical aspects of yourselves, though you shall move onward to other creations, traveling to other realms and evolving yourselves."

"Thank you, Father," the Children acknowledged with bows and smiles.

The new planet, Tara, floated serenely in the vastness of empty space… her own entity, a bright testimony to the Children's evolution through light. This final moment was filled with great joy and sadness for Divine Mother and Father.

Ama offered a prayer "May your new life be perfect and joyous always. May you enjoy all that you will feel and learn by having physical bodies."

It was the hardest thing she would ever do, to watch a part of her beloved children depart the ethereal realm alone, to manifest in a physical world. But she exhibited only confidence and her excitement for their journey, selflessly as Divine Mother would.

They both smiled upon all their beloved children one last time. I understood that it was time for them to return to their abode in the Highest Realm. The 144 children bowed reverently to parents whose light-bodies began to fade until there was nothing but empty space. They held their bowed positions for a long while like that even after they were gone. Like any farewell, it was a sad and long moment, and there was nothing more that could be done, nothing to say… at last they returned their attention to the planet below.

In unison they stopped and turned toward the planet. Their bodies radiated pure strength and serenity, holding their hands at their sides, palms facing forward, each focusing their attention on the planet.

Suddenly there was a soft tone; it grew louder and louder, producing a resonant, complex sound that rang out like a wave. This tone caused the new realm to rotate. Soon the entire sphere swelled and spun, encompassing the planet, and also the two moons created by the Children. These three spheres rotated around a golden sun in the solar system where the planet had been placed. Suddenly the tones softened and then ceased, leaving only a faint echo that would continue to ring about the planet as it rotated, encased by an aura of soft blues and violet. Far in the distance I could see the bright golden sun, and beyond the sun were little round balls spinning slowly. They looked indeed like other planets in Earth's (Tara's) solar system that I knew so well.

The scene drew closer and closer to Tara until I was inside the atmosphere looking down upon the blue capsules. Closing their eyes, the Children exited the 'capsule of creation' and re-appeared in their resting capsules.

In the next moment these 144 "pods" began to move slowly toward the surface of the vast blue ocean, close to the enormous continent covered in green. Brilliant, translucent blue illuminated the entire sky, and an excited soft buzz emanated from the capsules. The ocean below was a tranquil deep aqua, resting silent and serene. Sunlight danced on the ocean floor, a smooth blanket of white sand. Shining in purity and newness, the new planet truly seemed like a massive crystal. I was astounded; here I was gazing at the very first moments of our planet's creation, a planet so vibrant I hardly recognized it as earth.

There were quiet sounds, those of the soft wind, the gentle movement of the ocean, but also an extraordinary silence. It was a silence that could be felt and almost heard, as though it were the silence holding all the wisdom and power of the universe.

That type of silence could not be found on the current

Earth, except for faint whispers here and there, yet I felt the silence would always be there in the echoes of the distant past, beckoning all to remember. I had felt a trace of that profound silence in the mountains of California, the valleys of Kentucky, the desert planes of Arizona ... and now in the expansive sea of Hawaii. Even in the purest places, it was not the same as it first was; now with cars and signs and trash, and words carved into trees.

It made me realize that the noise pollution and wireless technology of the current Earth interfered with humanity's ability to feel the true source of spiritual nourishment - what a loss! The striking duality was concerning.

I could tell a great deal of time had passed for the Children of One, lying in complete stillness, harmonizing their new forms with the physical realm around them. Finally, it was time for them to emerge from the capsules. In the sea below the dolphins appeared out of the deep-waters, swimming in large circles below the bright blue pods. They seemed to have been awaiting the arrival of the Creator Gods. Their sweet voices began to rise in their own language, reminding me of a chorus of delighted toddlers. The capsules slowly lowered to the surface of the ocean, wobbling gently. Gathering around them, the dolphins slowly began to nudge each pod with their long noses toward the shore. Just as the capsules touched the pure smooth sand, the new bodies began to stir and open. The Children, still lying in their pods began to sing in unison.

It was a song unlike any I had ever heard. I knew this was their creation song, and it held within it the seed word of the land that was to be their home - LEMURIA. The sound was glorious and ecstatic. With their rising voices the capsules began to open. One by one the Children lifted effortlessly into the air, extending their open hands toward the land. Their eyes sparkled as they looked with complete awe upon the continent before them; their perfect forms radiated brilliant white, purple, and pink light as their song carried across the vast landscape. It was by far the most beautiful song I had ever heard and one I would never forget.

The Children of One were centered in the middle, each so beautifully adorned with their shimmering clothes, and gemstones, larger than life. Out from them stretched the 136, small dwarfs, large elves, delicate fairy-like humans, all beautifully adorned with all the colors of the rainbow. Their eyes sparkled with bliss and awe as they looked out upon their world for the very first time.

Each of the Children of One began to sing his or her own name, adding to the great song of the 'Motherland,' anchoring their signature onto the planet. An, the Goddess of Air, listened as they sang, feeling complete awe at the echo of all the names reverberating from the great mountains near the sea, and of the feeling of the human voice. Their language, I understood, was the one they had brought from the ethereal home, the seed language of light throughout all of creation. It was beautiful, not just words but song, tone, feeling, and energy as nothing I had ever before heard, though familiar, like a deep ache in my heart's memory of such perfect expression.

Behind them the capsules dissolved into thin air, their purpose complete. The dolphins seemed to laugh with joyful celebration as they took to leaping and flipping their great bodies into the air with tremendous strength.

An And Ayia slowly joined hands for the first time, sending a thrilling wave through their shining new bodies.

I could see sparks of light literally fly between their bodies. It was the moment in time that summed up everything one truly should feel when they stood at the altar of marriage, joining together in physical and spiritual union. It represented what so many people were truly searching for, that pure, undefiled love. After a moment the Twins of Air turned their luminous gaze toward the land again.

All 144 Children gracefully floated through the air until they were spaced evenly hovering above the long white beach at the edge of the ocean. As they landed, a wave of white light expanded out like a ripple on a pond over the planet's surface. I sensed an inward gasp among them as their feet felt the planets physical surface for the first time, although outwardly they did not utter a sound.

Slowly they began to discover their hands and feet and stretch their bodies this way and that. I marveled 'How will I ever describe such rapture to others?' Witnessing the splendor of the Children's self-discovery was like watching a baby realize its toes for the first time or experience its first taste of food. That expression of purity and the innocence of a baby; there in these fully-grown beings that had just come into form from pure thought, complete innocence and delight.

To witness them was to witness what life should be. In that moment I understood the meaning of life, the purpose of being incarnate in physical form. It was so simple, so perfect. If one could only learn to live in the moment, to be, 'as a little child' just as Jesus taught, a human being could actually be happy, be free! What other purpose could there be?

An's body scintillated and pulsed, her green eyes sparkling with gaiety. She was unsure how to even begin moving her body; there was so much sensation. She would have to will her body into further motion when she was ready.

The Earth was soft and embracing, warm and welcoming, her feet light and sensitive, and I could hear the song of each grain of sand through her skin.

'Oh,' thought An, 'The wind is sublime! It is so soft and loving, powerful and yet calm. It is everything I thought it would be in form.'

Wanting to include her beloved in her experience she sent him the thought, "Isn't it amazing? The sensations of the body are almost overwhelming, almost too fantastic for such a condensed energy-form."

Ayia called out in his mind, "So wonderful my love, together we shall experience everything this realm has to offer."

Summersara laughed out loud when she looked down at her long, graceful arms. A wave of pure bliss moved through her body, and she laughed again hearing the sound of her own laugher, feeling it shake her body, a wonderfully pleasant feeling. Slowly she lifted one hand and moved it over the surface of her arm. A gasp escaped from her mouth, as she laughed harder feeling how connected her voice was to her experience of sensation.

Seeing through the Water Goddess's eyes, I noticed a visible energy of dancing colors surrounding all the plants and every life-form, even around her own hands. With each breath, she really did experience being one with everything. Her breath simply extended out and out over the planet, and I felt everything as a part of myself, just as she did. It was a feeling of complete security and comfort, and at the same time vastly powerful. It was so incredibly different then the feeling I was used to of 'me', and then 'everything else'.

I recalled an experience that in some measure resembled what the twins were going through, when I had taken magic mushrooms with some friends in a redwood forest. Everything had felt so very alive, unlike any feeling I had ever known. I had seen beautiful eyes looking out from trees and felt the heartbeat of the Earth in the soil beneath my bare feet. My mind was raw and pure as though I were alive for the first time.

What I was experiencing in Hawaii with the water and the vibrant beauty around me was a heightened consciousness without the use of any mind-altering substances. Yet I wondered in that moment if those mushrooms existed on Earth to help people remember. It was clear that the Children were in such a state of bliss all the time. No wonder people sought out this state; it had once been so natural. A chill moved through me as I wondered once again what had happened, how such perfection had once been, but was all but gone from my world now.

Summersara turned her gaze from the beach and forest beyond to Sunta, gasping in delight. He was so beautiful.

She extended her feelings and thoughts to him at once, this way of communicating was so much more direct than simple words, and it felt something like... "Sunta, oh how perfect your new form is. Can you believe this, we are here!" Her innocent eyes glazed deeply into his.

Sunta smiled adoringly at his love.

Sunta thought back to Summersara. "Yes, it is incredible, beyond anything I thought it would be, the sensations are sublime!"

Using his mind to think caused his entire body to vibrate and to send out bright colors. Closing his eyes, he focused on his love for the Goddess. Suddenly, on the white sand in front of him, a brilliant blue crystal appeared. He reached out his strong muscular arm, and after a few tries, was able to control his movement enough to pick the crystal up. He turned and offered it to Summesara who clasped her hands ecstatically.

With that, he became aware of the blissful feeling in his heart, and another explosion of energy suddenly moved out of his head, causing his body to lift from the ground and start to float away. The others looked up and they all began to laugh outrageously. An could feel her laughter tickling and vibrating her entire body, a sensation that was happy beyond measure.

I thought again that the Children's experience was similar to a drug induced state, or a medicine journey as a shaman had once taught me to view it. But their experience was even higher. They would never have a "bad trip."

Sananda interrupted my thoughts. "Indeed Luna, the first humans did exist in a state of expanded awareness and oneness each and every moment. Think of how pure they were. They had no negative thoughts or limited concepts to prevent them from this natural way of being. They had not been taught that they were mortal and subject to disease and decay. They were free - the way they breathed, the gratitude within their hearts, their ability to stay in the present moment - all contributed to who they were. There are beings on your planet even today who have achieved that original state."

"Really, like yogis?" I inquired inwardly.

"Yes," Lord Sananda responded. "The yogis and other masters. They transcended all the conditioning placed on humankind and the density of the body and cells and achieved mastery. There are relatively few of them. This will become your destiny as well Luna."

This proclamation was shocking and unexpected. I had a great passion for the spiritual path, but I had never ever conceived of the notion of mastery.

"Me?" I uttered emotionally.

He laughed tenderly. "Yes you, you can, and you will."

I gasped. "I will?"

"In time you shall do just that. Watch carefully all that you see. Feel your desire to be like your ancestors grow within your heart."

I could only accept what he had said, though it was more than difficult to imagine.

Out of the forest walked, floated, and flew all the creatures the Children of Light had manifest in the ethers. Shimmering white unicorns gracefully pranced to the sand's edge. Little fairies numbering in the thousands, wearing tiny clothing and jewels, buzzed with elation above them. Great winged horses soared in the blue sky, their brilliant golden wings catching the soft sunrays. Gracefully they landed around the unicorns, staring at the Children with the silent strength and honor that is the hallmark of a Pegasus.

Circling high in the sky above this splendor were eagles, hawks, and a wide assortment of very colorful large birds. Slowly, they too began to descend to Earth in a clockwise spiral, some landing in tree limbs, others on the backs of the great horses. Other creatures now emerged from the forest as well. Giant cats, tiny ponies, enormous elephants, giraffes, and many other beautiful creatures soon lined the forest edge.

I understood that this great animal kingdom, created by the Children of Light, was one with them. There was no real separation between man and animal; their spirits were interlinked. I joined with An's awareness as I marveled at the unicorns, so splendidly poised and graceful, their soft white skin shining in the gentle rays of the sun.

"Greetings, beautiful ones. I love you! I love you!" An's emotions reached out across the space and felt the unicorn's strong bodies.

One of these glorious four legged beings who stood embracing her greeting called out, "Thank you, gracious Sister!"

The majestic unicorn began to prance, turning in circles. It made perfect sense to me that the animals could communicate just as the Children did.

Each group of the 144 then faced one another in silent, deep communion. Their eyes met and held each other for a moment. There was tentativeness for all of them, but, as it had been in the ethereal realm, they had agreed to spread out and diversify. The moment of sadness passed. The Children knew that they were One, that they would always be connected, and that they would see each other often. The groups moved slowly off in different directions to begin their new lives.

Fairies flew around the Children of the One, sprinkling stardust upon them, giggling in delight. The twins laughed as they began to carefully take one step after another. Soon they had adjusted to moving, and proceeded to run, falling again and again on the soft sand. They were so light that sometimes they basically leapt through the air, landing lightly again.

Watching all this made me long for my own Family of Light - for my tribe. I thought of my dear sisters and realized with amazement that they must be part of my own soul family! That would mean that there were perfect male counterparts for each of us as well! I wondered if they were alive, out there just waiting for destiny to bring us together.

The twins walked slowly away from the long sand beach toward the forest and the mountains beyond. After hours of walking, lost in fascination with the world they had created, they stopped in a small grove of trees shaped like a perfect circle. Long, limber branches gracefully touched the forest floor. It was a quiet place where wind moved on gentle breezes, whispering through the leaves. A hundred yards away the forest ended, and another flawless white sand beach stretched out for miles. Beyond it, again, was the endless, calm, sparkling sea. As the twins stood entranced by the great beauty of greenery and shade, hearing the sound of the waves close by, they smiled at each other knowingly.

An voiced the thought for them all, "Our first home!"

This was also the first time any of the Children had spoken a thought aloud; the language that was the same as the one spoken in the higher realm. It sounded melodious, always like a song. It reminded me of a time I had heard ancient Sanskrit prayers being recited. Perhaps Sanskrit was derived from that time; that would explain why it felt so holy, so powerful, and held such a spiritual essence.

The Children laughed and danced in the little glade, spinning each other in circles, clapping a rhythm as they went. Eventually they grew calm and laid down in a circle with their heads touching. Their spirit bodies left their physical bodies then and flew freely over the vast lands of Lemuria taking in the vast beauty from above. There was a freshness to all that they saw, a purity that nearly caused my heart to break as I thought of the current Earth covered with concrete cities, endless freeways, electrical lines, and polluted lakes and rivers.

Time passed, slowly the twins awareness returned to their bodies and they placed their minds together. It was time to create their new home. They formed a circle and began to chant. The sounds they created together began to form their abode. The sound moved out like a wave, spreading over the land. Their eyes were closed, and their arms reached for the sky. First a round wall began to encompass their circle, growing larger and larger. When it was as wide as they wished it to be the walls solidified into a soft, strong material. This wall was shining and glowed with soft pink light.

The ceiling was round, covered in golden stars and sparkling white gemstones.

They separated from each other, each adding their own special touches. With the power of her mind Summersara filled the room with soft silken pads to lie on and hung beautiful ornaments from golden arches. Then opening her eyes, she clasped her hands in satisfaction.

An seemed to think long and hard on what she wanted to add. With her eyes closed tightly she manifested her ideas into being. Crystals of all different colors and shapes lined the rim of the cozy room. In the center there stood a tall, clear pillar. She seemed to analyze her work. Thoughtfully she changed the ceiling to glass so that they could see the night sky.

Kané draped vines all over the wall, projecting them from his limbs. At the same time Sunta was busy creating a cascading waterfall in the center over the crystal. Observing all of this, Ayia realized they needed more space. He held his hands wide and mentally pushed the walls back.

As they opened their eyes, they began to discuss their co-created vision.

An asked quietly. "Is the ceiling fine? Does everyone like it?"

Everyone nodded eagerly and Sunraya offered. "I love it. We'll be able to watch our moons rise!"

She then pointed to the doorway. "Do you like the entrance way?"

Everyone turned and nodded appreciation at once. On either side of an exquisite carved wooden door, lilacs draped perfectly. Fiona moved to squeeze her sister's hand. Her red curls trailed behind her in sensuous movement. "It's lovely, Sunraya."

She kissed her sister's forehead and Sunraya let out of joyful sigh. "That feels amazing - warm and cool all at the same time."

Sunta smiled, his hands on his hips, "Our home suits us well."

She smiled with him. His was a smile that lit up the entire space. His strong, angular body reminded me of a giant Greek statue.

"Indeed," agreed Rasha in a deep baritone voice, jumping at the sound of his own voice, and then laughing as he put his arm around his brother's shoulders.

"There is nothing missing. It is complete." His deep emerald eyes shined with mirth. Together they both laughed, and the others joined in. I giggled; it was amazing to hear their voices for the first time, so melodious and pure, not unlike Disney characters. Once again, my mind wandered. Was this where all those stories came from, the stories of perfect love and princesses who could create a realm at the wave of a hand? I knew at once that it was, those weren't just stories, those were memories drawn out of the origins— how amazing!

Summersara began to spin in circles until her body lifted from the ground; she soared high above the others; her curved body displayed beautifully in the air. The others held their arms up, stretching to the sky as they laughed and danced in circles, singing her name over and over, "Summersara, Summersara."

Summersara twirled in circles looking down at her siblings ecstatically. "Let us play, play, and play!" Her giggles were like bubbles that lifted her body further into the air. She somersaulted, twirling her delicate hands about her body. Finally, she floated to the ground and lay on her new bed, covered in satiny pink.

Once more I understood there was no purpose to this other than a very delightful play, but I couldn't help but feel nervous for them, they were so vulnerable. What about Father's warning?

Sunta called out. "Is it not amazing?"

An replied, "There will be many times such as these, treasured by us all."

As the sky grew dark their precious home became a sanctuary of rest. Long into the night, they took turns surrounding each other with love. They took turns lying in the center of the bright little home; the others lightly feathered their skin with gentle fingertip caresses. I could see by the peaceful smiles of the recipients, that the sensations were quite blissful. They had no guardedness, no apprehension, and no wounds to prevent them from receiving this pure love freely. I thought of my flower child past and knew that such feelings of free love were what many of the adults around me had sought.

Summersara casually glided over to Sunta. Draping her arms around him, she rose on her tiptoes to kiss him on his lips. His entire body rose to meet hers in response to her electrifying touch. Holding out their hands toward one another, pulsing energy back and forth between them, as they looked deep into each other's eyes.

Nibbling on her ear he whispered. "My body pulses with desire to be with you."

Summersara shivered as she ran her hands over his strong chest, touching his nipples for the first time. "Your body is the most divine creation."

Slowly Sunta kissed each one of her perfect toes, and then her fingers, her eyes, and she shuddered blissfully with each one.

That seemed interesting to the others who then found the embrace of their beloved. The four beds around the room were quickly occupied as they snuggled and explored their bodies for the first time. Clearly, I was meant to witness this, so I looked on, noticing the stirring in my own heart. It had been so long since I had been intimate, and though I had been more than content with this, such pure love reminded me of the passion I had once longed to share with a man.

Fiona and Rasha began to passionately kiss, their erotic moans filling the room. Soon their hands were exploring every sensual curve. The sparks were contagious.

An and Ayia lay quietly, their body's naked, supple limbs wrapped around one another. They gazed about their world of nature in the same way they looked at each other. I admired the long, graceful limbs of Ayia's body, carved with perfect muscles and silky golden skin. He was absolutely perfect. Each breath he drew created feelings of peace and serenity, wonder and fascination.

One by one the other couples seemed to feel complete in their erotic, yet innocent, exploration. Slowly the twins drifted into a deep sleep. I understood that their need for sleep was different than mine. They needed to sleep because it was necessary for them to be able to fly free in their spirit- bodies each night. Perhaps, I thought, even though I had never been told this, this is why humans today really needed rest as well. My own dreams were often crowded with strange nonsense that seemed to come from the static of the world I lived within. I could see that the twin's dreamtime was very pure as there was nothing to convolute their experience.

The next morning the Children rose and went to the beach to greet their first sunrise. It was amazing to see how quickly they had become comfortable in their new bodies. Each of them walked with such grace and agility. The sun was just rising over the calm, clear sea. It was brighter and more golden than I had ever seen it in my world. At the same, time there was something gentler about its warmth. I wondered if that was really a difference in the sun or if the atmosphere had been different then. With complete freedom the twins tossed off their clothing. It was amazingly natural for them. Of course, it was, I thought, no one had taught them to be ashamed.

This display seemed much like the story of Adam and Eve and the innocence the experienced in their early days of creation. Standing side by side the women were a sight of magnificent beauty. Summersara smoothed her hands over the soft curves of her breasts and hips appreciating their silkiness, delighting in the feeling of her skin. Fiona stretched her long limbs and graceful fingers toward the sky, greeting the day. Even though their bodies had physicality to them they were still somewhat translucent and ethereal.

Sunraya turned to Fiona and took her hand. Together they walked toward the water. Soon all four women frolicked in the small lapping waves. They laughed and splashed each other, turned summersaults and sprung from the water like flying fish. After a while their play ended and they each turned to their own quieter activities. Summersara continued to play in the water, laughing with herself, spinning and floating. An stood silently on the shore enjoying the sensual feeling of her body caressed by the gentle warm breeze. She looked to the horizon as though contemplating the splendor of the light blue sky. I noticed that of the four women, An seemed the most introspective and contemplative. Summersara seemed more spontaneous and was often the first to experience new things.

The men had taken up a game of coconut toss. Fiona watched them, giggling from time to time as one of them literally flew through the air, catching the ball. Sunraya had walked to the back of the beach, lifting her perfectly toned brown body to sit in a tree limb, where she happily watched a near-by group of birds gathering seeds for the day. She began to sing and sway her limbs. Her body grew lighter, and she soon drifted above the trees where her beautiful song soared across the Earth. Her long arms swayed in a dance- like movement as though she were communicating with the trees below. The trees began to dance, first just their leaves quivering, and then entire limbs moving in unison with the soft breezes. Their limbs were the limbs of dancers, their strong solid trunks gently twisting to and fro.

The Goddess of Earth had her eyes closed even as her body twirled in a wide, slow circle as she sang praises to the very creation of the trees, the plants, and the flowers. Her heart poured forth this incantation of gratitude like liquid gold, showering tiny droplets of golden light as her body began to soar over the vast expanse of primordial forest.

As the Goddess flew, she turned for a moment and seemed to call out. Instantly her twin stopped his play and turned in her direction. Soon he was soaring with her, his strong deep voice creating overtones with her own strong song. With them I soared over the great land. It was far vaster in its reaches then the American continent I knew so well. They soared over valleys so deep I could scarcely see the wide, rolling rivers below. Enormous rock walls lined deep narrow gorges, often lined with crystals of brilliant pinks and purples.

God and Goddess had their eyes wide now as they took in the beautiful sights of their own creation. They soared over rainforest for miles upon miles, until at last they came to the higher mountainous lands. Here and there, calm lakes dotted the surface. Streams and rivers raced through the mountain crevasses making their way toward the calm expanse of the ocean in the far distance. Waterfalls over two thousand feet high plummeted to wide pools, creating a perfect dance of earth and water.

The Twins of Earth laughed blissfully as they rose over the highest peaks and glided quickly downward over their northern slopes, where their eyes were met with more splendid beauty. In green meadows below, deer and rabbits quietly nibbled violet and yellow flowers, and drank at the edges of little ponds. The space was calm and offered deep nourishment. I imagined they would frequent this beautiful area, for I understood they lived solely to experience the great pleasures of life. They lived to see all the beauty, to feel and touch it, delighting in the warmth of the sun, the refreshing touch of the wind upon their skin.

After what seemed like hours the pair landed softly in another peaceful meadow. Contented smiles radiated from their perfectly beautiful faces. Hand in hand they lay back on the soft ground with eyes closed. They seemed then to rest empty of thought, happy to just feel the joyful pulses of their breath and the solid ground beneath them.

I imagined they would have many, many perfect days just like this one. There was no need for money or work. They had everything they needed. There was fresh water in the streams, and fruit in the trees if they wished to eat. I understood that as light beings who were incarnate in form, the Children could eat for pleasure and added nourishment, but otherwise their bodies made everything they would ever need. They were fed by universal life force.

Back on the beach, the Goddess of Water had stopped her delightful girlish play with the waves. She stood and stretched her arms outward toward the sea. Her eyes deepened; they seemed to me like deep pools of water, like the very sea itself. Suddenly her form rose, hovering lightly just feet above the glassy surface. She soared then, her laughter trailing behind her. In a second, she plunged, breaking the calm, and sending a great wave toward the land. Just before it reached its destination, it seemed to gather itself into a ball of liquid that rose into the sky. It swirled above the beach where the other twins looked on. Out of the swirling motion the form of the Goddess shaped herself. She was vast now, over one hundred feet tall, and stretched out widely. I could see the shape of her delicate, yet wise, face in the molding of the silvery water. Her limbs swayed gently as her torso moved in slow undulating circles. The other twin's forms appeared tiny compared to this vast display of their sister. They looked up at her with pure delight. Fiona clasped her hands and laughed joyously as she called up, "You are beautiful, sister of light! Wonderful, wonderful, wonderful!"

She raced down the beach, running so fast she soon became nothing more than a blur of energy, and in the next moment burst into flames. The flames grew, rising toward the sky until they had reached the height of the watery Goddess. The sight was astounding, formed fire outlined by sky and sea all around. Soon the form swirled into the shape of the Goddess. Her sharp, sensual curves swayed powerfully, and her golden face appeared amidst that vast swirling red and brilliant orange.

Fiona moved toward her sister's form, and Summersara in turn moved toward her. They danced around each other gracefully, filling the sky in splendid power. The outline of their bodies brushing each others', mixing fire with water, incredible, perfect, perfection. I felt like my soul was soaring with them, one with them, this was how it was meant to be, how we were meant to be. I could feel it pulling me, a yearning so deep I thought I would die then and there, I wanted so badly to be that to be as One as they were! Slowly they danced away from each other reunited again and again. As the dance came to an end the sisters stilled their forms in the air. They turned to stare deeply into each other's eyes.

Holding each other for a moment in this gaze I could hear Summersara's thoughts. "I honor you my sister of light, for all time."

I was spellbound, remembering reading once in a text about Hawaiian spirituality, that the purpose of life was to balance the child self with the high self. I read that the middle self was our ego, the part of us that was logical, and could care for the physical form to keep it strong and in balance with the spiritual aspect. This self was meant to be in service to the child self and the high self, and nothing more. I had read that somehow over time this ego had gotten out of balance. It had somehow forgotten its true nature, and had taken over the body, blocking both the child self and the high self from existing.

Excitedly, I realized that the twins did have an ego (individualized consciousness) and that it was indeed keeping the physical and spiritual aspects in balance. I could sense how that part of their mind did exist simply to have thought, to change between the two selves easily, effortlessly. There was no struggle, no fear, no resistance from one or the other.

Days and nights flew by on the screen as I watched, completely drawn into the harmonious life of the Children. Their time was devoted to play and expansion, experiencing all the best their world offered. Around the continent the other tribes had created homes and lived just as the twins did, simply and in harmony with the land. Sananda communicated that the amount of time we witnessed passing was more then 900 years, though time moved differently then, faster and more fluid than anything we could really compare it to in our own time/space. The twins never aged, always appearing the perfect embodiment of youthfulness and vitality.

I was beginning to feel a strange disturbing sense of restlessness; on one hand I could watch the twins forever, on the other, I was distracted. Obviously, something drastic had occurred, and changed everything. As though in response to my feelings, everything was about to change and I would regret not waiting patiently, dwelling in the state of oneness the twins held. But alas, the time had come...

CHAPER EIGHT

Seek And You Shall Find

I came back to my body with a sudden jolt and fell into a
deep sleep for hours. When I woke, I lay there just thinking
about the twins, in love with them, their world. I loved how unique
the twins were from each other; Fiona and Rasha, so fiery, while
An and Ayia were thoughtful, Sunraya and Kané were quieter and
more inward, while Summersara and Sunta were like bubbling
rivers, boisterous and gay. I thought they very well could have been
the basis of some of the great characters of mythology.

I want to live like that, so free, so innocent! I shivered,
feeling the scars of my life, the toxins that raced in my blood, the
pollutants of my world, and the exposure of my mind to that which
was anything but innocent. My generation had been exposed to so
much defilement through media and conditioning, and it was only
getting worse. Would there be a way, I wondered, to remove all of
that, to live as the Children of Light had, truly? It seemed too far
away, too distant, too hard to get to.

Later, I found Gracie preparing a wonderful breakfast of
papaya, mango, and farm fresh scrambled eggs. The air outside was
warm and sweet. In the distance I heard the comforting call of a
rooster. I ate hungrily, among the kind- hearted people of the farm,
enjoying listening to the simplistic talk of the day's chores, but I

was beginning to feel a sense of discontent. There was a greater potential for humankind; I could feel that now. Will I be shown how that potential can manifest once more? I wondered this, as I drank freshly made guava juice. The juice's bittersweet freshness filled my mouth, reminding me to be content with the present moment, and all that was so good about the new world I found myself in.

Blue interrupted my thoughts, "Do you know where you're going yet?"

I nodded. "Yeah, I think the other side of the island, the rainy side. First, I want to stay on a beach for a while. A white sandy beach with lots of shade." I indicated my nearly burnt skin.

They were all smiling, and I could tell that they could in some way relate, but in another way, I was becoming different, even from these alternative people. For a moment I felt afraid of the changes I was going through. What if I could no longer relate to others?

Blue responded. "Hey, we know a great beach about an hour north of here, you could hitch a ride there. Just tell any local you want to go to 67 and they'll know the spot. You would be safe to camp there, and there's even a little store near-by for water when you need it."

My eyes lit up. "Why do they call it that?"

Blue smiled. "It's the telephone pole marker, the number on the side…"

I nodded. "Interesting way to name a beach. It sounds perfect."

We finished breakfast and it was time to say good-bye. Gracie and Joseph gave me a large bag of fresh fruit and mac- nuts. I was sad to leave new friends, and the mountain that had become so familiar in just one day; the rich smell of earth and flowers was intoxicating. I was also eager to return to the sea, and whatever I might discover, no, manifest next. Handel and Blue drove me to the bottom of the hill and pointed me in the direction I should hitchhike, explaining that it was pretty simple; there was just one main road that circled the entire island.

Handel hugged me tightly as I stood next to my backpack on the side of the road. "We will miss you so much, little sister. Your spirit of playfulness and wisdom will stay with us forever."

I squeezed his hands and smiled warmly, trying not to get emotional. "I will always remember you both, you've been a very special part of my journey. Thank you so much for everything."

He replied through teary eyes. "Believe me, the pleasure is all mine. Now listen. Hitching is cool here on the islands, but you are so beautiful and so young. If you ever get a bad vibe just don't get in the car, no matter what. Promise?"

I laughed, shrugging off the concern. "Yeah, I'll be fine. I grew up in California, remember?"

I turned to Blue. For a long moment we looked into each other's eyes. Blue held out his arms as a tear rolled down his face.

He whispered as we held each other tightly, "Promise to write?"

I whispered. "I promise. Be well, okay?"

Releasing each other, Blue nodded through teary eyes. I felt my throat constricting; it was amazing how quickly certain souls became bonded. We hugged silently once more, and then Handel and Blue drove away.

I stood alone, quickly resolving to let go of the sadness. I had to be bright and happy to hitchhike. Holding out my thumb, I arranged my bag and newly filled water bottle. I looked down at my clothes, a white gauze dress that came below my knees, decorated with tiny purple flowers, flip-flops, and my collection of necklaces. I looked less like the girl I had been a week ago, and much more like a local, at ease in the tropical splendor. Looking up at the sky, I prayed for a safe ride. There weren't many cars on the road, mostly what looked like sparkly new rental cars with concentrated faces behind the wheel. Only a few minutes passed when a beat-up old red dodge truck skidded to a stop in front of me.

Pulling my hair quickly up into a bun, I grabbed my pack and nearly empty water gallon jug, and walked quickly toward the vehicle, peering in the window. A man who looked to be about 30 something looked back at me. He too was tan, a bit unshaven, looking local and safe. His blond hair reminded me of the surfers back home. I thought for a moment that my parents, regardless of their "younger years as absolutely hippies", would be quite nervous to know what I was up to. Then again, they had never placed any boundaries on me, and this was the reason I was so confident in traveling on my own, coming to Hawaii. A neglected childhood had its benefits after all was said and done. People thought I was an extremely intelligent, healthy, and balanced 'young woman' considering the dysfunction I had grown up in.

It was a bit strange, with all the traumatic things that had happened to me in life, that I felt as safe as I did. Somehow those things had taught me that ultimately, I would be safe no matter what, as long as I used a little caution and common sense. If my parents had been more protective, they would have kept me from a lot of harm, to say the least, but still all the decisions I had made in life were mine. I had learned to protect myself, and how to be discerning, at least I hoped I had.

"Aloha," the man said with a bit of a local tone. "Where are you headed?"

I sensed I could trust him right away. "I'm headed to 67 you know the spot?"

The man laughed. "I know the spot, it's one of my favorites."

"Great." I loaded my pack into the back of the truck and hopped in.

The man introduced himself as Leimana and I offered my name.

"Actually, I also need food supplies. Is there a health food store between here and there you could drop me at?" I inquired.

"I can take you to the health food store and drop you off at your beach, I don't mind grabbing one of their awesome smoothies."

"If it wouldn't be any trouble, that would be totally great." I responded.

"Oh, no problem. Here in Hawaii, you'll find people have what we call 'Aloha', sharing with love. It is much different than the cold shoulder you usually get on the mainland."

I nodded eagerly. "Definitely. I'm already finding that."

I was grateful for the sight of the health food store. Being careful not to spend much of what little money I had, I got a loaf of bread, some cheese, a few carrots, and a cucumber. Before leaving the store, I decided to splurge on a large chocolate cookie. As I stood filling my gallon jug at the water purifier, my mind was drawn to the twins again.

Just then a revolving book display caught my eye. I finished filling my jug and put it down with my bags, walking to the display. All the books were the small pamphlet books common to health food stores. One book seemed to leap off the rack: 'Huna - the Ancient Practice of Hawaiian Spirituality'.

Quickly I picked it up. I began flipping through the pages, skimming the table of contents, aware of how much time I was taking and not wanting to keep my ride waiting, Hawaiian mythology, Origins. I turned the pages. My eyes felt on fire as my pulse quickened. It talked about Hawaiian mythology and a tale of how the Hawaiian people, and all Polynesian descendants, came from a lost continent known as Lemuria. This great continent, larger than Australia and North America put together; is also called MU by the Hawaiian people.

I could not believe what I was reading. The Hawaiian people came from Lemuria! So, this was why I came to Hawaii, it was all inter-connected.

I read on. It said the legends say that the continent was sunk in a great flood. All that remained of Lemuria were the high mountaintops. The Big Island was one of those 'mountain-tops'. One of the mountaintops, Lemuria had sunk; I wanted to know everything! The book was almost ten dollars. I couldn't spend any money buying books and reluctantly put it back, promising myself that I would be back, on my own time, to read more. I walked out of the store almost in a daze.

The Ride to the beach was back past the airport and another 10 minutes or so. We talked some, mostly chitchat. When we arrived, he pointed to a trail and mentioned I should be careful to not get cut and that if I did to take care of. It right away so I didn't get a staph infection.

I crossed the highway with no traffic in site, and I noted how unpopulated this part of the island seemed so far. It almost seemed too good to be true, like everything else on my trip. The mid-day sun was hot, and I shaded my forehead. Walking down the small dirt road, I could hear the ocean waves, and smell the sweet, salty breeze.

I had taken just one step onto the beach when I caught my breath. Polished white sand stretched out in either direction, with clusters of shade trees here and there. Beyond the beach, a completely calm bay sparkled in the sunlight. The landscape was not quite as luminous as it had been when the Children of Light first created the planet, but it was similar in its spectacular beauty. There were six people on the beach, among them a nude couple basking in the sun.

For a moment this startled me, and then I welcomed what this meant for me. I, too, could also be free. One person sat under a shade tree quietly reading a book. Another young couple played in the waves with their daughter.

Walking onto the beach, I felt like my feet were barely touching the ground. The bay was shaped like a horseshoe; turquoise water started out shallow, the sandy floor inclining gradually to the deeper blue waters in the distance. Lava rocks outlined the beach, and at the far end there were a few houses.

I sat under the palm tree, drinking from my jug trying to get my bearings. Spreading out my towel, I took off my clothes, revealing my teal bikini, and laid in the warm sun, which seemed to penetrate my very bones.

Once hot enough, I swam in the deep, cool waters, playing in the gentle rolling waves along the shore. I was aware of people's eyes upon me and found this difficult to ignore. At sixteen, sunbathing in a tiny bikini at the local river swim spot, I soaked up that attention. I had sought human approval from onlookers to let me know that I was beautiful, that I was alive. Now, I really didn't want that attention, only to be free.

Getting out of the water I scraped the bottom of my foot on a rock. "Ouch!" I whimpered loudly, limping across the hot sand and wrapped my foot in the towel. Leimana's words came back to me.

Strange, I thought, it was almost as though he had a premonition of this. I remembered Handel saying that things manifested faster in Hawaii because of it being such a special place. I thought about the twins, and how they manifested instantly. I had better watch my thoughts carefully. I only wanted to manifest goodness. One thing was certain—if I camped on the beach, there was no way I would be able to keep sand out of the cut.

For the rest of the day, I wrote in my journal about the journey of the Children of Light. From time to time, I took a swim or a walk, or just watched the waves. As a child, I had enjoyed finding balance in life, doing things that created harmony in my day. I remembered playing with my dolls, making myself snacks, playing with others in the community, but then happily being on my own once I'd had enough social time. In my recent life, I had found little opportunity for such things because I was consumed by the need to survive financially. Here at last, I alone, and not the demands of bills and society. directed my treasured time. It seemed I was remembering that sense of balance I once knew so innately.

I looked out at the sky. The sun would be setting soon. I felt content with this storytelling; there was no better gauge of truth than a child. It inspired me to think of sharing with other children too. For a while I sat just playing with her, both of us still thinking of the twins. When her mother got out of the water, I stood to say good-bye. I might have touched something deep in this little girl, but it was I who had really been touched. This little girl was really magical, and I knew I would never forget her.

When the sun began to set, I closed my book and entered the water. Everyone had gone. I was alone with the power of the sea and sky. For a moment this power frightened me, as though I could be swallowed by it, never to be seen again. But then I took a deep breath and felt grateful to be alive, to feel the coolness of the water.

The sun began to sink into the sea. I watched once more, admiring the golden red disk floating on the surface and then disappearing. It was so amazing to watch this, and I could do it every day. I gave thanks for the beauty of the day and prayed to be protected through the night. Here, too, there was no need for a tent. I sat on my sleeping bag eating a piece of bread, cheese, and a carrot. The simplicity and purity of this meal brought more gratitude to my heart then any five-course meal ever could have. I thought about how little money I had and how wondrous it was that I needed to spend so little.

I thought about the information that had come to me about the Hawaiian origins and knew the truth of human history was all around, amazed that it was right there in a book, in a health food store. It was there in the beauty of the mountains, the dolphins arriving on cue, and I imagined, in the stories of natives around the world. All one had to do was look and it was there. I smiled at this comforting thought. I was definitely not going crazy, I was being shown truth directly, raw, unabridged truth.

Not long after my meal I began to feel my third-eye pulse. I was being called. Laying back I surrendered to the energy and once more found myself in the temple.

CHAPTER NINE

Conception

Everyone's eyes were on me, welcoming me; they seemed somehow pleased with me. Lady Nada communicated that over 900 years had passed on Tara. During that time there had been only peace in the lives of the Children; they had enjoyed more of the beautiful existence I had already witnessed. I also understood through Lady Nada that time moved faster when consciousness was more evolved, so what for the Children was indeed 900 solar years, in all ways that one could compare it to in the current time cycle, would have felt like 100 of our years. Because the Children were immortal, they had not aged at all. Instead, their bodies had settled more deeply into a state of physical perfection as they had become more grounded and familiar with their realm. Lady Nada explained that there had been a soul agreement, which would allow them to begin having babies after 900 years had passed. Divine Mother and Father had thought that a suitable time, to evolve and enjoy their lives on Tara, before having babies and populating the planet.

The children sat around their little home excitedly discussing everything. Once again, I was fascinated by the complete purity. Four couples, and yet there were no inhibitions, no jealousies or insecurities. There was only comfort, ease, and joy.

Summersara lay on her back as Sunta combed his hands

through her long silky hair. "I want to have babies soon, don't you, my love? Remember how Mother described it, how we can choose to have children? Imagine it, tiny little babies."

Sunta beamed a smile, glancing up at the others. "Of course! We'll give birth in the water, maybe at the crystal cave." His excitement was contagious.

An laughed adoringly as I and the council looked on. It was just like her adventurous sister to want to experience something new immediately. For her she would wait. She knew Ayia would feel the same; being twins, this was always the case.

Sunraya was curled up in Kané's arms. She imagined giving birth deep in the forest, holding on to a tree-limb as her love caught their new baby. She squeezed him in delight just at the thought. A baby! They were going to have a baby!

Suddenly she sat up. "How many will we have? How many!"

Kané laughed gaily. "Dozens, dozens!"

The joy seemed to spill out from the room. As I watched, the image on the screen panned away from the twins to show similar scenes of rejoicing among the other tribes of Tara.

I contemplated what I had seen. I instantly understood how the gift of such creation was passed on from generation to generation within the 'Lineage of Light'. Modern day humanity, however, seemed to have lost so much understanding of this sacred gift. I thought back to all the parents I had known who saw their children primarily as burdens, to be sent off to school or sat before a television, or, worse, abused and neglected. In this sense, current day life could scarcely be more different than it had been in the early days of the planet. Clearly, these first babies would be loved and cherished.

The scene changed once more. Time had moved forward, and I suspected we were about to witness the first conception on Tara. Summersara and Sunta strolled through the quiet forest behind their home holding hands tenderly. In silence they approached the edge of a beautiful meadow. The sky was ablaze with brilliant orange and blues as the sun began to set. Where the meadow met the forest, a gentle waterfall cascaded into the warm waters of a natural hot spring. The couple stood for a moment, captivated by the beauty of their surroundings. Around the pool seven tall amethyst crystals shone beautifully in the dimming light.

They wore turquoise gowns created, like everything in their world, from pure thought. The translucent garments caressed the curves of their exquisite bodies. Summersara swayed her hands across the waters, giving rise to a warm steam that lightly encapsulated them in a circle of mist. A soft breeze began to move through the weeping willows that gently hung their limbs toward the edges of the pool. I could sense that the weather, as always, was warm and balmy, a perfect tropical paradise.

The lovers slowly removed the soft clothing from each other's perfect bodies. Together they entered the waters. As their physical bodies floated, their spiritual consciousness lifted up, freed from their physical awareness.

Gently they explored the warmth and excitement of each other's bodies. As their passion grew, they seemed to merge with one another, becoming a swirling dance of beauty and light. And so it was that the seed was planted within Summersara. She would give birth to the first-born child on Tara!

The scene moved at fast-speed and I witnessed Summersara's belly swelling with child. Pregnancy was easy for her it appeared, graceful. She spent her days playing in the sea, eating fruit under a shade tree on the beach, resting. Sunta often rubbed her tummy and placed his ear against her navel, smiling ecstatically as he listened to the baby's strong heartbeat. The other twins marveled at Summersara's growth. They too loved to caress her with gentle hands, and to feel the movement of the baby rippling under her skin.

Ten months later, Summersara's labor began. My awareness was brought inside a cave lined with rose quartz crystals emanating a soft pink light. There was a feeling of great comfort in the space, like it was the womb of Tara. Summersara sat in a fresh spring of warm water in the center of the cave. Around her, An, Sunraya, and Fiona stood naked, holding her hands and beaming wide smiles at their sister. Their skin glowed with the rose light; their nipples raised from the waters soft touch. The brothers sat around the water's edge, witnessing this moment of sisterhood.

An motioned to Kané. "Prepare the vase to bless the baby."

I still sensed such amazing innocence within the Children. Although they were completely matured and aware of the sacred importance of this act, their eagerness for life had not been lost.

Kané smiled at Summersara as he began to pour sacred water from a small waterfall at the side of the cave. He placed the water near the edge of the pool and then stood back again.

Warm wavelets caressed Summersara's fine, clear skin as her beloved Sunta now entered the water. His sisters gracefully stepped out of the pool, wrapping fine silk cloths around their hips. He placed his arms gently around Summersara, and together they swayed back and forth. Her large belly peeked above the water's surface. The other twins gently toned the melody of Summersara and Sunta's names, creating a beautiful harmony.

Outside the cave and past the smooth beach, the dolphins were singing for the couple too, calling out to their star homes for the blessings of the star-child being born. Summersara could feel their presence and she gave thanks for their support, which would help the spirit of the child as it came forth.

I thought about the typical birth process of the current day. In my mind's eye I saw an image of a woman in a hospital room. She was lying back on the bed, drenched in sweet, screaming at the top of her lungs. "Get it out of me! Get it out!!!" Her husband stood at her side, also yelling, but at the doctor. "Do something! Do something!" Suddenly the woman was injected with a drug and she lay back nearly unconscious, unable to feel her body.

Summersara spoke softly to Sunta. "Our baby is coming down." She smiled so tenderly. "I can feel her now."

Sunta squeezed her arms lovingly. The twins all had looks of wonder. I could then sense that for the baby it was a journey through a tunnel of brilliant white light, leading to her new home and first breath. Slowly her body was pressed down the canal until her head began to push through. Summersara's breath intensified, and she sank her chin into her chest, but unlike the anguish woman in the hospital birth, Summersara's face was tranquil. I could feel through her that the sensations were intense, but there was an element of ecstasy to them, and her deep concentration was fearless, without any hesitation for being a mother.

Suddenly the tiny head slipped completely out of the opening. With one more push the baby was thrust into the waters face up. Through the soft liquid she gazed up at her mother's face. As the infant's body wiggled in the water, Sunta held her under the shoulders and slowly lifted her until her face felt the cool air around her. Instinctively the baby drew in its first breath. It was the most precious sound! Just a tiny little gasp, and then regular, fast-paced baby breath. There was no crying, no trauma at all.

Summersara cried quietly with joy. "Welcome my daughter, welcome."

Peacefully the girl child gazed into her mother's eyes and then around her new, warm world. Here was her father, the glorious male being that she was a part of. Sunta smiled with amazement at his daughter's tiny fingers and toes, at her brilliant green eyes, so like the jade stone that was grown plentifully near the rivers of Tara. In a moment he realized that the galaxy she came from had at its center, the 'Jade Sun'.

Sunta held Summersara and the baby close to his chest as both parents silently wept with joy. Summersara telepathically communicated the babies name to her siblings. "Jade, Child of the Jade Sun."

An spoke gently to Summersara. "May I enter and bless our beloved child?"

Summersara nodded consent, and An walked slowly down the pool steps, gracefully carrying the vase. The newborn looked at her aunt with wide eyes and a small smile. Tears slid openly down An's petite, oval face. "Welcome, blessed one. Welcome to your family. Welcome to your home."

The baby made a small gurgling sound and An laughed, sweet laughter that filled the room. The others looked on in awe as An slowly poured the holy waters over the baby's head. As the pure water ran down her face, the child gasped in delight.

An spoke gently as her hands touched the baby's tiny head. Kané handed a soft cloth to Sunta who took the child in his arms, wiping her fine, translucent skin dry, and then handing her back to Summersara. The children then filled the room with a song of welcome.

Her small head slowly moved from side to side as she gazed up at them and the light of the cave. Her muscular legs and arms began to stretch out, welcoming the space around her body. She cried out in hunger, and Summersara intuitively brought her to the breast. The baby's tiny mouth quickly latched onto the round nipple and began to suck with great strength. Everyone watched openly in amazement. Summersara was radiant with joy as she looked up at her brothers and sisters. I could see the fascination and honor they felt for their sister.

When the baby seemed to feel complete, she relaxed and laid her head back on her mother's arm.

Summersara spoke softly to her baby girl. "Let us go to the sea, the dolphins are there, and they wish to offer their blessings."

Silently Sunta helped Summersara rise, and the group walked in succession toward the calm ocean, where, together, they all entered the waters. I could see the dark gray forms of the dolphins approaching in the distance through the clear turquoise waters. They swam slowly in unison toward the Children. There was such grace around this birth, such incredible sensitivity toward this child.

Slowly the group of twelve dolphins began to circle the humans. The baby watched, riveted, as the long, sleek beings of the sea rose from the waters as one to breathe, disappearing beneath the waters again. Suddenly several of the young dolphins leapt into the air, flipping and spinning. They seemed to have a special role in greeting this new soul, like midwives of the sea. The tiny babies deep green eyes were filled with love as she looked on in fascination. It was clear that this daughter born to the water twins would never be afraid of the vast ocean or the dolphins. She was so extremely aware, completely awake!

The council sat in reverence with this first birth for a few more moments, while I integrated that this was how birth was supposed to be. It was all so beautiful and perfect, the way the twins shared everything, and to think of these babies that would be so loved, so safe. There wouldn't be any parents off to work, babies in daycare, or even school for that matter. It was amazing!

The image on the screen then raced forward in time and I witnessed more magical births. A second child was born to the Twins of Water, this time a boy. Sunraya and Kané were blessed with two boy children, and Rasha and Fiona with a boy and a girl. Around the continent the other tribes were also delighting in the miracles of birth. Quickly the population more than quadrupled with the eagerness displayed by the Children of One.

As more time passed, the original children of the Children of One had grown to be adults yet had the same eternal youthful embodied by their parents. Some of them stayed with their parents, extending the size of the once small tribes. Others ventured out on their own, joining at times with descendants from other clans and creating new tribal families. Entirely new races developed from the merging of humans, elves, and dwarves, each unique in its beauty.

At times they played in the ocean, leaping over one another, laughing without inhibition. I longed to know that life they had lived, so carefree, without any burden of past thought, of trauma or attachment. Sometimes they simply rested in their small homes over many days. They spent a great deal of time dreaming of inner journeys, and even more time creating new life on Tara. As they would lie meditating, beautiful crystals would manifest in the forest above them, or a new type of flower or plant. Everything they did was simply for the experience; to fly, to swim, to hug, to laugh, to create, and to exist. There was no hidden agenda, no deadline to meet, no person to impress. There was certainly no money to be made, or material empire to feed. They ate only from the trees, and only very little. It seemed to me that their energy came from the spiritual universe, more so than the physical plane. Their way of life was perfect. They were perfect, perfect in beauty, health, vitality, and thought, and connected to the world they had created in complete trust and oneness.

Parenting was very different. There wasn't much of a distinction between the roles of mother and father. The children were equally bonded to both of their parents, and the entire clan was with the Children throughout the day. Sometimes uncles and aunts watched each other's little ones, giving their siblings a chance to rest, or be private for a time. It was common in these images of their lives for me to see babies happily passed from one adult the next. The babies were completely aware of their surroundings, and everything that was happening. They clearly understood what was being said to them, and in no time at all were speaking in complete thought patterns. Small children had the same powers as their parents. For example, they could fly, create through thought, and move objects through the air. Like their parents, all of this was simply delightful life, being experienced. This didn't appear to be learned from their parents in any outward way in terms of instruction, but rather adapted as part of their DNA, as it was so alive in their parents. It seemed most instruction of any sort occurred through direct transference, rather than word or action.

This harmony amongst the community was how I thought life should be. There was incredible simplicity, which left ample time for play, exploration, rest, and bonding. The babies and children exuded a glow of health that was unknown in my current time. Their eyes were crystal clear, and they never seemed discontent, though the small babies innately knew how to cry to get their needs meet. The adults were so attuned to the children that they responded swiftly and eagerly.

It was amazing to watch the little ones so free to explore though their parents were near and watchful. They were not watched in fear or tethered to a leash. There was no one rubbing toxic sunscreen on them or feeding them junk food. They were so perfectly cared for. There was such a different of parenting. I tried to imagine how the average mother would implement the type of changes necessary, if I could understand this way of perfect living. It would take a lot, but step-by-step it could be done. One day all children could be cared for as they should be, and then for the future generations it would just be natural again. Maybe one day we would even fly again!

I loved looking on as the twins curled up in bed together with their little ones, just watching every movement of their babies' precious little body. I imagined that some parents of the current time might act just this way, if only there was no job for them to rush off to, or underlying stress to keep them from enjoying the present moment. There were no cribs to separate, no pacifiers to placate. There were no powders full of toxins, vaccinations that might cause a child to become autistic. The babies were naturally potty trained, communicating by facial expression and hand gestures when they needed to be taken under a tree. They nursed, they ate fruit, they played, and they rested. All was perfect.

Finally, it was time for me to rest again. This time Lord Sananda communicated that this time I would rest in a special room designed for optimal healing. My own personal angel guided me to a small room just outside the meeting hall. A soft blue light glowed from under the door, which instantly opened as we approached. Inside the room was a capsule, one that looked just like the capsules used by the twins when they first incarnated. I gasped and the angel smiled, motioning for me to get in as she explained, "Yes dear one, this is a blue healing capsule. They are used throughout the realms of light for restoration and healing. You will find yourself more rested than ever here."

I could only nod, looking eagerly at the capsule as I climbed in. Blue light surrounded me, and a feeling of complete contentment crept from my toes to the top of my head. In a moment I was gone, feeling nothing but light. In the morning I wrote about all that I had witnessed.

CHAPTER TEN

Memories

I turned on my little flashlight and got up to relieve my bladder. Knowing I needed to write about all that had occurred, I quickly got out my journal and wrote as fast as I could, not wanting to forget anything. Then I added to my list:

- Learn about natural childbirth and water births
- Babies in native cultures, ceremonies surrounding birth
- Native Creation Myths

As I lay back on my sleeping bag, with dawn approaching, I was now swept into the painful memories of my own unplanned pregnancy and traumatic abortion.

When I was fifteen, I became pregnant with Tommy's baby. There was never any option for me to keep the child, we were just kids, and I was terrified of what my mother would do if she ever found out. More than that, I felt so ashamed and completely incapable of imagining motherhood would be the right thing at that time. I had stayed in another county with my friend Sandra so that my mom wouldn't suspect anything. Sandra had been through two abortions herself, so I looked to her for guidance. Sandra had driven me to the clinic, squeezing my shaking hand. I had been petrified at the thought of someone sticking a vacuum into my vagina and sucking a tiny fetus out, but I was certain I had no other choice. The worst part by far, was that I knew I was taking the life of a baby that grew inside of me. I felt a connection to that being, and I sent it thoughts night and day, telling it that this was the best choice, that they were better off not to enter a life that could mean nothing more than misery for both of us. When the doctor put the clamps on, I bit my lip, biting back the pain.

He muttered something about a twin, and I cried out, "Twins, there's a second one?" The grief that came through my moans must have been heard throughout the clinic. The nurse clamped cold fingers around my wrist with a menacing look that told me I needed to settle down. There was no compassion, no warmth at all. I cried softly, feeling my heart breaking. The doctor sucked and sucked and with each torturously painful moment my mind shut down a little more. Twins, twins. That was more than I could handle. When I was younger, and had envisioned the mother I would one day be, I had often imagined I would have twins. I remembered looking at old family photos. There had been several sets of twins.

For the next two days I lay on Sandra's bed enduring the most agonizing cramps I had ever known. I could have been on meds, but I refused them.

Those memories, though long behind me, were still in need of some healing. What could I do here in this place to let go more? I had a sense God wanted me to forgive, to accept that I was born in a time when the world didn't provide the right sort of space for teens to be healthy and thrive, and not wind up in challenging situations. I stood up, walked to the sea, held my hands at my heart and asked the ocean to help me heal, and sent prayers to the soul of the tiny fetus. If there had been more than one, I asked for further forgiveness and prayed that they were ok. Maybe I was too dramatic, maybe there was no soul at all, but I supposed it was better to feel remorse than to feel nothing at all. Later I rested in the baking hot sun, loving the warmth and the way it made my body so utterly relaxed. There was nothing I could do about the past but keep trying to heal, looking forward, looking up.

Soon, the beach was busy with people. Near-by a 30ish man kept watching me. It felt very invasive, and I thought about how

strange our culture was, that people could just sit and stare and leer
and have whatever kind of thought or feeling they wanted about
a total stranger, no awareness or care of how that might affect that
person. A little way down the beach a group of young women sat
talking very loudly and negatively about their boyfriends. Their
cigarette smoke drifted my way, causing me to feel nauseous. At the
water's edge, several sets of adults or parents played with children,
but many spoke roughly to each other.

I began to feel irritated. "Why?" I wondered, "Why does the
Creator allow people to be as they are, so arrogant, disrespectful,
and abusive?"

But I knew the answer, there was free will on Earth, so people
were free to do as they wished. I wanted to know more of what
had happened in the First Time to cause humanity to devolve
so very much. It wasn't that I could only see the negative side of
modern-day humans. Not at all, there was much about all people
that was wonderful and precious, but their habits and manners
could be so far from the reverence and respect for all life that their
ancestors had. How had people learned to do anything to dishonor
their own lives? It seemed to me it was a lot of things; Hollywood,
media, school… humans were up against so much that was totally
unnatural. As the cigarette smoke floated past again, I reminded
myself to look upon people with compassion and non-judgment,
but my thoughts continued.

Discontentment with the way things were was the only
way to create change. It was the only way to have enough desire
to become something greater, to evolve, and begin the process of
understanding the bigger picture. I prayed that one day no child
would be born into a life of abuse. This was the only way I felt I
could keep myself from falling into bad feelings.

Cautiously I approached this older man, somehow thinking
he might know what to do. I called out as I limped along, "Excuse
me."

He turned, surprised. "Well, Aloha! How are you doing
dear?"

I must have thought I was doing better than I was, because
in that moment of hearing another human voice asking about my
wellbeing I was overwhelmed.

Tears escaped as I replied. "I'm okay, it's just that I have this cut on the bottom of my foot and I'm camping here. I think I'm going through a lot, and all the people here… it's too much for me."

By the time I was done speaking the man had risen to his feet, aware that this was a serious situation. "Come, my dear. Come with me."

The man's compassionate voice comforted me, and I half limped behind him, grateful for the human contact. He motioned for me to sit on a log in the shade. "I'm Uncle Sonny. What's your name?"

"Luna," I said, as he motioned for me to hold my foot up. "Oh, yeah. That's an infection all right. I'll be right back."

He frowned with concern, turning for towards a tree with a stack of stuff under it.

I sat waiting alone, feeling relieved and yet overwhelmed. I had gone from feeling so bright and strong to weak and unsure in a matter of minutes. The vastness of the journey I was on was changing me and I felt panic welling up. There was no one for me to talk to. Certainly no one would believe or understand what was occurring. I began to doubt my ability to handle everything I was going through, yet my desire to learn and to grow and to be of service was so great. I knew I could not allow weakness to take over. It was okay to let the emotions well up and release, that seemed necessary. But on the other side of that emotion, even greater strength would need to arise.

Sonny returned with a bottle of tea tree oil and a damp cloth. Holding it up he smiled, "Here in Hawaii I never leave home without this stuff."

He began to clean my wound and dress it with some gauze he had pulled from his pocket. "Now, the big thing is going be how you'll manage to keep the sand out it. That's where the staph infection is coming from."

I began to cry uncontrollably, unable to hold back any longer. Uncle Sonny handled it in stride. As I tried to fight the tears back, he held my hand and said, "No, no. You let it out. Just let it out."

Even though his words were reassuring, I was uncomfortable. I wondered if I was going to bleed soon, that could explain this sudden change in my ability handle things without getting overwhelmed emotionally. After a few minutes I managed to stop crying and looked down at Sonny whose blue eyes were filled with gentle concern.

I laughed vulnerably. "You thought you were just going to help someone with a little cut."

Sonny laughed too. "I could see from the moment you walked up that there was something powerful about you. You look like an Angel, you're so very beautiful and pure."

I thought of the angel of light who guided my journeys, and thought I begged to differ, but I just smiled politely.

Sonny continued to wrap my foot. "You'll find that there are a lot of us around here that have been called to Hawaii for spiritual reasons. It is a very holy place. Pelé sometimes pulls people harder than they feel they can handle. I am a purifier and a wish granter."

I nodded with understanding.

He continued. "It feels like you're going through more than most of us. You must have a big purpose."

I looked silently at the ground. As much as I yearned to share what I was really going through with someone I couldn't, at least not with a stranger.

Sonny began to put away his supplies. "Listen, you just tell me what you need right now, what you really need, and I'll do my best to help you get it."

I was stunned by this generosity. Looking out over the calm turquoise sea I took a deep breath. "Well, I feel like I need a place where I can be alone for at least a week, somewhere safe, with fresh water to drink and bathe in. I'd like to be here near the ocean, but without sand. I know that's probably asking too much."

He laughed gaily. "Well, that is a tall order and one I bet you thought I couldn't fulfill! But this just goes to show you how the universe gives you what you really need. You see, I'm probably the only person near or far that could take you to just such a place. I happen to know of a secret hideaway about half a mile from here with everything you have just asked for."

All the people back home that had been afraid for me couldn't have been more wrong about the dangers of me coming to Hawaii alone to camp. I was safer here then I had ever been! "That's amazing. Thank you so much for taking care of my foot, Sonny."

I smiled through glossy green eyes, for a moment feeling I could see myself as he would. They always turned deep green when

I cried. I called my hazel eyes mood eyes, ever changing with my moods, even the seasons, the colors I wore.

Sonny smiled showing stained, aged teeth. "It is more a pleasure to me than you may ever know. I truly feel like I am serving an angel on a path of greatness."

It seemed so much like the interaction I had with Handel, I wondered at this similarity and the way they looked at me, almost like God was blessing me with grandfather figures. I missed my own grandfather and smiled at the thought of him with his big glossy blue eyes, and the way he used to just stare off into space smiling at something none of us could see or know. I looked at Sonny's aged body as he walked in front of me, leading me off of the beach. He was energetic but small framed, almost frail. I didn't think he would try anything with me, but even if he did, I was sure I could over-power him. He wasn't some crazy loon; he was pretty benign. Soon we were walking down the road. I didn't need to limp as much with the bandage and my flip-flops. My pack was heavy in the late day sun, but it helped ground me to the earth. Some days when I was feeling really light, I felt like I could just float away.

Sunny turned off the road onto a path lined with pine trees. I was surprised to see them in Hawaii, they reminded me of home, a comforting feeling. Their long limbs swayed gently in the breeze. After we had walked about 100 feet the path opened into a tiny grove beside a protected bay framed by lava rocks. I could see the water was quite shallow. The air felt cool now in the shade. I put down my backpack, looking around. The pine needles created a soft bed on the earth, clean and cushioning. Sunny explained that the trees were Ironwood, which were different then the pines I knew from home. There was a gentle peace about this place. It was perfect for my needs. Sonny could see the approval in my eyes and motioned to the lava rocks. "And that's not all. Come with me. Taste that."

Squatting down I cupped the clear, cold water in my hands. Startled, I looked up. "It's fresh water! How can that be, right here in the ocean?"

He giggled. "It's a freshwater spring! This is a holy place. That's why you like the energy. This place used to be reserved only for royalty because of the powerful energy and the fresh waters. Women used to give birth in this pool." Tears came to my eyes

as I thought of the sacred births of the twins, being here, this
manifesting was almost too much. It was a though I was in a place
much closer to the time of Lemuria, where my thoughts and wishes
were coming true very quickly. Perhaps some of that magic had
been carried on through the traditional Hawaiian birth practices.

"Wow," I said, looking up at Sonny with a wide smile. "It's
more perfect than anything I could have imagined. Thank you so
much."

Sonny looked deep into my eyes. "In Hawaii we say 'mahalo'
which means 'thank you with love'."

I repeated, "mahalo."

At that moment I looked up turning towards the land and
saw Mauna Kea, the sacred mountain I had read about, looming in
the distance. Over it, a beautiful rainbow arched itself toward the
sea. "This land is so magical."

Sonny replied. "Yes, the rainbow is an omen of great blessing.
This place welcomes you, Luna. If you would like, I could stay here
with you for a few days, if it would help you feel safer."

He sat down on a rock near the sacred pool. "By the way,
have you heard of the legend of the Children of the Rainbow"?

I felt a shiver move through me. That name was so similar to
the Children of Light. "No, who are they?"

He smiled and looked toward the vast arch in the sky, which
was growing brighter each moment. "Well, it is a Hopi prophecy. It
is said that in the end of this time cycle, before we go into the fifth
world, people of all colors of skin will gather from all twelve tribes
around the globe. They will be people that stand for living in peace.
They are the chosen ones, come to inherit the fifth world, the place
where there is only peace between man and animal, between the
physical and the spirit."

With that he reached out and touched the rainbow band
woven into my hair just behind my left ear. Two young girls at a
dead concert had braided that for me over a year ago, I loved it.

He continued. "It is said that they will come wearing rainbow
ribbons in their hair, and rainbows painted on their face. They will
sing and there will be great drumming and celebration."

I gasped. "Is that where the Rainbow Gatherings came from?"

Sunny laughed excitedly. "Yeah, yeah. Have you been to
one?"

My heart pulsed with enthusiasm. "Yes! Last year I went to a gathering in Kentucky near the town where I was born. It was amazing! There were thousands of people at a state park for over a month. It was near a lake and during the day I would swim and bask in the sun. At night there was a great bon-fire and hundreds, literally hundreds, of drummers. There were African drums, Congo drums, Native American drums... it was the most amazing drumming I had ever heard. There were women dancing topless with long flowing skirts with rainbows painted on their foreheads, and children playing everywhere. I would dance for hours into the night. The vast starry sky above was so magical, and the rhythm, the beat could be felt in the earth below. It was one of the most magical experiences I've ever had. When I would finally lie back on my sleeping pad too exhausted to move another muscle, I would listen to people calling out from the hillside and valley beyond, "I love you!" "Good-night, I love you!" It was truly a family, a Rainbow Family."

I fell silent then, realizing how similar that gathering had been to the lives of the Children of Light so long ago. It had not been as perfect, but it had been so deep and so very magical.

Sonny smiled, beaming. "That's incredible. You are a good storyteller. I bet you have had a very deep life. I can see it in your eyes."

I shrugged and winced a little, remembering times less magical than a Rainbow Gathering. I watched the quiet waters gently nudging the dark mud at the edge of the bay. My mother liked to say I had a life full of what life really is, the highest heights, the deepest depths...

Sonny was quiet for a moment and then interrupted my silence. "What do you think? I will give you all the space you need. I can go to the store for you and help you keep your cut clean."

I thought about the offer. I probably would feel safer at night and he seemed like such a nice man. "Okay, that sounds good. Thank you!"

He smiled and began to lead us back toward the trees. "Why don't you stay here and set up your camp. The store is just down the road. I'll go get us some provisions."

I was really hungry and nodded my consent. After he has gone, I sat listening to the quiet all around me. The place enveloped me in a space of safety. Listening to the quiet lapping of the waves, I felt I could almost drift off to sleep.

That night we ate blue corn chips and salsa and then shared a chocolate bar, it was all so good. I appreciated food here more than I ever had!

I went to bed early and then woke when the moon was high in the sky. Before settling down I got my little flashlight, which I was so grateful for. Opening my journal, I reviewed my two most recent lists:

Tools for Spiritual Growth:
- Prayers to Great Spirit
- Calling for protection from the Angels
- Positive thought
- Intention manifests reality
- Visualizing goals and health
- Living free of fear/confronting fears
- Eating well and organic
- Drinking lots of water
- Yoga, yoga, yoga
- Connecting with nature
- Seeing the good in all things
- Healing the past/letting go, forgiveness
- Seeking Higher Understanding
- Desire for spiritual growth
- Contemplation/meditation
- Learning from the past/clearing karma
- Using crystals to bring energy to the body and align energies

Goals:
- To be happy with things the way they are, yet to hold a balance of striving for better
- To know life's purpose
- To serve God's light
- To help children remember light
- To feel completely healthy
- To be free of worry, concern, and doubt
- To have only positive interactions with everyone
- To fly, literally!

- To experience light the way the Children of Light did
- To know Divine Mother and Father
- To swim with dolphins and understand their message!

Feeling content with what I had written, I happily snuggled down in my sleeping bag. After a few minutes I felt the familiar sensations rising in my body. Suddenly I was being transported down the tunnel of light once more.

CHAPTER ELEVEN

The Dark Lord

I was in the temple once more; the screen displayed something ominous, I almost didn't want to look. At first there appeared to be nothing but dark space. Then I began to see a small dot in the middle of the screen, swiftly grow in size. Soon its image filled the screen; a barren red planet hovering alone in this isolated, lonely place of cold, empty space.

Slowly our attention was brought to the barren surface of the rocky planet. Ahead of them was an enormous, gloomy- looking cave in the side of a large mountain. There was an ominous, steel-cold feeling about all I saw, and I found myself squinting to look inside the dimly lit cave. Deep inside I could see something moving. A large form stood watching a calm pool of water in the middle of the dirt floor.

As the image became clearer, I was shocked at what I saw. Standing in the middle of the dark cave was an immense reptilian-looking being. He must have been at least eight feet tall with a wide, muscular frame and a short, spiky tail. His scaly skin had a greenish hue, and he looked in most ways like a giant lizard, yet he stood upright like a human. Atop this massive body, his pointy, snake-like face looked disproportionately small. His long tongue occasionally shot out of his mouth, and he seemed to be talking to himself. He had a small nose with two little holes like those of a large snake. I was shocked to see a creature that was so ugly and animalistic clearly displaying human-like qualities of intelligence.

The creature was looking into a dark pool in the middle of the cave. It took a moment to realize that there were images of what looked to be Tara there! I could see the beautiful sparkling sea and the long white beach, starkly contrasted against the glooming pools edges. There, the children were displayed, playing delightfully, running along the beach, splashing in the waters. I shuddered. What was going on?

Rubbing his webbed hands together, this repulsive being watched them vigilantly. Suddenly, he threw a rock into the pool with a yell of fury. My mind felt distorted for a moment. These images were jarring, and I was beginning to feel this creature's mind. I understood, to the degree that he did, what he was feeling.

"I will destroy what they have!" His heaving, wretched breath grew heavier as his mind spun in envy and loathing.

I was surprised that I could understand his garbled language just as clearly as I had the sacred language of the twins.

Images raced by on the screen and I saw that this wretched reptilian-like creature had been watching all that occurred on planet Tara. He had become obsessed with the Children of Light. Their naïve innocence and happiness made his blood boil. To him, the light and the eternal love they shared was repulsive.

From time to time, he left his cave and gathered in another, larger cave with more reptilian beings that clearly saw him as their leader. The dark lord was called Tarcon, and his followers seemed to worship him as they might a god. He called his servants Zygotes.

I came to understand, through a rapid mind transference, that there were about 100,000 of these beings. Some were smaller and quick moving. Others were larger than Tarcon and lumbered along slowly.

It seemed that a plan was being devised. Tarcon only came out of his cave to report the latest stages of his plan. This seemed to satisfy the Zygotes enough. Each time he left their presence I had the feeling they were spending their entire days and nights simply awaiting his command.

Tarcon had begun to focus on one Tarian. He was fascinated with her; drawn yet repulsed. One day he sat watching her in his pool of magical sight.

His breath became heavy as he stalked her from afar, watching her dance alone on a long stretch of white-sand beach. An laughed and jumped, her graceful body somersaulting in the air, landing softly on the sand and then running, singing out with joy.

"She is ignorant, like a child. I don't care that they can create entire worlds. They are stupid. They are nothing, nothing compared to me!"

Tarcon made a menacing gurgled sound in his throat. "I am a great Lord, holding domain over an entire planet myself. I will destroy her type of consciousness, and her planet, as I have so many have others, and enjoy feeding off their fear!"

He reached his slimy webbed fingers out toward the image of An, laughing and playing. "I have shown others in this universe that love does not exist. I have shown them that they would betray those they thought they loved, and even themselves, once they realized the greatest deception of our creator. Love does not exist!"

His hand reached into the waters and the image of An blurred. He seemed frustrated that he could not simply capture her in his hand. What it was he wanted with her was confusing, even for him.

Grunting, he stormed about his cave. "I will become the Master of these little children. I will show them that my powers are greater than theirs!"

He grew silent, plotting within his mind what he might do to gain the attention of the twins, by invading their silly little world. They were oblivious of his watching-eye now, but he intended to change that!

'Oh no!' My mind cried out. 'This can't be what happens!' Tragically, I realized that it could be. All the great myths of the current planet had some sort of battle between good and evil. I wondered if they had all arisen from what I was about to witness. I knew that somewhere in time everything had changed drastically from its original state to what it was today. Still, I wanted desperately for the perfect world of the Children of Light to never be disrupted. I wanted that innocence to be protected. This emotion touched a deep cord within me. I had been so innocent and free as a child myself, but that innocence had been corrupted, definitely not protected.

The Council called for a short break, giving me a few minutes to integrate all that I had been witnessing. The next thing I knew I was surrounded by this great healing, soothing light, and I heard the council letting me know to relax, and that what I was seeing was important, but to not be too effected. They seemed to create that ability in me; I don't think I would have had it on my own! When we reconvened, I knew more was coming and braced myself…

The screen zoomed over the planet again. This time I was able to see more of the planet's surface. For vast miles there was nothing but barren red desert. Here and there large rocks and hills jutted toward the dull, hot sky. Soon I saw what looked like metal structures, large and rectangular, spread out over at least 100 miles. I could see reptilians walking between these structures. They appeared emotionless, almost zombie-like. Suddenly the screen showed what looked like a large, deep hole in the ground. It was the length of a football field at the diameter and was so deep I could not see the bottom. Along the sides of this enormous abyss reptilians were perched on metal structures, hammering away more and more rock. Clearly, they were digging the hole, but for what purpose I could not see. There did not appear to be anything around the hole that they were mining.

There was vast expanse of the desert like land beyond the cave. There, more reptilians were building what looked like enormous cages made of iron. A truck-like vehicle with a long flatbed was pulling one of these cages toward the abyss. The cage was enormous. My mind recoiled at the thought of what such grotesque creatures possibly needed cages for. I wondered in that moment what exactly they ate, and what was inside the large building. At that moment Lord Sananda pulled my mind away. Clearly, I had seen all that was to be seen for the moment.

Once more I saw Tarcon pacing back and forth in his cave dwelling, his reptilian tail swishing violently back and forth above the floor as he walked. His enormous webbed and scaly feet pounded the ground, images of the Children of Light faded in and out of his pool.

Suddenly he called out in his deep raspy harsh voice. "Zante, come here now."

Another reptilian creature appeared outside the cave.

Awkwardly he shuffled his large body into the room, breathing heavily as he did, stooping before Tarcon with a bowed head.

Nearer!" cried Tarcon turning his own large scaly head to place his gleaming eyes upon his servant.

Nervously, Zante lumbered close to his master, clasping his clammy, reptilian webbed hands together.

Tarcon looked into the pool with his enormous yellow eyes as though entranced by what he saw there. "Today our plans begin. There will be no more waiting. I have watched the foul humans long enough."

A greedy smile came over his face. "Tell the others that they will feed soon. The fear that will wash over Tara will be so great; our thirst will be well satisfied."

Bowing to his master, Zante left in haste to gather the Zygotes, preparing their spaceships for departure...

Suddenly the scene disappeared entirely. In abrupt contrast, I found I was looking at group of six glorious angels sitting cross-legged on what appeared to be a violet cloud, with nothing but a soft pink sky around them. Their eyes were closed, their faces looked deeply peaceful.

I was deeply drawn to the serenity of their presence, but in that moment one of the angels opened her eyes in alarm. The others opened their eyes and looked to that angel who had made the sound, shaken from their meditation, "What is it, Ariel?" One of them asked.

Ariel looked frantically from one to other and spread her enormous rose-colored wings wide behind her. "There is a dark Being, his mind watching Tara! My mind was resting peacefully above Tara when I sensed danger. I followed the trail of cold, dark consciousness to a distant planet."

The other angels gasped in horror, wide-eyed with concern.

Ariel continued. "He's watching Tara, planning to attack it. I was fortunate to catch him in the midst of devising a plan. I don't know how we could have not felt this before."

A male angel responded quickly; his fists firmly planted on his hips. "Ariel do not despair. At least we know now before anything has happened on Tara."

Another added, "We must first consult Io and Ama."

The others nodded and together they closed their eyes. In a

moment, a great, white pillar filled the middle of their circle and the images of Io and Ama swirled within it.

Ariel quickly explained what had been discovered.

The contented expressions of Divine Mother and Father quickly turned to concern. This was their fault: the Children were far too innocent, and they should have realized this was possible, rather than carrying on with their own existence, trusting that the incarnation on Tara was going well. In their time it was but a blink of an eye, but they should have caught this!

Quickly Ama sent Io the thought as she searched his eye, "Could it be? Tarcon? How?"

Io looked back with the same searching gaze. "It is my love, it is him. I don't know how, but clearly it is so. He is alive and he has sought out the light of our children." Knowing there was no time to spare, they turned toward the angels with looks of focused concern.

Ama spoke abruptly to Ariel, "There is no time. This dark-lord…" She hesitated, "he was once our brother in light. He turned to the darkness. There is no doubt that it's him. He's sought out innocence and found it in the Children. He perceives this innocence to be ignorant and naive. He will never accept innocence as the highest form of worth."

She turned to the other angels. "Deep inside there is longing for that highest purity within our brother, but he has no memory of this. He has pushed it too far away."

The angels nodded at once, grateful to have some understanding of what was going on, still concerned for what this information might mean.

Io exclaimed suddenly, "Go to the Children, explain to them that there is an impending threat of darkness invading their planet. Tell them to create a shield of protection, remind them of what this is, how they must gather together, holding hands. They should visualize a golden shield around their planet that will not allow any malevolent force to enter. At that time their thoughts must all be the same. They must intend with great conviction that they will not allow any other presence to enter their plane of existence. This is their divine right."

He looked worried, pensive. "Go now and make them understand what we have told you."

Bowing, the angels quickly departed from the Angelic Realm, willing their consciousness to the planet Tara.

Seconds later this group of 'Arch-angels' appeared over the lands of Lemuria and separated, each traveling to meet with a different tribe. Ariel soared into the field where the Children of Light were gathered on the beach. They looked up giggling and clapping, delighted to see their friend as she hovered above them.

"Beloved ones," she began, "I bring to you a message from Divine Mother and Father..."

After hearing the message, the Children sat in silent contemplation, trying to understand the importance, for as yet darkness was of course still unknown to them.

Sensing this, Ariel continued patiently, trying not to sound despairing. "I know dear children, that the meaning is foreign to you, but you must trust your beloved parents and carry out this most important task."

She looked to each one as they slowly expressed their agreement, although it was clear that their understanding of the message was incomplete. Though their consciousness was as vast as all the suns in the galaxy, they did not sense darkness, could not. It simply was not in their nature or experience. Ariel smiled graciously, accepting their confusion and honoring their openness, trying to remain patient.

"Listen, I am a guardian angel because I know these things from experience. I understand the need to protect light. You must gather with the other tribes. Sit in meditation and focus your collective will power. You must make sure that you are all holding hands. Together you must create a shield of light that cannot be penetrated by anything that does not resonate with the light. The voluntary participation of each being on your planet is vital. Without even one of you, the shield cannot be fully created. Know that once you have created the shield, we angels will be able to return, as will all beings of the light. But without the shield, if darkness were to come here, it would become much harder for us to be near you, to care for you as you might need."

She seemed to want to express much more, but closed simply by saying, "It is up to you. It is your free will that you must exercise now. But please, you must make the choice to do this," she implored." The others have been given the same message. We must leave your realm now while you make your decision, but we will be near and ever watchful."

CHAPTER TWELVE

Listen Well

The Children turned their attention back to each other, playing with the little ones, turning flips and chasing after each other. I felt like I was watching young children who, when told to brush their teeth and go to bed, easily forgot and went back to their play as soon as the parents left the room. These divine beings, for all their vast powers of light, simply could not fathom the seriousness of the situation! Sadly, I realized that Mother and Father had underestimated their lack of ability to take matters to heart. Through their innocence, they were most vulnerable. At the same time, I knew they had to do it alone, it had to be their sovereign choice as free-will beings.

An last seemed to tire of the game. Turning to Ayia, she sent the thought, "I don't feel like playing any longer. I want to be in the forest for a while, I'll return soon."

Ayia replied with a wide smile." Yes, I will see you when you return, my love." With that he effortlessly sprang into a back flip, sharing his joy with An.

An giggled as she began to skip away. "I shall be back before your games are through."

Ayia looked to the others running up and down the beach playing. He seemed to hesitate for a moment, turning back to watch his beloved slip into the forest, but he soon shrugged and turned to resume play.

Quickly the screen scanned the lands. The other tribes were having similar responses. So delighted were they in their own play, all had easily forgotten the urgency of the message, as though the moment of importance had slipped away. It was as though with their linked consciousness, they all responded with the same innocent forgetfulness, or lack of taking it too seriously.

An glided over the forest floor, her white dress brushed gently against the brown earth blanketed by fallen violet flowers, her feet not touching the ground. The fairies came out from their flowers high in the treetops and eagerly surrounded the Goddess of Air. As the procession moved through the forest, all creatures sang out to greet her. I could see several deer, birds, and in the far distance a beautiful herd of unicorns prancing about, as though playfully awaiting An's greeting.

Despite her carefree nature, An was actually reflecting the words of the angel Ariel. She knew that everyone thought the request of Divine Mother and Father strange, but she trusted them, they all did. Oh well, she thought, soon enough they would gather and create the shield. Still... she wondered if it was right to forbid some aspect of creation from coming to Tara if it so chose. There was reluctance in her to completely surrender these independent thoughts.

She cleared her mind. Regardless of what she thought, she would of course join with the group later. She and the others would have time to share their reflections about what was happening then. Leaping into the air, An laughed and began a game of tag with three fairies. They all giggled delightedly, skillfully moving beyond her hand's reach.

Unexpectedly, An stopped and floated back to the ground with a look of confusion. The fairies fluttered apprehensively as well. Suddenly, An decided she was ready to rejoin her siblings at the beach, though she didn't know why. Turning to go back, she spun on her heals. A roar bellowed from behind her. An enormous beastly creature leapt from behind a tree, pouncing on her back, violently throwing her to the ground with a high-pitched roar, flipping her body violently around as he pinned her down with huge, webbed claws.

An had no way to move, the monster's huge body was heavy on her small frame, his large, scaly head twisted from side to side revealing huge, jagged teeth. Looking into his cold, gleaming yellow eyes An let out a cry of terror as she tried to shriek away, but the beast held her captive with his huge, dagger-like front claws. Quickly he ripped into her flesh, tearing apart her gown until she lay naked, vulnerable and completely defenseless. With another blood-curdling roar he penetrated her with his beastly organ. An yelled out in agony again and again; her terrible screams echoing throughout the forest.

His foul breath was like a poison vapor, causing her to float adrift in a sea of terror, unable to move. While raping her body, the dark lord flooded her pristine consciousness with the most wretched, hateful thoughts of guilt and shame. He planted the seeds of self-destruction, ensuring that An would blame herself for this violation. Stricken by pain and the oblivion of vapors, the Goddess of Air soon fell unconscious.

His brutal act complete, Tarcon rose from An's twisted form, letting out a satiated laugh that echoed through the woods. The fairies had long since fled, hiding in the trees, petrified for An. It had all happened so quickly.

Tarcon walked slowly and methodically through the forest his mouth turned up in a wicked sneer. He entered a small, metallic spaceship and quickly disappeared. I could still hear his wretched laugh blanketing the humid forest.

As I watched the screen, I held my hands to my face in disbelief. Tears running down my cheeks. "Sweet An, no, no!" I could not believe that An's perfect body lay there, bleeding, twisted and broken, perhaps no longer even alive.

The twins should have acted quickly with the plans they were given! I wondered if they could they have moved fast enough, Tarcon had acted so quickly. Had Tarcon's thoughts already been with the children at the beach? Had he caused An to enter the forest at that moment? My mind raced. In just one moment of time, everything had changed. I sensed it would never ever be the same again.

The scene moved over the forest quickly toward the beach, where the Children abruptly stopped playing their game, as though frozen in time, listening to something inwardly.

Ayia suddenly turned toward the forest and yelled in panic "An!"

Surprised by his yell the others tuned into An as well. An overwhelming feeling of nausea washed over each of them, a completely unfamiliar sensation. Ayia raced toward the forest, the others close behind. Only Fiona remained on the beach, holding the small children in her embrace, bewildered by what she felt.

They ran in different directions calling out, unable to hear her thoughts clearly. The fairies, stunned with fear, watched from their hiding spots. Ayia raced through the forest pausing only to concentrate on sensing where his twin was. A rising sense of terror gripped his heart. Racing through the sacred grove of oaks he suddenly tripped, falling hard. Quickly turning around to see what caused his fall Ayia moaned, shaken to his core. His beloved lay twisted covered in blood, naked and torn apart. He could see no light around her, only a dark shadow.

He collapsed to his knees, his body trembling as he burst into terrified sobs. Not knowing what to do, or how to think, he swept An up in his arms and cried her name over and over. Her limbs were limp at her sides. There was no response. Panic was new to him. The feeling of fear was completely misplaced in his being. There had never been anything to fear. What was wrong with her? What happened? Terror and shock took over his being. Helpless and out of control, he sobbed wildly over her body as the others gathered around in much the same state of disarray.

The beast had left An, having torn her precious womanhood brutally open, thus accomplishing his terrible goal. She fled her body unable bear the pain and shock.

For a moment she hovered above the broken form, looking down in horror. Then with a flash, soared through tunnels of light, her every thought upon the angel that had come to deliver the message, her soul seeking her out in confusion and despair. She woke, confused and dazed, to find her spirit-body lying in the embrace of four angels. She winced at the bright light around her, golden white and all embracing. They were smiling down at her, these vast beings of such tremendous love.

Pain of the memory of what happened seized her quickly, gripping her in its power. She looked around frantically. Where was she? The angels held her body as she began choking out endless sobs. One stroked her head silently.

She shrieked uncontrollably, realizing fully what happened to her body, and that she had left it. Had she died? She'd never died before, never had a body… Was this what death was? "No, no, no!" she cried.

Much time passed before An finally spoke through her haze of grief and incomprehension "What, what was that? Was that darkness? Was that what Father warned us of?"

The angels nodded at once, silently acknowledging this truth. As they did so a look of great shame came over An. "I should have listened! Why, oh why didn't I listen?"

Ariel was at her side, holding An's sweet though painfully stricken face. "Dear one, you were innocent. You didn't know. None of you fully understood. Do not blame yourself. We could equally well blame ourselves for thinking you would create the shield right away. We should have stayed longer."

An looked searchingly over the faces of the concerned and loving angels, shaking her head back and forth. "No, it is my fault. This would not have happened if I had listened. The Law of Karma for not doing as we were told punishes me! I will never, ever forgive myself."

With great concern Ariel looked the other angels. It was up to them to help An and all of Tara. "No, An. No, you must not blame yourself. That is what the darkness wants. An, this darkness believes that innocence is in some way bad, that every living thing should be wise to the wicked ways it lives by. Do not, please do not let the darkness in!"

An's eyes got even wider. "Who was it than, that being of darkness?"

Ariel responded quietly. "He is known as the dark-lord on another planet far from Tara. He is the leader of the planet Stella, and it seems, dear one, that he has bad intention for your world. This is why Ama, and Io wished you protected, because of beings like him. We are so sorry."

An shuddered in disgust. "The dark-lord, why would he do such a thing to me? I, I don't know him, I've never done anything!" She cried again and the angels waited patiently for An to grow calm again. She spoke again nearly spent of all energy. "So, it's too late, this dark lord will now be on Tara, doing whatever it wants?"

Ariel hesitated. "You must be strong now, An, very strong. Do not blame yourself, or the others. That will cause you to separate from Oneness. That is exactly what the dark- lord wants."

Ariel offered. "No, An, but now that he is there you will have to fight to regain what you have lost, restoring light to your body and soul. Then you must all work together to create protection for your world."

An shook her head adamantly, "I will not go back to that body."

Angel Michael hovered behind his sister, and calmly responded. "My love, you must go to the others. They need you now. You must be together."

An stared blankly, "It is too late. What is done is done. This thing, I cannot forget. I am forevermore changed."

He offered. "You can heal An, you can. With the help of the others, you will all be okay."

An looked skeptical. "Why didn't Io and Ama remind us when we forgot to create the shield in the beginning?"

Ariel looked beyond, and for a moment, to some place in her own mind. "They didn't realize, An. They assumed all would be well. Do not blame them, An. That would be the worst thing you could do. It would cause you to turn away from their love. This is exactly what the dark-lord would want!"

But An did feel betrayed by her parents. They should have done more!

Ariel rushed ahead with her words. "Think of this now, An. Divine Mother and Father were torn, even in asking you to create the shield. They were torn between their honor of your free will and innocence, and their own desire to protect you."

An lay in silence, too confused and angry to respond, these feelings were all new, what was happening to her?

Ariel stroked An's brow gently. "Can you love them for this, An? Can you love them for their love of you, and their own striving to learn and understand the right path?" She paused, "Life is a mystery An. At every turn it presents itself to itself, as it tries to learn, to grow. Divine Mother and Father are on that path of growth, as you are. You are one with them, as am I. We are all parts of each other. We cannot always predict how consciousness will seek to understand or evolve through us."

An nodded as a tear fell. "I understand the process. It is difficult to not regret their choices, as I feel they should have created the shield for us!"

The angel of light held her hands to her heart searching for the wisdom she could offer An. "An, if you allow your mind to think about what you would have done differently, you will only live-in resentment. You will lose the ability to have compassion and to realize that you are one with everything. Place your mind upon why they made the choice they did, not upon how it could have been different. Indeed, because of free will, Divine Mother and Father could not have prevented you from your own path, from choosing to forget, because you didn't really want to turn away any life force. Nor would they have wanted to. Even if it takes you a thousand lifetimes, And you have to strive to overcome this; this is how you must use your light."

An looked more responsive, as though a spark was reigniting.

Ariel eagerly continued while she had the ability to get through An's anger. "Mother and Father would have so loved to keep you in the ethereal realms where you would be safe always. And yet, they let you go. Beyond their own desire to protect you, they let you go."

An's eyes searched Ariel's angelic face. "I understand, I do. It is just so hard to let go myself. I want to erase what has been. This can't be the right path for us!"

Ariel responded calmly, smiling at the beautiful light being before her, this ability to overcome was who she was, she knew the Children would do what they must to heal and move on.

An whispered desperately. "My body lies broken, and I cannot erase the memory and the bad thing!" She struggled for words she didn't have. "It is my fault that this, this darkness came, and I would do anything to make it go away, but it can't! I feel what it is. I feel powerless, unable to create through my thought or feeling anything that would be good now. It has already shattered our innocence!"

The angel looked at An more cautiously realizing that she could not imagine the torment, the duality that now tugged at her soul. "Yes, you are in pain An, and I do not want to take away from your feelings. They are valid. The hurt done to you was not right. This is the way of darkness. It takes, and it violates the laws of free will in doing so. All I am saying is that, perhaps, through your journey of working to understand what is happening to your world, you will find a way that none before have found. You will find a way to bring healing to darkness, the most wounded of all creation. Remember, time does not exist. Not truly. There is no limit to how long the journey of this kind needs to take for you. You yourselves can choose how that journey will be." The other angels looked on with nods of agreement.

An wished she could just believe the words, but she could not erase the thought that it was her fault, that it never should have happened. All at once she longed for her mother's embrace, but she was so angry that the Children had not been protected. She wanted to accept and to have only understanding, but the wrongness done to her and the others was too great. She just couldn't get beyond that, and didn't think she ever would.

Ariel placed her hand on An's head and pleaded with her. "An, every moment is precious now. You cannot stay away from your body for too long or the energy will grow too weak for it to survive. You must go to the twins. They will need your help to understand what has happened. You must allow their love to help you through this."

An felt her beloved calling, desperate for a response from her body. Oh, her beloved, so betrayed by this act. He would surely never understand.

They looked at An expectantly. "I will go. But I don't understand what this feeling is. My heart pulls me back to my family, and yet I long to stay here."

Ariel responded, "What you feel now is just the fear An, remember emotion is simply that; you can change it, you can be with it, but it will never become all that you are. Be aware of it. Be true to yourself in what you feel, and you will not get lost in it. You will find the strength to know what to do with the others."

An wanted to smile, she wanted to feel the love, the joy she had always felt. But all she could manage to feel was devastation, an eternal sadness and concern for the others. For their sake, she willed her consciousness back to her body.

Ayia knelt in the dirt, clinging to the limp form of his Twin. "And what has happened? Where are you? I cannot feel your spirit!"

When she did not respond, Ayia wept, touching his face to

her broken chest. They were the first tears of grief spilled out on the soils of Tara. The others, hearing his moans, came running to his side. They looked upon their sister in disbelief, not understanding why her body looked so limp and lifeless.

As she came back to her body An felt the others around her. She did not want them to see her in such a way; they must already know that the pain suffered was her own fault for not taking their parents' warning seriously. When she finally opened her eyes, she could not bear to look at Ayia and so stared up at the treetops vacantly. Ayia reached out with trembling hand, eyes frantic with worry, to wipe the blood from her brow, but she quivered and withdrew.

"Oh, my sweet love." His heart pounded and his hands shook violently. "Please my love, tell us what has occurred. I try to read your thoughts but cannot, I...." In that moment he knew, knew something but he didn't know what it was, she was guarding what happened. How else would he not feel her memories? This pain, this separation, he could not bear.

An whispered, "There is nothing I will tell you of what has occurred. The fault is mine and mine alone. Because of me this has happened. I would never give you more pain."

All watched in silent despair as their sister closed her eyes. She fell into a deep, disturbed sleep, so burdened with her own pain that she had already forgotten the words of the angels.

Summersara quietly spoke, trembling with fear. "Darkness did this, it must have been that. We didn't create the shield quickly enough. I think she believes this is her fault because she went into the forest alone, but it is the fault of all of us. None of us took the warning seriously." She looked down for a moment thinking back to their parent's first request that they shield their planet.

Ayia stood abruptly, shook his fist, crying out to the sky. He cried out as though to the heavens, "What has happened here? I will find out who did this to my beloved!" He was feeling anger for the first time.

But he could not take back what had happened, could not erase time. This limitation was unbearable. He collapsed to his knees, weak and despondent. Why had they not been better warned about what could happen in the flesh? These feelings were awful, and they could not be removed, not with any amount of love.

He spoke out. "If Divine Mother and Father had spoken more to our higher selves about the darkness, would not they have understood, would not that understanding have transferred to us all and caused us to remember what to do when first we came here? If the angels had been more clear about what the results would be if we did not listen, we would have known to take it seriously!"

With some part of his mind Ayia received an understanding; Father had wanted to say as little as possible in the hopes that they would never have to experience it. He had, quite simply, wanted them to listen, or else to make their own choice to accept the danger that was to come.

Ayia pushed these thoughts away in frustration. None of that mattered. All he wanted was to see his beloved back again, whole and complete, laughing and playing. Would that day ever come?

Sunta realized his brother felt even more than he could for his dear sister; perhaps it was up to him to take control. "Ayia, we must bring An to our home and gather there!"

Ayia nodded through teary eyes. Ever so carefully Ayia lifted An and slowly walked out of the forest while the others hurried on in front. Her limbs fell limply at her sides, her chest open to the sky.

Tarcon watched from above in his spaceship, gazing into a dark crystal ball, satisfied with his first moves.

Across Tara members of the other tribes were being attacked by Tarcon's Zygotes. In response, the fairies, plant- spirits, and other magical beings of the land were disappearing in rapid succession, leaving the physical plane for the safety of the ethereal-realms. In their place, blackness began to creep through the very veins of the land.

An's dream body hurled through the atmosphere of Tara, her eyes painfully riveted to the scenes below. Within the oceans the cetaceans sang a song of sadness so great that the waters began to roll violently in response to the darkness. Some of the tribes could be seen running, hiding in caves with their children, struck with panic and fear. So many tragedies occurred that fateful day, and there were many, like An, who would feel shame, and blame themselves for the fall.

Around and around the globe An flew, finding no respite from the spreading darkness. She longed to return to her body, to fill it with love and forget what had occurred, yet in shame she allowed her mind to be controlled by the dark presence that had imprinted itself on her soul. Never again would she be the same. She could not erase the memory her mind and body now held. It was too strong, too vivid. As night came, she mournfully recalled the magic that had once been experienced by the beings of Tara; how she and her beloved would watch the sky deepen from blue to purple, how the fairies would dance beneath the majestic glow of the two moons. Now darkness came forth as never before and endlessly she felt herself falling....

The twin's had taken An's body to their home, washed her and tended her wounds. She lay on her soft bed, her family gathered around her. I could see a bubble of golden light around the twin's home that had not been there before. The poor little ones were so sad and scared. They wept, held in their parents' embrace. Ayia's blood still boiled with anger. In response the wind outside blew furiously as he kept vigil beside his beloved throughout the night.

Just before dawn An fell into her body with a sudden snap. Daylight was coming, yet the world was foreboding to her now. The soft bed offered no comfort to her aching bones. The deep cuts to her vulva and limbs still stung. Feeling her twin next to her she longed to fall into his arms. Her throat ached as she longed to let the cries come forth, but she withheld them. For the sake of her beloved, she must endure this alone. He cannot know the extent of this pain, she thought.

Ayia felt An return to her body and began to whisper of his love for her as he covered her face in kisses. "Please, my love, let me take this pain for you. I will take it and burn it in the flames of my eternal love." Realizing she was wincing at his touch he withdrew. The thought that he might cause her more pain was unbearable.

Finally, An opened her eyes and gazed into the clear, pure eyes of her Beloved. She had once known those eyes to be so free of any burden. Now they were heavy with grief and rage, though she knew Ayia was trying to withhold this for her sake. Unable to bear the depth of his love she withdrew to a silent, cold place within. Far off she could hear him begin to sob despairingly.

How could she share what she was feeling with him? The attack was in the past, yet it replayed unceasingly each time bringing more pain, confusion, self-anger and hatred. Something far worse was happening than this tragic rape of all that she was for deep within her womb An felt a burning fire, a life beginning to stir. So great was the pain of this knowledge, and she feared so deeply, that her soul would be lost forever in a sea of eternal chaos and self-blame. There was nowhere to run, no way she could deny what was happening; the dark-lord's seed grew within her. He meant to bring his cold hatred to Tara through her. She would not have it!

Through the cold unbearable numbness of the past days, An felt a boiling inside her heart, seeking its way to the surface of her being. She could not allow it, could not be angry, hateful like him. She had to remain who she had always been, loving, gentle. There was no choice but to battle the evil within, never let it come out and harm those she loved. The gift of birth, it had been given to them by their parents so graciously, but there was no limit to it. She had wanted to carry the seed of her beloved, now she would never be pure enough to feel worthy of such divinity. Was this tragedy the result of her careless regard for the instructions given by the angel? Shame washed over her again.

She had only herself to blame. How could she have lost her will, fearfully fleeing her body and seeking the embrace of the angels? She could have stood strong in the face of such violation, not allowing this unspeakable act to occur. If only she had called her beloved with all her strength! He would have been there!

Tormented, as her thoughts were, An wanted to stay inside her own mind forever, never to face Ayia and her siblings. It seemed in some way safer, but there was no time. She understood from Ayia that the twins had meet telepathically with the other tribes. Perhaps it was not too late to create the shield for protection. It seemed that all the Children remaining agreed that although they would like to help, they were afraid and confused about how to do that. She had to force herself to help create the shield.

That morning, all across Lemuria, the tribes gathered in sacred circles to implement Divine Mother and Fathers' plan. An silently joined her siblings, using all of her strength to stand. Her body ached, her legs shook tremendously, as though the attack had drained all her energy; she leaned on Ayia for support. The twins looked worried, sad, fearful, and confused. But they could not wait, could not fret with their own emotions, they just had to do what they had been told to do to begin with, each knowing that darkness had already entered their world. Mother and Father had said the shield had to be in place before darkness came; perhaps it was just denial, a false glimmer of hope, that their action might somehow still make a difference, correct what had gone wrong and return their world to the perfection that had been all they ever knew.

Joining their hands of light in the inner state, they created a grid of protection around the planet. Aware of the importance and seriousness of their action no one rejoiced in the occasion; it was so unlike every other sacred ritual they had performed.

Tarcon had no power over their freewill but he did not fear it, he had already entered their world, confident that the seeds of he had planted in the bodies, hearts and minds of the Tarians would spread and grow like wildfire. He knew that his energies were powerfully contagious and corrupting, even in small amounts. For every step the Children made he would make three. When they slept, he would be awake, shadowing their dreams. Already the negative thoughts seeded by him were weaving themselves into their shield; the doubts, fear, denial, all that was negative weaved its way into the matrix of what they would attract to their world. In a way this created even more power for darkness to grow. He laughed wickedly, watching it all from his hidden lair, knowing his work had been done, and with such mastery!

After a time of great concentration, the Children of Light saw that the shield was not successful, not in the way it needed to be. They had already experienced darkness, and it was on their planet. But the collective awareness of their free will, the united power of their love and wisdom, indeed placed into a collective thought-form around the planet, like a matrix of golden light. Despite the negative emotions they now carried, their desire for peace and love would shine brightly for all time, a place of light their minds could connect to forever more, a field of love and unity they would draw strength and connectedness from. There was nothing more to do but accept what had come to be, to find the way to let go of the anger and move forward. The tribes returned to their work at hand, that of healing themselves and seeking understanding about this new wave of energy called 'darkness'.

I had seen enough, and council closed the session. I was to

return to my body at once.

CHAPTER THIRTEEN

Integration

I returned to my body with a tremendous jolt, breathing heavily, deeply shaken by all I had just witnessed. I didn't rest well through the night, haunted by horrible visions of Tarcon, so that when daylight came, I welcomed it's bright embrace. For a long time, I lay motionless, not knowing what to do with the grief and bottomless ache in my heart for the twins and all that had been lost, for An, and the terrible thing she would live with.

When my bladder called, I got up and headed for the forest. Walking over the soft bed of ironwood needles, I knew how to deal with the pain in my heart. I had to give it a place to reside. It was in that moment of epiphany that I knew without a doubt I would indeed write the story of Tara. It was helping me understand so much, to believe in purity and that humans were that, could be that it could be this way for others as well.

Sonny kept his word and left me to my inner-reflections and writing that day. But when the sun began to set, his direction took an abrupt change…

Lying on my side, still writing in the dying light, I felt a hand on my leg. Startled, I jumped, and found myself looking down at a blood-shot eyed 'Uncle Sonny'. He shrank away from me as though surprised by my response.

I yelled and pulled my legs back. "How dare you touch me? Get out! Out!!"

He was nearly panting, and I surmised that lust was the culprit that possessed him. Adrenaline pumped through my heart; I was not safe.

Sonny cooed, "Luna, you are so beautiful. I could make you feel so good."

I was disgusted. He was so old and frail, I could overtake him, and he had no weapon on his body. "I trusted you, Sonny! Don't you realize how fragile a young woman's trust is?"

Inside, anger began to boil within me as I thought of the horrible act done to An. Now my own reality was mirroring the events I was witnessing of so long ago. I knew all too well the rampant danger of a man under possession of lust for flesh and control.

I realized that the abuses I had faced as an innocent child and adolescent, indeed, all such abuse, reflected that original time. Was evil truly behind the strange acts of mankind? Did man not possess his own being? If originally man was pure and innocent, as the Children of Light truly were, then something else had happened to humankind. Either they had changed themselves so drastically, or something else had possessed them. Hadn't I seen now what that was through the Council? But there was more to see. What did become of the Children, did they overcome anything at all?

Mankind in his divinity was not evil. Evil had been brought upon mankind. All the lies about Eve having destroyed purity, humans paying the price for their inherit sinfulness; I was sick with it. None of that was true, what happened was not the fault of the twins! It was the fault of Tarcon! Was that who Lucifer was, or was he another evil God that came later? What mattered was that people needed to know that their true nature was not sinful, it was pure and divine. If they could feel that they could begin to feel themselves more worthy, not accept bad and terrible things that happened to them like it was their fault, they could achieve a higher existence. They could strive to get the darkness out, to restore goodness.

Only a few moments had passed. I felt as though my rush of adrenaline, the fear-response to protect, had caused time to stand still, allowing me to use this moment of darkness to find deeper wisdom. Light truly could arise from any experience.

Sonny looked sheepish and surprised, as though my emotion had pierced through the evil within him to his true nature, the person I had known and trusted. He had not expected such strength in the young woman who had appeared so vulnerable and in need. He had expected that I would be submissive. "I just thought…"

I yelled. "Well, don't! We can't be friends now. Leave me. You need to go!"

Sonny looked almost afraid now and began to gather his things. Anger still raged in my body. "You should be ashamed!"

Sonny simply gathered his things and nearly ran into the forest. I sat down, heart beating wildly. How would I feel safe now? The night was coming, and I had nowhere else to go. I forced myself to stay calm, to think rationally. Sonny was just a lustful old man; he was not going to come back and try to rape me. I would have to overcome my fears.

I shook my head. I should know better. Sadly, this experience showed me that I still had not cleared one of my most bizarre patterns. With all that I had been through in life; I should know not to trust people so openly. Yet, there was something overpowering about my trusting nature. It had always prevailed in my life, often to my detriment. I promised myself I would be more careful, much more careful.

I thought about my family. If they knew of this, they would believe that all their fears for me had been validated. I could just hear my father. "See, I told you. The world isn't all love and good. People will crush you down when they can."

I thought about the angels' words to An. 'Darkness wanted the Children to lose their innocence, to dwell in distrust and separation'. I understood their great predicament. How could one trust and be innocent in a world consumed by darkness? I didn't sleep well, half believing Sonny would come back, possessed by some dark spirit, this time with a weapon; but he didn't return and by the morning I was sure he would not return again. I had really scared him! A woman's emotion could be powerful. I thought about a time when my mother and I were walking across a street at night when a mugger grabbed her purse. Filled with anger, my mother had yelled and held onto to her purse so tightly, the huge and dangerous man had run off into the black night.

I set out early that day with a few belongings, prepared to hitchhike; I needed to find a safer place to camp. This time it was a couple visiting the island from New York City who stopped to pick me up. I found that there wasn't much to talk about along the way. At first, the attempts at superficial conversation followed by long periods of silence were uncomfortable. The couple seemed nervous themselves. It almost seemed like they had come on vacation not quite knowing what they were there for or what to do. It made sense, as the world they were from was nearly like a different planet. It was a long two-hour drive and after a while I simply accepted the discomfort and settled back into my seat to take in the scenery.

We drove through windy gorges filled with lush tropical foliage and flowers. Beautiful white birds flew in circles above the flowery treetops. Clear waterfalls cascaded down enticing rivers toward the ocean every few miles. This was paradise. I could imagine just hiking upstream somewhere, pitching my tent and melting into the sublime natural surrounding! There was a vast difference between the rainy side of the island, and the dry, sun-beaten lava fields I had left behind. Finally, the long journey ended at a small town inland from the sea. This was as far as the couple was going.

It was approaching dusk when I found myself curbside again. I prayed I would get a ride before it was completely dark. The town I had been left in was not a place I was comfortable remaining. The run-down buildings and some shady-looking characters lingering on the corner made me focus even more on finding a ride quickly. I didn't know where I was going exactly, only that it was a beach where I could connect with the dolphins. There was a bit of panic welling up. I had no plan, no place to be if nightfall came. Maybe my father was right; I was foolish to come alone like this. I didn't have much food left but had filled my water bottle when the couple stopped for gas. I ate some of what I had left, my one hand in hitchhikers pose the other shoveling bread and a carrot in my mouth.

But before long a woman in a small Honda pulled over and offered a ride. Along the way I described to her what I was looking for. The woman lived out on a papaya farm with her family smiled knowingly and claimed to know just the place.

After a half-hour drive, we arrived at a cliff-side parking lot. Beyond the short, bushy trees, was the ocean. Unlike the tranquil waters on the leeward side of the island, the waves here were enormous. These dark, choppy waters were not so inviting, yet there was a power here I could feel. The woman described a steep lava rock path that would take me down to a black sand beach cove. Once again, I couldn't believe my luck, or my guidance, whichever it might have been it certainly felt like spirit was guiding me.

"The dolphins come here frequently," she said, "and it's safe to camp. You probably won't see another soul until morning. Tomorrow being Sunday, the beach will be full of people. There will be a man cooking pancakes over an open fire for any who would like them. There will also be drummers, dancers, children, and lots of people body surfing."

I grinned happily. "That's sounds amazing! Thank you so much for the ride!"

As I retrieved my pack from the back of the truck, I thought how magical this beach sounded. Perhaps I would find my spiritual family here, my tribe. I was exhausted as I walked down the long lava cliff path.

By the time I had reached the sand, dusk was waning; soon it would be quite dark. To my back loomed a majestic lava cliff. Above it I could see a rim of trees, coconut palms and other, lusher foliage. The beach was indeed pure black and stunning in its contrast to the blue sea and greenery. The enormous waves crashed down with mighty force on the shore. I had never imagined anything like it and was amazed to think that lava had created it all. The sand was incredible, dark black, pure, clean, with specks of silver and shimmery gold.

The power of this place was mysterious and magnetic. I rolled out my sleeping bag and found a flat spot on the sand in the middle of the beach, pulling my sheet over me. Once more I was alone, surrounded only by a scattering of coconut trees and the coming night. The giant waves crashed so close I felt as though they might just carry me away as I slept.

I certainly did keep choosing vast experiences, but that was the point of this journey, to move beyond the comfortable and known. The sand was dry, and I looked at the firmly rooted coconut trees nearest my sleeping back and decided I would be safe from the tide. I allowed myself to be absorbed into sound of the waves until my mind was empty, and all I could feel was the powerful rise and fall of their unending movement.

Time passed and I felt the ocean beckoning… the moon was rising, creating a soft glow on my beautiful surroundings. Unable to sleep and feeling the need to connect more with where I was, I stood with the wind pulling gently at my long white dress. I stood at the shore of the great sea, the powerful surf pounding at my feet. I reached my arms out to my sides, energized by the nearly electric energy of the water.

Suddenly, a feminine voice echoed in my mind. "Call to us, beloved one! Call!"

I raised my hands as though entranced, understanding automatically how to respond. With an incredible force of love, the first song of the Children of Light came pouring out - LEMURIA. The vibration of my voice moved over the sea with such strength is seemed to move into the ethers beyond, breaking the barriers of time. I began to feel a rumbling in the waters of the deep. A glow began to break through the surface of the waves, brilliant pink and white. The song echoed back to me, the voice that had called to me, only it filled the entire sky. There was a part of my mind that couldn't believe what was happening but another part that was getting very used to all this 'power', and concentrating on that feeling, acknowledging the part of the mind that couldn't believe, but letting it know it was ok, and that I needed to do this.

A tremendous burst of this pink light surged to the surface and I stood transfixed and fully energized, as the light beamed at me. A giant triangle of pure white light swirled with dazzling pink, just above the waterline. It looked like it might be a giant spaceship. I pushed through a feeling of being overwhelmed and fear at such vastness, and continued the chant, power coursing through me. The omniscient voice echoed back as my own - LEMURIA. In the space before me a massive eye formed in the center of the pyramid. It seemed to look deep into my eyes. In that moment I sensed who this was. It was the very soul of ancient Lemuria and the very land I stood upon now. I understood in that moment that Hawaii was indeed a remnant of that ancient world!

The Goddess' voice called soothingly. "Beloved daughter,

remember and call, call to us, let Lemuria rise."

The melodic voice filled the moonlit sky above. I sang out again the sacred word of the land that once was. I felt my spirit float out of my body and across the waters, merging with the powerful spectacle before me.

My soul called out. "Mother of All. Oh, Motherland, I am returning Home!"

The voice called back to my mind in waves. "Not now, daughter. You must send for the Children of Light, that they may awaken. The time is at hand."

With that, the Goddess of the Motherland disappeared beneath the waves, and I surged back into my physical body on the shoreline. The jolt knocked me to the ground. For some time I was not aware of my body, identity, or location. I simply was, unlimited and without thought. Slowly, I became aware of the sound of the surf and I remembered what had taken place. What did the message mean? How could the Children of Light be called and who was I to call them? I was changed again, I wasn't sure how, but I had taken another leap in evolution. I wouldn't be the same.

Crawling back onto my sleeping bag I collapsed as though I were suspended in the air, held in a capsule of light. I watched through the dimensions as young children of otherworldly beauty surrounded me and began to massage my body and sing. The littlest one sang, "Sister, we heal you now. We make you well now. Heal now and be as one."

The eldest spoke. "You have journeyed far, remembering much. Return to your body."

I was only half-conscious. I didn't fully comprehend. Were these the Children of Light as they had been even before they had created Tara? Were the Children of Light reincarnated somewhere on earth? My mind reeled. How did this relate to all that I was being shown with the council? Whatever was happening was beyond reality. I felt different, as though they really had healed something deep within that place of pain and haunted childhood memories.

CHAPTER FOURTEEN

The Hardest Choices

I slept, not knowing how much time passed. When I woke, I felt the call of the 'council'. Having grown accustomed to the change in vibration and awareness, I immediately found myself amongst them in the temple of light.

They sat in silence; everyone's attention returned to the screen. I remembered all too well where they had left off, the evil deeds had been done. There was no returning to the perfect light. All around the globe I could see dark clouds covering the landmass and sea.

The screen focused once more upon the twin's forest home where An still lay in her bed. The trees still swayed gently in the breeze carrying the eerie feeling that held all the land in its firm grasp...

An willed her mind into quietude. Although she was still feeling weak, her mind was focused. She knew what must be done; she had to repel this being that had been implanted in her. For the sake of all on Tara, she must sacrifice the love of life she had always known. She had to willfully deny a growing life, casting it away from her body and her dear planet.

She had to tell her siblings what was occurring. She could not have them bear more pain for her, or watched her tormented body suffer without understanding why. This all had to come to an end. They needed to move on, and as much as possible, return to the way life had been. Inwardly she gathered strength, preparing to tell them all of the events that forever more would change their lives and their beliefs about creation. When she was ready An called to the others in her mind.

They gathered around An's place of rest. Little Ra, Summersara's second child, touched An's brow lovingly, wanting her to come and play. An winced at the touch, undone by the sweetness. She began to cry uncontrollably.

She fought to regain control over her feelings of shame and despair. There was no time to waste, she must do what must be done. Summersara was the first at her side, holding her hand tightly.

"An, my dear sister. Can I get you anything?"

An tried to smile for her sister and to appear strong. Summersara was so loving, and so devoted to her recovery.

She shook her head no and looked hesitantly around the circle of loving faces. The twins moved closer to An in response to her signs of openness, sitting around the edges of her bed, massaging her feet and legs. Eventually An pushed away their loving caresses, relaying the shocking account of the attack, averting the penetrating gaze of her beloved and the rage that she felt within him toward the one who had destroyed her purity.

As she neared the end of her tale An looked to each of her siblings, gauging their responses. She met their eyes, not with the deep sight and unity they once cherished, but with darting glances and apprehension. Silently they looked to her with a mixture of confusion, anger, hurt, and compassion. Knowing no one would speak until she finished, she quickly confessed the most tragic aspect of all, the seed implanted within her, and her plans to expel it. She could not bear to watch as Ayia collapsed to the ground, screaming out in anguish. Sunta was at his side in a quick moment, gripping his shoulders, trying to support his brother's heavy weight.

An closed her eyes, exhausted from the output of energy, unable to bear the pain her beloved now shouldered. She felt herself being tormented by the dark lord who had forced himself into their awareness, into their very existence. She could hear his oppressive voice, willing her to surrender to his mind.

"You would kill life? You would destroy something that is a part of you, too?" Tarcon taunted her.

"No!" An responded fiercely in her mind. "I would not kill anything that was truly born of my will. I wish this were not the choice I must make, but it is better that I release this growing thing, whatever it might be, for it would bring only destruction."

Anger rose as she sent her thoughts sharply toward the dark presence. "It is obvious that this is your plan, to bring more destruction by bringing your seed here, becoming one of us. Do you think I don't see this?"

Tarcon recoiled in his mind from her insight and willpower. How could she suddenly have this kind of discernment? Was there more to her soul then just the naïve innocence he had been so intent on destroying? Amazingly, Tarcon only found himself more drawn to An at these signs of strength, knowing he could destroy it.

Instantly he shot back to her mind. "My seed could only be planted within you because you already had darkness within you. If you had obeyed the command of your Creators, you would not be in this situation." Tarcon laughed tauntingly, "You will never forgive yourself for that!"

An knew her will was strengthening, though now it grew from hatred and defiance. She would withstand any level of torment or threat, remaining strong in her determination to rid herself and all of Tara of the seed of destruction. She would not ever give into the controlling logic of the voice in her mind, no matter how difficult it became.

"Darkness will grow regardless of what you do. You will feel the torment of guilt forever!" He laughed menacingly. An opened her eyes, willing her awareness away from his threats.

Rasha was the first to speak. "I am too stunned to think clearly. I don't know what should happen here." He looked to the others who only nodded silently.

An responded listlessly. "Yes, you all need time to think about this. It has come so suddenly to you. Please take what time you need, leave me here to rest."

She had said what was necessary. The others would need to decide if they would agree to her plan. She would not act on her own, without their consent, and she would need their energy to banish this being from her womb anyway.

Ayia looked around the room, pulling himself together. He too needed time to think, but he would not leave An. He would never let her be alone, would never trust anyone but the twins with her, not ever. As the others slowly moved out of the room, Ayia held An's hand tightly. Alone with her beloved, An was once more uncomfortable. Ayia's grief and anger was too much for her, only causing her to feel more guilty and ashamed.

"Please, Ayia." She whispered already closing her eyes. "Please leave me for now. Return with the others when the decision is made."

He sat for a moment, stunned by her aloofness. She had never before wanted him to be away from her. His heart recoiled, hurt and confused. He wanted nothing more than to be one with her in this experience, even though it was so painful. Together, he knew they could get through it. If only she would allow him to hold her, to comfort her, all would be made right. But she would not let him in; her heart had a wall around it now that he could not penetrate.

The scene shifted to the ethereal plane, where Mother and Father watched over everything that was happening. The sadness they felt was palpable. Mother watched her precious An filled with grief and compassion.

Io reached out to her lovingly. "My dearest love, they have made their choices. They are strong. They are so much more than our precious children. They are of the same eternal source as we, that which always grows and always seeks to evolve."

Mother slowly turned her face away from the scene before them, remembering when they had been children themselves. She smiled as she recalled the first planet, she and Io had helped to create. They had been so young then, so fresh, but her smile quickly faded. They had endured their own journey with darkness, and it had changed them, but it was nothing like what the twins were enduring. It was in part because of that journey that they had deepened and grown into the beings of wisdom they were.

She sighed. "I know. They will grow. They will not be lost, but as their mother, there is a part of me that fears for them. I don't want to doubt them, but I struggle with the instinct to protect them. It was difficult indeed. We never understood what caused Tarcon to hate innocence so much, what triggered him to believe that control and hatred of anything that appeared naïve was the right path for him."

"If he had not rebelled against the light so suddenly, before any of us realized what was happening, perhaps we could have understood … could have helped him." Io exclaimed sadly.

Ama sighed. "I still feel the pain of not knowing if our love could have somehow saved him. If only we could have prevented him from rebelling; so many would have been saved from his violence."

"Surely this is a part of what is happening now," Io spoke strongly again as the understanding dawned on him. "Our children are a part of us, through them light is trying to understand what happened. The light of the one, of which we are all a part, is seeking to rectify what has been."

Ama acknowledged the truth of this. "Yes, the light is seeking the answers and the healing that we could not create with Tarcon. But this is not what he seeks; he seeks the total destruction of light. It is a battle of good and evil, being played out within the lives of our children! I am afraid for them even though I know they will not be lost to light. I will not allow it to go too far!"

She recalled for a moment a time when Tarcon had turned his anger at her. He had claimed that her love for Io was selfish, that she did not truly love all beings equally. This had been so confusing for her. Ama remembered contemplating his words for so long. She thought of the love she felt, it was for all things. There was nothing that she did not cherish. Before she could ask why he had taken such a strange and distorted view of her, he had fled. He sought something elsewhere, answers he could not find with his close brethren. At the time she had not known, could not have known, the misery he would later bring to their universe.

She still didn't understand why his view of her had taken the shape it had, why anger drove his soul when she and their other siblings felt only love. Why had he not been able to know love? How had the strange seed of confusion come to exist?

For a few moments they sat in silence, working to remove the fear they felt for the Children. Finally, Io spoke with the solemn detachment that was much more familiar to him in his current embodiment than an emotional state.

"No amount of fixating on the past will bring aid to our

children. We must not interfere now with their attempt to bring healing to Tarcon. This is their chance to overcome darkness and deception"

Io could see by the look on Ama's face that this thought terrified her.

"My love," he continued, "we will keep watch to see that these events remain within the bounds of what the Children can handle. We will see them push their minds and emotions to grow, which is what needs to happen. But, if ever the danger grows too great, and we see they might become damaged beyond repair, then we may intervene with their permission."

Ama sighed, trying to align with what she knew was the only choice. "Yes," she replied softly. "Tarcon does not abide by the laws of freedom in our universe. Yet we ourselves must have the permission of our children if we decide it necessary to bring about some form of intervention. We will have to wait for their hearts to open to us."

CHAPTER FIFTEEN

Leap Of Faith

I woke with the rising sun, feeling a great pull to look at the sea. It was calmer than it had been the night before. The night ... I remembered with startling awareness, my vision and the voice, but I had only a moment to think of all that had occurred, for just beyond the surf break, only fifty feet offshore, the blessed dolphins swam in unison directly toward me! I had been through many intense experiences in the past days, but nothing overwhelmed me as this did. There must have been at least sixty of them. Their sleek gray bodies were dauntingly powerful and perfect. My heart began to race. I had no time to integrate the initiation of the night before, what An was going through, the relationship between Tarcon and Divine Mother and Father... Somehow the dolphins being here in this moment was no coincidence, all was connected somehow. The power they exuded was beyond anything I'd known, and there was no doubt they were divine beings, fully conscious and more powerful than humans.

"Come," was the one word I heard.

They gracefully, silently, and as one, turned and began to swim out to sea. Pulled magnetically toward them I stood and looked up and down the black beach. The sun was low on the horizon, a beautiful display of purples and orange through the passing clouds. Above, the sky was clear blue; it would be a beautiful day. There was still not a single person in sight. Once more I felt the overwhelming impact of just how alone I stood. Was there no one else to be with me in this journey? I was being pushed beyond all my comfort zones to overcome all my fears. I took deep breaths seeking to transcend my human-self which felt faint with fear. Watching the waves carefully, I approached the water. I could hardly believe they were there, that all of this was real and not just a dream, but it was more real than anything I'd ever gone through.

A large wave broke, and the cool waters tore at my feet. My body began to tremble. How could I force myself through the waves when my body seemed glued to the spot, certain of its imminent death should it be forced to comply? I planted my legs in a wide stance, forcing my breath down though my feet, willing myself to not run away. I would have to time it perfectly or be tumbled under their mighty strength. Beyond the break, dark blue waters looked unfathomably deep. I was all alone, asked to embrace my greatest fears, the wide-open ocean, the threat of sharks, monsters of the deep, the pull of a rip-current … All this, after seeing a spaceship the size of a football field rise, from its depths, claiming I was to call up the greatest land that ever was.

The dolphins were willing me to come, I had to trust their judgment. This, perhaps more than anything, was why I was in Hawaii. Before leaving California, I had read that sharks never attacked people with a dolphin pod around, and besides, the dolphins were well-known for killing sharks and chasing them away by ramming into them over and over.

They looked so peaceful, their bodies rising on the crest of their unified movement, disappearing, only to surface back again. But they also felt, well serious … It was the only way I could describe the empathic feeling that rose within me, as though they carried all the universe of concentration, knowledge, and mind-power. They were massive, truly massive beings! It wasn't like how some people described who had seen them at sea-world. They didn't appear just playful, flipping this way and that, backing up on their tail-fins like flipper, trying to chat to me. No, they were vast, nearly as vast as the stretch of ocean before me. Together, the ocean and the dolphins made a daunting pair.

I seemed to stand there forever, heart racing with fear,

contemplating all this; it was beginning to feel like too much. But I wouldn't go back now, this is what I had come for, I just somehow had not expected it to be so much! Calling up all my strength, I took off my dress, stood naked before the rising sun, the daunting sea and the huge pod of dolphins speaking directly into my mind.

I took a deep breath and dove under the next reasonably sized wave. Cold water rushed over my body, shocking me into the reality I had just plunged myself into, causing me to feel even more shocked and aware. I gasped for breath, my heart absolutely racing with fear, but there was no turning back.

I thought I could feel the dolphins facing me in the pitch-black water in one long power line. I couldn't see them, but I knew they could sense me with their sonar, in fact, they could see more of me than a human could, inside my body, my energy-field. I was more naked than ever, soul deep naked. Rising above the surface past the break, I struggled to take deep breaths, petrified with the action I had just taken. There they were, moving right towards me, just 20 feet away. I could see the streamlined shape of their bodies, the eternal darkness of their eyes, like black pools of forever. Then, at once, they disappeared, and there was no doubt about it, they were under me, all 60 of them!

My heart would surely pound right out of my chest. Had I just made the greatest mistake of my life? Would they attack me? These were not the playful creatures seen at sea-world, after all, they were wild, wild mammals, and I was way out of my own element. Fear tore at my mind, that I would not make it through the scary waves. That itself was an overwhelming thought. How would I ever convince myself to make it out of this water past the dangerous surf!

The dolphins circled me, just ten feet away, if I wanted to, I could reach out and touch them. No, I didn't want to touch them, I wouldn't dare. All I wanted to do was remain as still as one could in moving waters, holding my breath.

They were beckoning me out to sea, testing my courage, my devotion, and my trust. They began to make larger circles around me, as though sensing my fear, backing off a little so I didn't feel quite as frightened by their power. Slowly, I began to swim out, following their rhythm. At each crest of a wave, I could see them coming toward me, all together.

Yes, they were so close I could have touched their beautiful, silky bodies, but I understood intuitively that this was not the right way, even if I weren't still afraid. I looked deeply into the dolphin's warm eyes of love, and then laid back, allowing my body to float. I closed my eyes and began to surrender into trust.

I could hear their tones, soft, yet penetrating sounds beyond speech, the highest form of communication I had ever heard. The dolphins continued to send frequencies into me, surrounding me on all sides and directly below. I knew from reading that the dolphins were sending me healing sonar. Seeing my body, inside and out, as energy, they could see what needed to be healed and dissipate it. There was something so powerful, and so vulnerable about being seen so completely. I felt that as the dolphins saw all of me, that reflection came to me as well. I could feel, suddenly, how vast my spiritual presence was, as it was for all humans, I could also see how much pain I carried, childhood traumas rose and fell away from my awareness. That was the gift the dolphins were giving me, clear vision, telepathic ability, and empathic ability.

Drifting in and out of an altered state, I felt deeply tranquil, like I was simply dissolving into water and light. From time to time my human awareness would rise to the surface and move into fear again; the enormity of the great powerful creatures, the waves, and the ocean itself. I knew they were gentle loving beings, much more evolved than humans, but the fear was still there. What if they bumped into me, or took me so far out to sea that I couldn't find my way back? When such fears arose, my body would begin to tremble, and I would lift my head to make sure I could still see the shore. I was alone in deep mysterious waters, unable to see to the bottom, with no humans around, and by now, at least 150 yards offshore.

A few hours passed, literally, as I floated in the cocoon of love created for me by the dolphins, surrendering more and more to their love. Whereas the water had felt a bit cold when I first plunged through the waves, I quickly adapted and realized the temperature was quite perfect. I probably could have stayed out for several more hours. With my ears under the water, I could hear their high-pitched tones, causing me to really know how close they were. When I opened my eyes, there they were, circling me, with perfect grace, always seeming to know exactly where I was. They didn't run me over or even graze my skin, yet they often came within mere inches. Even with the surrender, there was hardly a moment I was not shaking with fear to the very core of my being; not a moment that I forgot how vast it all was, where I was!

Finally, I knew it was time to return to the beach; I needed to rest my body. Time seemed to stand still … the dolphins had become so familiar to me. I didn't want to leave their watery world in a way, but in another way, I couldn't wait to reach the shore, to get out before anything bad did happen to me. With a feeling I would be with them again soon, I reluctantly said good-bye, giving many thanks, which I was sure they could hear. They put on a wonderful display, leaping and flipping high in the air. They cleared at least three to five feet above the ocean. It was so incredible; their bodies were so strong. Nevertheless, I was still basically and mostly petrified out there in the deep.

They seemed clearly sad I was leaving and swam along with me as I turned toward shore. My own ability to swim was not a fear. Ever since I was three, I had been nearly more comfortable swimming than walking, it was just easy for me. I loved it more than anything and always had. I'd swim in anything, just to get in water, a tiny pond, a small river, any swimming pool, but my favorite was lakes. Nothing though, compared to these warm yet refreshing waters with the sun rising, filling the sky with bright hues.

Making my way towards the shore I was surprised to see a few people on the beach. Had they been watching me? This lone crazy girl, but more so, how I would be seen? This dripping wet, youthful beauty … I had experienced it my whole life, the staring crowds, and yet I'd never be used to it, never fully comfortable with the intensity of energy, but there it was, reality. So hard to let inhibitions go, watched by the world; when I wanted to throw my arms up and yell for joy, I held back. I still had a way to go to become totally free, that was for sure. I didn't want to have to get out, through the huge waves. I felt awkward about getting out of the water wearing nothing. I reached close to the shore, gauging my timing making sure I didn't take a big wave, risking getting pulled under, or crashed on the rocks. Finally, I caught a small wave, nervous every moment, and onto the warm black sand. I could feel people looking at me. I looked up trying to be unafraid. The staring was a bit much, so I turned my gaze to the sand, acutely aware of the thoughts and the feelings had by others. Was I getting more sensitive? I kept my eyes to the sand as I walked toward my stuff, pulling back my wet hair.

Quickly wrapping my towel around my waist, I stuffed the sleeping bag into my backpack and leaned it against a tree. I spread out my towel and promptly laid down on my stomach, noticing that I was trembling from all the fear I had moved through. Closing my eyes, I felt as though I was still swimming in the waves. I could see the dolphins in my mind, wow, it was so amazing ... I soon fell into an exhausted sleep.

When I woke the hot sun was beating down on my back and sweat was rolling down my burning face. I heard the sound of deep drumbeats and human voices all around me; people talking, laughing, and playing in the surf. I opened my eyes, surprised I could sleep so long surrounded by all the sound. Glancing side-ways I took in the bizarre and amazing scene. At least 300 people sat or stood along the beach, most of them naked, some with dreadlocks. There were clusters here and there of people just chatting. Others were dancing to the rhythms. Children played on a rope swing at the far end of the beach. A man with long hair was twisted into a complex yoga pose just feet from me.

I smiled. It was just as I had imagined it would be. These people looked free and happy. Perhaps they would be people I could relate to. Twisting my head, I looked toward the ocean. More people were swimming in the surf, some on boogie boards. When a large wave came people simultaneously yelled excitedly as their bodies rose on a wave or got tumbled in the crashing sea foam. I was amazed to see an entire beach of people so liberated and open. Was this what the message had meant? Were these the Children of Light, right here in front of me, just perhaps not knowing consciously who they were? Was I meant to bring some message to these people? I knew I had to be careful not to think too much. The human mind could make things quite complicated.

Then I remembered I was naked. Nearly everyone else on the beach was as well, but still I felt self-conscious and was certain I had finally managed to burn my skin, badly. I reminded myself that these people were here to feel free, that they would not behave like typical beachgoers. I would once more need to overcome yet another type of fear. I sat up slowly, trying to feel at ease with who I was in a new world!

My head began to throb, and I realized I was completely dehydrated. With shaky hands I found my water bottle and drank thirstily. The sparkling ocean looked very enticing.

A group of young women were looking directly at me, though they weren't talking. They looked natural, beautiful, and at ease as though this were their turf. To the right several naked men were drumming, many of them just openly staring as they did so. I of course, made a point to not look down at their hanging parts.

I walked the few steps it took to my backpack and reached in for a piece of bread and ate it ravenously as I watched the sun dance on the water. After eating, I put on one of my sundresses and decided to try meeting some of the other beachgoers before I retreated too far into myself. Otherwise, I might never poke my head out again.

Walking over to a group of young women sitting in a small cluster watching the body surfers, I contemplated my next move. Most of them were naked, but a few had sarongs wrapped around their waists. I observed them without them noticing they were being watched. It wasn't my first time in a nude scene, in fact I had sought them out for their freedom of expression and acceptance. Sure, there were always men watching, but it was so different than mainstream. They might be admiring but they weren't jeering or being rude and ridiculous with come-ons.

I sat down on the outskirts of the group, crossing my legs. Everyone looked up at me, some smiling, some vacant of expression, some as though I had no place being there. I smiled brightly looking around the circle, and then introduced myself to a young woman closest to me.

"Hi, I'm Luna."

"Hey! Rosie," said the young woman bluntly and resumed her silent observations of the surfers. From the look on Rosie's face, I felt I was invading some inner circle. But working against my intuition, I tried to further the conversation.

"I'm new to the island. This place is pretty amazing yeah?" Rosie looked at me with the same look of indifference.

"Yeah, it's cool."

I hadn't expected this response. I realized I had hoped to

find a group of bright innocent people who would welcome me into their world. A pipe was being passed around, the smell of pot filled the air. Looking more closely, I saw that everyone in the group had that 'not-fully-present' look of one cast adrift on a sea of transcended bliss.

For a moment I wanted to be accepted. But I was glad I didn't smoke, and fitting in here would require joining their ritual. I knew that burnout feeling all too well and I never wanted it again. The high I got from just basking in the sun, or watching the clouds pass by, was far more satisfying, and the world of the council, the dolphins ... so far beyond what marijuana could achieve.

Seeing how beautiful and perfect life could be without any of that stuff allowed me to see my own attachments and the suffering of the world with a clarity I never had before.

No one else made a move to welcome me so I said "see you later" to Rosie who just nodded good-bye. I got up and walked down the beach, finding a quiet place to sit in the shade of a large coconut tree. I tried to relax, but I felt unsettled, out of place, even after my amazing night and morning. I had been so happy in Hawaii thus far despite my aching foot, but it had been a week since my last shower. My sun-drenched skin was turning to a painful burn and I longed for a hot meal and someone to talk to. Although I had been taking the journeys with the council in stride as much as possible so far, I suddenly felt I could take no more. I felt so alone in my experience, like I just couldn't go through more without something comforting, normal, and a break from the intensity of the elements.

As though in response to my despair, a voice interrupted these inner musings. "Aloha."

I looked up to see a young man with tinted glasses and long reddish-brown hair quickly approaching me.

I smiled back tentatively, "Hi."

The man sat down in one decided movement. "I was up at the cliff this morning. There must have been at least seventy dolphins out there. Was that you I saw swimming with them?"

I was surprised, not having realized that the bay could be seen so easily from the cliff. "Yeah, that was me. How did you know?"

The young man laughed. "Well, I admit I'm a bit of technical person for this part of the island. I had binoculars."

"Oh, that's how."

The man had turned to face me by then and I noticed I could see his eyes easily through his glasses, a light hazel. "That must have been one amazing swim. I've never seen anyone brave enough to swim alone with them like that."

I looked at him curiously. "Have you swum with them?" "Oh, yeah! My friend Michael and I swim with them all the time, usually later in the morning or early afternoon.

"I'm David, by the way."

I shook his hand, smiling. "I'm Luna."

He was looking at me smiling, his head cocked to one side. "What's your story?"

I told my story in a nutshell, leaving out my journeys with the council and ending with my arrival at the black sand beach camping alone.

When I was finished, David responded. "I think the dolphins are preparing you for something!"

I nodded like I knew he was right.

David continued. "Hey, we have a house up on the cliff. If you would like, you can stay there with us."

I was surprised at this generous offer. He seemed so friendly, and I didn't sense any hidden agendas. I wasn't even sure if he was straight or gay, but his mannerisms were gentle, and I had noticed that he didn't look up and down my body while we talked as most men did. Men were more open and generous with me, women generally seemed threatened

… I missed my sisters!

I replied. "That would be great. I could really use a shower." I pointed down at my cut, which still had not healed. "Maybe I can take care of this too."

David winced. "That looks like staph potential. You need to watch that carefully."

I moved in with David and Michael that night. Michael was fifty-five, a very sweet science professor at the University of Hawaii, in the nearby town of Hilo. He had the largest head and protruding blue eyes I had ever seen. The house was small, built of sweet-smelling cedar with a high ceiling and lots of windows.

My friendship with these two men was very healing. Previously men had never just been friends. They were always coming on to me or taking advantage. But I had been wanting this to change. It made me think of Blue and how special that friendship was. Already I missed that time on the lava rocks. But a house, a shower, hot meals, this was amazing too!

I felt so comfortable with both David and Michael. They doted on me, cooking dinners and tending my cut foot while they talked about their past, the island, and the dolphins. There was an innocence about their connection, which allowed me to relax and be myself with them. I danced around the house to Bob Marley wearing only a sarong and napped on the couch completely at ease.

For the first time since I was a little girl, I began to feel free of the limitations of the modern world and other peoples' expectations about what I wore and how I acted. Each day I felt a deeper understanding of how life was meant to be lived. People were meant to be free, loving, kind, not bound by judgment and control.

On the fourth night at David and Michael's, I lay awake on the couch for a long while praying that the dolphins would help me keep healing. As my consciousness drifted closer to the dream state, I contemplated how strange it was that more people didn't try to understand who they were and why they were here on Earth. So many people I knew just moved through life with superficial purposes, not seeking, not yearning. How could humans have gotten so disconnected from their own divinity and the divinity of all life? Was it darkness that kept people dampened down this way? I felt that it must be, for now that I was breaking free of the darkness, all my heart could do was yearn. I fell asleep with the words on my lips, "Who am I, Who am I?" The council called.

CHAPTER SIXTEEN

Reflections

I found myself in my seat in the temple chambers as though no time had passed since the last witnessing of Earth's ancient past. The children had separated so that they could seek understanding of their new situation.

Fiona stood at the very pinnacle of one of Lemuria's great mountains, pacing in fury. Rasha sat calmly on a boulder, appearing deep in thought. Fiona stood before him and blurted out with her hands on her hips. "I will not take this anymore."

His eyes opened with a start staring at her with surprise; her hair flared out behind her, caught by the wind, her eyes near to darting flames.

Fiona stated, "I see it all so clearly. If we cannot let go of what has happened, then we will create more and more darkness ourselves through our anger and fears, but I cannot stop being angry!"

Rasha seemed to sense that he needed to be the calm one for the moment. He responded softly, cupping her face in his strong hands, "What is it that upsets you so?"

Fiona pushed his hands away in exasperation; he recoiled in shock from the coldness of her gesture. "Why do you think I'm upset? I'm so upset I could blow up that mountain! Mother and

Father should have warned us more. They should have prevented this from happening. Now it is for us to live with!"

Never before had his twin treated him with anger. Fiona was just as shocked as he was that it had happened at all and recoiled from her own movements speaking fearfully.

Rasha was pacing. "Well, they did what they could to protect us from our own openness. They did not want to further interfere with our choices. Perhaps they thought that in our choice to welcome the dark, something different, something healing would take place that had never been before."

Fiona was further enraged by his calm demeanor and turned to face the mountain across the valley. Taking a deep breath in she let out a deep piercing scream. The moment she did so the top of the mountain exploded into pieces. Rasha jumped up and stood before Fiona with a look of great displeasure.

"Fiona, this is dangerous! We cannot misuse our power. Try to calm down!"

She only glared at the ground, her body tense with emotion, yet thinking how good the release of energy felt. The children had only ever used their powers to create in goodness. Could they, if they chose, use those same powers to destroy Tarcon?

She yelled, "No!" pushing the thought away. They couldn't become violent like him. That would be just what he wanted them to become. But this thing had already happened, and she was filled with shame and remorse.

Rasha's face softened. "I am sorry I further provoked your anger by being so calm. I too feel upset. Fire burns within me to see you unhappy, but I was trying to remain calm for the both of us." Embers seemed to glow in his green eyes.

Fiona retorted quickly, gripping her muscular hands together. "Well, don't. Seeing you so calm only frustrates me. How can any of us be calm? Isn't this what that beast wants? For us to be so weak that we allow him to take out his anger on us while we sit back and do nothing? I know we can't just be angry and violent, but we can't just stay calm and afraid and do nothing!"

Before he had a chance to reply she continued. "Do you truly believe this to be the end of his actions? This is only the beginning! I can feel it to the core of my being. He will not stop until he has destroyed all that is sacred to us!"

Fiona hit her fist lightly upon on his chest, as though doing so would make things better.

Rasha quickly swept her into his arms, sitting down, with her wrapped up on his knees. "Oh, fiery Goddess, so beautiful, even in your fury."

Fiona seemed to soften at his gentle words.

"My love," he said, "fire is strong. In the past, we always used it to create, to feel magically alive and powerful. I have just witnessed you use that power destructively for the first time ever. This can't happen again. Do you know this?" He looked passionately into her eyes.

Fiona looked into Rasha's eyes with more sanity now, as she allowed his love to engulf her. "I know, and it scares me, but I don't know what else to do. I can't hold this anger in my body, it will destroy me."

"Yes," Rasha replied passionately. "That is so, the anger will destroy you and you can't hold it in. Anger is in the dark-lord and it spreads through the very veins of our land." He suddenly looked out toward the setting sun, searching for understanding there. "Somewhere along the way he grew so angry that he wants to pull everyone and everything into the agony that he himself feels. Do you truly think that fighting him will make a difference? Do you see how he penetrates your own being with his emotion?"

Fiona gazed regretfully at the mountaintop she had just destroyed. She could hardly believe she'd done it, destroyed life that was so precious. Her siblings would be so upset with her.

"I know it in my heart and sitting here wrapped in your warm embrace I can feel calm. But I will feel the anger again when I think of An, and the pain she now lives with every moment. I want to fight him, to have him feel the pain he has created. I want him to see the wrongness of his ways. Yet at the same time I want to somehow show him that he can have love and appreciate the preciousness of life. With that part of me I understand that he must come to realize and embody the light, to heal whatever is broken within him."

Her eyes caught the sunlight, brimming with passion and deep sadness. "How can I live within this strangeness, this twoness? I feel two things at once, and the struggle between them. Is that what we are in now, Twoness?"

Rasha responded hastily. "Yes, we are in duality. That is exactly right, my love. No longer do we live just within light, in Oneness. But that light is still here, alongside the darkness. Consider what you said a moment ago. What if the dark lord doesn't want love? How could you trust that any measure we would take to extend love or healing toward him would be safe for us? I believe the best thing to do is to protect ourselves, to expel the beastly being growing in our poor sister's womb and to ignore any further taunting efforts he makes. We should show this dark-lord that no matter what he does we will never lose love or our desire to fill life with goodness and purity."

Fiona smiled as she felt herself drawn into Rasha's optimism. For a moment they sat silently looking into each other's eyes, tenderly kissing, pulling back to talk more. Both had the same thoughts and Rasha spoke them aloud. "Strange that we lived in such purity only but a blink in time now past, with no understanding and no language for any of this. Now it grows familiar to us, as though somewhere within us we already knew it. How else could we have these insights?"

They sat in silent contemplation, gazing at the burning sun as it sank into the horizon, finding no answers to the big questions, only more questions. One thing they were both certain of, they had to help their sister in her plight, a plight they all shared.

Summersara stood talking with her nearly grown children as they stood under a grove of trees just near their house. Jade and Ra were both stunningly beautiful with long, sandy-blond hair, and the same tranquil light blue eyes as their parents. Their skin browned by the sunshine and their bodies sleek and muscular. They didn't fully understand all that was happening, their parents shielded them from as much as possible, but they felt the energies and their gaze was weary, fretful even.

She left their side, asking them to go into the house. When they had gone, she sat down on a log. "I can't stand to see my sister like this! I want to run away and to never feel any of this again!"

Saying it she realized for the first time the depths of her own grief and exhaustion. She was overwhelmed, and now, finally allowing herself to feel the pain that had been welling up.

It was so awful to want to leave Tara. "I know we can't go home to the ethereal-realms, no matter how much my heart aches for them. We have a responsibility for what happens to Tara, to our children and all of life here." The enormity of that responsibility weighed upon her unbearably. They had to make things right, but how could they ever in a billion years do that? How did she come to feel so tired? For a moment she could see her own reflection, she looked different, not so perfect.

A look of terror overcame her. "Without the pure love that we were, this body will change. It will wither and die! We will no longer be immortal! Will the repercussions of this darkness never cease?"

She cried out in despair and anger; there was nothing she could do to control any of it. What had happened to free will? Had it just fled the planet when the darkness came? How could darkness cause the greatest rule of the universe to be altered? The thoughts were maddening.

Hearts grew heavier but they still had power, it was not too late!

Summersara garnered her strength for a moment. "I cannot think like this. It is as An says, the dark lord wants us to believe we are subject to his commands. I must be strong for An. We do have free will. We do!"

Finally, she collapsed in exhaustion. Lying there looking up at the clear blue sky she yelled out. "Take it away from An. If such pain has to be for one of us, let it not be she! Let it be me!"

In her state of compassion for her sister she no longer realized what she was really doing. She was literally using her power to manifest upon herself something negative. This would not help at all; it would only make things worse! This was the power of chaos. Out of it grew only more chaos.

In that moment I understood life in a way I never had before. Thought truly did create. Not just a little bit, but entirely. If the Goddess of Water could not clear away her emotional mindset, it would bring havoc upon her. If not in that moment, then at some point, somewhere.

My dismay deepened. Moment by moment all the emotions and thoughts of all the Children of Light were continuing to manifest life on Tara as they always had. They were so caught up in their own experience they didn't see the results … From my vantage point I mourned as more and more of the sensitive beings, the little flower fairies and unicorns, literally vanished from the physical realm. And worse, other creatures born of fear and confusion came into being. I felt frantic. Would the Children realize what was happening? The darkness Tarcon had brought was creating a ripple effect that no one on Tara could escape.

Summersara knew she would aid her sister; at the same moment her twin knew the same. Deep in the forest Sunraya and her beloved had reached the same conclusion. It would be done.

The screen faded to white. It appeared the council was taking a short break from their viewing so that Lord Sananda could speak directly to me. As always, the kind lord seemed to understand all that I had been reflecting while watching the screen. He took my awareness now back to the image of Summersara facing her changed reflection in the pool.

"Yes, it is true. It is thought and emotion that create all. They can cause the body to whither and age. In your day and time, aging is also created by the stress of your societies, the fear that people live within, and the pollution of your bodies and world. The memories of stress and fear live within the cells. Your cells also hold the toxicity of your parents and theirs, your genetic imprints. All of this contributes to the lack of perfect health and harmony in the body. Most people have no idea what health really looks like or feels like, so how can they wish to feel better? They have no point of reference. But you, dear Luna, can see what is before you and what has been. You understand how high the potential for the human race truly is."

I struggled for a moment to take in the enormity of what he meant. "You mean that we can return to that way of being? We can be as perfect and as immortal as the twins once were?"

Sananda beamed his bright, calming smile. "Yes. You are all offshoots or fragments of the original beings. Their DNA is yours."

I frowned, troubled. "But what we are as humans is all there in our DNA, generation after generation of fear and stress and trauma."

I winced, "The consciousness of our ancestors, is there in that same DNA. How could we ever feel that, with so many layers? This explained so much about why it seemed so hard for people to act consciously rather than un-consciously."

He responded intensely. "That's just it Luna. The original

DNA is there, as pure as it ever was, deeply hidden, a buried treasure if you will. You have to want to heal, want it so bad you would give up all that prevents you from knowing your true self. You are the healing of the your lifetime. Sometimes you have to walk through the darkness to find the light."

A chill moved through me; I needed to understand more. "Why can't we just return to that original state?"

Patiently he replied. "Because of free will, because of the memories that you hold of darkness, because of learning. Think about how much you will learn if you explore all facets of yourselves, of your ancestors?"

I thought about how much time had passed, millions of years! "It seems impossible. It seems like so much work, to heal that much."

His energy seemed to embrace me assuredly. "As humans you are always working, are you not? People work at jobs, they work to resolve conflict, clean their homes, and take care of their children. Humans even work just to feel the suffering they are in. Work cannot be avoided. This is just another type of work, and the most important work you can do. Eventually it becomes fun and infinitely more rewarding then 'normal work'. If your race continues on the path, you are on, imagine how toxic the DNA will be one generation from now, or two? Soon, the body will not be able to live with so much filth in the DNA. Luna your race will die if you do not change, and soon. First, you will become sterile. Then your bodies will die of disease, and viruses, and other contaminations. It is up to people like you who care about life to preserve the DNA, to resurrect it. We hope that more and more people will begin to really care…"

He continued, "Also, if enough people don't create change, those in control will make sure that you can't find purity. They will pollute your air, water, and soil to the point that you won't be able to exist without mutations, and your world will eventually die."

I nodded. It was overwhelmingly depressing, scary even. We returned our attention to the images moving again across the screen…

Night had come, and the weary twins gathered around An's bed. None were able in those hours to find understanding of what had occurred or why, but they shared their insights and agreed that the best approach was to create healing and to move forward with watchful awareness. They would have to work hard to put the past behind them, to restore the lightness that had, so recently, been their reality. All feared that no matter how hard they tried, it would lie on their souls eternally, that there would never be a way to cleanse what was happening to them, not fully, not ever.

Sunraya stepped tentatively towards An embracing her sister's trembling hands, trying to send her healing energies, but found no acceptance. Exhausted by the day's emotion, she began to weep, crumbling to the floor. 'Why can I find no trace of my dear sister's openness, her light spirit and joyful laughter? Will I ever see her again, can I do nothing to make her better?'

While her sister cried, An stared blankly at the ceiling. Finally, Kané came to the aid of his twin, looking down at

An with his big, sympathetic brown eyes. "My dearest An, we are all sad, so sad to see you this way, faced with the hardest decision any of us will ever have to make. We weep for you, and for all of Tara. I wish that we could take from you this pain and replace it with pure bliss once again." His eyes searched her listless expression for any response.

Seeing none, he continued. "We have decided to aid you in the decision to rid your body of this growing embryo."

An blinked in recognition but showed no emotion. "We truly wish there was another way, but none of us can foresee what such a birth would mean. We sense that it would only bring you more torment, perhaps even death, and we can't allow this to happen. It would mean more destruction to our world, the very off-spring of the evil one. It would not be your child dear sister…" His voice broke off into soft sobs.

An spoke flatly, "I am grateful for your love. I wish that I could feel as I once did, but I cannot. I can only hope to accomplish this feat and end this suffering. I do thank you all, and hope that I will not cause you further pain."

Sunraya knelt next to the bed, her legs curled to the side. "Can you remember that we are all One! What you endure, we do as well, as much as we can. Please know, that we do this in love, with no resentment. You did nothing to bring this upon yourself. You were simply the one this being chose as the recipient of his darkness."

An's kept her face firm, blocking her deeper emotions, thus holding back tears of vulnerability, as she looked at her sister and said only, "Let us accomplish this act now before the dark-lord devises another plan."

Kané could feel that An was determined in her decision, but he could also feel that she would only blame herself more, once the seed was cast out. Hers was the worse plight, the one in which either decision was terrible; this the lesser evil of the two, the noble thing to do. She was brave enough to ensure darkness would not come through her, to bear the burden of guilt and shame. He hoped she would transform it into forgiveness as well.

More than anything Kané felt desperately puzzled, not understanding how this situation had come to be in their world. It was true that, until now, their lives had always followed the 'Great Law', which states that all action and thought brought forth its own likeness. But Kané knew his sister's soul. He was one with her and they were of great light; to question her was to question them all. There was no seed of darkness inherent within An that could have brought this suffering into their world. He was certain of that. They were all still pure light within, despite what had come to be.

Tarcon, ever watchful of the twins, seized this opportunity to inflict more of his darkness, reaching into the God of Earth's consciousness, twisted his thinking, instilling doubt, doubt even of his own mind, and inner knowing. In the very second after his assured realizations, Kané questioned himself, perhaps these events were his fault. Was there some thought he had created that had brought this dark fate upon them all? Were they all defiled within? Were they making the right choice?

These thoughts were unfamiliar and confusing to Kané. With some effort, he pulled his mind back to the present moment and squeezed An's hand assuredly. He needed to focus on helping his sister, that was all.

Summersara, Sunta, and Rasha joined Kané, Sunraya and Ayia in creating a circle around An, preparing to banish the being from her womb with their combined energies. Fiona gathered the young children and took them to the meadow.

The twins began to create a protective golden circle around their home, one that Tarcon could not penetrate during these moments. Ra and Jade sat outside the house, meditating on protection and light.

Fiona sat in the meadow watching the precious children play and began to send her sister a loving prayer. In those moments of tenderness for her sister, Fiona's heart reached out to their parents. She wanted to fight the anger she felt toward them, to let go of the hurt and distrust.

She cried out, "Oh, Divine Mother and Father. Take this pain from us. Forgive us, for we did not honor you. Divine ones, please may we be forgiven by you?"

At An's bedside the others stood in silence, while Ayia took his beloved's hand and looked deeply into her eyes. Here he found his deepest test, he was overwhelmed with love and emotion for his An. He too felt pain, for she would not let him in. This separation created a chasm that spanned an entire universe. Ayia controlled the fear within his mind that they would no longer be together, that his soul, their soul, would be forevermore fractured, torn into pieces and thrown across the galaxies. Everything was connected, and he knew that their experience on Tara would affect all future aspects of themselves. He had to will himself to concentrate his life force upon this most unspeakable act. He had so wanted to have children with An. Now that probably would never happen, she would not allow it.

Focusing their awareness on An's womb, the twins willed the embryo out, no bigger than a tiny cluster, still nothing but cells fused together, the very beginning of life, not even a fetus yet. Summersara found herself wondering what kind of soul this life force would have, if any. At least An had realized she was pregnant early on, before the life had truly come into being.

An cried out as the egg was ripped from her womb. Blood gushed from her, spilling into a bright red pool around her and onto her silky white legs. A wave of anger and grief could be felt washing over Tara, as the implanted consciousness detached from the physical egg and spun through the planets ethereal field. A piercing scream seemed to tear through the dimensions.

Tarcon paced in his cave, yelling with a mighty fury, unable to penetrate the bubble around the twins, but he was certain of what was taking place. He had hoped they would be naïve enough to believe they were ending some precious life, when in truth he knew it was nothing but a cluster of cells as of yet, not an embryo with nerves to feel, a brain to know its life was ending. Still a part of his soul was there, attached to that blood-mass. He blasted hatred towards Tara, sending a storm over Lemuria. Rain began to pour down in the meadow, and Fiona ran with the small children to a near-by cave. There they huddled together, concentrating on protection.

Tarcon knew that regardless of An's success, he would find other ways to get what he wanted. For a moment he felt a strange, deep longing. His mask of anger cracked for just a few seconds, and he felt within himself an intense desire to be a part of An, to be inside of her, or with her somehow, anything that would bring him closer to her. Hurling the thought away, he stormed out of his cave in search of something to hurt or destroy.

Summersara held An, wiping her brow and her body with sweet healing waters from the crystal cave. The blood washed away easily, revealing the deeper wounds that still remained from the attack. She winced, shaking, uneasy with the sight of blood and empathically feeling her sister's deep pain.

It was all over, and An slept. She seemed to fly through empty space alongside a strange consciousness. It felt like it was a part of her, though it wasn't. The energy was heavy and dark, lost and despairing. An's dream was far from the journeys of light that she had once known. The consciousness grew and grew until it manifested as a great ball of burning light. A tail streamed behind it as it hurled through space, searching.

None of the Children had ever imagined that the life form growing inside of An was also a part of her, it was only the darkness to them. Only from this perspective could they have allowed themselves to dispel it. It held An's light, somewhere deep inside, but closer to the surface it held her confusion, fear, and anger. It also held Tarcon's dark hatred and rage, but on an even deeper level it carried his most hidden memory, that of unity with the divine.

Now, this infantile consciousness propelled itself through space at great speed, seeking it's home and it's parentage. Time spanned out and though only moments had passed on Tara, to this consciousness, it seemed a long, long while. It drew near to Stella in the vast reaches of cold space, and then in a moment of terror, it fled.

In her dream-body, An soared beside the strange ball of

light seeking understanding. Why was she drawn to this creation, longing to embrace it in love, while at the same time feeling repelled by it? The ball of light grew and grew with the intensity of its parents' thoughts and confusion.

Soon this being was nearly larger than Tara herself, and filled with a most intense desire to find 'home'. It drew near to Tara again, feeling a sense of recognition and almost comfort, but then it withdrew. Although it remembered being on this beautiful planet before, it could sense that it was not welcome there. Again, it hurled his massive body through space, filled with a deep, agonizing shame and loneliness.

"No!" An awoke with a start. Her siblings watched her fall back into a fevered sleep as her mind continued to drift between realms searching for answers, giving each other worried glances. The women took turns wiping her sweaty brow with the cool cloth. Ayia looking drained, and exhausted. He lay down on the floor, curled into a ball and fell into a deep dreamless sleep.

An however could not stop dreaming and for an indeterminate amount of time floated in empty space, alone and cold, filled with fear. Everywhere she turned she found herself in most horrific worlds where souls moaned her name, beckoning her to come near. If she looked directly at them, they appeared as monsters and swallowed her whole, taking her into even more frightening realms in which she found herself drowning in molten lava and broken body parts.

Whenever she returned to her body she remained in a state of delirium, unable to see her surroundings, screaming in terror, then falling into a deep exhausted sleep once more.

For weeks, her beloved twin waited by her side, watching as her body became frail and gaunt. They all tried everything they knew to bring her back. Some days they sat around her bed, singing songs, telling stories about the days of light, trying everything they could to remind her spirit of it's true nature. Their attempts to draw her back to their love appeared useless, and as her body withered away to nothing more than skin and bones, they feared the worse, that even after all had been done as she wished, she would still die. At night, while the others slept, Ayia wept until his emotion was spent, and then would fall into a deep slumber, always without dreams, without An. She seemed all but gone to him.

The scene faded and we were left to ponder our thoughts for a moment, then I was moved to the healing chamber.

In that space I felt more refreshed than words could describe, reborn, really. I had no idea how much time had passed before I was returned to my body.

CHAPTER SEVENTEEN

Healing Crisis

When I woke up it was dark, the lamp was on, and David sat at the edge of the couch looking down at me. I looked out of sorts to him I could tell.

He asked, "My dear, are you okay? You look a little pale?"

I nodded my head and shifted to a sitting position on the couch. Trembling, I began to cry. Once my sobbing subsided David beckoned me to the bathroom where he drew me a hot bath. I sat on the edge looking up at him sheepishly.

"I'm sorry, I've just been through a lot, and I guess I didn't realize how much." I squeezed my arms, feeling chilled.

He squeezed my hand smiling. "Don't be sorry, we're just happy to have you here with us!" Michael brought in a bowl of warm oatmeal and a few slices of toast with butter. Reaching for my hand he asked. "Are you going be okay now? David and I were planning to visit a friend on the other side tonight. We'll be gone until Sunday."

I nodded trying to reassure him. "Yeah, don't worry about me. I just need to rest. Thank you so much for everything."

"You're welcome," both men replied. David kissed my head and they left me to the bath.

I stripped off my clothes and entered the soothing waters.

Candles and incense had been placed around the bathtub. Silently, with the vulnerability of a baby, I ate the warm food and sank back into the nourishing waters. That's when I noticed a red line moving up my leg from the cut on my foot, which was again caked with black sand from my last swim. I recalled being told it was the sign of a severe staph infection.

When I woke the water was lukewarm, my skin pruned. I rose from the tub, wrapped a dry towel around me, and walked into the main room where I curled up on the couch again and was soon fast asleep.

In the morning, feeling somewhat refreshed I ate some cereal and headed for the beach, I walked barefoot through the middle of the street watching the pink sky, ignoring the pain in my foot. I wore only a purple sarong, there was no need for clothing on the beach, and it doubled as a towel. Needing so little made me feel very free.

There were many people on the beach, including a group of boys, wild and rugged, like the island, beautifully tanned with long hair, mostly blondes. They tended a fire and joked with each other. I noticed they were passing around a bottle of some strong alcohol. They couldn't have been more than twelve or fourteen. Near them a local man and his son were pulling live fish they had caught onto the sand. I sat on a rock above them, at a safe distance.

I spent the whole day there, swimming with the dolphins, this time not alone but with five other people, eager to catch a glimpse of their streamlined bodies or be delighted by the more playful side of the Cetacea, a flip or leap. I lay on the beach absorbing sunlight, watching the waves, then sitting on a wooden swing while watching children play in a small tide-pool, the only safe water for little ones at this beach.

When the sky began to grow dark, the group of boys made a huge bon-fire that sent flames leaping into the night- air. The sound of the waves absorbed all but the occasion burst of laughter from the boys.

Closing my eyes, I felt how weak my body seemed. I just couldn't seem to shake the feeling of sadness. Looking out at the horizon I began to see what looked like dark spirits, large burning, angry eyes and monstrous forms filling in the entire stretch of ocean. They seemed to stare at me menacingly, sending a message.

Was I going crazy, or were they trying to warn me not to share the story of Tara with the world?

The boys on the beach were again passing around a bottle of hard liquor. Several of them were taking turns leaping over the flames while the others urged them on. I began to see dark shadows above them, like dark spirits provoking them to defile their bodies with poison and abandon reason, thus risk their lives to a childish game. How had I not seen all this darkness before? I blinked my eyes, but the dark figures were still there.

Down the beach the father now sat smoking a cigarette next to his young son. The fish lay listless on the sand, but still alive. Anger whipped through me brain. Darkness. It was the answer to everything that was wrong in the world. I saw the purity of the twins in my mind, the way they had cared for themselves and their world. There was nothing dark about their world, no cigarettes or alcohol, no meanness or competition. There was no disregard for the blessing of life they had been given. Darkness was not natural to humans, only to beings like Tarcon, so far from the light, preying off unknowing humans.

I leapt to my feet and began racing up and down the beach, my body moving at a high speed, once more ignoring the intensified pain in my foot. I felt like Pelé was burning through me, seeking to destroy all that was evil. I yelled into the sky at the dark beings.

I was certain I saw them, "You will not stop me! You will not stop the light!" I didn't think to ask for protection and had no idea why darkness was suddenly appearing in my little world.

I heard a piercing evil laugh, mocking, provoking.

I ran toward the fisherman and yelled. "Those fish were innocent. Couldn't you have given them a peaceful death at least, instead of leaving their bodies to burn in the sand? Don't you know that being out of the water burns them? They are suffocating to death!"

The man and boy just looked at me completely bewildered. Then the man smiled a devilish toothless grin and laughed at me. The boy followed his father's example. I ran from the beach, scrambling up the cliff. At the top I sat beneath a tree and stared defiantly towards the horizon. I didn't feel like myself, yelling at that man. That wasn't like me. Suddenly I felt quite ill as though I might throw up. My foot not only ached, but it was also beginning to feel numb.

I forced myself to get up and walk toward my temporary home, no longer excited about my night alone, and mad as hell at all the defilement, all the people who just refused to respect life, and there being nothing I could do to control it. I limped barefooted in the darkness, wrapping my arms around my chilled body. When I got to the front door, I went to open it, but it was locked! I yelled out in exasperation, "No, no, no!"

I checked the windows, but Michael had closed them all in preparation for a coming storm. I sat down tired and dizzy, frustrated at my own absent-mindedness. In my down and out state I hadn't even thought of grabbing the key before I locked it. Down the street I heard music. I was out on an edge, not really knowing what was happening to me. I had to do something. Slowly I walked toward the sound, nervous and unsure. Four older men sat on a porch under a bright light. They were playing guitar, laughing, and drinking. I stood in the shadows watching. The sight of them was in some way welcoming, a reminder of my childhood with men gathering around at night to play music and sing. But the alcohol also made the scene intimidating.

There was no choice but to put the needs of my body before my intimidation. I felt I was near to breaking. Slowly I walked up the steps. For a moment I felt I could imagine what it was like for these middle-aged men to see this young woman wearing nothing but a sarong.

One man called out. "Welcome, honey. Do we know you?" I heard one of them whisper. "Sure, would like to." Cautiously I walked toward them and stood still about five feet away. "I'm Luna, I think I'm hurt."

I meant to be strong but my voice broke and I choked back tears. I asked for the one thing that had always made me feel better. "Can I take a hot shower? I've locked myself out of the house, and I've, been through a lot." I was crying despite my efforts to appear strong.

Another man with thinning white hair and aged blue eyes walked toward me. "Oh, honey, let me guess. You're new to the island and she put you through a dandy hard time."

I nodded, unable to say anything, afraid I would cry even

more uncontrollably, that was the least of it.

He put an arm around me; his hand was rough and calloused. "It's going to be okay. I've got plenty of hot water, shampoo, even conditioner."

I heard a slight southern accent in his voice, and this comforted me too. Suddenly I missed Kentucky, the place of my birth, the summer rains, grandma's cooking, and my grandpa sitting on the porch. I missed California, my friends, and restaurants ...

"It'll be alright. Jake will take care of you."

I felt relief flood through my body. While I was in the shower, I would think about what to do about my predicament. I couldn't very well ask to spend the night. I was so weak, I felt nearly delirious. I was just barely clinging to the reality at hand, holding at bay the dimensions of both light and dark that seemed to surround and press in upon me. Jake flicked the light switch and reached into a closet, pulling out a washcloth and towel. The bathroom was simple and pretty clean, though I hardly noticed.

"Take your time, there's plenty of hot water." He gave me a fatherly smile.

I mustered a thank you and closed the door.

Quickly I took off my sarong. I turned on the water and adjusted it to steaming hot. Hopeful that the soothing warmth would take away the uneasy feeling of impending danger, I stepped in. I wanted to wash my body and hair, but I was so weak my hands trembled and all I could do was stand and cry and cry. I cried for the twins, for the darkness I had seen above the water, the drunken boys, the fish, and for the locked door. I cried for everything, for the loss of light to my world, for what had been and would never be again. How had I not been crying the whole time, just handling all this vastness on my own, it was crazy!

Something inside of me told me these tears were the best form of release I could experience. Perhaps they could even release the weakness I felt, and I would find strength again. But time passed and still I could only stand there under the hot water, unmoving.

I felt my head sway, and suddenly it was as though all the energy and all the consciousness I had ever been was being sucked into one dark hole. I heard a high-pitched sound, and my head began to pound with a mighty force. Then all I could see was blackness. Somehow, I knew I was dying. But it wasn't the right kind of dying, not the right time. It wasn't the death I expected, where there was a light at the end of a tunnel and angels everywhere. I was sinking into an abyss of nothing.

Somehow darkness had found me, and I had but a moment to seek help. With tremendous force I suddenly felt my entire soul enter my body. There were no words in my mind for what was happening. I just knew it was so. I was in danger, and my soul was calling forth all its energy to keep the body alive, to keep my consciousness from dying.

I heard my own voice, as if from a great distance, calling out feebly for help. I tried to breathe, my hands gripping the edges of the shower. I tried to call out again, but nothing arose in my throat. I was falling and I couldn't stop it. My body fell hard, as I was falling there was nothing but blackness. I was afraid I would forget everything I'd been shown, everything I'd learned; that darkness was trying to steal my soul. I fell hard straight forward hitting my head on the side of the tub. I knew nothing, was nothing.

There was a pounding on the door, and I came back to find my body lying there, twisted and shaking, cold water pouring over my crumbled form. I was shivering, nearly blue, and unable to move.

Suddenly the door opened, and Jake said, "I'm sorry honey, I've got to come in. Good gracious! What happened?" There was no answer.

He pulled back the shower curtain enough to see me slumped there. I could not say a word. I could not care that my breasts were borne to this man I didn't even know. Time seemed to stand still as I understood inwardly that I had died and come back again. Darkness had tried to take me, but my soul had battled. I knew this with certainty. I had gone to a place where something deep inside of me had been released, and something new had come into my being. This gift I had been given was like a protective shield or a wand of light that I now possessed. But these men would have no way of knowing what had happened, and I was far too dazed to communicate anything. I could barely move.

Jake quickly turned off the water and grabbed a towel. Slowly he lifted me up until I sat limp on the tub edge.

He wrapped the towel around me and grabbed another from the closet as he called out to his friends, "One of you get in here and help me. This girl's in trouble."

I closed my eyes, feeling pulled back to the endless darkness. I could hear the voice of Jake though he seemed so distant. "Don't you leave us. Stay with us, you hear?"

I felt my body being lifted and soon I was lying on my side. The darkness still pulled me down, down. I saw burning eyes there. I knew then that I had tried to handle more than my human body could integrate. All the journeys with the council, and on top of them the dolphin swims, the staph infection, the sun, the dehydration, traveling alone, Sonny; it had been too much. What was more, I had alerted the dark forces. I didn't know how they found me, only that they had, and I no longer wanted to be so alone. Why wasn't I protected then? Was it because I was sick? Did this weaken my protection? Did I need to pray for it? Was I not always protected without asking for it?

I heard the men around me, calling me back. One spoke. "I can't imagine what's wrong with her. She looks fine."

Another said, "Do you think she might be diabetic?"

I was trying to shake my head. No, I was not diabetic.

I felt movement on my arms and Jake saying. "No, she has no marks."

Another said, "She could be falling into a coma. We need to get her to eat!"

I remained partially conscious of my surroundings, touched by their concern. Humans were so far from the grace they had once known, but they could still love and still care. Perhaps that was my lesson of the night; to keep seeing the good in everything, no matter how much darkness I was being shown.

I knew that I was not diabetic, but the infection had certainly weakened me. I did need to eat, to be nourished. Jake moved something under my nose that smelled awful. I opened my eyes, squinting at the bright light.

Jake held my jaw. "You need to eat, Luna. Sit up, please."

I nodded and felt myself being lifted to sitting. My eyes closed again, and I drifted away. Something was placed against my mouth and I heard the words, "Drink this."

I took a sip and felt the familiar taste of cold apple juice. It was the best thing I had ever tasted, cold and a bit numbing.

I pointed at my cut, trying to lift my foot.

Jake drew a deep breath in. "Lord have mercy, this girl's got a serious staph infection."

Everyone gasped peering down at my foot and another man said, "I see one bad like that last year. It got so bad they had to amputate the leg."

I was startled more awake by this alarming comment but all I could do was stare at my leg. Jake lifted my foot and placed a pillow under my heel on the coffee table. The men gathered around inspecting the oozing cut still filled with sand and dirt, and the deep red line that ran up my leg.

Jake began commanding the others. "Frank, get the antibiotic ointment from the kitchen cabinet. Joe, you get a warm bowl of water, a rag, rubbing alcohol, and tweezers. It's all in the bathroom."

While the men pulled the debris from my raw wound I was fed crackers and cheese. It took my mind off the pain, but I still winced and yelped now and then. It was pretty painful and I regretted letting it get this far. When they were done, I looked from face to face. Each man wore his life on his tired, wrinkled countenance. I could see joy, pain, sorrow, regret, and wisdom.

Smiling meekly, I offered, "Thank you all. I don't know where I would be without you."

One of the men jested, "Without that pretty leg, that's for sure!"

I made a feeble attempt to laugh. Jake looked serious. "Where is your house?" I had almost forgotten my predicament.

"I'm staying down the street a few houses, with David and Michael. Do you know them?"

"Oh sure. We all know each other around here. Why aren't you with them?"

I explained that David and Michael had gone on to the other side of the island and left the house to me, but that I had locked myself out.

Jake laughed, "Oh, that's easy. I know where they keep the spare key."

A few of the men escorted me down the lane. I limped awkwardly on my bandaged foot. At the doorstep Jake reached

under the floor mat, pulled out the house key, and opened the
door.

I turned to them. "I'll be okay from here. I am so sorry I
ruined your music night."

Jake replied with a wide smile. "Not at all. You brought more
excitement than we've had all year. Take care of that and if you
need us just give a yell, ok?"

They all said goodnight and I entered the silent, dark house
alone, too tired for anything, and fell into a deep dreamless sleep.

The next day passed and I did little but rest and write in
my journal. I still felt that I didn't have a handle on all that was
happening to me.

That night Michael and David arrived around dinnertime.
They both saw once again that something was different with me.
They wanted to know everything. As they sat at the coffee table I
explained. Both men were clearly very concerned and encouraged
me to just relax for a few days. I assured them I would try.

After hugs and dinner preparations the three of us sat and ate
together. When it was time to go to bed, Michael went to his room
as usual, but David had fallen asleep on the futon chair reading
while I was in the bath. I decided not to disturb him, and after
quietly making a makeshift bed on the living room floor, I quickly
fell asleep.

A noise outside and a light awakened me hours later.
Opening my eyes, I was paralyzed by what I saw. Three men with
very pale faces and beady, inhuman black eyes stood before me,
motionless. They wore black, well-pressed suits, black ties, and
white shirts underneath. I felt like they were holding my mind,
keeping me from moving, from being able to speak, that they
were reading my mind, the memories of everything I'd ever been
through.

I wanted to scream out for help, but my voice was frozen. I
had no memory of having seen such men before or ever hearing of
them but somehow, I knew them. My mind called out frantically.
They were the Men-in-Black! How did I know that term? How did
I know exactly who and what they were? The Men-in-Black were
robotic, barely human beings that were part of a control system on
Earth. They had been sent to repress my memory of my journey
with the council. They were either to erase it from my memory or

make sure I didn't believe it was true. They were here to prevent me from ever sharing the story with anyone. They were trying to crush my spiritual memories so I wouldn't keep evolving.

I knew I had to fight their mind-control, but how? One of the men directed a beam of red light at my head from an object in his hand. I felt the light crushing down on my brain. It hurt. It stung. An electronic ringing sound filled the room. My eyes moved to David. He, too, lay there wide-eyed, unable to move or speak. A voice inside my head continued to tell me that they wanted to take my memories. I would have to be strong, to push an energy-field out from my head back toward them telepathically, letting them know that I could not be controlled.

My head felt like it would split in two. I felt myself losing consciousness and fought back with greater resistance. In my mind I yelled out, "No!"

There was a flash of white light and they were gone. I slumped onto my side, exhausted with effort and trembling with fear.

David rushed to my side. He too was shaking. "Luna, are you okay?"

I looked up at David's worried, confused face.

David sat back, dazed, as though allowing the shock to hit him. "I can't believe what just happened. Do you know who those men were?"

Still shaking with fear, I looked around the room. "I think I do. I heard a name, the Men in Black."

"Yes." David replied surprised. "The Men in Black. They came for you, because of who you are."

I stared at his face trying to take in what I already knew. "How do you know that?"

David sighed; his face still covered with fear. "A few years back I became friends with a man in Chicago who had worked for the CIA. After he resigned, he began quietly to tell people about the secret government and these secret agents known as the Men-in-Black. There sole purpose is to monitor human consciousness and make sure no one realizes a greater reality or enlightenment than the government permits."

I sighed and said only, "Wow."

David replied softly. "You need more protection than we ever imagined."

Neither of us wanted to talk anymore. We were both still deep in our internal thoughts and fears. But David wrapped his arms around me, and we slept tightly bound together as brother and sister for the rest of that strange night.

In the morning we both still felt dazed, confused and a little scared. Would the Men-in-Black come back, what would protect us? When we asked Michael if he had seen or heard anything he only looked with innocence and spoke. "No, nothing. Why? What happened?"

Once David told of the visitation a look of great concern came over Michael. "Luna, how are we going to keep you safe?"

I shrugged, my hands trembling. I spoke more to myself then to him really. "I don't understand much of what is happening at this point. I don't know what can protect me. I guess I'll have to be really strong." David's eyes searched me, filled with dark fear and worry. This wasn't helping.

Excusing myself, I went for a long walk along the cliff. My foot still hurt but it was clean and there was no longer a red mark going up my leg. Once I had reached a place far from houses, I stood in the middle of the black road, a field to my left, the ocean cliffs and pounding surf to the right. I felt afraid, not knowing what would happen next or how to proceed. I needed to clear my mind of those men, if they were even really men. I needed to know how to protect myself.

I felt dire urgency. I didn't know why but I had to discover who I was and why I was alive. In fact, the thing I found must unbelievable was that I had gone through my entire life without asking this question.

I looked around me, reassuring myself that there were other people nearby, that I was safe. Dropping to my knees right there in the middle of the road I cried, arched my head to the sky, opening my heart, with my arms reaching outward. "Please, please, let me not walk this journey alone any longer. I cannot take anymore and remain sane. It is all too much. Please, please, Universe, bring me a teacher, someone who will understand what I'm going through and know what to do. Surely I'm not the only one." I truly hoped that was so.

My prayers were as simple as that yet spoken from the depths

CHAPTER EIGHTEEN

A Man Named Sid

The next morning David and Michael offered me a ride to the near-by town for shopping. I walked through the health-food store grateful to be buying the food my body so desperately needed. As I looked for peanut butter, a young slightly, middle eastern looking man, walked toward me. He wore a large, pointed straw hat over his long hair, and a long beard framed his wide smile. He stopped a few feet from me. "What's your name, sister?"

I smiled openly. "I'm Luna."

"Well, I'm Sid. This might sound strange, and I don't know why I am supposed to tell you this, but I am, so I'm going to." He laughed at himself.

I tilted my head with curiosity.

Sid continued. "I live on this farm, a commune of sorts. It's a bunch of folks trying to do organic gardening, and one day we want to be a place of magic for children. There's this man there, Orion. He's a spiritual teacher." He paused smiling almost mysteriously. "I think I am supposed to introduce you to him."

"That amazing!" I replied, beaming. "I have been praying for a teacher. I really need one."

Sid beamed back. "Well, there it is, the Great Universe in

motion. Let me scribble some directions for you."

As he took out a pen and ripped off a piece of paper from a pad, I waited patiently. Sid handed me the directions and said, "Here it is. It should be easy to find. Do you want to come up the day after tomorrow? That would be Sunday, I guess."

I responded quickly. "Definitely. My friend will bring me over around ten?"

Sid nodded. "Great. I'll see you then."

I left the store with a racing heart. Was this the moment I had been waiting for? Was I really going to find a teacher, just like that, an instant response to my prayers?

I headed for the payphone to call Julia, who was in India. Thankfully, I had received a letter from her just before I left letting me know where to reach her. I didn't have a lot of money on my phone card, but I couldn't resist talking to her. There was a lot of crackling on the other end, and finally an answer. It was a strong Indian accent. After some time, Julia was brought to the phone.

"Luna?" Julia's voice sounded like a bubbling spring. I was so happy to hear her voice.

"Hey!"

Julia laughing, joyfully, probably jumping up and down. "I miss you so much. Where are you? Tell me everything!"

I laughed too; it was so good to hear her voice! "No, no. You first, please. How were Alaska, Thailand, and Egypt! Wow, I can't believe it's been so long. And now India!"

"Oh, it's been amazing, Lu. Where to begin? Okay, well, in Alaska I met my true love. I'm sure of it. His name is Billy and he's amazing. We're here together living in this ashram. I think I mentioned that in the letter?"

I offered quickly. "You sure did. Tell me more."

"Well, he's great. I mean, really great. He's handsome and sexy as can be. Well, at least to me." She giggled. "He takes such good care of me, and I adore him. The best part is that he's so spiritual. We spend all of our time doing yoga, massage, and talking. For the first time, I can really say, my lover is also my friend."

I cooed, "I'm so happy for you, Jewels! You deserve that." I wondered if Julia had found her twin flame.

"Thank you, sweetie. I miss you though. Nothing can ever replace sisterhood."

I felt a tear roll down my check. "I miss you too, so much. Tell me more, more, more."

"Okay. Thailand was incredible. I stayed on a remote island while Billy went to a monastery to practice yoga. It was so beautiful, probably like Hawaii. Calm waters, endless white sand beaches … I had a great little bungalow for just a few dollars a day. I spent all my time just relaxing and swimming."

I was smiling, it did sound familiar. "That sounds great!"

Julia continued, "Egypt was incredible. I kept feeling you there. You feel like a part of the Goddess Isis to me. The pyramids are so powerful. You can really feel how life used to be in the ancient days. But then we got bored there because the culture has been destroyed, and everything is so chaotic. India, though, oh, it's like my spiritual home. There is nothing like it. It's so hard to describe. There is life and death everywhere in the street. You feel like you are breathing spirituality, and you just can't get enough. Right now, we're in an amazing ashram. And this part, well I've been waiting to tell you, this will sound strange coming from me, because you know I've never been into spiritual teachers, but … I have found my guru. He's amazing. He's completely enlightened, and when I'm in his spiritual presence, I feel my whole body filled with light."

I broke in. "That's incredible!"

"Yes. He has taught me that all that matters is love. So long as we have love, and we are in the moment, we are enlightened. It's so simple really!"

I laughed. "Well as far as I'm concerned, you already were enlightened. You must be floating now."

Julia giggled. "Actually, I really feel like I am. But now, what about you?"

"It's interesting the way our paths always have such parallels. I have been having a lot of experiences with teachers, ones that are non-physical."

Julia asked. "You mean like spirit guides?"

"Yeah. Also, I've been swimming with the dolphins, and they are teachers as well. They are such high beings and purely loving. I've grown so much. I've been feeling so free, really trusting of the universe. But I've also gone through so much so fast, that I have prayed for an earthly teacher to help me, and just today someone I met in the health food store said there's a teacher I should meet!"

"That's perfect!" Julia exclaimed. "You always manifest what you need."

The computerized operator broke in letting me know I only had a minute left on my call. "Oh no. I'm out of time, but it was so good to talk to you! Please send another letter and my stepdad will forward it. I'm so happy for you!"

She sounded suddenly sad. "Okay. Well, big hugs and kisses. I love you. Take care."

I got off the phone elated and also sad at the same time. Nothing made me happier than my connection with my sisters, and I missed them so much. After recharging my card, I called Alexis who was planning to arrive in Hawaii in just a few days. We made arrangements to meet and spend a week or two together before she went to stay with her boyfriend, who was on the island as well.

I was so excited about seeing her, and this idea of a teacher, that I nearly ran back to the farmers market where I was to meet David. I excitedly told him about what was going on. He was just as excited for me, thinking this might be the answer to how I could get some protection. I couldn't help but wonder why I wasn't having protection anyway, when it seemed like I had before. Did spirit want me to take the next step and find out how to protect myself, so angels weren't always doing it for me? Or had darkness worked hard to find me, breaking any protection I did have? Was I meant to experience the darkness? It was all so confusing.

Back at the house I took a late day nap, waking up an hour later, dazed and disoriented. A gentle breeze floated through the living room screen, reminding me I was still in Hawaii, never wanting to become dull to that fact, but rather to cherish it each moment. I showered and packed, making sure I had gathered all of my belongings and what little food I had bought.

When it was time to go, Michael held me tight. "We will miss you so much. Come back soon, please precious one?"

I nodded, in my mind, thinking I would indeed. I'd miss them and the dolphins too much to stay away for long, but the memory of the men in black, and the darkness over the ocean, sent a chill through me.

On the drive to the commune David seemed suddenly

apprehensive and shared his concerns. "You have been through so much, especially during these last few nights. You don't even know these people."

"Actually, that's exactly why I have to go," I explained, telling David about my prayers. " I need a teacher. I can't go through this anymore without some guidance. And the way Sid came up to me as though God was speaking through him...I don't know my friend, but I have to try. I'll be fine." I reassured him.

David had no choice but to give up. When we arrived, Sid was standing near the driveway entrance, smiling brightly. David simply opened his door, gave Sid a rather distrustful look and spoke. "Take care of her."

Sid looked back with an open smile. "We will."

I walked over to Sid and quickly embraced him with a tight squeeze. As David drove away, I looked back and waved, reassuring him with my eyes that the hug wasn't what he thought it was. I could feel Sid didn't have motives with me, he was just a friendly person.

Sid told me that the teacher was doing a massage workshop in town and wouldn't be back until around dusk. We walked the land as Sid described what they were doing with the gardens. I found it healing to breathe in the rich smell of soil and plants. It was wonderful to see fresh kale and chard growing everywhere. The only drawback I could find in the location was the mosquitoes. They were everywhere and swarming wildly. This took away a good deal from the peace I might otherwise have been able to feel. Enormous trees surrounded the property, which Sid explained the residents were clearing by hand.

Sid asked about my story, and I found myself surprisingly open to sharing with him. He was amazed at everything that had been going on with me, though I didn't mention the Council. Sid said with enthusiasm that Orion would be very interested.

He shared with me his understanding of the spiritual growth people were going through from an astrological standpoint. I learned that the planets had been aligning in a way that they had not for over 2,000 years. Sid believed this was the reason some people were changing so quickly.

As we passed the hours away, walking and talking, I began to feel this was my initiation through patience. I grew more and more intrigued by the idea of meeting this mysterious teacher.

Sid showed me the truck he lived in that had been converted into a house truck. It was like a little home on wheels.

"This is nice!" I told him. "It reminds me of my childhood. My family was always doing things like this. I was raised in communities all over the mainland."

"Well, you are full of surprises! You're going to fit right in here!" he said, amazed.

He shared with me that he had moved to Hawaii from New York City with a dream of living off the land. He had met this group of people and joined their farm, though he struggled with giving up his love of technology. I nodded with understanding as he spoke, and he seemed relieved to share his thoughts. As he was speaking, I began to think about how I might propose that Sid give me time to rest.

Finally, I found a silent moment to break in. "Wow your story is amazing Sid. It's really inspiring. Hey, do you think I could lay down somewhere for just a little bit?"

Sid smiled wide and his accent came through a bit. "I talked your ear off, didn't I?"

I laughed. "No, really, it was great. Nothing could have been better than your company as I await the suspenseful arrival of Orion."

Sid joked. "Yeah, you're right. What else are you going to do, huh? Do you want to set up your tent and have a rest there?"

I clasped my hands. "That would be great."

Sid showed me to a flat spot. There were a few trees around, and some upturned soil that I supposed was for more garden beds. Sid left and I quickly set up my simple little tent. Crawling inside, I laid back. At once I felt the Council calling my name. I felt the familiar, but uncomfortable shaking coming on; zooming through the tunnel of light, I arrived at the temple.

CHAPTER NINETEEN

Reign of Terror

R est was anything but peaceful. An lay helpless, unable to move, or control her mind, incapable of turning off the rapid imagery, filled with defiled horrors, that haunted her dreams. Somehow, she felt she deserved it. How could it be happening if she did not? She did not yet understand that this complex web of terror was already beginning to weave its way so deep, into the very fabric of her being, that there would be no way of releasing it.

She cried out as though awake, but there was nothing anyone could do to stop her nightmarish sleep. Long days had passed since that terrible day that would come to be known as "The Fall".

The inability to help her agonized poor Ayia, as he helplessly squeezed her twitching hand. He whispered that it was just a dream, just a dream… How could he have known the protection she needed? She lay like a wounded patient on the surgical table, cut wide open, baring her innermost parts, susceptible to further infection.

She sat huddled in the corner of some dark cold place, a place rank with dampness, isolated, as though no light could penetrate, like a cave. She could not remember how she got there, where the entrance was, or what the wretched smell of rot could be. She stifled her breath, resisting the urge to vomit. Inches away an abyss fell into forever, black dead waters. She had a glimpse of it when the light of serpent beings rose to the surface. All was dead silent, void of all love. Fear pressed in, fear that she would always be out of reach from Ayia, too racked with guilt to find him. Where had he gone anyway? Anger overcame her. Why wasn't he there? Did he think her vile? Had he indeed abandoned her? The voice, the terrible voice that filled her mind spoke that it was true, her twin had forsaken her.

She didn't know she was dreaming, that her physical form wasn't there. Slowly she inched herself along the wall finding footholds here and there, small places to clutch onto with tensed fingers. Something grabbed at her from above, a spider's mouth, she thought, then her hand slipped, and she fell headlong into the abyss. Freezing black water surrounded her, as though pulled by a magnet she sunk deeper and deeper, she tried to rise to the surface, until she no longer knew which way was up, and her lungs filled with the deathly water.

She was dying, and all she could think about was Ayia and how he had left her, blaming her for everything. He must have left her, but she couldn't remember when or how. A hissing sound filled the blackness around her, a serpent again. She could see nothing but red eyes and the faint outline of the long body. Fangs snapped at her waist, and she felt herself being swallowed, slime all around her, a piercing pain in her side.

She lay covered in cold dark earth with only her head sticking out. There was sky above her, but it was red and dull, not like the bright blue sky of her own world. He stood over her, panting, drool oozing down his scaly chin, just as he had during the attack. He tilted his huge head back and laughed, an evil mocking laughter that filled the cold sky above.

Raising his arm high above her with a long sword ready to strike, just once, he drew it down, hard, across the neck, just above the collarbone. Her head flew through the air, eyes wide open in terror, felt the slice, the burning pain, bone ripping apart, then nothing. Her soul cried out in anguish, agony.

Consciousness… she was only consciousness, as her body was no longer alive. She lay beheaded, her precious body, under the earth. Blackness closed in on her until she could not see even the faint form of Tarcon, she could only smell his breath, rank with death. Images flew at her in rapid succession; her siblings strung up in chains, blood pouring down their swollen limbs, their children tied to steely slabs, screaming for help, screaming her name. Where was she seeing this? She tried to yell out to them, but her voice was frozen.

Was this really happening, had he taken her family? Was she bound to him in this prison of death?

But wait, there was a voice was calling her, frantic with worry, a voice she knew better than any in the wide universe, her beloved Ayia. "Can you are dreaming, open your eyes my love, come back to me, now!"

She was dreaming then. Not dead at all!

Tarcon's voice boomed all around. "You are dead, mine now. They are gone to you forever, say good-bye"

Something felt wrong, she could almost feel it, her body, in her cozy home, on her world, her precious Tara, the warmth of Ayia's strong assuring hand on her arm, calling her, calling her to come home.

Eyes snapping open as her breath caught in her throat. There he was, leaning over her, those beautiful brilliant green eyes filled with purity, love; all that was right in her reality, this was real. He glowed so brightly she winced. Silence was all around them, and she could smell the sweet flowers of their homeland floating in the window above the bed.

She quivered, trying to summon courage. "Leave me alone, leave our planet!"

Tarcon laughed, making it clear she was no threat to him, she recoiled even further, feeling for the wall behind her. "What is it that you want from me?" Her question rang with desperation. Perhaps if she could give him what he wanted he would leave Tara, forever.

He walked towards her then with menacing steps, though she could not see him, she could hear the slippery sound of his feet against the wet earth.

Pressing her hands on the cold wall behind her, she listened with rapt attention.

"I want you to see who you really are, weak and ignorant. I want you to see that you are nothing, your life is nothing but a senseless waste of life-force."

It was just a dream. She was back on Tara lying next to her sweet beloved. Tarcon couldn't harm her, not truly. Surely, he knew that she could create another body, but not another mind. It was this he sought to ruin with his relentless captivity. She could not him keep him away nor will herself out of the dream or cause herself to wake up.

She swallowed hard. "It's not true. If I believe you, I will lose all my powers, the power to create light. Is that what you want?"

Tarcon only grunted. She pushed on. "You want to extinguish light? To convince us that we are unworthy or that light isn't real?"

She laughed. She knew light to the core of her being, it was all she had been. This, this terrible darkness, a contrast she could not even fathom was really happening. As though her soul would live in nothing but shock from that day forward, unaware, lost, betrayed, little more than a struggle to survive, cling to some semblance, some faint memory of herself. He may have traumatized her, made her stand still in time for a long moment, wondering what in the world had happened. But light? That was what she was. She would never forget the feeling, the awareness, and the 'beingness' of all that light was. That he could not take from her, even if it was but a faint whisper!

Tarcon responded violently. "I will not give up, but you will. Do you think I will grow bored, find something else to do?"

He laughed again, filling the damp space with a haunting echo. "There is nothing else for me to do. I will taunt you like the plaything you are to me, until you surrender to my wisdom. I don't care if it takes a million eons. There will come a day when all of Tara will be subject to my rule."

She could almost feel his scaly flesh against her smooth human skin. He continued, "All that you stand for, all that you think you are, it will be gone, vanished without a trace. Your grandchildren will not even remember who you are. Their cells will shrivel up, becoming nothing but slaves to my will. They will know me as GOD. I will be the only power!"

Ayia couldn't stand the torment of his beloved unconscious like this. What did she dream of? What was so terrible she could not wake herself?

For hours, days, he sat there, but at last could take no more. He needed a tiny break, just a few moments… something.

Calling Fiona to her side he left their protected home. Outside, he sat with Rasha under the brightness of the healing sunlight filtering through the large weeping willow shading their front lawn. He was aware of its beauty, but it did little to ease his agony. How could it matter when his beloved could not be there to feel this with him? She

would perhaps never be there again… With that thought, his body, spent with grief, gave way.

Ayia pounded his chest furiously, letting out a loud mournful sob. "She will not speak to me, nor let me into her thoughts."

His face had the look of a man in utter torment as he cried out. "I would rather die a thousand deaths, endure any type of pain then this, this I cannot bear."

Rasha held his head low, solemnly exclaiming. "Brother you do indeed bear the hardest pain I can imagine. She loves you, and one day she will let this self-blame go out from her heart. And when she does, she will be in your arms once more."

Ayia looked up to his brother, as a small, wounded boy would. "What I would not give, my brother, to take it away from her, to endure for her what she did, would that I were the one."

Rasha knew this might not be the right moment, but time moved too quickly and speak he must. "You know you couldn't have been the one brother. An was attacked because she is woman, born to bear fruit, and clearly this is what the dark wants, to bring his seed here. Brother, I know you are hurt. She will come back to you soon."

He paused looking at his brother's hopeful gaze. "Right now, we must think of the future. We must learn to protect the women, to ensure that this never happens again. What An did, to will the wretched being from her womb, took strength and bravery. It is not something she or any of our women should ever have to go through again."

Ayia drew in a deep breath. "You're right my brother. Let me not dwell in grief. Let us seek council with the others, we need to learn how to protect ourselves."

He returned to An at once, unable to stay away for long. Her face was distorted into a fitful expression, the anguish of her dreams apparent. Kissing her brow, he took her limp hand in his. Squeezing it, he began to calmly sing her name, calling her home, back to his loving embrace as he searched her body for a sign; nothing changed. Still, he sang from the depth of his heart, knowing she would eventually awaken. His strong gentle voice filled the room with the essence of his deep love for her.

Hours later, with dusk approaching, An finally stirred, slowly opening her eyes. Weary with effort, Ayia thought he was only imagining it, then realized that she was really there. Her eyes were distant, and for a moment he feared she didn't recognize him at all.

Passionately he whispered in her ear, his voice cracking. "An. Oh my precious love, please stay with me. It is here in my gaze that you will find solace. Please do not close your eyes. Stay with me!"

It had been months since he had heard her speak. He longed to hear her sweet voice once more, even just one word, but she said nothing. She could hear him. All the resolve she had felt in the face of the dark lord began to fade. How could she ever face her beloved again? So, defiled was she, so unworthy of his great love and unending compassion? He had always been there, she could feel that now, she had never been abandoned. She could not bear to give in, to trust, to be there, to be present after all the darkness that had torn her heart apart.

"Are you angry at me; angry that I ran away?" His words were timid now as his green eyes searched hers, the perfect match to his.

Her eyes focused on him faintly, filled with despair. "Ayia, don't make me come back," she whispered. "I cannot bear the pain of seeing you. I cannot return to what we were, not after what I have done. It is my burden to carry. I am not angry with you, not at all. When you ran, it only proved to me that I was causing you too much pain. Please move on with your life. Let me go…"

He was losing her all over again. "No, no! We are one, never to be apart. An, remember without each other, we die, we die forever. I would never leave you, no matter what you might say! Please don't ever say such things, please I beg of you, don't break my heart like this."

He searched her empty face. "Don't you realize that is what the dark-lord wants? He is jealous of a love so deep. We must prove that our love is stronger than that."

An recoiled, tears rolling down her pale cheeks. Fearing that she might withdraw again, he softened his voice. "I know it's difficult for you to allow yourself to return to this love, your pain is so deep. But your soul is in danger. You must look into my eyes; you just have to trust me."

She was openly crying, refusing to look at him, as she buried her head in shame. "You cannot truly believe that I could ever be happy to leave you to the misery you are in. If you do not listen to me, your body will die An. Your light will leave your body and you will die! Is that what you want?"

Ayia held her face in his hands, kissing away her tears, his face determined. An willed herself to look into his eyes. She saw the light of all they had ever been. Hawks and eagles flew through clear blue skies, sunlight danced with butterflies, and beautiful tiny birds flitted amongst flowers. It hurt so much to see that, to remember all they had lost. It felt as though her soul were torn into a million pieces, never to exist in that perfect oneness again. She could see the light, feel the memories, but they only hurt, for they were no longer all that was.

Ayia felt as though he was looking into an abyss of torment, but still the beauty and wisdom she carried was there in the depths.

He knew she would heal, that all the dramatic words only reflected the terror she was in. "An, sweet being of light, please give to me all that you have seen. Give me the pain that you have known."

She began to retreat again, not wanting him to ever know the pain she felt.

He continued. "Dearest, I am strong and my love for you can conquer anything. Give it to me, beloved."

Like water breaking over a dam, An pushed herself through the block that had been there for what seemed like an eternity, she missed him so much and could no longer bear the separation she was creating. "You want to see? You want to understand how I could wish you to leave me, so that you could continue and find peace? Here it is, look into my mind and you will know."

For the first time the barriers she had held so strongly fell away and Ayia rushed into her consciousness. He was determined to take the pain away by feeling it, knowing it. She had wanted so much to protect him from this.

Ayia's mind wanted to revolt as he went through the inner dimensions of his beloved's consciousness. He was shocked to see how much self-doubt, anger, and shame she held. He had to be strong; the journey revealed to him that An had been influenced and controlled by the dark lord. In her innocence and empathy for life, her soul had been swept away in terrified awe of all she had seen.

As she allowed the memories to pour forth, An began to feel stronger. She could feel his love pouring into her soul, like no other could. It felt like crystal waters, bathing her mind in the light of purity. She willed herself to come through, to be as strong for him as he was for her. He was right, to withdraw was what the dark lord wanted.

She whispered. "I will show you the face of he who has done this."

Tumultuous memories exploded in his mind as Ayia felt himself being sucked into a deep well of anger. He wanted to destroy Tarcon with a fury he had never known. Was that darkness too? Was he failing her by allowing emotion to take control?

An wept, "I knew this would happen. I could not have expected you to feel and see so much. I wish that I had refused. Promise me that you won't do anything out of anger. Promise me!"

At first, he shook his head stubbornly, but for An's sake he had to concede. "My love, I can move through this. I promise I will not act on anger or hate."

He held her hands tightly as their gaze locked. "Our lives have been altered from this experience, but I promise you, we will grow from this. It is the nature of light to grow, and of the light we are born, never to be separated."

A faint smile came to her lips. Seeing his beloved smile after so long Ayia could do nothing but weep and hold her body close to his.

Finally drawing away, he said tenderly. "You need your nourishment now. I will send for your sisters. They will be relieved to see you. I must seek the wisdom of my own heart."

This time she would be present, she would be who she was to him, Tarcon could not take that from them. Lifting her head, she kissed him deeply, loving the warmth of his smooth lips, lips made to fit hers perfectly. He smiled, the smile that lit up her world, their world, squeezing her hand he left the house, in need of sharing his good news with his brothers. They stood guard, speaking in hushed tones about the dark and how to conquer it; they would not venture far. Who knew what monsters hid in the trees and beyond?

Shortly after, her sisters arrived, each carrying a bowl full of fresh fruits, herbs, and healing oils. It was time to welcome their sister back to the world. One by one they kissed her brow.

Summersara held her head up and spoke. "Drink, sister. Drink and grow strong."

An sipped slowly and then laid her head back. Sunraya began to gently rub sacred oils from the flowers and plants of the forest into the soles of her feet, calling her energies down into the Earth. For the first time in months, she felt her sister open to her love again, and her hopes soared.

Fiona brought a piece of ripened fruit she had picked from the orchard. An smiled as the soft golden fruit touched her tongue. Fiona also felt a restored hope. If they could surround their sister in all the beautiful things of Tara, she would realize that life could be good again. It would be hard, but it would be good again someday...

Tarcon felt An gaining strength. "She must not slip from my grasp!" He yelled into the abyss of his cave.

For months he had succeeded in controlling her mind, flooding her awareness with wicked dreams. In the pit of his stomach there was an aching, a vulnerability that he could not understand, and this infuriated him.

He stomped his massive, webbed foot. "I will get what I want. This is certain!"

His goal was not to kill the twins. He was obsessed with them, determined to dominate their planet under his own reign of terror. He had to prove love did not really exist, was no more real than anything. Perhaps if it really did, he could not justify all the terrible, horrible things he had done without a care. He knew it wasn't real, wasn't ever, not then, not now, not in a million years ... not ever would it prove to be real.

Storming out of his cave, he looked over the thousands of steel cages lining the walls of the bluffs to the horizon. They held countless men, women, children, and even babies, imprisoned and awaiting torturous death; they screamed in agony, he felt a deep satisfaction that filled his mouth with juice.

In the center of the ravine there must have been over a thousand reptilians mulling about an immense cauldron, smoke drifting into the still, lifeless air. A woman held down by monstrous razor-sharp claws of an enormous male, screamed and cried out as a mallet swung violently through the air, landing on her shoulder. Her blood-curdling scream rang throughout the heavy space. The monsters relished her torment, throwing their monstrous heads back with a most chillingly evil laughter. The mallet came down again and again until the woman's body was nothing more than a bloody mess, limp, with tissue and bone sticking out, until she finally, in one dreadful yet relieving moment; dropped dead on the dirt beneath her.

An enormous female reptilian ran towards the body, grabbed the bulk of it, and scurried quickly towards the cauldron. Inside, hundreds of human body parts - limbs, heads, eyes, and dismembered babies all swirled around in a boiling broth.

Tarcon suddenly appeared before the cauldron, reached in with bare hand, took out a bloody hand and devoured it, emanating a wide range of grotesque sounds as the bone cracked under his merciless jaws.

I was outraged and petrified at the same time. Their leader, with all his darkness, was intelligent enough to hold a consuming obsession, to see human beings as game pieces to conquer, yet for his heartless followers, humans were simply their prey, their food - nothing more.

I could never understand these wretched beings. Could not handle anymore. It felt as though my mind were ripping in two, unwilling to take it in as real, yet knowing it was a real as anything I had ever witnessed, terrifyingly so. As though the council understood that I could not handle more and remain sane, the screen drew black, it was over and yet it was not. It would haunt me forever; I was sure of that.

The ability to handle pain and complexity while maintaining sanity was a survival skill I'd developed through my childhood, as though my life depended on it. But this, I didn't know how I would handle this. I wanted the power to stop all evil. Why did freewill have to exist? It could make sense, but not when this kind of evil was free in the universe. It had to be stopped, it just did! I tried to calm my mind, remembering how I had overcome personal evils in my own life; when my step-father (the second one my mother had married when I was thirteen) had choked me nearly to death and thrown me against the wall, coming after me as though to end my life … then the night I was nearly raped … the countless times I had been beat-up at school, being molested at age seven … no matter how much darkness I saw or felt in life, some deep calmness inside of me always kept the sanity, saw me through to the light.

With a few breaths I forced the vision of Stella to the back of my mind. If I was to share this vision with the world, I must not be consumed by it. I opened my eyes, graced by the presence of these master beings of light once more. How patiently they awaited my completion, my acceptance of all I had been shown.

Lady Nada gave me an approving nod and gently motioned towards the screen. I rested my terrorized eyes upon the soothing image there, a panoramic view of Lemuria from above, the continent still so beautiful even after the invasion. The Great Motherland shined, truly a jewel surrounded by the perfect sea …

CHAPTER TWENTY

Starseed

When I woke it was nearly dusk and I could hear the sweet jungle sounds around me; the birds telling their songs of the day, the soft wind in the treetops high above. Several hours had passed and the sun was almost touching the horizon. The air was considerably cooler. I wrapped my arms around me for warmth. Disoriented at first, then remembering where I was, I began to worry that Sid would think I had taken too long of a nap. Getting up from the platform, I walked toward the shape of a tarp just visible in the dimly lit sky through the coconut trees. I found Sid engrossed in a book, lying in a hammock under a few tarps held up by bamboo. Clearly not worried about my naptime. There was a fire-pit nearby and a few old chairs and logs for makeshift seats.

I spoke quietly. "Hey Sid."

Sid jumped. Startled as he was, he smiled his big, white-toothed smile, as he seemed always to be doing. "Oh, hey there! You sure are quiet. Did you have a good siesta?"

I yawned. "Yeah, I feel really refreshed. So, is he here yet?" I must have sounded so eager, I was!

Sid shook his head. "Not yet, but he should be soon. How 'bout some tea?"

I nodded eagerly, thirsty and hungry. As Sid made a fire and put a pot of water over it for tea, I took some nuts and raisins out of my bag and offered some to Sid. "No thanks, I'm on a fast right now. Just tea for me."

I ate my small meal and waited while the tea brewed. The sun had already begun to set, but Orion had still not appeared. Anticipation grew as I thought more and more about this unknown teacher. Was he really the one I had prayed for? Had he really appeared in my life just one day after my desperate prayer? What would he think of me? What was this tumbling feeling in my solar plexus? My mind raced like never before.

A few others from the community came back and they all sat around the fire, eating avocado and coconut while they chatted with me. There was an older man named Carlos who talked hurriedly about the sun being his solar energy, and how he didn't need much more than a daily charge-up of that free energy. I could easily understand this notion. With Carlos was a woman named Brenda, who had a twin sister back home in Minnesota. Brenda had come to the community to learn about permaculture and communal- living. She hoped to start one of her own when she had learned enough to return home. She did miss her twin terribly, but they both thought it healthy to be out discovering life on their own for once.

Then there was a man of about 40, with glasses, who didn't say much but I had managed to learn that he had been in the military and seen some strange things. He had muttered something about trying to find the meaning of life. From what I could see in his face, he was trying quite seriously.

Finally, there was a car coming up the driveway. Sid stood up excitedly. "It's him."

I still felt a bit panicked, and very, very nervous. This was a very big moment. There were butterflies in my stomach, like the first time I had danced on a stage. For a moment I was self-conscious, looking down at my attire. I wore a rainbow tie-died shirt that was cut in such a way that it fell off my shoulders, revealing tanned, vulnerable skin. I nervously tousled my hair loosely around my face. Was I really doing that? What was coming over me?

The car lights remained on for a few minutes and everyone waited silently. Finally, a door shut, and the car began to drive away. A man began to walk quickly and purposefully passed the campfire. I could only see the outline of his form.

He called out in a deep voice as he began to pass by. "Aloha everyone. I'm going to my tent for the night. It's been another very long day."

Sid nearly ran toward him calling out. "Orion wait!"

He stood in front of the man, blocking my view, talking quietly. I couldn't hear what was said and nervously jingled my dolphin necklace. Suddenly, the man began to walk toward the circle with Sid, again at a swift and determined pace. I could see what he looked like more clearly as they approached. My heart was beating out of my chest.

Orion wore a button-down shirt sleeve shirt, with a little collar and slack-shorts and I could see the outline of his strong chest and shoulder muscles. He had black flip-flops on his tan feet. He was carrying a briefcase, which could not have seemed more out of place in the jungle setting. His long brownish hair was tied back in a ponytail. In the firelight, I could see streaks of blond here and there. His skin was a deep, golden brown. I thought he looked about 5'9. He had a very muscular build, and well-built perfectly healthy body, broad chest, large biceps, strong calves and smooth brown skin.

Orion strode into the circle. He looked at me and held my gaze from several feet away. I looked back at him for a timeless moment and noticed that I was holding my breath.

Finally breaking the silence, he gasped and slowly walked closer, my heart thumped louder with every step. He sat down on a stump about five feet from me and motioned for me to sit too. Relieved, I found the chair behind me and quickly moved to it.

His first words shocked me. "I have been waiting for you." His face was dead serious. The life force emanating from him was incredible.

My eyes widened questioningly; I was truly speechless. He didn't ask my name and I struggled to integrate what he had just said. 'I've been waiting for you.' This line struck me as one out of an Asian film where the ancient teacher greets the young student in the same way, followed with, "When the student is ready, the teacher will appear."

"Tell me your story," Orion said, cutting off my thoughts.

The others were still seated completely spell bound. I could feel their presence there, but I felt like Orion and I were suddenly floating in some other dimension where we could only be observed. I didn't wish to be observed, but there was no choice. The flames of the campfire rose gently into the air. Everyone was so silent, watching as I looked into the flames. I felt like I could see myself as Orion did then; my long hair fell loosely around my shoulders. My mind seemed suddenly very calm as though I had found myself in another familiar feeling of the synchronistic moment. I realized right away that Orion was a "to-the- point" kind of person. He certainly wasn't wasting any time.

As I found my words, Orion simply stared, not distracted or concerned with those around him. He took in all parts of me; I could feel it, hear it in my mind, my heart.

Slowly, I lifted my eyes to Orion. I saw something there that was unlike looking into anyone else's eyes. There was a familiarity there, like I had known him before, but could not remember. I sensed that revealing my story to him would lead to understanding. I could trust in him.

With that thought I opened myself up to him, and for that matter, to everyone there. Clearly, they weren't going anywhere.

For the next hour I spoke about all that had happened on my journey to that point, leaving out the part about the council. I needed to guard that for the time being. To that regard, all I did disclose was that I "was guided by dolphins and beings from other worlds." Orion studied my eyes intently.

Occasionally he would interrupt with a question, wanting to learn more. My body was filled with vitality; sharing my story and this feeling that somehow this person, this teacher, understood like no one had before. It was a relief after the long months going it alone. In fact, I couldn't remember ever feeling so calm, yet so energized at the same time. I could feel my face glowing in the firelight. At some point I became aware that I felt like I was seeing myself through his eyes, but also hearing how he felt about me, what he saw in me. I had never experienced anything like it. I felt beautiful, truly, deeply, as a soul, not just a person, or even a pretty face. When at last I was done, the small unmoving crowd finally stirred in their seats.

Orion held out his hands. "Can I look into your eyes?"

I got up and walked toward him, sensing that something very special was happening. I sat before him and to my surprise he reached over to a little makeshift wooden table and turned on a flashlight. Asking me to stare into his eyes he then focused the sharp beam directly into my eyes. He held my face tenderly as he peered into my hazel eyes.

"Can I see your hands?" he asked.

"Yes," I said, curious, holding my palms out. Palm reading seemed a bit out of place, but I soon realized he was doing something else.

Orion's eyes nearly closed as he gazed openly at my hands. He seemed to move into some altered state for several minutes. Reading my energy-field, he saw it there again? Finally, he placed my hands on my knees and sat in silence for a few minutes closing his eyes.

I looked back to the fire, respecting his withdrawn state. I had never really been with a spiritual teacher before, but somehow, I intuitively knew to make this show of respect. I glanced at the others who were waiting breathlessly for what would happen next. They were looking at me as though I were so special, or perhaps from a different planet.

Suddenly Orion opened his eyes. "Did anyone ever tell you that you are a Star Seed?"

My heart pounded in my throat. I still wasn't comfortable revealing the council to all these people, as open and spiritual as they may have been.

"It's someone who comes from many different higher planes to help out on earth. Is that right?" I asked.

I sensed what he was saying was very important. His expression was one of awe and reverence. Orion nodded and looked deep into my eyes again and spoke in a deep serious tone. "It is time for you to remember who you are."

My heartbeat even faster as I thought, this is exactly what the Council wanted, and what my prayers have been, with a mixture of elation, amazement, a little fear, and marveling at the synchronicity of what he was saying.

"I would like to remember," I said quietly.

Orion didn't break eye contact for a moment. "As I said, I have been waiting for you. You realize that the story you tell, the things that have happened to you, are extraordinary, don't you?"

I looked at him wide-eyed. He thought it was amazing that I had been brought to Hawaii by dolphins and almost died on a cliff, realizing I would never die unless I was meant to. He didn't even know the rest of my story, and still he was amazed!

I replied, once again ever so quietly. "I know a lot of people are going through spiritual awakening, I don't really know if what I experience is that different."

Orion laughed slightly. "Very humbly put. Yes, people are changing everywhere, but the higher the soul, the greater the gift. You are in for one grand acceleration."

I blushed at his words, spoken in front of so many people. The familiar feeling of being under a spotlight was uncomfortable. Orion looked around the circle and quite simply said. "Goodnight everyone, Luna and I will begin her studies now."

As he said this, I thought that he had an air of command and authority about him that I had only seen in old movies, where people were direct and curt, but it came across as kind, yet powerful.

He stood and motioned for me to follow him. I looked to the others and said goodnight, almost shyly, after all the star-studded attention, or at least that's what it felt like. I felt dazed and excited at the same time. I barely noticed the arm squeeze from Sid, or the words of awe around me.

Orion led me to a small tent, held the flashlight in one hand, and unzipped the tent with the other, motioning for me to come inside. I nervously knelt down and slowly crawled through the opening, feeling a sleeping bag beneath me. I watched as Orion lit five candles around the tent.

He sat cross-legged facing me and motioned for me to do the same. I sat across from him as he reached into a corner pocket of the tent and pulled out a tattered book. He held the cover in front of me. "Have you ever seen this book?" Orion asked. "Or the image on it?"

I looked at the drawing for a long time. In the center of a circle there was a man with his arms and legs stretched out. There were triangular shapes drawn around him. "No. It seems familiar, but I don't think so."

Orion took a deep breath. I once more thought he was very

different than anyone I had ever met. His eyes seemed to be on fire with an intensity I had never seen; yet he also felt familiar to me.

He spoke seriously "This is DaVinci's Man, and within this book are the keys to alchemy of the self, and of immortality. It's a very old book and I'm going to loan it to you to read. Luna, this is what I have to help you remember. Inside - deep inside -you already know all of this. You must simply remember who you are."

Orion's words sounded so important, otherworldly. Yet somehow what he said made me want to cry. He continued. "I have so much to teach you. Remember when I say teach, I always mean that I will help you remember." He laughed. "Believe me, there is nothing I know that you don't already know! In fact, one day you will be my greatest teacher."

I felt like I was swimming in non-reality. My mind reeled in the small tent. The candlelight played with the shadows, making everything move. The whole situation was disorienting and overwhelming at the same time. Not only was this beautiful, mysterious man telling me grand things I could have no way of understanding, believing, or not believing, but I was also witnessing his image change. One moment he looked like a native chief, and I felt I had known him, the next he looked like an ancient priest, that ruled over some vast kingdom or something grand like that. It was as though my memory was searching for when that had been, but I could not quite give it words. In my mind I saw a tribe. I saw myself as a native woman, carrying a baby on my back. Around me I saw my people being shot and slaughtered. I stood on a hill crying. In the distance Orion was on a horse, wearing warrior clothing. He yelled out to me to run to save myself, the child on my back and the two children at my feet. Everything was happening so very fast. My mind searched for something. I was part Cherokee on my mother's side; six generations back she had a full-blooded grandmother, and my great-great-grand-mother on my father's side was full Sioux. I had never really explored that connection but suddenly it was certain, I had been Native American in my past life.

Orion paused. "What's happening?" I muttered. "I see things."

Orion said only. "You are remembering. The Ancients are with you now. You are going to need to be cleansed and prepared for all that they have set before you. Your purpose is greater than you can imagine right now. It is one of greatness, courage, and above all, transmutation."

He looked at me with such seriousness, such intensity, stopping to take a drink of water from a glass jar. "Do you know what this word transmutation means?" I shook my head. "No, I don't."

"It means to take one thing and to make it another. In the case of human transmutation, it means to take what has been limited, conditioned, and asleep, and transform it into the Spiritual-Self. This is the Self that is unlimited, capable of greatness, omniscience."

I nodded, eager to understand what he spoke of. "If it is okay, I will begin to read your cellular structure now, and to help you clear your emotional body. I will need to hold acupuncture points on your body."

"Ok," I said, wondering what this would bring. I had to trust the process.

Orion motioned for me to lie down on my stomach. I laid down, excited for the healing that was to take place, closing my eyes, seeing the candlelight flickering beneath my eyelids. Behind me I felt him begin to breathe deeply. My inner world became suddenly dark, deep. Suddenly Orion pushed my shirt up to my shoulders and pressed deeply into a point at the middle of my back. Another finger pressed deeply into the spot opposite this. This was all happening so fast. I had just met him, and his hands were touching my bare back.

Sudden deep pain moved up and down my back. At first, I tried to take deep breaths, handling the pain. Soon it was unbearable, and I whimpered. "Ouch."

Orion's voice became extremely deep, reminding me of an ancient Greek film when the God of the Underworld spoke.

"There will be much pain. Can you handle it?"

"Yes." I whispered, squeezing my eyes tightly.

As he moved from point to point the pain grew deeper and deeper. I was astounded at how much pain was held in my body. Images flashed through my mind of things that happened as a child. I saw my father yelling at me, a girl in school pounding my head into the toilet in the bathroom. Images raced forward and

I saw a boy trying to rape me, a teacher scolding me, my mother coiled up in pain and depression on her bed, unreachable. I asked. "Is this pain emotional memory held in my body?"

"Yes." Orion replied.

I had a sense now from the pain and the images that there was so much releasing now.

Orion let me know. "This is just the surface. The depth of darkness and suffering your life has been saddens me. For a life-force such as you to hold so much pain… But you took it on in order to create the possibility of transformation for others."

I didn't understand everything he said, not logically, but felt it somehow and was so amazed he could see and feel all of that in me, without me saying a word. I winced with pain and at times cried spontaneously from the memories and emotions welling up inside. Finally, Orion's pressure eased off and I could breathe with ease, glad the worst was over. I felt l was drifting in a sea of tranquil liquid light when Orion stopped pushing on the points. There had been so much grief in the visions of the past. The moment before it had seemed unbearable. Then, a calm peacefulness washed over me, and I knew the journey had been worthy of the pain. I could then feel Orion's soft, strong hands moving gently over my back in long, slow strokes.

I could hear his deep voice whispering softly, yet it seemed so far away. "It's okay. The pain is gone now. Feel the deep energy of peace."

I felt peace deeper than any I had ever known. I felt safe and warm. I lost sense of time and how long I lay like this. I began to feel that I was somehow in an altered state, like the time I had tried Opium, or too much marijuana. There was no boundary between altered consciousness and me. I floated, into a deep safe place, a place of infinite peace.

Orion lifted my body to his and sat me in his lap, wrapping my legs around his. I could not open my eyes, still floating freely in my altered state, but I felt my body being moved, vaguely. Suddenly some part of my mind began to call me out of that serene place, nearly screaming.

"No, this isn't right! What's happening?"

Orion's voice was soft, yet deep, almost inhuman, godlike.

"I have waited so long for this my love. Drink deeply of my

Divine nectar."

Again, part of my mind alerted me "No! What's going on?" Yet I was entranced. I had partially returned to my body but was not yet fully in it. I was unable to control my body and cause it to move.

Orion wrapped his hands around my cheeks and pressed my lips open. Pressing his lips upon mine he transferred some type of sweet liquid from his mouth to mine. I almost choked and found myself swallowing against my will.

My thoughts were coming with greater strength. "No! This is NOT happening!" I tried to will myself into wakefulness, yet I floated somewhere between the ocean of light, the ocean I had trusted, and one of despair and confusion.

Once more Orion's intoxicating voice washed over me. "It's okay, don't be afraid. I am here now. I will take care of you; I will cherish your every breath."

Again, I struggled to hold onto consciousness, his voice really did still sound like a god to me. I didn't even know what this meant really, but it definitely didn't sound human, like it was in many places at once and taking me there with it. I forced my eyes open and saw a soft white light around Orion. It too was alluring, yet my mind called out with warning - danger, something is wrong!

I was torn between the voice of my mind and Orion's soft tone. "We can be one. Let us be one now." He placed my limp hand over his heart and began to breathe deeply. I could feel his heartbeat and warm muscular chest under my hand. Again, I struggled to be more conscious. His actions, his coaxing voice, it was all strangely familiar to me, dreamlike. Suddenly I was able to withdraw my body, recoiling from his embrace. He held me firmly. I knew what this was. My mind was brought back to seven years of age.

My mother had come for a visit in the community where my little brother and I stayed with Johnny. My mother and Johnny had gone on an overnight hotel date, leaving my brother and me with a teenage boy who lived in the commune. He was sixteen and had been my friend. In the night he had come into the screened-in porch area where we were laying sound asleep. I woke to feel the boy touching my vagina. I had been terrified. I thought of the twins and of poor An. This feeling in me of rape, or violation, it must be a trace of the devastation the Goddess of Air had felt. Yes, the memory and the pattern of rape still replayed itself again and again on this planet. It was not going to happen to me here, not with any trace of consent. I had to be strong.

Suddenly, I felt horribly embarrassed. I was seven again. What was he doing? I had felt that I had to pee, that I was going to pee right on him, and this was even more embarrassing. It was so dark I couldn't see anything. I quickly closed my eyes.

"Let him think that I am asleep." I had thought. That would be less embarrassing, and maybe he would stop. I couldn't let my brother wake up; it would be so traumatizing for him. I bit down on my lip and tried to not breathe. I tried to not feel anything, but the embarrassment was still there. I couldn't stop feeling, so I forced it deeper and deeper into my mind, where it wasn't so real. For my brother I had to endure.

Just when I thought he might stop I felt his warm lips and tongue all over my vagina. I was so embarrassed. What was he doing and why?

So that's what I did, enduring it until he left. I was so scared. There was nothing I could do. No parent to go to. No adult to help me. Later I couldn't remember if I got up to go pee or if I lay there terrified until daylight. I couldn't let anyone know what terrible, confusing thing had happened. I was grateful my brother had not been startled awake; it was he that needed protection. I would have endured anything to keep him safe from the thing that happened in the middle of the night.

My mind raced back to the present. How was this any different? This man, this supposed "teacher" had caused me to trust him. He had touched me when I was most vulnerable. I had needed desperately the healing touch of the massage he had offered. It had moved past all my boundaries, all the fears and distrusts of men. He had made me feel safe when no one else ever had. And then he had violated me. It was no less horrible than rape or molestation. He was no different than any man who had ever violated me.

Anger pulled me back to my body, and I shrank away in anger. "What do you think you are doing?"

Orion's voice cracked. "What do you mean? I was giving you my love. I have nothing to hold back from you."

I was scared to think that he could perceive what he did as being acceptable, even good. What was wrong with him?

Orion continued. "I have waited for so long. It has been an eternity waiting for you. I only assumed you must feel the same."

I could only see the shadow of his large muscular body, his long hair hanging loosely around his face. I was once again disoriented. Did he really think that was supposed to happen? Did he think he could just draw me into some intoxicated state and then be sexual? Something was very wrong.

Orion seemed to realize I was very upset and tried to reach out to my hand. I quickly withdrew. "How dare you do that to me? No true healer should ever take advantage of someone in a such a vulnerable state!"

I could hear his deep breath. "I, I am so sorry you are offended. Your body is full of pain and trauma. I wanted to take that from you. You are afraid of my love because of your pain."

I was livid with anger. "No, I am afraid of what you just did because it is no different than molesting a little girl who is confused and scared. What you just did was not healing. It was violating." I was so angry I was certain nothing he could say would change my mind.

"Forgive me, forgive me. I was overcome with my passion for you, my love for you", Orion pleaded. "If I am to learn that you will never trust me, I will never forgive myself. When I look at your life, what I see in your aura, Luna, you have no idea the effect you have on people."

Was that supposed to make me feel better, like this was my fault?

"Please I beg you, give me another chance. I will not touch you again without your verbal consent."

I wanted to flee right then, to never see this person again. But I was also confused. I had seen great light in him at the campfire, had felt with all my heart that I had known him before. I had known that he was meant to be my teacher. I didn't even know what that entailed, but with all my heart and soul I knew that to be true. I felt I wasn't safe with any man that would do what he just did, he didn't really deserve another chance. Yet the other part - the teaching part - I knew I had to receive that. How could this be?

I blew out the breath I'd not realized I'd been holding and

said forcefully "Don't ever, ever do that again. If I am going to be your student - if you are to help me heal - you must never cross that boundary again!" My body was shaking with adrenaline.

Orion's voice was relieved. "Thank you for giving me your trust. I hope in time you will forgive me for allowing my passion to overwhelm me. I would never want you to feel unsafe."

I squeezed my hands together tightly, trying to clear the events from my mind, being strong. "I have always had a forgiving nature, perhaps too forgiving. I'll try to let this go. I'm going to my tent now."

I got on my knees and crawled quickly toward the tent opening. I didn't say another word, only quickly unzipped the zipper and fled to my own space.

I lay awake for a long while, confused and tired, trying to process through everything that had happened. I wanted to cry but was too angry. I had wanted a teacher, had called out for one, and here he was! He had opened so much so quickly, trusting that he was 'the One'. And now this! How could this be what I was meant experience! I felt like ice moved through my veins. I had wanted to not feel alone and now I felt more alone than ever. Had he been so overcome with his own emotion, he didn't really know what he was doing? Could I reach below his human instinct, to that place where his soul had made me feel so safe, so understood? Why, why was all of this happening? Angry and confused I tossed and turned all night, unable to find the peace I so desperately sought. Already I was clinging to the edge of sanity in my mind. There was no one else to understand me. Could I forgive him? This one person who could know my soul and perhaps held the keys to really embodying all the Council had asked me to become, or was it too late?

CHAPTER TWENTY ONE

Inner Strength

I didn't expect to be called to Council, but called I was. I didn't seem to remember what was going on in my personal life while there, as though all that was shielded, to protect the council from the human drama and keep me focused.

The screen rotated, displaying the great beauty of Lemuria from the air, still as surreal as ever in a way, as though no change had come.

The Twins of Air walked cautiously through the forest towards the beach. An's strength was coming back with the aid of her siblings, she could stand, and even walk a little on her own. Ayia carried a sword, forged by Sunta under a great fire just days before. They had all agreed upon weaponry, had called up the vision of a sword from the records of all time. They had not the luxury of innocence anymore. In need of knowing their enemy they had searched the past, found the records of planets where light and dark had fought. A sword, forged of pure gold, seemed a noble weapon. If a serpent were to arise from the great sea, An would be far enough from the water's edge to remain safe, and Ayia knew his anger was enough to bring certain death to any creature. Putting aside all thought of how terrible it would be to bring harm to anything, Ayia held his sweet love's hand, immensely grateful for the leap in strength she seemed to be taking.

An's trust was fleeting though, as fragile as a leaf floating on the wind, never knowing where it might land. It wasn't Ayia she didn't trust, not truly; she no longer had trust in herself, as she believed that she was the cause of all of this. Sometimes, she didn't know if she would ever find that trust again. She would not abandon them, to do so would be no less wretched than Tarcon! This is what he would want, to prove her weakness, to destroy all that they were - unified light and love.

There was no time to waste on such thoughts, each moment spent allowing the darkness to gain control meant the spread of its terror, the manifestation of negative thought appearing all over their world. It meant more light beings fleeing the planet; the fairies, the unicorns, and all the magical ones, gone forever. With the darkness that lay on her soul, the soul of their world - such light could not be called back. All she could do was salvage what was left, to act quickly before more was lost.

For the first time she gathered the will power to leave their little safe haven; she needed to feel the wind and breathe pure air, to feel its strength. Ayia's strong arm lent support to her shaking, bruised and scarred body. They took each step slowly crossing the wide beach before them. When they reached the edge of the sea An sat down to rest on the beach, aware of Ayia's concerns. She was nearly exhausted by the walk that was once an easy trot, or effortless flight. Knowing this pained her; so long as there was fear and heartache she and her siblings would never fly, never soar on the winds of Tara again.

The calm ocean drew her gaze - so beautiful, so serene, even with the turmoil that waged war on her world. Ayia stood nearby watching her every move, still sick with worry. He tried to smile as she looked to him for reassurance. 'You are safe, sweet love. Do what you must.' Oh, he thought, she is still so beautiful even now! But a shadow still lingers. What I would give to take that away from her!

She stood on the beach with Ayia at her back and vowed to reclaim some power. Her body was beginning to decay and that was not acceptable, she had to be as she had always been; immortal, restore herself to perfection. She took the breath that restored all and shot out of her body.

Her body rocked back and forth spontaneously and An's delicate fingers sank into the sand supportively so she would not fall over. Each cell filled with the ecstasy of the experience of the divine breath, overflowing the boundaries of her body. After months of contraction in the throes of fear, she felt her energy fields expanding as her being merged with the surrounding environment. Instantly, she returned to the beginning of Tara's creation, where trees, rivers, rocks
      - everything material - was pure spiritual consciousness. Therein was the feeling of wholeness that was all the Children of Light, creating life from the innocent love and joy they shared.

A sound of mournful longing escaped her lips as she exhaled. She felt the depth of longing for Oneness once more consume her. Darkness would not conquer her. It could not, for it was not who she truly was. Her innocence might be gone and with that so much that was precious to her, but she would never be darkness! She could still feel the reverberations of the breath in her cells, opening them again to light and the unrestricted movement of energy. She praised the breath in that moment. It was and would always be their greatest gift.

Ayia watched over her with expectant hope. Before his very eyes the long slashes on her arms, and the bruises on her lower legs disappeared. The dark circles under her eyes cleared. A flash of white light moved over her slight body, and at once she was all that she had ever been - radiating her most perfect beauty, grace, and serenity.

She called out, "I want to be home, home, home ..." The mournful words rang out powerfully over the sea. "How do we return? Take me home. Take me home!" In those blissful, deep, yearning moments An knew she would breathe life again! Her voice rang out in song. "All I want is to be all that I AM again, forever - I am One with my brothers and sisters. Nothing can take that away from us. Nothing can take me away from my beloved Ayia. Ayia, Ayia" Her voice was filled with deep love for him. The song rang through his being and he fell to his knees, weeping in gratitude. He knew her love would bring her through the terror. The sound of her voice carrying his name meant everything to him. She would never let him go! Forever the sacred winds that they were would be as one, never apart. With the wind at their backs, they walked hand in hand, unified and undividable.

That night the twins gathered on the sacred beach. Around a solemn fire built by Kané, each of them holding a golden sword with a different gemstone cast into the cross- point. They stood, looking stronger than they had through it all, innocence and that unmistakable essence of complete freedom gone, each focused on the burning embers, deep in thought, their gaze filled with the newness, anger, wisdom, discernment, loss, longing, resolve.

An's family gazed at her in amazement, her wounds were gone, and she had clearly managed to create some incredible healing within herself. This gave them all hope.

An broke the deep silence. "I feel as though this entire sequence of events is my doing." Unable to explain further with the words stuck in her throat, she began to sob uncontrollably, desperately sad that even with all the clearing work earlier, she was still racked with guilt and shame. Ayia put his arm around her holding her tight. He could find no words of comfort.

Kané responded after a time. "Dear sister, I wish only that we could convince you that none of this is your fault. So long as one holds love, there is nothing they have done wrong. This is what we have learned from the disruption of the dark-lord."

She cried out sinking to the ground, hitting the sand with her small fists. "I cannot believe that anymore! I did have only love but look what happened to me. There must be other reasons one can call harm to themselves!"

She paused and took a breath. "I did not listen, from the beginning - I was childish. It is clear that something wished for me to grow, to be more evolved. I should have heeded the warnings we were given! I grieve for the loss of that innocence we all once felt, the freedom, the openness of our consciousness, the love that we knew. Now I feel we must always be guarded, wary, and aware of consequences to all our actions! How can this be freedom? How can the light exist in this state? What could possibly be the purpose for such growth?"

Sunraya came to sit before her sister, looked into her beautiful green eyes, the fire dancing in them. "An, please dear sister, perhaps it is so. You should have listened. We all should have taken the words of Divine Mother and Father more seriously. But we did not know! How could we? We were so innocent! Nothing like this was in our memory or experience before life on Tara. None of us had experienced anything but light in the higher realms."

An looked back at her strong earth sister, taking in her scent of soil, tree, and flower. "If this is the case, then we have all learned through direct experience, what we could not have otherwise known. We are now more mature souls. We are watchful and will never again make the mistake of not heeding the words of wisdom. We can see what results from such folly."

An slowly began to smile, knowing the words of her sister to be true. For a moment An felt relief and probed her sister's eyes for clarity, as Sunraya continued. "There is pain in your heart now, An. You must heal that first. One day we will all feel free again. We will understand the process of this healing."

An nodded, absorbing the strength of Sunraya's clarity. Quietly, she said, "I know this, and I am striving to be light. It is painful to me that no matter how light and happy I may feel in one moment, I keep losing it."

Sunraya nodded with compassion as An continued. "The fear and all the memories always come back. I can't make them go away. Believe me I too long for the innocence that we once were, I am just doing all I can to overcome this and be positive."

An looked from one to the other, and for a moment hesitated to speak, but suddenly she spoke rashly. "There is more. The dark-lord has told me that he knows our beloved parents, that somehow they are responsible for what is happening to us now!" She winced at her own words.

Around the circle everyone looked at her with gasps of shock and disbelief.

Rasha blurted out. "No, don't believe him An! You need to guard your mind. He is only trying to create more separation and doubt!"

An retorted quickly. "If that is so, then how would he even know them by name?"

The group looked startled, their eyes searching. Rasha's voice was shaky. "He - he knew their names?" A memory came to him then, vague but unmistakable ... the moment they were creating their bodies and he had felt a strange energy but dismissed it. Just as much as An might blame herself he too should blame himself. For was that not darkness he felt and pushed away?

An nodded. "Yes, he knew their names". She said looking away from her brother's searching eyes back towards the fire.

Ayia replied. "Why haven't we called upon the assistance of our beloved parents? I know we are all confused. In some ways we have blamed them, or at least wondered why they allowed us to make our own choice in the ethereal to 'welcome the dark', but still, they are our parents, Divine and Holy, infinite."

There was silence for a moment and then An spoke quietly, her eyes still burning with anger. "I've been so upset with them, blaming them in part, but it is time to make peace. Let us call upon them. Let us ask them for the truth."

All of them stirred and shifted in their spots uncomfortably, hesitant to initiate the process.

Finally, Sunraya offered, looking from one to the other with her deep, brown-eyed gaze. "Listen. The only way we are going to understand this is to ask them directly. We must call to them together; it is the only way. They will not come if we do not summon them together, right?"

Within a matter of minutes Io and Ama appeared above the Children in a circle of golden light; their light-bodies floated gently in the space above the beach, wrapped in white silken robes.

An winced again as she looked from Mother to Father, filled with unfathomable pain, guilt and the abandonment she felt. It was she who would have the greatest challenge to let her heart trust again.

Rasha immediately began to cry, and release much of the fear he felt, comforted by the loving embrace of his parents. "It is okay, my son." Mother spoke compassionately. "Be not afraid to feel as deeply as you can. You must speak."

Any anger the twins had felt began to dissolve in the perfect love of their parents.

Summersara asked shyly, "What shall we do, beloved parents? We are trying to heal, to understand, and grow, but we feel so lost, so afraid!"

The circle of light expanded and Io hovered above his sweet daughter. "Beloved daughter, do not allow thought to consume you. It is natural and good for you to contemplate everything you experience, but you must surrender to the light. Do not fear the darkness. Shine your love."

For a time, the Children remained quiet, surprised by this simple answer. Rasha was the one to call out then. "That is all? Shine our love? This is what we thought to do, but surely there is something more? All we have received is pain and anguish!"

Ama opened her hands of light in a gesture of love over her son, reassuringly. Then slowly she moved to An who quickly recoiled in a ball. Ama looked pained; not her own pain, but the pain she felt in her daughter, it was for her to feel as well. "Dear one, we do not know all of the answers, our hearts feel much, and we see so much, yet still we do not hold all of the answers."

She paused here for a moment, seeming to hesitate, but then continued. "Remember how we tried to warn your higher-selves about the dark?"

All quickly nodded yes. "Well," she continued, "that is because we ourselves had an experience with darkness. As your thoughts ask of us... yes... we knew Tarcon long ago. Indeed, he was our brother in the light."

All gasped in utter disbelief. An slowly lifted her head, squinting as she listened.

Ama smiled sadly at each of them. "It is true. Once Tarcon was another being entirely, light like all of us. Something happened inside of him. He went away from us. We tried to stop him, but he fled from the world of light we then inhabited in bodies much like your own. Later, we tried to find him; he had become a very dark and angry being. We tried to come near him, but he would not allow it, his anger was too great. Then he was gone. We searched the Cosmos but never found him. We thought perhaps he had destroyed himself with his destructive ways, though we sensed his presence. It was not until the angels found him that we realized he was still alive, had become the Beast known as Tarcon. It took us a few moments to realize it was him, but then we were certain. This great beast was our once dear brother."

An burst out. "Why didn't you tell us about him before?"

Ama looked compassionate. "I know, dear daughter, that you are angry. You have every right to be. Please understand that you were completely innocent. It was all we could do to warn you of the dark, to offer you the choice to protect yourselves. To give you more information would have been to defile your purity with those thoughts and images.

Ama hesitated for a long while, but then began slowly. "I want to tell you, to somehow aid you in your journey, I just don't want to confuse you. I don't want to plant seeds within you that are like those that Tarcon came to have so long ago. Even discussing it I risk that."

An called out desperately, bravely breaking down the anger in herself. "Please Mother, what seeds he wished to plant, he is already doing. Your words can only bring us understanding!"

She nodded, knowing it was true, but still felt reluctant to add more. For a moment she closed her eyes. "Io what should we do?"

Io calmly offered. "They must hear the truth they seek."

Ama opened her eyes and looked at the beautiful, eager faces of each one. "Tarcon somehow came to feel angry at the love I had for your father. He told me that my love was conditional, that therefore it did not really exist. He said that everywhere he looked there were conditions on love. You see Tarcon as a soul never separated into two parts, some of us chose this, to remain as one and not express our self-love as two. He lost the light of his feminine side deep within and then began to look for that love in the wrong place. He looked for it within me."

Mother closed her eyes in pain. "I tried to talk to him, to make him see otherwise but it was too late. When he left, I sensed that he had gone out into the universe to prove that love did not truly exist, that it was fleeting and temporary. This was to move toward darkness, for darkness can distort anything to such a degree that it might never again be seen clearly."

Mother opened her eyes, and calmly looked again from one to the next. "There was nothing we could do but move on, to continue to evolve. That was a time long before we became Mother and Father, we were in many ways, young and unknowing. We fear dear children that Tarcon seeks to disprove love in you, our beloved children. He despises innocence. He may be so far from love now that he doesn't even remember why he does what he does." She shuddered, feeling just how dark and corrupt Tarcon had become.

The children sat silently contemplating the vastness of what they had been told. It made sense. Perhaps with this knowledge there was hope that they could not only protect themselves, but also bring a transformation to Tarcon and help him see clearly again.

Sunta humbly expressed on behalf of them all. "We are grateful dear parents. Your love is eternal, and we have something to hope for now. Perhaps through time we will bring Tarcon and those of his kind to live by love once again."

Mother and Father smiled at their children, seeing that eternal spark of light.

Ama offered final words. "You will do well in all that you endeavor with, please don't hesitate to call upon us, and know that we are grateful for your understanding and forgiveness. It is the light that you are and always will be."

Slowly their images faded. Weary but hopeful, the Children returned to their dwelling place for the night.

Lying next to Ayia, An reached out her hand. He was startled - she never touched him in bed anymore. Immediately he sat up. "What is it my love? Are you thirsty? Is there anything I can get for you?"

An shook her head. "No, my love. I just, I just want to tell you that I am sorry. The dark lord would have me believe that you do not really love me. He told me that if you had been truly one with me in love, you would have known what was going to happen, and prevented it."

She had barely gotten the words out when she broke down in tears once again. Oh, how it felt endless! "I am so sorry to have doubted your love. I know you didn't feel me, and it was my fault because I went away into the forest alone."

Ayia squeezed her passionately. "No, my love, no. If only I could convince you to stop blaming yourself. I did not know what was going happen. I too, have wondered at this. We are so infinitely connected; how could I not have? I think the dark lord was upon us all the time. He knew how innocent and open our minds were. I think he caused us all in those moments to not take the words of the messenger seriously. He distracted us all somehow causing a separation of our consciousness. Otherwise, I know I would have felt you."

An nodded eagerly, agreeing. "Ayia, he wants us apart, but our love is so strong that his lies have the opposite effect. They brought us back together with our parents, and now they draw us closer again. I knew today that I would not give up, not ever."

Ayia smiled warmly. "We must be so strong together. This is the true power we have. We must not ever allow him to separate our love, not ever. Promise me that you will stop separating from me."

She nodded, moving into his strong embrace where he held her until they both fell into a deep, exhausted sleep. Tarcon was unable to pierce through their protective shield that night, for they had found the source of their greatest protection: their united love. That, coupled with a warrior stance against darkness, and it stood no chance.

The scene shifted to an aerial view of Stella. Tarcon stood on some sort of platform with many of his followers gathered at the base. Behind him was a screen, at least that is what it appeared to be. Tarcon was talking and motioning to the screen.

His gruff voice rang out in the otherwise empty room. "I have implanted one of the Tarian scum with my orders. He will serve as leader of their kind. He will bring them to me, under my command."

"Already the descendants have moved away from the Law of the One. They believe their creator has betrayed them. Now we enact a plan that shall encompass millennia. We will make them our slaves."

"First we get them to act against each other. Then, we teach them to own land and conquer each other's lands and possessions, focusing more and more on the 3rd dimension." He laughed sardonically. "We'll introduce technology, moving them further away from their own mastery. They will look to us for everything. Over time we will manipulate their very DNA until the day comes when they no longer even know who they are or why they are alive. We will dictate everything they do, but they won't even know it is we who are in charge of their very life force. It doesn't matter what they might try or for how long. We will always conquer them!"

The followers were spellbound as Tarcon sped forward. "They will believe that everything they do is free-will. This is important, for free-will rules the universe, doesn't it?" He laughed again and the other jeered him on. "We will control what they think, when they eat, what they eat, how they breed and when; everything. They will believe everything to be their own choice, because they are so stupid. I will feast on this control, this mastery of manipulation!"

He commanded. "There are rules you must obey about how many Tarians you consume. Remember mistakes learned from other planets. If you feast too greedily, you will obliterate their race. You must allow them to continue to live and to breed healthily enough to continue their genetic stock. We take selected individuals, as we have from other planets, enough for you to feed and to bring me their pure blood. And no one, no one is to touch the twins, none of you!"

The crowd grunted their consent.

"You are to take no more than 5% of the population underground for ritualistic feeding. You are to bring me the blood of an additional 2% each week. To gain control, you will crossbreed with 50% of the population. Only 10% of this may result in shape-shifting abilities for you and for your offspring, within whom you must implant your consciousness. You may bring another 2% here for breeding and hybridization."

Turning, he motioned to the screen and then turned to another reptilian male, an electronic display of these numbers in pie fashion appeared. "Hanta, you will keep these numbers in records, and oversee all that is occurring."

Hanta grunted and bowed his head low. Tarcon turned back to the crowd. "Remember always as I have said, leave the Children of Light for me. They are my prey and no one else's."

His orders clearly complete, he quickly dismissed them, turning back to his cave with great satiation. The crowd scurried and shuffled out of the room.

The images changed back to Tara.

There was a young man with red hair, a descendant of the original Children of Light. A crowd of people gathered around him in the forest near the sea.

He addressed the crowd in a gentle, coaxing tone. "Why should we always act by the Law of the One, thinking only thoughts that others can readily hear, striving to make things right since the time of the great dark invasion? Why should we make all of our actions righteous for all living beings and not create more for ourselves?"

The group sat breathless as he continued, "The Creator gifted us all with our own thoughts, our own bodies, and our own will to act. Why should we not have thoughts that no one else knows, live in lands where no one else can live, and create our own laws?"

Gasps of shock and amazement arose in the crowd, no one had ever spoken in this way before.

One spoke for them all. Kaya could no longer bear listening to Marduk. "You cannot speak this way! You bring danger not only to yourself, but also to all of us. We must honor the ancient way and never think such separated, evil things!"

Marduk calmly looked to each person, gauging his or her response. Then, knowing he must act quickly before her thoughts turned them against him, he responded. "For so many years our people have sought understanding, searching for the answers about what happened to us on this planet. We have all wondered why the darkness came and brought harm to all."

He watched the group closely, using his hands and body to express the intensity of his message. "The Creator always told the original 144 that they would have tests in life and that they would need to know for themselves what to do in certain situations so that they could evolve."

Everyone nodded in acknowledgement of this truth, curious where he was leading them.

He squatted before them, placing his hands on the Earth. "The Creator knows that we are creator gods, we are unlimited and can do anything. Why has no one ever thought that perhaps we needed to create in our own ways to evolve ourselves? I think that we need to make our own rules and live as we wish. Then we will truly be fulfilling the role of creator gods!"

The group sat in sheer astonishment at this determined, puzzling man. They were a part of him. How could they not in part agree with his logic, when he was trying so hard to convince them? Murmurs arose as they spoke in small groups, considering his speech.

They seemed to go in circles for some time when one called out loudly. "Perhaps Marduk is right. Perhaps we were always meant to express ourselves freely, not just as we have been witness to in others, but in our own ways, creating our own rules to live by. This would be true freedom, would it not?"

At this point, Kaya quietly removed herself from the group, backing into the safety of the forest. Then she turned and walked quickly away to find her parents and warn them of the plans the group was considering.

In the end they all agreed to the plan. For the first time an entire group of Tarians would think and act, as they liked, without a care for how this affected anyone else. Excitement coursed through Marduk's veins. He knew this meant power for himself. He would help the group devise ways to create a new way of being. As others saw the freedom involved, more would gather to follow him.

Divine Mother and Father watched all of this from their place on high.

Io sighed. "I pray the Children can show them the faults in Marduk's logic before it is too late." Mother replied sadly.

Io shook his head. "It is concerning indeed. If there is too much independence, too much rebellion; the understanding of Oneness will be lost, just as it occurred with Tarcon so long ago."

Mother felt a shudder move through the very core of planet Tara. Io continued, "The polarities are shifting already. If darkness outweighs the light any more than it already does, the fields surrounding the planet will be seriously affected, and the magnetic polarity may shift, spinning the planet into a reverse turn on its axis. Massive destruction will result if that takes place. The tribes don't realize that the planetary consciousness and energy-field always react to the thought and emotion held by its inhabitants..."

Mother finished his thought. "We cannot directly interfere and do not wish to alter the course of learning, but perhaps simple suggestions... perhaps the Children can begin to teach the descendants to return to the light, to withstand the darkness. Then they will no longer be influenced by such thoughts of independent action and separation."

Father responded. "That is a wonderful plan. If it is not successful, we can attune to the changes that would take place with a pole-shift and direct the Children to safety, only if they wish. They will never consent to the complete destruction of their world and rebuilding a new one surrounded by light. They still blame themselves too much and carry the burden of the dark, in need of sorting through all that has come to be."

"Yes, the twins must know of Tarcon's horrific acts and future plans at this point. It will be shocking for them to learn the truth, but they must teach the tribes to protect themselves from cross-breeding, enslavement, and..." Mother's tone hushed she completed. "Worse."

My thoughts returned to the present with the council, and I asked Lady Nada. "What became of Tarcon? Will I see how he was vanquished from Tara? It just feels like too much to wait, can I see now?"

"Tarcon is still in control on your planet, now more so than ever. The evil he is inducing each and every moment is far, far worse than what you see happening with the Children of Light. This is why you must understand what happened in the beginning. See it closely and never forget it is real."

It was all so much to take in. I wished with all my heart the world that had once been could somehow come to be again. The journey into the past had been long and I welcomed sleep.

CHAPTER TWENTY TWO

Discernment

It took a moment for me to realize I was in my tent, safe, and alone. My body was shaking and covered in sweat. Taking a few deep breaths, I tried to steady myself.

I went outside and looked up at the vast sky above, relieving my bladder under a giant mango tree, slapping mosquitos away. I stood under the cloudy sky listening to the soft song of the crickets before going back to my tent. Before long I had fallen into a deep sleep.

It was late morning by the time I finally woke. The sun was hot on my tent, the air stifling. I stretched, opened my door for some fresh air, remembering nervously what had taken place between me and the 'god-man'. I was embarrassed, tense, and eager to see him all at the same time. Besides, I was very hungry, so I headed for the kitchen. Halfway there I realized I was also quite thirsty and made my way back to my tent to find my water bottle. Gulping down water as I walked to the kitchen, I looked around. Orion was nowhere to be seen and I wondered where he would be.

I had not expected to see Orion in the camp. I had been so involved with my inner process, that his presence was a surprise to me when I looked up. He turned and smiled at me brilliantly. Inwardly, I shuddered as I remembered the liquid he had put in my mouth from his. He was beautiful, stunning even, but I felt no real attraction to him. From his response I could see that he had clearly moved on from the night before. Perhaps he thought I had as well.

I forced a smile back, uneasy. The feeling of awkwardness reminded me of movies where two lovers had come together for one night, and in the morning realized they had shared something very deep and powerful yet didn't really know each other at all. The discomfort though was clearly all on my part. Orion seemed so relaxed with me, as though he knew me well.

"Good morning, can I get you some medicinal tea?" I shrugged. "Sure, what's in it?"

Orion held up a hand full of what looked like thick grass. "This one is lemongrass." Picking up another bunch he pointed to each one, his bright eyes sparkling. "This one is noni leaf. This one is goldenseal, and here we have licorice. They are all great for the immune system, the blood, and the digestive system."

I folded my hands behind my back. "Sounds great," I said, detached.

Orion turned back to his preparation and gestured toward a pile of fruit. Before picking up his knife he reached behind his head, quickly pulled out his hair-tie, shook out his long hair and retied it in a ponytail. He seemed unselfconscious but I wondered if he had done it for my benefit.

He smiled up at me. "Help yourself to the papaya and mango there. And if you feel like you need more substance, there's some avo."

My eyes lit up. I was starving, and the appearance of avocado and fresh fruit had an inspiring effect on me. I was so uncomfortable with him, but at the same time I so wanted a teacher, and I'd always been really forgiving. I think my history helped me understand that lust and desire could get the best of any man. I only hoped it was the last time with him. I decided to use the morning to get to know Orion more, to try with all my will to let go of the night before and give him another chance to prove himself to me.

"Do you eat mostly raw food?" I asked as I made my way toward the fruit. There was a knife and a cutting board, and I quickly cut open a mango and began to eat it enthusiastically.

"Yeah, I do. Raw food has the highest vibration of all." He

paused. "Because of all the transmuting I have done, I can eat anything I want. It just moves through my body. If you practice what I give you, that will happen to you. But truthfully, I just like the vibration of raw foods better. Though, I do like a good batch of popcorn. I add nutritional yeast, sea-salt and soy sauce - it's great. I'll make some for you later."

I looked up from my fruit, noticing the innocent joy he exuded about the popcorn. "That sounds nice. It's so great that you can eat right off the land. Did all this fruit grow right here?"

Orion laughed at some inner knowing. "When I first came to the islands, I thought you could just walk down the beach or go into the forest and pick all kinds of fruit and just eat it. But it isn't quite so easy. There isn't anything growing on this land yet, just a few veggies and herbs. We have to either buy or trade for everything we get."

I sat silently thinking about what he had said. I too, had thought it would be easy to live off the land. Aside from the beaches, I understood from David, someone owned every piece of land. It was part of America, after all. Soon, the smell of the sweet tea filled the air and Orion offered me a cup. It was too hot to drink but I held it in both hands and took in the strong aroma.

I asked. "Do you think you could tell me more about your spiritual experiences, just different things you have gone through?"

Orion smiled eagerly, as though he had been waiting for this question. "I would love to share everything with you!"

I was taken aback by the strength of his response as I remembered the night before and looked away blushing.

Orion sensed my reticence and continued more casually. "I know it will help you understand what is happening to you and what you have to look forward to. Why don't we go for a walk?"

I replied in an even tone. "Sure."

After finishing our tea and fruit we put down our cups, and slowly walked out the driveway together.

He suddenly said. "I do yoga almost every day, it's a big part of spiritual practice, and one I hope to share with you.

I offered, "That would be great, I do a yoga practice that's kind of my own style. I hurt my back really badly in a car accident many years ago. I was unable to move an inch without a lot of pain. The doctors said I'd never be ok, but I had this feeling from the one yoga class I took that I could heal it with yoga, so I created this really gentle routine. I still do it all the time, but I'd love to learn another practice."

He smiled, so I asked. "What?"

"I'm just not surprised that's all, given who you are, that you would come up with a yoga practice to heal yourself with just one class."

I didn't know what to ask about but was sure that if I could get to know him more, the trauma of the night would go away. "Tell me, tell me about your life." I skipped ahead turning my head to look back at him.

He laughed seeming to enjoy my light-hearted eagerness. "It will take a long time, perhaps a little each day?"

I nodded happily.

He began as he walked looking at me as he did. "Well, my mom's side of the family is the Navajo side, but my dad, he was Italian. I grew-up an only child, living in Las Vegas. In the summers I lived with dad's mom in Santa Barbara, or on the reservation with my grandmother and the elders. My father was an alcoholic and very violent."

Orion paused and stood still, taking a moment to catch his breath. He looked back over his shoulder. "We've come pretty far without water to drink. We should probably turn back."

I nodded, agreeing as he continued. "I turned to martial arts. At first, maybe I thought I would spend the rest of my life defending myself from someone or something bad, because of my dad. I had great teachers. Along the way I think it became a way to release or harness the anger I had about my mom. I missed my mom a lot and I blamed my dad. I haven't spoken to him since I was sixteen. As far as I'm concerned, he doesn't exist. I began to spend the summers with my tutu - that's Grandma - on the reservation. That's when the old ones began to teach me of the ancient ways. I learned how to use Shaman powers for healing and lots of other things."

I noticed that his eyes looked very distant and haunting somehow. I thought maybe it was just the memories of the anger and violence.

Orion continued once more. "I got really good at martial arts and began to compete. One day my Sensei in Aikido said he thought I should go to Japan to train in the old-school way. So I went there. That world is so different than the West. Really, what they are teaching is about how to purify the ego; anger, pride, resentments. My training was hard and intense. I learned that I liked it, there was something about intense discipline that suited me well - my fiery nature I guess."

He paused to catch his breath and then continued. "I will go into much greater detail later, but basically from there I went into Tibet and the Himalayas where I meet my high teachers. They were masters who lived in remote caves. I had to go through a lot of initiation having to do with remembering who I am. I had to do things like sit in a cave for a month with no food or water with a blind-fold doing nothing but intense breathing. When you do things like that you begin to experience the Void, higher consciousness, and you understand that the you that you think you are really doesn't exist."

I asked. "Enlightenment?"

Orion responded energetically.

"Yes, enlightenment. At that point I had purified so much that nothing mattered anymore. All I wanted was to stay in that state of bliss and nothingness. But, my teachers said I must bring their teachings here to the West.

He looked distant and sad. "I knew they wouldn't live much longer, but I really didn't want to go, I was so blissful all I wanted to do was stay there forever."

His face looked suddenly drained of life. "Leaving my teachers was the hardest thing I have ever had to do."

I looked at him with awe. "Wow. Your story is incredible!"

I noticed as he smiled broadly how very white and straight his teeth where, how deeply pink his lips. I had no idea how old he was. He seemed ancient and yet fresh like a small boy all at once.

He added. "So I came back to the west to offer what I could, but along the way I went to India and studied in-depth yoga, and then to Thailand practicing meditation in the temples.

When I came back here I studied natural medicine and homeopathy, and opened a pretty amazing clinic in Cali with a partner. I worked too hard and eventually came to Hawaii where

I met my Hawaiian teachers and studied Huna. I left Hawaii for a while and went to Europe were I studied alchemy and massage and other holistic therapies, teaching what I could along the way. I also do shamanistic healing taught to me by tutu and the other elders of the Navajo."

His pace seemed to have quickened and I rushed to keep up, breathing hard. "Have you heard enough for now Luna? I feel like I've talked your ear off. But I just want to say…" He had a soft look. "I have so much to offer you, I can't wait to share all of those things I just talked about and more!"

I shook my head. "No, you didn't talk my ear off. Thank you so for sharing with me. I had a feeling you really were my teacher, even before I met you, but understanding some of what you are about is helpful for my mind to digest. I can't believe all you've done, and you still look so young and vibrant!" I was beaming by that point. "It seems like you can teach me everything I'd ever want to learn and more!"

On the walk back I decided to be brave and tell Orion about the council. After describing everything I looked over to see him grinning widely. "I know Luna, I knew about all of this long before you arrived here."

I was shocked. "You know them? You've met them?"

Orion smiled a bit mysteriously. "Yes, and they told me you would be coming, but they didn't tell me everything."

He continued, "They told me - that's how I knew you were coming – they told me they were going to bring you back through the entire history and that you were the memory keeper."

I felt chills "The memory keeper?"

He looked almost stern then. "Yes Luna, the memory keeper. The gatekeeper to the threshold of time and the borders of our reality."

I was petrified. I didn't want this purpose. I could feel it was going to mean so much more in my life. I thought for a moment about the Native American name I'd been given "Shaoini." The meaning (she who remembers) had a completely new feeling for me. If knowing the history of the world meant being attacked by dark-forces and men in black I didn't want it!

There is so much for you to know." He said.

I gulped. "So, it's true, I need protection…" my voice trailed off.

He looked so serious. "What do you mean, how do you know that?"

I told him about the night with the dark and the fall in the shower, and the men in black.

Orion said quickly. "This is part of why you are with me, I have to protect you and I have to teach you to protect yourself. You need to know more, right now, about my training and what I can teach you … the masters in Tibet taught me the breath that activates our energy-field, and allows us to travel beyond time, among many other incredible things."

He continued, looking so serious it was unnerving. "Once I learned how to use that breath I began to travel through time and space. It was then that I remembered who I really am. Once that happened, I sought out the Galactic Council. I had remembered them from other planets where my soul lives in higher vibrations, I knew they were masters of our universe. I wanted them to explain some things to me about our planet and my purpose. They did that much and more. It was because of all I saw when I was with them that I began to go on certain missions."

He paused, gulping down water from his steel bottle, and I took the opportunity to do so myself. I sat down, asking if we could continue at a later time. It was all too much and I just needed to be alone.

Orion left for the day to teach his students at the dojo, which also explained how he was so fit. I spent the day resting and calling friends and family back home. Alexis would be arriving so soon, it felt like an eternity since I'd come to the island but in reality, so little time had passed! That night I joined a quiet circle around the fire. Later, I quickly fell asleep, feeling like I had made the right choice.

CHAPTER TWENTY THREE

Reunion

The next day I hitched to town to meet Alexis at the airport. I easily spotted her, waving wildly at me and I ran to her with a lump in my throat; embracing her.

There were probably few women of such beauty and grace I could share this child-like innocence with. There was no pretense between us, no need to be "cool", or talk superficially as I had found with most others over the years.

Suddenly a male voice interrupted. "Hey, you two!"

I smiled back. "You must be Jerry. Al also speaks ever so highly of you. Isn't it amazing that we are both in the same area of the island?"

Jerry put his arm around Alexis and squeezed her tightly. "Well, I know Alexis is more eager to spend time with you than me, so I guess you get her first."

She nudged him playfully and kissed his cheek. "Yeah, friends before lovers, you know."

We followed him to an old beat-up white van. Alexis climbed into the front and I hopped in the back. It was carpeted, and there was a bed at the back and a few boxes of books.

Back at the land, I showed her around and helped her set up her tent. Just as we were finishing a car drove up, it was Orion.

My heart raced again. Suddenly, I was nervous for the two of them to meet. Why did I worry that he would judge Alexis somehow? I didn't know, but I tried to quiet my heartbeat.

Orion strode toward the two of us with his usual confident, focused stride. He put down his backpack and walked straight toward Alexis, holding out his hand, smiling brightly. "Welcome. Aloha."

Alexis shook his hand and then ran it anxiously through her hair. She seemed surprised, nervous even, which was strange for her, she was always so at ease with everyone. "Nice to meet you."

Orion shifted his attention to me and spoke softly. "It's nice to see you too. I'll see you in the tent in a little bit?"

I shifted my weight uncomfortably. "Well, actually I wasn't planning to do any studying tonight. Alexis and I have a lot of catching up to do."

I gave him a look that said I assumed he would know that, but his eyes looked disapproving and somehow yearning.

I was still very uneasy with this part of his interest in me. I worried for that part of him. In my past, many young men had told me that I was responsible for their deep unhappiness when I showed disinterest in them. A few had even resorted to self-destructive tendencies and claimed to be suicidal because of that. Even though I knew that no person could truly be responsible for another's obsession, not when they tried to discourage it, I still carried guilt.

Orion abruptly picked up his pack. "Okay, I'll see you two in the morning, then." With that he strode away at a quick pace.

Alexis gave me a bewildered look. "Luna you never mentioned on the phone yesterday that he is absolutely gorgeous beyond words. Nor that he is in love with you!"

My mouth dropped.

"Orion is not in love with me." I was shocked. "I don't know what that energy is, but one thing is for certain, the man is my teacher and that is all."

Alexis looked at me with concern. She sensed, no doubt, my unease - anyone would. It kept coming in waves, one hour I was excited about being here, being his student, the next repulsed.

Alexis smiled cunningly. "Yeah, chemistry is either there or it's not, but he clearly has it for you, that's what is so strange."

"Well," I offered slowly. "It is confusing. He is the one who is so evolved. I'm only just beginning to awaken, to heal. But you know, no matter how dysfunctional I was in the past, I feel that I have always been able to know things through my intuition."

She smiled compassionately, "Well I'm here now sis and I've always got your back, if he tried to get crazy with you, he'll have me to deal with."

I felt a tug of guilt, not wanting to share with her the violation, it would make her want me to run from this wild scenario.

I smiled back. "We should rest now. Remember, we have to work on the land in exchange for our stay."

Alexis asked, "What will we be doing?"

"I think we'll be digging a garden bed."

Alexis nodded and we hugged good night. I returned to my tent and, even though I was exhausted from so much talk, I couldn't sleep. Once more waves of energy filled my body and I felt my spirit pulled out of the tent and beyond.

CHAPTER TWENTY FOUR

Final Decree - Guidance

Divine Mother and Father hovered above their children. So much happened on Tara. The man chosen by Tarcon to be his puppet had convinced many of the tribes to begin to act in defiance to the Laws of Oneness. More havoc was being wreaked as people began to fight each other and chaos seemed to be taking over.

Divine Father initiated the meeting, opening his arms in a fatherly gesture. "Welcome dearest. Come sit close."

Io and Ama quickly explained that to regain balance, their world would most likely turn on its axis due to the imbalance of energies on the planet. This would mean a great destructive energy would potentially displace most of the landmasses and re-arrange the structure of the planet itself. Many would die.

The group sat silently for some time, reflecting all that this meant. Really, they were barely able to take it in.

Summersara spoke for them all, with calm despair. "I didn't know the darkness had influenced people to this degree. What can we do?"

Divine Mother responded. "We can only offer suggestions. Watch the others carefully now."

Io added, "As you seek to learn from the experience, ask

yourselves to remember what you know of Tarcon. See if there is a way that you can develop a plan to bring healing to this energy, and thereby bring all back into light, along with your planet. They are too far from light for us to reach them, but perhaps you, as their older siblings, will break through and one day we can reach them directly as well."

The children were quiet, and it was clear that they were all at the same place in awareness. It was a lot to take in and there was very little to say.

The screen blackened and I understood it was time for question and answer. "So, the Children of Light were able to remain more connected than their younger siblings even though they had endured so much trauma?"

Sananda nodded. "Yes, for they were the most evolved, having existed in the realms of light far longer than the younger ones who were simply newer souls. As they invited them to experience Tara, they were in that sense responsible for them."

"Was there something biologically different about the twins from us? Something that they did, or absorbed, that we don't?" I asked.

"Before the moment Tarcon invaded, all Tarians used a certain breath that is longer in use today. When darkness came, everyone went into fear and stopped that breath."

Sananda pointed to the screen and I saw an image of the human body in its energy form. Lines of energy pulsed through. Down the very center of the spine from the top of the head to the base of the spine was a golden cord of light."

He continued. "It was the main way they were connected to oneness and sustained a high vitality. This breath was not of oxygen, but of pure energy, it kept the mind in a place of oneness rather than duality. Later the twins remembered that they had stopped breathing this way, but it was no longer innate. They had to consciously do this breath. That breath was carried down through lineage and is still on your planet today. Your teacher, as you know, will be giving this breath to you."

I looked surprised. "You sent me to him then, it is true?" He nodded, so it was true, how amazing!

At the moment I knew it was the breath lineage that Orion spoke of. "You mean there is a lineage that goes all the way back to the Children?"

Sananda smiled, loving my excitement. "Indeed Luna. You see there are aspects of their teachings around the world. They could not simply keep them all in one place for the dark would easily destroy them. So they created many different paths and hid the teachings within them. Now we are coming to the exciting part. First, I want you to ask Orion about this, about the breath he mentioned to you. He will begin to instruct you in the lineage that he carries, one of the most sacred on the planet. More importantly, you will use those tools until you achieve mastery with them. One day you will travel around the world gathering all the ancient teachings. It will be the greatest treasure hunt ever, and the most important."

Sananda continued. "One day you and your family will create the highest spiritual path this planet has ever seen, a path that will lead people directly back to the light. You will do this after having gathered the teachings. It will not be a religion in the sense that people think of religion today, but True Religion, a path to be followed with utmost loyalty. It will result in the return of life that was lived by the twins."

That was so far beyond anything I was able to really take in, but years later I was to see it all so clearly.

The session ended. It had been shorter in comparison, but so huge.

∞

Back in my tent I opened my eyes quickly. It was getting harder for me to journey so far. I was beginning to feel restless, like I needed some old part of my life back.

Orion was in the kitchen, as though waiting for me. He seemed to see in my worried eyes that I had gone through something pretty big, I felt depleted and exhausted. He held his arms out in a welcoming embrace and I fell into them, feeling safe in the strength of his muscular arms, the strong beat of his heart.

I would never be too sure how I had so easily forgiven him for the night in his tent, and came to trust him.

When Orion offered to cook me breakfast, and to give me a healing session, I couldn't resist. Deeper still, I knew I needed help.

I ate silently while Orion sat next to me, reading a book. For the next hour he did a Reiki healing on me. I felt my body beginning to balance out. Images of the twins, the dark reptilian beings, and Divine Mother and Father passed through my mind, all mixed up.

I spent the rest of the day and evening walking and talking with Alexis. As the sun began to set we headed for the kitchen. Alexis made a big batch of popcorn while I made guacamole out of a bag of avocados Orion had picked the week before. They were finally ripe! My mouth watered. They were going to taste so good with lemon and onion, and a bit of salt. Just then Orion came in, looking up I instantly saw a familiar look of focus.

He gave Alexis a hug and sat on the bench next to me. "Before the meeting tonight I need to do some work with you."

I could feel Alexis tense a little; she wasn't entirely comfortable still, even with all I'd said, with the whole spiritual teaching aspect. He was referring to the community meeting. My heart was beating a little faster. "Okay, when?" I had just gotten comfortable with him and here I was sweating again. Hopefully that would end soon!

He looked down at the bowl of avocado, smiling. "That looks good. Why don't you eat and then come over to my tent?"

I nodded, returning to my work as he walked away.

It was already getting dark when I stood outside his tent and called out. "Hello?"

He unzipped the zipper as he looked out. "Come in."

He began immediately. "It's time for you to start learning about the MerKaBa."

I remembered that term from our first session, pushing away thoughts of what else had occurred then.

He continued. "You remember we talked briefly about the meaning, the vehicle of light?"

I nodded as he continued. "These teachings come from Lemuria. They were carried down through all the eons of time, held sacred by masters who guarded them well."

I couldn't believe it. Did he know what the masters had said to me? Everything felt suddenly very surreal. "Orion, they told me you would be teaching me these things."

He smiled. "I know, it's all been so well planned for you. When I was given this practice in Tibet I had to do many things to deserve receiving it. For you it's given with so much more ease. One day: I hope you will teach it, teach many. I will lay it in your hands and ask that you carry on this sacred lineage"

Intrigued and surprised, I squirmed in my position. "What kind of things did you have to do?" I couldn't imagine teaching as that part almost went over my head. Years later, I would understand much more my responsibilities; when I would find myself on my own, no longer with a teacher but needing to be my own teacher.

He looked like he was transported to that time and I saw with him... "I had to sit in below freezing weather in the snow, naked for twenty-four hours. If I had one thought of limitation, of believing in the body's frailty I would die, that's how high their tests are. But I accomplished the task. I had been trained well, to control the mind to harness the emotion."

"I need you to take a vow that you will carry these teachings with the utmost respect and secrecy. You are not to share them with anyone until the day I decide you are ready to do that."

I nodded holding my hands to my heart, my face flushed with color. "I vow to keep the teachings safe and to hold them as sacred!" At that time, knowing nothing of their true power or where it would take me, was probably a good thing.

Orion smiled. "Good, then let us begin."

He sat up even straighter. "Some of what I say you may have been told by the council but its still important that you hear it here, in your body. There's a golden cord of light that comes from the universal light, about the size of a dime that enters your crown, it goes right down the center of the pineal gland, and right through the center of the spinal column and directly out the tailbone, connecting deep into the earth. When the breath is activated, prana or universal life force travels up and down that cord, in both directions at once. There is something about breathing prana in two directions at once that causes us to see in Oneness, to feel our connection to that. This breath activates all the other energy flows in the body, through the meridians."

I was completely still, captivated and excited all at once, thinking there's so much we aren't ever taught, what if the whole world knew these things, would it make a difference?

He smiled, continuing. "That's just the beginning. You know how you saw the Lemurians flying and traveling into other dimensions, doing incredible things?"

I nodded, "Oh yes, I would never forget, it was my greatest passion."

"Well, they were able to do that because their MerKaBas were activated. That too was lost to the average human over time. But that energy structure still exists around each person; it is a part of our genetic heritage. It's just dormant in almost all people. My teachers carried the understanding of how to activate and utilize the MerKaBa."

"The MerKaBa is the most sacred of all things. It is the fountain of youth, the Holy Grail. My teachers carried the understanding of how to activate and utilize the MerKaBa."

I was amazed. How rare he must be, to know these things, to be a person from the West, carrying something so… well, so holy.

As if in answer to my thoughts, he continued. "There are only three other people trained by my master teachers."

He held his head low for a moment. "My teachers are no longer alive and it is up to us to keep the flame burning. Their masters and those before them gave instructions that in this time period, the very one you and I are a part of, teachings had to go out to the world. They understood that the star-seed would incarnate now, traveling back in time to gather the teachings they planted here."

There were tears in his eyes and I could feel the deep love he held for his teachers, how he missed them dearly. I could imagine them, little old Tibetan monks, so pure, so ancient, so holy.

"So now I pass these teachings to you. Believe me, Luna, I am as excited as you. I have waited for this a long, long time."

I knew he was referring to what he had said when we first met, that he had been waiting for me. It still felt strange, overwhelmingly strange.

"That's not all." Orion continued, "The MerKaBa is the most sacred of all things. It is the fountain of youth, the Holy Grail. You've heard about the quest for such things and how people both good and evil have searched the world looking for some item, some relic?"

I nodded. I'd heard of these things, but had never known what people were really searching for. I'd always imagined some type of goblet or device.

The candlelight flickered on Orion's glowing face causing his light blue eyes to sparkle. "Well they all thought it was some type of relic, but in truth it's all inside. It was really the teachings they were searching for, the key to open the greatest gift of all, immortality, perfect health, omniscient wisdom and sight, teleportation, travel beyond time and space without space craft. You can travel anywhere and learn anything instantly, you become like a walking encyclopedia of universal knowledge. But the best thing is, Divine Creator guarded these teachings from those who would use them for harm. You see the only way to activate the field is through an open-heart, through love."

I wasn't even blinking at that point. This explained how he knew I was coming. Orion held the key to immortality? That would explain so much about him, how he had done so much in his life but looked so young. How he knew so much and had so much energy all the time. I wanted to have energy like that, to not feel tired, to be immortal - to be forever young - wow, Wow!

He was still beaming. "The best thing is, when you activate your MerKaBa the feeling you have in every cell of your body is one of great bliss and ecstasy through all of your cells, there's nothing like it. That's the best way to describe it, but words can't truly relay how incredible it is, you'll have to experience it yourself. The thing is, not everyone activates, its up to your higher self and whether or not one is ready for that."

I nodded. It was good to know there were sacred things the dark couldn't ever take away. Orion looked at me intensely. "Even though dark can not use this tool, they know how powerful it is, and they don't want anyone else using it. They have other powerful tools and they can destroy anyone, anytime if you are not careful, if you are not protected. They also have this idea that one day somehow they can find the way to access anything because they don't believe love protects anything. Do you understand this all?"

I nodded.

"Do you want to learn this breath?"

I took a deep breath. "I would very much and I understand how careful I will have to be."

Orion closed his eyes and seemed deep in thought. When he opened his eyes he spoke gravely. "We will begin your studies soon. We will begin your studies soon. I'll meet you in the gathering place for dinner and discussion."

CHAPTER TWENTY FIVE

Revelations On The Planetary Control Grid

People were gathered around the fire pit, where a small fire warmed the space and kept the mosquitoes away. The group of ten, including Alexis, sat around on the stumps and old chairs. The weather was clear and warm enough, but I found a fire comforting at any time. As I approached, wearing the long velvet red dress I'd brought for special occasions, I thought about how lovely it was that such a great dress could roll-up in my backpack so easily and come out completely unwrinkled.

I loved the way it hugged my body ever so slightly and the way the shoulder straps rested in just the right place. It was a dress that made my feel grounded in my femininity, strong and alive. Orion looked up, not concealing his adoring smile. This did not go unnoticed by anyone. Clearly, we were a subject of much needed gossip. Suddenly I wasn't so comfortable with my femininity, I found myself curving my spine, drawing it in, my normally very correct posture being replaced by one that I hoped would somehow hide me from watchful eyes.

I imagined the group wondered what was going on with Orion and me and I hoped they knew I had no romantic interest in their leader.

There was one man there that I had not met. As I sat down,

he stood up and reached out his hand. He was a round fellow with short red hair and small, gold rimmed glasses. To my surprise he spoke with an accent. "Hi Luna, it's so great to meet you, Orion has told me all about you."

I looked at Orion with an upturned eyebrow, jovially but with question. He continued. "My name's Bill. I understand we hail from the same parts?"

It took me a moment to realize what he was saying and then I burst out excitedly as I shook his hand. "You're from Kentucky?"

Bill laughed. "Well, yes, you bet I am. I come from a place about one hour from where you were born. Have you heard of Cumberland Falls?"

I beamed. "I have indeed, I've never been but yeah. This is amazing. I'm shocked! I never meet anyone from Kentucky anywhere other then Kentucky, and here you are in Hawaii of all places. In the middle of the rain forest."

Bill nodded laughing. "Well, don't I know it? When I heard about you I just had to met ya'."

I wanted to understand. "How ... well why, are you here, in Hawaii I mean?"

Bill laughed again. "My big brother Jackie, he lives about 30 minutes from here. He moved over here five years ago with a friend. They've got a tomato farm going. I have a community of sorts myself in old Kentucky. I came out to see how these things are run. One day over at Jackie's I met Orion here and we two got to talkin'." He winked over at Orion. "It seems we know a lot of the same things but Orion knows a whole hell of a lot more than me. So that's why I'm here, to rack his brain."

I looked over at Orion who was clearly enjoying watching this, and then looked back at Bill curiously. "What do you mean know the same things?"

Bill shook his head a bit and adjusted his glasses. "Well, I'm Christian you see, and I believe in the Bible's Revelations, the end-times if you will. I believe we are seeing the signs of Revelation coming true."

I looked around the group. Everyone was watching so attentively. There was little in the way of entertainment out in the sticks, and they were clearly enthralled by all this.

When I didn't say anything Bill rushed on. "Surely being born in Kentucky you would have read the bible and know all about the apocalypse?"

I shrugged, uncomfortable under Orion's penetrating gaze. "Well, I lived in Kentucky nearly every summer of my life. My grandma is just about the most god-fearin' Christian you'd ever meet. But, you know I tried to stay above and beyond all that fear. The idea that only a "saved Christian" won't go to hell but that other good people will, or people with other beliefs will, well that just never sat right with me."

I smiled, enjoying a little accent coming through me. I did love Kentucky so much; its rich essence had always raced through my blood, as though I were really a part of its river gorges and rocky expanses. I had Sioux blood on my father's side and Cherokee on my mothers. The land I was born in was sacred to them and I always felt my deep affinity to it must something to do with that blood. Usually I couldn't keep myself away; my pull to the land of my birth was so strong. Every summer I would wind up there. But this year was different. Yet here was this man, reminding me of the sacredness, and the longing began to grow again, pulling me to the rich hills, the old people, the graveyards, streams and river.

I pulled myself back to the present. Bill was chuckling, clearly delighted by my straightforward response. "Well I figured you were liberal so that's to be expected. Don't worry now, I'm not like everyone back home, I've got an open mind." He motioned towards Orion. "That's why I'm here, to find out more about the mysterious "New World Order" Orion is said to be an expert on."

I looked at Orion questioningly. Orion smiled calmly at me and then looked around the group, taking on his teaching tone. "Bill asked me to talk tonight about what is really going on in the world, in America, who the government really is, and so on."

He paused taking on a very serious look. "Nothing that I say tonight is going to be easy to hear. It's all pretty intense, and it's all very real. There are dangers in our world that you have no idea of and things to come that we all need to be prepared for. A lot of what I talk about causes people fear, so I just want you to all check in with yourselves. If you don't want to be here, or need to leave at any point, that's fine."

I looked around the wide-eyed group. It was quite a tantalizing statement he had made. Who could not resist such mystique?

Everyone sat still. Sid offered. "Well, I want to know what's going on. I've experienced some strange things in my life. I've heard the words "New World Order", but that's just about it."

Everyone seemed to nod in agreement. Orion plunged in. I noticed that Bill settled back in his seat. His arms folded over his side girth, his face serious and concentrated. "There's no easy place to start with this subject so I'll just jump in. There are two forces on our planet - good and evil, light and dark."

I could see from the look in his eyes that he had moved to a focused place. His body seemed to emit a lot of energy as though when he talked like this he was doing more then talking, like he was truly giving away energy.

The group was already captivated as he continued, which wasn't surprising to me. "Throughout all of history light and dark have battled. In this time dark has waged a battle far greater then even the darkest of times past. Revelations speak about a time when certain signs will be seen, when the earth will change, and the mark of the beast will be upon us."

He made eye contact with each person. "There is a secret government made up of elite families in Europe and the US, throughout the world really, that rule the governments you see. They are the government behind the government. They are responsible for all the choices that get made, when we go to war and why.

They control the monetary system through the World Bank. They control the medical world, the pharmaceutical world, farming, third-world countries, diseases like AIDS, education, health, media." He was counting them off on his fingers. "Everything you see in our world, expect for remote little operations like this, is controlled by this elite. But even we are affected by what they do and you will learn why tonight."

I was fascinated watching Orion. He was a storyteller of great suspense. Somehow even just being connected to him made me feel more significant.

He was saying. "This government has been there all along, planning things, leading up to complete control. They have a strategy that has spanned eons of time, going back even before known civilization.

He smiled over at me knowingly. "For now let's stay in the present. Their goal is to create a one-world government, one that controls all people, under one common rule. They're agenda is nothing short of frightening. They plan to control food, which they are already implementing. They have corporations that have developed genetically engineered food, supposedly this food is resistant to bugs and the like, but truthfully it only adds to the problem. What's worse is that some of these crops actually have plastic molecules in them and other cancerous, immune-weakening agents that cause the human being to mutate, horrible, and at best, to be easily controlled. Once they change the food sources, there will be no turning back. We've already seen this, for example in cows that have eaten genetically modified grains. There was a cow born last year with two heads."

I cringed, along with everyone. "They are actually patenting these seeds."

He paused, noting that he had everyone's rapt attention. "So that's like, say you have a papaya seed that you want to put in the ground, but this elite group has the patent on it, they can charge you with theft if you didn't buy it from them. Then think of the average farmer, his entire crop could be considered stolen. He would have to either pay or destroy his crop. They will eventually gain control of the world's food. Organic food, herbal, medicinal … it will all disappear. And they are doing this with animals as well."

Bill interrupted. "So you mean, one day we farmers won't have any seeds left that aren't contaminated."

Orion nodded passionately. "Yes one day there will have been so much cross-breeding that you won't be able to tell the difference between the tomato seed you planted, growing from a healthy seed and the one that blew in from the genetic field next to yours. And the same is true with salmon bred in farms, getting away in the open water and cross-breeding with a non-genetic fish."

Bill let out a big sigh. "Can you explain to everyone why they are doing this?"

Orion nodded. "They want to weaken the human-being to the point that everyone is completely controlled. People are controlled even now they just don't know it. But what they have in store is complete enslavement. They want humans to be a controlled race for work, and as a energy-source."

Bill sighed. "What do you mean a race for work and an energy-source?"

Orion clasped his hands looking around at the others. Everyone had looks of great concern and fear. "How's everyone doing?"

Everyone nodded eager for him to go on no matter how unbelievable it was.

"Well, as for the work force. If they control all the food, money and land, then they can dictate everything. They can create a communist world in which everyone works for them, they choose who does what. I know this is difficult to imagine but it gets worse. Before I go too far with the energy-source aspect, lets talk about the 'mark of the beast'. In the bible there is a prophecy about the end-times, in which a world-leader who is actually the antiChrist will take total control by implanting all peoples with the mark of the devil - otherwise known as 666. Well you all know what a barcode is?"

Everyone nodded and he went on. "There is a barcode on everything we buy now, this gets scanned into a computer and the price comes up for the teller right? But there is more of a purpose. This information gets feed into a giant computer, named the 'beast'. This machine monitors who buys what and when. This information is for the 'New World Order'. They track the habits and buying power of all "supposed" free American citizens. Well guess what three numbers are in all of these bar codes?"

I could tell Orion really enjoyed storytelling, but at the same time was dead serious about this subject. "666 - the mark of the devil. One day they will do away with money all together. They will stage something to make everyone believe there is some need for this to happen. Everything will go to an electronic system. People will be implanted, literally with a barcode, under their skin, in their hand or on their forehead. It controls and tracks everything they purchase, everywhere they go, when they sleep, breed, eliminate, whom they talk to and when. They will have complete control. Anyone who refuses this implant will be considered an enemy, they will not be allowed to purchase food, water, anything."

"As the bible says that the day will come when the 'mark of the beast' is implemented and everyone will have to choose. It will be a hard choice because if you take the mark, knowingly or not, you will have sold your soul to the devil. If you don't you will be found righteous in the eyes of God and be protected. However you will undergo many great tests, and only the strongest will remain resistant to the dark."

He continued. "Given their agenda, it is frightening beyond imagination. They will control what goes into the water, and even make you pay for water. They already put things in the water that are supposed to be good for you like fluoride. But guess what? Fluoride weakens the DNA and the immune system. So do a whole host of other things in the food and water supply. Even the fillings in your mouth serve the purpose of weakening the DNA. They have a plan for everything you can imagine and beyond. They will control who can travel and when, scan your body, see through your clothing, taking away all your basic human rights. They will initiate a level of holy wars in the middle-east that no one will understand. No one will know who is behind it or what's really going on. All countries that are not already a part of the 'New World Order' are being assaulted as we sit here, whether silently, like the war against Africa, which I can go into later, or overtly, like Iraq. These are beings that don't rest, they are relentless in their pursuit of total control."

Orion was really heated up; veins pulsed fiercely on his neck and arms. "While we are all happily asleep", he laughed, "they are plotting, devising. They are in a race against time to complete their plans and put them into action. There is still time though for all of us to realize what is happening and make sure we don't become their pawns any more than we already have been."

Alexis broke out. "Orion, I have never heard of anything like this. If it's true, it's really scary. I feel like I don't want to know about it, want to just forget what your saying!"

Her eyes looked nearly frantic, I could tell she was really panicked.

Orion smiled compassionately at Alexis and the rest who looked just as scared; the feeling of fear was palpable. "That's just it, Alexis. These beings feed off our innocence, and our ignorance.

They know that as a race, we would rather not know, to remain in the illusion of how peaceful our little safe lives are. They planned it that way, creating our need to deny truth. That way they go about their work unnoticed. They know that if we really knew what was going on, if we weren't being subjected to mind-control, we would be strong and powerful. If humans knew the truth about who they really are they might, just might, want to become that grandness, that unconquerable strength and then no one could control them ever again."

Alexis tried to smile but her brow was still furrowed. I almost felt she resented Orion for being so open with it all. I imagined this job of his, trying to get people to see, often put him in the position of being seen as the enemy. Orion smiled at me, seeming to communicate that it was okay to feel what I was feeling. I smiled back with understanding but held my head low, eyes fixed on the flames.

Sid called out from the other side of the fire. "I've seen some things in my life that make me think what you are saying is true. Plus," he touched his tummy; "I can feel it in my gut, but how is it that they control the mind?"

Orion laughed almost sardonically. "Media is their biggest tool. They fill the mind with propaganda that makes everyone believe what they want them to. They sell the American dream, the falsified idea of security, domestic enslavement. Take commercials as the first example. Keep in mind that the human consciousness, and especially the subconscious, is very programmable. Take for example the hypnotist who can program the mind of the suggested to levitate, with just one sentence. Now compound any commercial with not only repetition but also subliminal messages behind it. They tell women that their place is either at home or in a professional career, away from their children and the care they need, either way their plan is a success. They fill their minds with all the ideas of what they should be."

He raised his hand in the air, naming off. "Pretty, perfect hair, dyed even, make-up, panty-hose, heels, white teeth, nice smile. If she's not thin she should take diet pills, if she's got PMS she should take a pill ... then they teach her how she should keep house, they sell her all kinds of products for that, making it look like all that convenience makes life so happy and so easy. She doesn't think for herself, doesn't focus on growing or knowing the true power of a woman to create and be connected to earth and spirit. Rather she sends the kids off to school where they are indoctrinated from kindergarten with how they should be; quiet, obedient, staying within the lines. Again, not thinking for themselves but following the rules. She lives a life of domestic enslavement. When she has time she watches soaps, which further lull her mind to sleep."

As he spoke I got angry. This was the trap I had felt I tried to escape my entire teen years. The magazines, the idea of being perfect, flawless beauty with no mind, with no expression that was anything other than poised and calculated. I had worked so hard to be beyond that. But, I knew from eleven to seventeen, I was enslaved. Most people around me didn't realize it so they didn't seem to think anything was wrong. But for me the feeling of wrongness had been painfully strong and maddening.

Orion continued. "Little does this typical American woman know that all the products she bought are not only weakening her health, but are also the very thing that caused the breast cancer she is now fighting, because they are so full of toxic chemicals. They are also poisoning her children and the very reason they keep getting sick is because their immunity is so low. She doesn't have any idea that these toxins are destroying the planet, that in a decade from now the rivers will be so toxic fish will start dying and cancer rates will increase by say 80% worldwide. She doesn't know that she part of the problem, that by the time people start realizing what is happening the ice-caps will be melting and the oceans will rise, that storms will rage across the lands, causing famine and drought. She just goes about her happy little life. Meanwhile, she gets all her food from the store, again toxic poison, and very little, if any of it, is actually nutritional and fit for consumption."

He stopped for a deep breath. Everyone was still riveted. "She doesn't know how to grow food, or about her great grandmother's old herbal remedies, the ones that could truly heal her cancerous tumor, she never knew because every time they got sick they just took some suppressant or antibiotic. She doesn't know ten years from now those antibiotics will no longer work on a whole host of bacteria's that have grown in resistance to them."

He sat back allowing them all to take it in, there was dead-silence for a good two minutes.

Bill offered. "You haven't said much about who these people are, other than that they are the elite. Its hard for people to understand why they would do such a thing, its their world too after all."

Orion sat upright again. I noticed his right leg was bouncing up and down a little. I could see that these topics created a lot of energy in him - his warrior side. "Good point friend. In biblical terms these beings would be the fallen ones, Lucifer and his legions of darkness, the devil himself. What I am about to say will be for most of you the most startling of all. If anyone wants to leave, to take a walk, please do so now."

I looked around. Everyone was scared and angry, but they were awake. No one moved; they wanted to hear, no matter how hard it was.

He continued looking from one person to the next with his blue-eyed piercing stare. "Some of these are human beings, those that have sold their souls to darkness for money, power, and the promise of ever-lasting life. But most, most of them are not human at all. There are two main groups that control the planet, and they have since the beginning of time, and lets just say they don't need the same things nor the same atmosphere to survive that we do."

Orion continued. "As I talk, always remember that there is light and there is dark. When we talk about dark, we bring light; we release ourselves from the illusion. We should be informed, inform others. Then we should always return to light. If we focus on light, we bring more light, we create more light in ourselves. We should never stay focused on dark alone."

He glanced at me knowingly and went on. "Most of these beings are actually not human, they are over-seeing spirits controlling human-bodies, or they are shape-shifters, or cross-breeds of alien races. There are those known as the 'grays'. They come from a planet where their race is dying because they forgot how to love. So they searched the universe and found humans. They were so curious about our breeding abilities, our pro-creation." He laughed, "Because we are so good at it."

I noticed that he had glanced at me with that statement and

wished that he hadn't.

He continued. "So they began to observe us, then they began to actually manipulate us, doing experiments on countless children and adults around the world. They've taken hundreds of thousands of people up in their spacecraft and underground trying to understand us, trying to breed us and cross-breed us."

My body tensed, remembering what I'd discovered just a few days before. This reality was getting more and more surreal. Everything was so accelerated. I thought about the dolphin dreams and how they kept saying there was no more time. They wanted me to understand everything. I was beginning to see what that was about, at least I thought I did. The planet didn't have time. I was meant to help others understand, before this plan of the 'New World Order' took complete control. No wonder Orion's leg was bouncing excitedly; he was on fire with this need to teach, to help. I was almost numb with the realization that he knew everything. The universe, creation was so very complex.

Orion moved forward quickly after taking a drink of water from his thermos. "Some time ago, these grays made an agreement with the elite families that control the governments behind the government and the money systems, they became a part of the plot. They agreed to give them their high technologies, ones that offered space-travel, virus control, genetic-modification and cloning abilities, and highly advanced weapons of destruction, in exchange for underground space on earth, right here in America, for their experimentation and the use of human-beings; whom they take and choose as they like. They also made an agreement to use animals, particularly livestock. Believe me, the ways the 'NWO' uses these trades are unimaginably horrible. They are literally using and plotting to use even more deadly viruses, ones that keep humans submissive, ones that obliterate entire populations. They are breeding and cloning a massive army to take over when they are ready to implement their world agenda and declare martial law. This is just some of what they are doing. These underground facilities really exist. The biggest one is in the middle of the Nevada Desert in an area known as Area 51. They have a place there that is top-secret, and there are at least nine levels underground, each one is more terrifying then the next."

Alexis gasped and this time he asked. "What is it, what's

happening?" I hadn't expected that, and I could feel everyone's eyes on Alexis expectantly. This was all so very much for them. I hoped no one would blow a circuit with all he
was telling them.

"It's just that, last year, Luna and I ..."

She glanced at me. "Once Luna and I, and another friend of ours, to 'Burning Man', this big celebration out there in the desert, and that's where it was, Area 51. We went in these hot springs and I got the strangest feeling that we were being watched. We looked up in the sky and there were these strange glowing lights, like huge orbs, just hovering above us and we got the worst feeling, remember that Luna?"

I nodded thinking about what Orion had already told me about Area 51.

Orion nodded eagerly. "There was a reason you were there. Everything happens for a reason, always remember that."

Alexis nodded, looking at me with concern; this was a lot for her but she was handling it well.

Orion went on. "Anyway, the other race is a reptilian race."

I laughed out loud shaking my head. It was too much, too much. What was this, the universes way of confirming for me that everything I was being shown was so very, very real. Was Orion even a real person? Or was he just a hologram in front of me, there to make sure I didn't lose sight of what the masters had said. Sometimes I felt I was getting more out on edge since I met him, not more grounded, but I had to remember, he wasn't the information, he was the messenger. I should feel reassured, more than reassured, the whole thing, the way I'd met him, it was amazing.

He went on, seeing I wasn't going to speak. "That's right, imagine big lizards." He was smiling, that little boy smile that said in some way he was enjoying this work. I imagined that with his Native American heritage, that warrior energy and his expertise in martial arts, he really truly wasn't afraid of all this. "Yeah, just think of big lizards, with tails and slotted eyes, and big teeth, only they stand up, have arms and hands and are very intelligent. They're ruthless creatures, cold, calculating. They use humans, manipulate them, feed off their fear. They can look like us, they even bred with us, hybrids they're called. "

He continued. "They are the ones that truly control and dominate the elite families. They are in fact these elite families. That's right, the kings and queens of old and present are really reptilians, disguised as humans, so they can manipulate the rest of us."

Everyone seemed to be either shaking their heads back and forth or staring at Orion unbelievably. He concluded rubbing his hands together. "Okay, I think that's enough about all that for tonight. Does anyone want to talk?"

For a moment everyone was quiet. Then Bill asked. "The bible says that those that don't take the 'mark of the beast' will be protected, like you said. What more can you say about that? If they come out with this implant chip and force us to take vaccines that aren't really vaccines and all that kind of stuff, what are we supposed to do, if we can't buy food at the store, or buy gasoline or anything else?"

Orion smiled. "Well you're doing it. Starting communities like this one and the one you have in Kentucky, grow your own food, have your own water source, and essentially are not in any way dependent upon the system. I know that seems like a lot when you think about how much we rely on consumer products. We have been conditioned to think that without them we couldn't possibly be okay, but

think about our ancestors just a hundred years or two ago. They lived off the land, cared for their families, they knew how to survive. It is just harder for us because we were spoiled, so it's like detoxifying our material attachments."

Bill nodded eagerly. "That's exactly what I thought you'd say. I'm tryin' real hard. I got a few boys livin' out there with me. We're planting orchards and we've got a big garden. It is hard as could be though. I was raised on soda pop and fried food, lots of junk, my body's addicted to it."

Orion shook his head eagerly. "That's what happens, that's why cleansing is a good idea, once you get all that stuff out of your system, you won't be able to stand the sight of it."

Bill cringed. "That'll be the hard part for me, but I'm a willin'."

Orion offered. "There's more to it then just having a

community, you have to be strong inside, learn how to combat mind-control that will one day soon move through all the air ways, lulling us all back to sleep. And one day there may be a need to be mobile too, not just staying in one place."

Bill nodded, everyone else kind-of partially nodded. It was still so new to them. Orion checked in with each person then, making eye contact, letting everyone know they should make prayers before they slept and think about positive things. I knew it would be a hard night, and probably the next day too, for everyone, but it was good.

Slowly, everyone got up. People hugged each other, seeming to assure one another that nothing would get them in the night.

Bill walked directly to me. "It was so nice to meet you. Here's my card." He placed

a business card in my hand. "If you ever come back home, you have a place, anytime."

I nodded. "Thank you, I just might do that. I just can't get over the synchronicity, you being from Kentucky, right down the road from where I was born, too."

Bill shook his head smiling. "It is somethin' ain't it. God's plan in action I believe."

I shook his hand smiling. "I hope everything goes well. This was a lot to integrate wasn't it?"

Bill nodded eagerly. "It sure was!"

He turned to Orion. "Thank you so much. You have given me much validation, about all my concerns and everything."

Orion shook his hand and placed the other on his shoulder. "Be strong, walk in the light, it will prevail. It always does somehow."

No matter how things seemed, where there was love, it was always strongest, still I couldn't help but think, would it really prevail this time? The darkness seemed so strong.

While everyone else headed for their tents I decided to take a walk, look at the stars, ground myself in light before sleeping.

Orion said in a deep voice. "I imagine you're tired and don't want to talk more tonight?"

I smiled looking at the fire. "That was definitely a lot, I'm not going to sleep yet but I can't talk or process more tonight."

Orion smiled longingly. "Okay but I want to hear what came

up for you, with all those sighs, there was a lot happening there."

I looked in his eyes searchingly. "Okay then, thank you so much for talking, that must take a lot of energy."

He smiled back. "It does take a lot, but I know how to recharge my batteries. I'm fine, it's also energizing in a way. I just want people to get it. Sometimes I feel silly, talking to these little groups of people out in the jungle you know, but they are the ones that will listen. Hopefully one day there will be auditoriums full of people ready to listen."

I nodded understandingly, holding out my arms to give him a friendly hug, making sure my chest didn't touch his. When he held on a little too long I disengaged and abruptly said goodnight.

After my walk I ate some papaya, and washed off with the barrel and pail that caught rainwater from the tarp over the make-shift kitchen, returning to my tent. I laid down and drifted off easily, exhausted from the day. The council called once more...

CHAPTER TWENTY SIX

Manipulation

Where the scene picked up I learned we were watching the process of Tarcon's plan. The reptilian minions Tarcon had left upon Tara began to give birth.

In the months that followed I witnessed the horror of many births of Tarian/Reptilian offspring. Their bodies were human-looking with few noticeable reptilian features, but their spirits were born of their evil parentage. I wondered if these children would hold any grain of the light and love of the departed spirits of the Tarians.

This was one of the secret successes within Tarcon's master plan to take over Tara, for it greatly accelerated the plot.

We witnessed one of these first meetings, wherein one of the couples entered the tribal area of one group with their new child.

The couple approached Marduk (Tarcon's chosen, controlled human) lounging near a stump in the shade of his forest grove.

For a moment, even Marduk shuddered as he looked into the strange, vacant stares of the couple. The baby in the woman's arms cried and she looked angrily at it. From her mouth came a strange disgruntled utterance that Marduk did not recognize. He began to frown in suspicion, sitting up straighter.

The female of the couple quickly realized she had slipped and entered Marduk's mind binding him toward her will. He would not remember what had just happened.

The male stepped forward and spoke awkwardly. "I am Tanuka. My beloved and I live near the Great River. We come with wonderful tidings."

Marduk perked up, "What news do you bring to us?"

Tanuka said. "There are Gods that have come from the sky. They have come to protect us from the dangerous enemy. And they have also come to teach us the way to show the arrogant elders of our world how things should be. These Gods offer us protection, but we must remain indebted to their graciousness."

Marduk looked at the mother: "What debt must we pay?"

Tanuka smiled tensely. "We must simply obey these commands, giving them what they ask for. But what they offer you is much greater. As leader of these people, you will hold more power than you have dreamed of!"

Marduk looked down at the ground apprehensively. "I would like to meet them."

"Good then," replied Tanuka. "Come at midnight this very day to the cave near the great river. They are great Gods, powerful in stature, so be not alarmed by this."

That night, Marduk gathered a group of over 200 people to walk to the land near the river that soared swiftly out to sea. Later that day the twins sat in their grove listening to a report of all that had occurred by one of their elven brothers who had spied on Marduk.

After he left, the group discussed what to do with grave concern.

Fiona stood pacing before their small group, a long red dress caressing her ankles with each step. "How could it be? These Gods offer protection, from whom? Surely it can not be true, or they would have come to us as well."

The scene jumped forward, and were back with Tanuka and the group that had been gathered. "Fellow Tarians," Tanuka began, his voice echoing throughout the cave, "We are privileged to be the honored ones to tell you of the new gods who have descended to the planet." He paused, enjoying the suspense that filled the air. "We indeed believe you will all be as excited and thankful as we are. These are great gods, powerful beings who came from a distant planet. They have had experience with those who want to conquer Tara!"

"Now, bow to your new gods, show you humbleness as they come forth!"

Slowly, the Tarians all kneeled and bowed their heads to the ground.

Seven large reptilian creatures with scaly, human-reptilian faces stood behind Tanuka. One next to the other, they stood with their hands folded before them, exhibiting their controlled manner.

Then, Tarcon entered the cave from a tunnel in the back, his huge body lumbering across the cold stone floor. He strode proudly toward the others and sat on a large rock carved like a throne.

He motioned to Tanuka to give the word. Tanuka commanded the crowd. "Rise now, and meet your new gods."

Gasps erupted from the shocked onlookers.

Tanuka silenced the crowd with a simple hand gesture. "Listen now, and learn of your duties."

Tarcon waved his hand in the air with an exaggerated gesture and exclaimed. "Greetings Tarians, we are honored to be here on your planet." His deep, powerful voice easily filled the cave and moved out into the night air. "We seek your permission to help you make peace with the beings that have brought harm to your world." (Oh, how treacherously deceitful he was.)

The crowd stood with mouths open in utter confusion and fear as he continued. His words were smooth and so convincing, but nevertheless his size and look was all too intense for them to not fear him. He continued.

"Those that brought the destruction are the Stellian race. We have come to know them all-too-well on our home world. Their warriors killed most of us. We could not understand what they wanted with us."

Tarcon went on. "If you trust us and allow us to remain on your planet, we will teach you what we have learned. We will protect you."

Tanuka ordered. "Now, bow before your protectors."

One by one, they all bowed. "Good." Tarcon bellowed. "Now go quietly. We will come for you tomorrow."

Surprisingly, the session was over and I fell into my body with a huge shock. Realizing where I was, my heart beating with adrenaline. I was raging with anger, all the bad things that had ever happened to me, that I had pushed down so far racing to the surface. I cried uncontrollably, till all tears were spent. It felt detoxifying and yet exhausting. All I wanted to do was stay in bed and hide away.

CHAPTER TWENTY SEVEN

Serving

Work-trade was a serious part of me being here, and I couldn't neglect responsibility, so I willed myself out of the tent. Alexis and I worked hard in the garden, digging endless lava stones out of the extremely rich soil. The hard work was good for my body and it gave me a way to channel all the anger I was feeling. After lunch we found Orion at the edge of the forest using a machete to cut back the encroaching jungle. His burning intensity was as present as ever, his muscles bulging in the hot sun. He seemed deep in thought.

Seeing us approaching, Orion put down his machete and picked up his water bottle, taking a few large gulps.

I blurted out. "We're about to head for the beach for the day and then hitchhike into town."

He looked uncomfortable.

Alexis offered. "Do you want to come with us?"

His look almost seemed one of offense.

She tensed, "I'll give you two a few minutes while I go get my stuff."

I didn't take my eyes off Orion who responded as soon as Alexis had begun to walk away. "Why do you insist on going to that nude beach?"

I threw my hands up in the air. "I go there because I love it there. I love to swim with the dolphins and I love to be naked and free!"

Orion quickly retorted. "How can you be free when there are stoned and drugged men watching you from all directions?"

I retorted. "It doesn't matter to me how they look at me. I don't go there for that kind of attention, I don't want it. So it's easy for me to ignore it." My hands were on my hips defensively.

Orion took a deep breath as though he was losing patience. "Luna, just because you think you can ignore something doesn't mean it isn't there, or that it doesn't have an effect on you. You don't know what might be looking through the eyes of those men."

I asked. "Do you mean they might be possessed?"

"Yes, that is exactly what I mean," Orion responded, relieved that I understood.

"Well," I reflected, "Even if they are, all they are doing is looking at me. That doesn't affect me negatively!"

Orion looked exasperated. "It can and does affect you in many ways. Again you are supposed to be allowing me to teach you but you are so stubborn that you won't listen."

I searched the sky. "That's because I can't tell if you are teaching me or trying to possess me. Can't you see that is why your attraction is so confusing for me? How do I know? How do you truly know that you don't just want to prevent me from meeting someone else?"

Orion visibly withdrew his body, stepping back as though he had just been slapped. "So that's what this is about."

I sighed with frustration. "No! Anyway I have no interest in meeting anyone right now. There will be a time when I am ready, but it isn't now and it isn't with you. You are pushing me to hurt you by not respecting that I don't feel the same about you."

"That's because you ..." Orion began.

I held up my hand rejecting his words. "Oh, I know, I know, that's because I don't know who I am, right. You know what?" My voice was raised now, in anger. "I'm gonna go for a few days, probably a week. I need to be away from you for awhile. You're too intense for me. I am sick and tired of hearing about 'who I am', I'm a girl, I'm 19!"

Orion looked really hurt and turned his head away.

Apologetically, I offered, "Look, I'm sorry. I don't mean to be harsh. That's not who I am. You just keep pushing me. Don't you see?"

Orion looked suddenly like a young boy that had been shamed. "I'm sorry if you feel that I'm pushing, I just care about you so much. I want to be with you Luna, to feel you in my arms, to have you as my wife."

I was stunned beyond belief. "What? Orion…No, no, you are meant to be my teacher and nothing more." I was boiling with anger.

He gave me a such a look of devastation but gulped back tears. "Luna, you just don't realize yet who we are to each other. I can't control you. I just wish you could see it."

I was staring at the ground impatient and too upset to utter a word.

Realizing he wasn't getting anywhere he only said. "Will you still be gone for a week?"

I hesitated, wondering if I should just leave for good, but god I needed that breathwork. I knew it held the key to everything. He would just have to get over himself. I resolved to make sure I did everything I could to not be attractive to him and never lead him on.

I said only" I gotta go." My tone was cold and I hoped he'd get it. I was not for him!

Orion nodded and I saw the look of fear in his eyes. "Will you really come back?"

I nodded yes and he tried to muster a smile. "Can I hug you?"

I hesitated but he was just so sorry looking, it was to much. He held me way to tightly, not wanting to let go, I pulled back quickly and simply said. "See you in a week."

I sensed the tension in Alexis. "Sorry that took so long, I didn't mean to keep you waiting."

Alexis saw that I was very distressed. "That's okay, I was just beginning to wonder what in the world was going on between you two! It feels like blazing fire. Are you sure that isn't passion?"

I pulled back and smiled through my tears. "I don't even know how I'm handling it, it's all so intense. I just don't feel that with him, he is beautiful and a dream for lots of women, I'm sure Lexy, but I see myself with someone else. I can't describe it, but I feel it."

She hugged me tightly. "He's intense alright!"

We laughed and went to get our stuff.

As I was leaving my tent Orion suddenly called out from behind me and I spun around. He put down his tool and reached into his pocket, pulling something out, looking into my eyes searchingly. "Here, hold this and close your eyes."

I looked down at the small crystals as he placed them in my hand, noticing that he had a few in his hand too. At first the crystals just felt smooth and cool. Closing my eyes I felt energy racing up my arm. It was tingling, almost electric.

Opening my eyes, I saw that Orion was turning one of his crystals over and over again in his palm. "The energy you feel is our connection. I was sending your crystals love through this one. When you go on your journey, wherever it is you are going, I want you to take your crystals with you. If you keep yourself protected in all the ways you need to, the crystals will never leave you. But if you do anything that puts you or your energies at risk, you will instantly lose the crystals."

I once more thought he was being very dramatic.

I smiled. "Thank you. They are very beautiful," and then confidently, " I won't lose them."

Later that day, after hours of hitchhiking, we arrived at a nude beach on the Kona side of the island that I had heard of. It was a small beach, set back in a tiny cove. The white sand was smooth and warm beneath our feet. A small inviting bay gave way to the vast sea. Beyond, the sun was just beginning to set.

I turned to Alexis: "Have you ever been in the ocean as the sun sets into it?"

Alexis shrugged no. "Well," I suggested, smiling. "Let's go."

Taking off our clothes we ran toward the calm turquoise waters. There was no one else on the beach and I felt so good to go without a suit. This was how it should be!

Sunset was amazing! The huge glowing ball of red gracefully sank into the horizon. I gave thanks for the incredible beauty of Hawaii and for my sister companionship; it was nice not to be alone. Laying down on my bag, I fell into the familiar trance state and lifted off.

CHAPTER TWENTY EIGHT

The Teachings

Tarcon had not been idle; the moment had come for him to implement the next stage of his plan.

We watched on as Tarcon stood before a group.. "Tarians, you have done well. Be proud of yourselves."

They slapped each other on the back and smiled goofily at each other.

He continued. "You have shown yourselves worthy of our knowledge."

He carried on. On our world the gods took over; after more than 1,000 years of their tyranny, we finally understood how we could appease them."

The crowd was unflinching, hanging on his every word. "The gods, as we have come to know them, need food, they need nourishment just as you need nourishment. Theirs is simply a different kind of energy."

He chose his words carefully. "While you need only fresh fruits and water to survive, the gods need emotional energy to live, they feed off the adrenaline and sheer fear that terror, bloodshed, and death creates."

The crowd gasped, shuddered, and winced. "This is why they harm others and create chaos. It is not personal to anyone or anything in the universe. It is simply what they need to exist."

The crowd was shocked, but with such innocence. I wanted to scream in my seat, it was too much to see, all of it.

He was manipulative in such a way that they were so coaxed and it seemed he held control over their minds already. "Listen carefully, for I am about to share with you the greatest of all knowledge. We learned that if we offered something as often as the 'gods' need it, they leave us to our own lives."

He said nothing further, only looked over the crowd with a solemn expression.

Tanuka moved the suspense forward. "What is it, O Great One, that you gave?"

Tarcon didn't hesitate, showing that he expected the group to believe without any thought, "Sacrifice."

The group, confused, looked to each other, it was a word spoken in their language but not one they had heard before. "What does it mean?" Someone called out from the back.

Tarcon resonded. "To offer something up… in this case, a human life."

Gasps of astonishment spread through the crowd and they began to speak over each other.

Tarcon continued, breaking through the loud panic. "Think about it! You can either live in fear that any day you or your children could be walking through the forest," - at this he snickered to himself, "and be attacked, left to die alone …"

Once more the crowd responded with gasps and muffled shrieks. "Or, you can choose someone to offer to the 'gods'. The honor you show to them will appease them greatly."

Knowing where their thoughts were going, he concluded. "And think of the one who offers their life, how proud they should be to have such courage, not fearing death or pain. It is not about the lives that one saves but the sheer courage they exhibit. Surely this does not go unnoticed in their next life, where they will gain more power for the sacrifice."

The crowd grew silent, each person contemplating the shocking revelations.

"Rise," He commanded. "The 'gods' are already appeased for now. In two days we will meet here, for the first ritual sacrifice."

In the next days, the followers lived on, but there was nothing they thought they could do but agree.

The twins were alerted to the situation and held council with all they could, only to be meet with dead ears. Tarcon held them under his sway and there was nothing that could be done about it. It was all so new to the twins, they themselves were petrified as well. How would they stop this?

Marduks group had been convinced, that was all there was to it. That third day the crowd entered and knelt before him in obeyance. Tarcon was pleased with how easily they took to it.

After a few moments, he told them to rise. As though in a dream, the group methodically stood up, arms hanging limply at their sides. To the right of the throne, an altar had been created. A large flat stone now lay on the ground. That was all - no ornamentation - just a cold flat rock.

Tarcon held his hands over his head. "Call upon the dark-lord now, for he is watching! Offer yourselves up to him, show him your strength and worthiness. Like you, he requires sustenance. Just as life has been given to you, so too shall you willingly give it!"

The group began to wave their arms in the air, some gyrating their bodies, all calling out their praises. It was clear that each one thought it a noble cause to give to - something they should be proud of. The energy in the group rose to a frenzy of excitement mixed with fear, none knowing how entranced they were by the powerful sway Tarcon now held over them. He sat back and let his head hang. All were so involved with their own actions, they did not see the reptilians shake as they let the mounting energy course through them. Without motioning for the crowd to stop Tarcon pointed out a petite woman in the middle of the crowd to Tanuka. In a frenzy, she screamed out to the unseen dark-lord. "Take me! I am worthy, take me!"

Tanuka sauntered through the crowd, stopping at the chosen woman, pulling her by the arm through the crowd.

The petite woman with brown hair and slanted eyes stood before the throne, nervous and aroused.

Looking across the crowd ominously, Tarcon hid the sheer pleasure racing through his cold blood. "Here is your first sacrifice. A woman of great courage stands before you."

He taunted them, provoking them to want to please him and the dark-lord even more. "Bow down before your unseen 'god'."

Tarcon motioned Tanuka to the altar.

"Send your praises with your sister. You are one with her in her noble endeavor."

He called out over the bowed crowd. "Through her life you will gain appeasement in the eyes of the dark-lord."

"Not one of you look up. This time you shall not see the sacrifice with your eyes. You must build your courage for that."

The crowd didn't flinch; he was provoking their horrid curiosity.

Suddenly one of the reptilians handed a dagger to Tanuka. He looked into the eyes of the now terrified woman, and his eyes changed, no longer human but slanted and yellow - 'reptilian'. The steel knife pierced violently into her chest, blood squirting everywhere.

The sacrificial woman let out a blood-curdling scream that echoed in the hills beyond. In the moment of death she saw the truth, who he really was, how they had all been fooled. Tarcon withheld a laugh, feeding off her mounting fear. Tanuka plunged the dagger into her heart just as she let out another blood-curdling scream.

With wicked grins three of the reptilians dragged the body from the altar to the forest. None were to see what occurred there. Silence hung over the crowd as they awaited his word; terrified.

Tarcon solemnly spoke. "Rise now. The deed is done! You can feel it in the air; the dark-lord and his kind are pleased."

Suddenly the screen was blank leaving me with the council a moment to integrate what had just been witnessed. I was sick beyond anything I'd ever known.

CHAPTER TWENTY NINE

Hope

I woke to the warm sun on my face; the soft lapping waves a sound so soothing after all I'd just seen.

I got up and walked into the water, swam and then lay in the early morning sun aware of eyes on me, but undisturbed. Holding the crystals Orion had given me, I wanted to wash them in the water and pray about all I'd seen. How could I ever make a difference in this world, to wake people up to the truth of our world, our potential. How could I become that potential, more than a limited human but somehow powerful and invincible, capable of leading others, even. Something was waking up in me, a fire, a will that I had never known. I walked toward a tide pool, thinking I might cleanse the sparkling stones, as crystals loved saltwater and sunlight.

Suddenly I tripped and the crystals went sailing through the air. Baffled as to why I stumbled, I quickly resumed a graceful composure. I needed to be so perfect, that was still there, I might not wear make-up, but I still believed I had to be perfect in the eyes of others. Luckily I saw approximately where the crystals had landed and quickly moved toward them, searching the surface of the sand, moving further and further out from where I was quite sure they had landed.. Frustrated and panicked, I sat back on my heels, searching the surface for anything glistening - there was nothing.

I got a sick feeling and, as I looked to the back on the beach, where there was grove of trees I knew why. Sitting on one of the logs there, a naked guy was openly watching me. He held his erection in both hands and was stroking himself rapidly. I felt like I was going to be sick.

I gasped and called out in disgust, alarming Alexis as I ran for my towel.

Alexis yelled out. "Yuck!" Quickly she threw her sarong around her shoulders.

I ran towards my friend and we sat hugging each other quietly in disbelief, both of us trembling. After a few moments we both sat back, both staring wide-eyed out to sea. We were together, and felt safe to camp, though a little uneasy. It would take me a long time though to shake that terrible image of this guy masturbating as he watched me.

In the morning we would make our way back to Orion's. I knew this was not the night, I just needed more time out of his fiery presence.

CHAPTER THIRTY

Attack

Tarcon stood again before a group gathered basking in the silent trance he held them in. He snickered to himself thinking about what he was going to do next.

"Many of you know," he began from his throne, "that those that will not join you live among the dwarves and elven beings. This is not right. You must all be united in your intentions. The dark-lord may decide to still attack given their rebellious nature."

He paused for added suspense. "You must drive away the dwarves and elves."

Cheers rose in the crowd, drawn in once more by Tarcon's power. "They are too selfish to offer themselves as sacrifice for the good of all of you. This is not acceptable."

The crowd clapped again as all began to see his clever logic. "You must capture one of the elves, bring them here for sacrifice, then you will see how they fight and selfishly wish to live while one of you must die!"

Anger mounted as he continued gripping them all in his form of hypnotism. "Bring one to me at once. Warn the others that if they remain there, they too will be offered as sacrifice." Without a word, the large crowd ran from the meadow, jeering each other on, racing in single file toward the elven lands. They looked dirty and corrupt, a far cry from the beauty of the original life on Tara.

I watched in agony as two men pounced on one of the delicate, fair skinned elves. Tanuka rushed forward and tied the hands and feet of the struggling elf. He motioned for the two men to drag him to the circle. The other elves stopped in their tracks, but their captured brother cried out passionately for them to save themselves. Reluctantly, they ran for the forest while tears of grief ran down their pale cheeks.

The following events sped by quickly. The elf was sacrificed, and the crowd cheered wildly, glazed with the power of their evil new leader.

The following morning, Tarcon had organized the same ritual, only this time with the dwarves. The dwarves ran for the mountains and the caves that Divine Mother and Father had instructed them to go towards in case of danger. Just as with the elves, one of them was caught, while the others, having no choice, fled in fear.

The twins sat in circle, on the quiet white sand beach. At first they were quiet, watching the calm sea, the turquoise waters bringing them a sense of safety. It seemed that yet another wave of darkness had begun to move over the planet. The twins felt within their collective wisdom the depth of oneness that they knew; it was so loving, so loyal and holy. Separated, independent existence was so different, so cold, and very frightening for each of them. It was only in their protected circle that they felt completely at ease.

The twins talked about how much darkness had grown and how it had been impossible to reach those who had succumbed to the terrible trickery of Tarcon.

Sunta cried out to the heavens "How can we forget, how can we let go of all that we cherish?" Her voice rang out with deep passion, the passion born of leaping flames and dancing embers. "Tell us Great Spirit, show us how, how to let go, and be strong."

Sunraya stood and joined her sister, adding her chant. "Let us never forget, never forget what has been. May we seek always to find higher and higher light, and bring that back to Tara once more."

The twins sang out to the night sky. "Water, Air, Earth, Fire, and Spirit, we all are one, we are one."

Io and Ama appeared. They looked sad. Io began. "Indeed,

children darkness has gone too far and the poles will shift."

The children wept, the thought of their world rent asunder.

Their parents shared their plan, how they, the Children of One would be protected. It was a long night, as they listened attentively, cried, and mourned their world.

In the morning they awoke, lying hand in hand, their bodies often overlapping each others', a maze of smooth skin, soft curves, deep beauty. The sun rose majestically over the Lemurian Sea, flooding the earth with a soft red glow.

Wishing only to fulfill the guidance of Io and Ama, the Children withdrew from their place of deep prayer. They traveled across the lands, sticking together. They first approached a group under Tarcon's rule that lived deep in the jungle nearby. They hardly recognized these people, their bodies were covered with dirt and their hair was disheveled, faces were distorted into strange shapes, revealing the thoughts of the darkness they now held.

Walking silently up to the group, they caught them by surprise. Several turned and gasped at the brilliance of the twins, a few even winced. One woman began to shrink back towards the shadows of the forest, as though afraid of them.

Ayia stepped forward and began with a loving smile, reaching his arms out towards them. His brothers and sisters stood strongly behind him, the small children held safely in their arms. "Dear friends, please do not be afraid. We bring warning from Divine Mother and Father. All of life on Tara is in danger because of the way you are acting and thinking. You must all choose to begin the process of returning to the Law of One, whereby you act for the good of all, committing to this within your hearts. Otherwise the magnetic poles will shift, causing the ocean to rise, drowning our Great Motherland under the sea."

This drew little response, so Ayia continued. "Your bodies will die and you will be forced to see the results of your careless actions. Divine Mother and Father will sit on high and send forth love and compassion. If you choose to find humbleness you will find them there, you can return to our parents, for you are also their children. With forgiveness, they will show you the way of the light!"

The group snickered and sneered while the twins looked on with shock and compassion.

An rose her hands towards the sky as she spoke. "Again, we

give you warning, within one day this will all happen. You have
a choice, return to the light, promise to live in oneness and work
diligently to create this from this day forward!"

The group made grumbled comments that they either did not
believe the threats, or did not care. The twins left, unable to make
any difference, they gave up hope.

At the end of the day they had returned to their beach. Once
again, they stood in a sacred circle, sending prayer to Tara, awaiting
the next orders from On High.

The screen slowed and turned to blackness. The session
was over. It was all so very sad. People couldn't even reason
for themselves, to choose light when their minds were so muddled.
I had seen enough in any case, rest was a welcome reprieve.

CHAPTER THIRTY ONE

Desire

I woke once more to the rising sun. It was time to head back to Orion's camp. It was nearly dark when we finally arrived, after a long day of hitch hiking across the large island. Alexis headed immediately for her tent, tired from the long day. I unloaded my food supplies in the kitchen and went to Orion's tent. I saw his sandals outside and knew he was there. I noticed that my heart beat a little faster, anticipating our reunion.

Nervously I called out. "Anyone home? Knock, knock?" Orion quickly unzipped his tent and looked up at me, smiling radiantly and clearly overjoyed. His hair was wet, hanging loosely around his bare chest.

His deep voice offered warmly. "You have returned just as you said you would." He smiled that smile that hinted of a little boy inside the vastly mature male adult.

I smiled down at him, cocking my head to the side. "Did you think I wouldn't?"

Orion gulped. "I prayed with all my heart that you would." I looked deeply into his soft, blue eyes. I had resolved after the crystal incident to try to be more open to him, less defensive.

Breaking the silence I asked. "Is it okay if I come in?"

I suspected the difference in my openness was obvious. Orion didn't hide his excitement. "Yes, yes. Come, please." He moved to the side, making room for my entrance.

I crawled inside the tent to sit down across from Orion who quickly pulled a tank top over his head. I could feel his gaze upon my body. The silence seemed to span eons between us as we held each other's open gaze.

Finally he whispered. "You are so beautiful. You look like a Goddess right now. You always do. And now your eyes look even deeper, clearer."

Touching my bare knee gently, he asked, "Will you tell me of your journey?"

I realized I had been very excited to talk to him about everything.

He indeed had something to say. "If I had been there, I would have taken his head off."

I smiled, touched by his warrior protective nature. His eyes burned. "Now, will you believe me, will you please just let me protect you? You are like a jewel to be cherished."

He sounded very serious, almost desperately so. "There is something inside of you that must be protected. Can you allow this now?"

I puffed out my bottom lip and blew my breath out, giving Orion a rather mischievous look, mixed with acceptance and resistance. "Yes, I will listen more to what you have to say. I will be humble."

Orion laughed. "You mean you won't be stubborn?"

I laughed throwing my head back, blushing as I did so. "I will try, I will try. But just so you know, I am not so special. I'm just a person like anyone else."

Orion offered. "Humility is a wonderful quality, but insecurity is not. We will work on that. Are you ready to move to the next level of your training?"

I nodded enthusiastically and he continued. "It will mean that you will have to stay here, no more running away."

My blood was beginning to boil, as hard as I tried to stay calm around him. "I wasn't running. I just needed time."

Orion put his finger to my lip and I grew silent. Once more he took on the deep serious tone I had grown used to. "You will have to stay here and practice. You can't waste more time. I need to take you to other parts of the island."

I felt excitement rise in my abdomen as I clasped my hands together. "I want that with all my heart, to just focus and become the highest I can."

For a moment I thought of Alexis and added. "I guess Al will be okay. She's going to stay with Jerry tomorrow and soon she'll be going home.

Orion took a deep breath looking deeply into my eyes. "Desire, that fuels the path. The greater your desire the greater your growth. Time does not exist; how fast you grow only depends upon your heart's desire. Always remember that."

Orion closed his eyes for a moment and I respectfully looked away, watching a candle's soft flame. I looked up only when he had begun to speak again. "We must begin by giving you an experience of feeling your energy field and knowing yourself beyond your body. For that we must go outside. Do you have some pants you can put on?"

I nodded and Orion told me to meet him on the martial arts platform.

He had put his long hair up in a bun as he looked down at my attire.

Motioning to my pants he asked. 'Can you easily move in those?"

I nodded, I could. I looked up at the bright moon above, smiling.

"What I am about to do with you usually takes someone several very disciplined years to build up to. But because of who you are, you are going to go into this very quickly. I am going to hold an energy field for you, open a door if you will. All you have to do is focus and work hard." I nodded, sensing that something huge was about to happen, feeling anticipation as adrenaline began to rush through my veins. Orion walked around the platform in silence. I felt he was praying. He then asked me to close my eyes and make a prayer to connect with my higher self, that part of me that existed beyond time and space, and also to my spirit teachers. The prayer, he said, should be one of respect and asked for assistance in my growth.

I closed my eyes and felt the familiar connection and I could feel a higher presence with me, though I could not have given words to the experience.

When I opened my eyes Orion was standing at my side. He indicated that I should get into the same wide, low stance that he was in. I did as he had and focused eyes on the dim horizon.

Orion spoke deeply. "I want you to focus your breath, let it intensify as the stance becomes harder to hold. Don't come out of the stance no matter what. Allow it to purify, to cleanse you."

I focused on my breath, feeling the strength of the stance. My face tensed with pain. Then, I began to feel my mind panic, the burning was too great. I could not bear it. I wanted with all my heart to hold the stance but was ready to give up.

Just then I felt Orion's knees under my legs. I could not lower my legs. His strong hold was keeping me there. Through the pain I heard his words, deep and calm. "Don't give up, keep breathing, you need to keep going."

I wanted him to move, to let me drop out of it - it was way too much!

I cried out. "Let me stop." My voice shook through tears and racing panic.

Orion's words were calm and steady. "It is only sensation. You must make your mind strong. Use the pain to learn to control your mind, and your emotions. Then they will not have control over you. If you harness the emotions something will happen, you will begin to experience your body as pure energy."

I wanted to be strong. I spoke with a panicked, but determined tone. "Let me go, I'll hold it on my own."

At once his strong embrace dropped away, I felt like I was gong to fall over but kept my mind steady, burning through the unbearable pain.

I moved and suddenly the pain was back. My body shook.

As though aware of that thought Orion spoke sharply. "You must learn to keep your mind unlimited, don't focus on limitation. Hold longer. Be determined."

The sensation of pain had returned in the moment I thought of limitation. I kept breathing though my mind yelled out with pain. The burning was within my whole body. I shook violently though I could not move out of the stance. Finally Orion slowly released his knees and pulled me up to standing.

DESIRE

His voice seemed to echo throughout my body "Breath calmly until you feel stable."

The experience had been so intense I fluctuated between wanting to cry and feel comfortable, to feeling powerful beyond humanness

Orion eventually said softly. "Come with me."

In the tent I lay down, feeling every cell become ecstatic, one with everything, separate from nothing, vast, incomprehensibly vast. I felt my mind soar beyond limitation to a place where I knew all things as one. It was a place where all information was known and understood. It was a place of eternal wisdom and eternal strength. It was the place of pure knowing. It was the Beyond.

Life, existence I understood; I remembered, far more than just the physical realm - it was eternal, brilliant, and vast.

CHAPTER THIRTY TWO

Focus

That morning I found Orion in the field, chopping away at weeds with a passionate stance. Orion offered me a coconut as he began to speak. "I want to take you to the island of Molokai to continue your training."

He explained that it was the most sacred island, home to the Goddess of Air; that was so unbelievably amazing to me. He said that it was the most powerful of the islands and because of that was used by the spiritual masters to train. We were to camp on a beach and do nothing but practice and climb coconut trees. Interestingly, it was the beach where the sacred dance of Hula was said to have been created.

We were to leave the next day. Though this was all so sudden, I was ready for it, a change would be so good!

The next day, Sid dropped us off at the airport. The flight was quick and easy. We arrived on the tiny island mid-morning. I enjoyed the cab ride from the tiny airport into the small one town street. Later we got a cab to the other side of the island. There was a large, really nice lawn to camp on, just before a long beach, as Orion had explained it to be.

We pitched our two little tents and made camp. The rest of the day was spent with Orion teaching me how to climb a coconut tree. He said it would be one of the greatest lessons I'd ever had. Given that I'd always been fit and agile, I started out cocky, thinking it would be no sweat.

I looked up the long lean 50 foot tree and smiled, excited for something new to learn. But I couldn't get up more than three feet without breaking into a sweat, panting and whining. It was so incredibly difficult, every muscle was shaking and burning. After about twenty tries he said I could give up for the day. I had three days to learn the art of climbing and gather my own food, and therefore be able to eat. The training had been stepped up and there was no going back. I was determined to break through limitations, stop the whining, and focus my mind. I would climb a tree if it were the last thing I did.

At day three I finally made it up my first tree. I could hardly believe I'd finally made it, my muscles had never been so sore, and I had never felt so scared but I had done it! And having done it I realized what a challenge it was, I wondered what most people would have done, thinking a lot of people would have said this is crazy and headed for town. But the feeling of victory of self was also not one I was meant to keep. Orion helped me understand that also had to be released, just do what needed to be done and be humble, and… I could eat!

For the next two weeks of unrelenting practice from 3:00 am to 10:00 pm I trained: rising before the sun, doing my breath practice for four hours on the beach, before eating a single coconut, which of course I had to climb for. Those first days were so hard, I thought I would die, but eventually I grew strong in the difficult act, and though it was never effortless, it was manageable. I spent the day hours training in martial arts with Orion, learning combinations of many styles and their philosophy, The nunchucks were my favorite, and I soon developed an adept ability to swing those little weapons around without knocking myself silly.

I loved the camp spot so much I felt I could just live there, set back from the 4 mile long white sand beach, which was breathtaking and extremely powerful.

After two weeks I could laugh at myself when I thought of the first day I tried to climb the tree. My body and mind were strong and unyielding. No matter that my ego wanted to yell and kick and scream each dreadfully early morning I got up, shaking it off and headed for the beach. The first thing I would do is look up at the sky. Every morning it was filled with cloud beings, tiny little faces watching me, there was no doubt about it. No matter 'my ego' wanted to eat chocolate cookies rather than sit in breath and focus all day, I overcame all of its little antics and even it's most desperate strong-willed tantrums. I felt clear headed and light. Not eating anything but coconuts had made my body pure. I had never even imagined I could have felt so pure in my whole

life. I had so much energy sometimes I had to run up and down the beach just to expend some of it. Orion reminded me often not to waste the body's energies, but to let it fuel the purification of the cells and use the energy for purpose, but it felt like I had energy for that and energy to run.

The day of my test came and I stood side by side with Orion watching the choppy waves. "Don't you know how badly I want this? What more do I need to do to prove my desire?" I was nearly breathless with yearning.

Orion's stance was wide and low, his piercing gaze burned through me. Since we'd come to Molokai he was nothing but teacher, true and pure. I found it relieving though I knew in my heart his hope was that when I came through the training I would rise as what ever being he thought it was I was meant to be, and stand with him as the woman who wanted him.

"You must want it so badly that it aches, that every fiber of your being is yelling out for freedom." His eyes burned with so much fire, I flinched, not feeling I held the same passion.

I was nearly panting, searching his eyes. "It is all I want. I want to return home, to soar on the grids of light."

Orion smiled, his arms folded boldly across his wide chest. "Bring your stance low. Look to the horizon and find your spot. Let the fire burn through your cells awakening memory of light, purifying all that seeks to pull you down."

I held my gaze steady, knowing if my eyes shifted I would never make it through the stance. I could feel the pull of weakness within me, the voice that said, 'but we are nothing more then a little helpless girl, we are not strong, not wise.'

I steadied myself, "Don't let it control you, burn through it." I sharpened my mind. Why did it hurt so much to focus, why did the mind panic wanting to be anywhere but present? I wondered this even as the burn set in with more intensity. There was no space to think, never-mind, just focus!

The back of my legs instinctively found the parallel alignment with the earth. My gaze burned into the horizon out beyond the reach of the stormy sea, much like the maze of my emotion. The burning sensation came, first lightly, and then with such intensity it was like fire.

Orion stood still at my side attentively. "Repeat within your mind, Fire, Fire, Fire. When the burn is so great you want to get out of the stance yell - fire! Don't let go."

I held the stance until my legs shook violently and sweat poured down my face. My eyes burned, my throat burned. The weak one within taunted. 'This is not us, we can't be that strong, that brave. Just let go, let go.'

Orion whispered in my ear. "Strength is in the light of your own mind. The pain is the illusion. The only thing that truly exists is this moment. When you get in your stance, you are in the moment, not the pain the moment before, or the pain in the next moment."

Orion's words were like a burning light in my mind. "Beyond four minutes you will experience your body as light, you will have crossed the threshold of controlled reality. When you can do that, you will be able to do anything."

I yelled, piercing the empty sky with rage filled strength, "Fire, Fire!" There was never a soul on that massive stretch of beach, I was so grateful to the solitude it offered, and the great expanse.

That was it; I was out and beyond. There was the first sound, the sound of all creation, there were the masters downloading me with information at the speed of light, seeding it into my cells. And then there was void, pure consciousness, pure silence - covered by the continual echo of the sound of all of creation oscillated at once. There was no way to describe how I even knew this was what I was experiencing, not logically, not humanly, it was pure knowing, omniscience, and it was more like home than anything I had ever known. It was home, the place I had come from, would always return to.

Orion stood smiling gleefully. "You did it. See I told you that you could do it!"

I resumed my discipline. "I won't lose my focus. What do I

need to do now?"

Orion pointed to a cliff at the end of the long beach, his gaze serious and deep. "There is a cove there, a place where only the highest Kahunas trained, even up until the recent past, it is the place my own Kahuna Teacher took me for the highest initiation. These Teachers both present and past are with you now. You have passed your test and will train under their guardianship."

I nodded, noting how different I felt, my unyielding stance, my mind no longer full of ceaseless chatter, I felt somehow ancient, wise beyond my twenty years, reverent - that was it, I felt reverence.

Orion motioned for me to follow, his gaze still a steady stream of focus. We climbed over ancient lava rock for a good ten minutes before he stopped, pointing to a ledge. "That is the spot. Stay here until it is done." His voice gave no hint of emotion.

I peered carefully over the ledge. The spot he had pointed to was nothing but a five foot long, three foot wide little ledge, about five feet down the cliff. I could see there were footholds to get down, but not easily. The drop from there was about 50 feet, to jagged cliffs below.

I looked out to sea. The sun burned high in the sky but the wind was strong, keeping me cool enough. Orion handed me a water bottle. "Look over there". I followed his gaze to the right-hand cliff. "Do you see it?"

I relaxed my eyes and looked with a soft gaze. An enormous male face was etched into the entirety of the enormous rock cliff. It looked like an ancient chief. His eyes moved and I could see his nose and jaw move with breath. I attuned myself to this powerful being, staying beyond fear's intimidated reach, in reverence, in the moment. I closed my eyes, bowing. "Who are you?"

I felt the great one's words in my mind. "I am the ancient guardian Kahuna of this sacred land. I will watch over your travels while you train here."

I turned and Orion was gone. I brought my gaze back to the cliff. The Kahuna still watched me. It was so overwhelming but I centered my thoughts.

I straightened my back, uncrossed my legs, then re- crossed them, and brought my hands to my heart. From the vantage point of the Kahuna, I must have been so very tiny.

I offered. "Divine Mother, Divine Father, great kahunas,

dolphins, and whales protect and guide me. May I release my lineage's bound karma from my cells. I send them all my love and compassion. Now it is time for me to breath freely, to be free."

I placed my hands in the position for opening breath. I did not end the cycle until my body burned with fire once more. Sweat poured down my face and I felt my cells begin to spin faster. The moment approached and came. I drew the activation breath, eyes steadily closed. I was gone, flying in the corridors of ecstatic energy. My upper body shot forward, actually nearly leapt with the power the breath created. My head slammed hard on the rock, my arm dangling over the cliff, only I didn't feel it because I was gone, completely gone. My body wobbled in the activation, shaking back and forth threatening to fall off its already precarious perch. First I felt the ecstasy, and then heard the primordial sound.

I flew to the far reaches of the controlled reality. The dark-lord's demons were there guarding the gates. I'd never heard of them, never seen them, but somehow I knew them.

They were caught unsuspecting. "I see who you are. You are nothing to me. You will never stop me."

I flew past them feeling invincible at that point, thinking I was probably laughing gleefully.

I came back to my body wobbling but that wasn't anything new. I had hit hard. Hard enough that I would have fallen were it not for the angel that kept me held safely there, that was certain. How amazing, I would never forget this, ever! I was hanging over the cliff.

I had fallen and an angel had caught me, held me there - this topped everything I'd ever gone through. I knew it more than anything I had ever known; if I had not been watched over and caught like that, I would be dead. My broken bones and blood would have been shattered below. I laughed and laughed until tears streamed down my face. I had soared beyond the guardians of time, gone further than ever, I had a feeling no one had done that in a long time. I had set myself free. I knew without a doubt what this was. The physical was not what people were taught to believe it was. I would never die, ever. Not until I was meant to, and even then, the soul lived on.

I yelled out, unafraid, to the dark-ones and all their kind. "You see me here? I feel you watching me now. You will never stop me, never! I will never die!"

I stretched my arms out to my side in triumphant victory. "I remember who I am!"

When I returned to the camp I found Orion reading on a picnic table. He watched me walk in, striding joyfully. I sat and told him the tale, a big smile on my face throughout. He told me then that I was different, that my entire voice was different. He knew I had remembered who I was. That night, I lay under the stars, feeling free, liberated. The Council called once more.

CHAPTER THIRTY THREE

Keys Of Light

I found myself in my seat with the Council, ready once more to travel. I felt I was receiving a quick review of the past events. I remembered then that the twins were preparing for their departures. My heart sank low, but I forced myself to look at the screen.

As usual the entrancing images there pulled me in. I could not look away, no matter how hard or shocking anything with the twins ever was. I was spellbound.

Over the next several days the twins spent time in constant meditation, seeding the information into the planet for the future. The other original Children of One that had remained true to the law of the one joined them in the important endeavors.

On the first day, deep in concentration they gathered in a cave high up on the side of one of their great mountaintops. They sat around a quartz crystal the size of a refrigerator. Placing their hands on the smooth surface they sent the entire history of the planet, including the creation and origins, into the molecules of the crystal. This crystal was to become the earth keeper, and would hold the information sacredly, bringing the knowledge forth to the right people in a future time. Perhaps to the lineage of the Children of Light, or even themselves in their very same bodies, or possibly reincarnated.

On the second day they created a symbolic language based upon sacred geometry, which also held the keys to the history and the light of the inner-self. These symbols were inscribed upon rocks at various places of great power on Lemuria's mountaintops. These coded symbols would be read and understood by those of future times who were in some way a part of the lineage of light.

On the third day the group gathered with the whales and dolphins that would remain on the planet. These beings had agreed to be the keepers of memory as well, constantly radiating the memories through the oceans of the planet for the future and what might come.

On the fourth day they visited their favorite places across the great land, always surrounding themselves in a circle of protective light, offering respects and love. The protective shield took a lot of energy to sustain and was not something they could endure for long.

After saying farewell to their extended family, the twins rested in their precious little home near the sea. They needed to be rejuvenated and prepare for what was to come. The next day the circle of eight and their children sat on the beach, waiting to be greeted by the Divine presence of their beloved parents.

In the midst of their sacred circle the images of Ama and Io appeared. "Greetings Children," Io said tenderly as he smiled at each of them. "We know that you have wished to receive our guidance. We can help you create new life here, but it must be you who issues forth the divine call for this planet, you must make many decisions in the times to come that will seem of great immensity to you. The seed of darkness is already within the off-spring of the tribes, and by free-will that must be as it is, already done, a sad but true fact for all of us."

They all nodded with grave seriousness, attentively awaiting the guidance to continue. "My Children, as you know there are other lands separate from the Great Motherland. These islands and the smaller continent to the north exist uninhabited and unexplored by any of you. It is now an option that some of you journey out to these new lands to begin anew. If you choose the plan we've created, six of you will go forth with your children, and two of you will stay to hold energy here."

There was a pause as he gave them a moment to breath in all that he had said. "The people of this land must choose their destiny. It is no longer your responsibility to carry energy for them."

There was silence for a long time as the twins integrated what this meant for them.

They had to focus on being positive, imagining the opportunity this was to create anew and to be released from the karma of the other Tarians, at least for now.

Father gave further instructions. "Ayia and An you shall journey, with nothing more than your bodies and the clothing you wear, out into the great western sea. You will be guided to a small island where you shall live in harmony with the elements and each other. There you will heal the wounds of the past and evolve as you must."

The Twins of Air felt a shiver of hope and fear move through them and then simply bowed in acceptance and understanding.

"Fiona and Rasha you shall stay here, along with your children, living high atop Crystal Mountain. There you will remain in safety regardless of what will happen as the planet cleanses. While you are there, you will be able to heal the pain and separation that you feel. In time you will see what you must do". Fiona and Rasha also bowed in humble acceptance of their fate.

"Summersara and Sunta - you shall take your children in canoes to the eastern seas and follow the guidance of the whales who sing the history of your world. You will come to a great and mighty land, becoming the first inhabitants there. Living in harmony, you will come to know the mysteries of the land and sea until one day further understanding of how you will evolve life will come to you as well."

The twins bowed and returned to their inward stillness as they awaited the guidance for Kané and Sunraya.

The Twins of Earth were soon addressed. "Kané and Sunraya - your task is to journey far into the earth. Follow the caverns at the top of Emerald Mountain. Take your children and remain safely there. Connect deeply with the inner-earth and ensure that no memories are lost. We know you will greatly miss being with the outer world, the trees and all you love so. One day you will be reunited with your brothers and sisters again. Can you do this?" The twins nodded humbly.

Their instructions having been given and accepted, the Children bid farewell to Divine Mother and Father and returned to the present moment and task at hand.

On that beautiful long white beach, the very place they had first stepped foot on Tara, the twins created a dance that was the perfect embodiment of beauty and grace. They danced in honor of the earth, sky, sea, fire, and the Great Spirit within all things. They wove around them a shield of protection strong enough to endure throughout the ceremony.

Torches had been lit to honor the element of fire. Crystals had been placed along the shoreline, blessed by the refreshing waters of the sea.

The movement of their bodies was sensual and enticing as their spirits flowed with passion and great love, hips swayed like the tree limbs in the wind, feet stomped lightly to the beat of the Earth. In circles they turned in rhythm to the great sea's waving motion.

Their voices rang out with powerful harmony, giving thanks to the sun that brought them life and the fire that burned eternally throughout creation. The moon seemed to watch in silent wonder as these most beautiful Creators of the great blue planet called out with their dance.

The vision of each pair of twins, so perfectly matched the beauty of their element, combined with the fresh, youthful energy of the six children who were a part of their circle. They captured the very essence of the sea and sky around them.

The following morning, the Twins of Air sensed that the time was swiftly approaching for them to depart their beloved homeland. Though filled with dread and misery, they disciplined themselves to find the inner visions of what Mother and Father had described. Facing each other under a coconut tree sitting cross-legged they began to breath softly, like the gentle breeze that embraced the cloudless sky. At once the vision came to both of them, set in the distance from their Great Motherland lay an island, a small, quiet place, where no one had ever before journeyed to. They would be for the first time, alone in their union, separated from their dear siblings, whose fates they were to accept as well. On that one fateful day, too young and innocent, and in their own eyes too self-serving to listen, they had turned their backs on the wisdom of their elders.

As An looked into the deep emerald eyes of her strong and gentle Ayia, she knew the strength they gathered would surround and protect them once and for all.

Standing upon the golden sands one last time the Twins of Air held their hands to their hearts, giving eternal thanks to the Great Motherland, soaking up every last moment and offering their prayers for peace and wellness for all.

They turned toward the sea hand in hand. Wearing simple silken white garments and a few of their most treasured gemstones, they walked serenely into the sea, looking to the vast horizon.

They walked slowly forward until only their heads were above water, and then turned to look upon the great land once more. She loomed mighty and silent before them.

The twins turned and walked directly toward the center of the sun. They were being reborn through the sun's energies as they entered their new world. They swam silently, surrounded by dolphins, guiding them towards their new home. Their hearts were heavy, and as the sun began to set they feared for much.

Finally in the distance the twins saw a tiny speck of land, like a log floating on the open sea - their new home.

The magical island was a perfect new home; everywhere bright flowers stood to greet them and the trees provided abundant fruits. Ayia knew that their deepest healing would come from this solitude, from finding the playful nature they once shared so freely. There was much he wanted to learn and to evolve into but it was laughter and joy that he most wanted. He wanted more than anything for An to feel free of guilt and fear. They found near the sea a great waterfall with a deep pool. Together they leapt into the pool, laughing with delight. Later they lay near the pool on a soft mossy bank, slowly making love, knowing there was no one to disrupt their freedom.

They explored the island, finding magical streams filled with crystals, adventuring deep into caves, and resting on the warm sand.

Ayia and An had been gone from the Great Motherland for a time that felt both momentary and eternal to them. One morning as they awoke, they heard the call they had been expecting, and preparing for, from Divine Mother and Father. They were to spend the day walking to the top of the highest peak on their small island.

Each step would be one of prayer, of memory and gratitude for what had been. This would be the day their precious Lemuria would sink forever more below the sea.

Together they stood on the beach looking up at the majestic mountain. Covered entirely in lush greenery, its peak jutted out toward the pale blue sky, as though a finger pointing the way upward.

Hand in hand they walked to the forests edge and then turned first to face the sea, gazing out towards where their great land still stood strong. Their bodies trembled already with grief unimaginable to me. A blanket of darkness covered the motherland. They knew that they would never be truly safe or free in the way that they once were, until the darkness had been removed from their world. So there was no choice but to accept what was to come, as they had hope for their new life with the coming child. In that moment they realized that although some time had passed since their departure, and they thought that they had let go of what had been, they had not fully let go.

They stood at the top of the mountain at the center of the island. The sight of these vast gods standing at the top of this powerful pointed mountain peak, surrounded by a sea of green and the pale sky above, was awe-inspiring to say the least. They stood holding hands looking out towards the sun, united. Their outer hands turned palm face forward in surrender.

There was in one moment, complete silence. It was a silence that seemed to circle the entire globe. I could feel this through the twins. I felt the knowing of the land, that it would be gone in but a moment. Theirs was surrender and sacrifice of such grand proportions. So much loss, so much love.

In the next moment there was a great roaring sound that seemed to rip though the fabric of time. It was a sound of great release, yet so vastly tragic I knew that I would never, ever forget it, nor would the planet.

The land beneath the twins began to tremble subtly, like a small earthquake, and then tremendously, as the roar continued to reach across the globe. My eyes were wide- open as I watched the twins hold their focus inwards. Their forms hovered above the mountain, slightly, so very slightly. The trembling grew violent and the waters began to churn. All at once the world grew dark, pitch

black. I could feel, but
    not see, the great land sink below the waves, for there was no
sun.

I could see the moment of release in their eyes and how their
hearts ached with pain. They longed to be the innocent children
they once were, to fall on the ground and cry out with their pain,
as any child would. Yet, now, responsibility was their calling. They
had no time to spare.

Quickly the scene changed and I saw the Twins of Water,
with their two children standing in a like position atop a great
mountain in a new land, a land as wide and far as Lemuria had
been. It was surrounded by waters as far as the eye would see. My
throat felt choked. It was so good to see them.

Across the sea, where only moments before the great Lemuria
had been, were tiny islands, the mountaintops of that great land.
At the apex of one pyramid shaped island stood the fiery twins,
their arms reaching up powerfully towards the sky. The sea was full
of debris, trees limbs, logs, sadly dead bodies - sea creatures and
humans alike. I winced at the sight of death, but reminded myself
to be strong like the twins, to endure the pain of what I was seeing.
Death was liberation. Death was not the end. Those tribal people,
who had chosen not to heed the call, would have a chance to be in
light. It would have been better if they had heeded the call to be
sure.

These images, seen from the vast vantage point of beyond
were terrible and yet awesome. Here and there atop other of these
small islands, I could see some of the tribal members had survived.
Most sat clinging to each other, sobbing unceasingly. I could feel
their shock and loss. I would never forget those trembling forms,
wrapped around each other, weeping. I felt hopeful for their
transformation through such humility. It would stay with me
forever that in one moment there had been an entire continent,
larger than any of my current world, and in the next it was gone,
forever.

I then saw Tarcon just before the sinking. He heard the roar
that raced across the land and felt the trembling begin. At first
he gripped his chair. Then he yelled out, understanding what was
about to occur. He quickly said some words to a few of his highest
in command and they all raced toward his ship. He had heard the

tale through the

tribal people of what the twins had warned of. Though they did not heed it, he awaited its coming; always one step ahead of his once brother and sister's foresight.

His ship lifted into the sky and raced out beyond the atmosphere so quickly that it became a blur.

As all became silent, his ship quickly re-entered the atmosphere and soon landed on one of the mountaintops. I watched angrily as he got out of his ship and shook his fist at the sky triumphantly.

I was stunned, yet also amazed at the vastness I had just witnessed. The Great Motherland lay beneath the waves of the sea, its memory clearly still there, even to this day, I understood; there to always whisper its story, surfacing on the tides around the world. It was astounding to realize that somewhere out there beneath the waves, the land of Lemuria lay in ruins, indeed right off the shores of Hawaii, in the deep waters I swam in, the waters the dolphins lived in.

Time moved forward, as though to pull me out of the deep space of stunned silence the past scene had caused. Spread out across the sea the mountains floated as isolated islands of light in a watery world. Time passed and new ways of living came forth.

The Twins of Fire stood atop their mountain and bid farewell to their children, already then grown into adulthood. They had chosen to leave their human forms. Silently they rose into the air, and then before my very eyes they melted into molten lava, which then sank down into the rocky mountain crevices below. Quickly then, the brilliant red and orange liquid light fell back to the surface and began to ooze down the mountain side slowly, the image was mesmerizing. I could feel the great powerful spirit of fire and there was also a deep peace, almost calming in some way.

I watched in reverence as lava began to cool and take marvelous black shape across the land, beginning to extend outward in the sea as new cliff ledges hardened over once sea level white beaches. Indeed, I understood, there were many ways to create life.

The tribe members that had survived upon the great mountaintops quickly found humbleness. They began to listen attentively to all that was around them. Through this the Lemurian survivors began to notice the power of the lava that now flowed gently down the hillside. At night the Fire God and Goddess could be seen soaring above the flames.

Worship of these beings of light began to take place. At night the tribe's people gathered, calling out to the fire beings. Slowly they began to hear the messages offered by the gods. The tribes began to understand that they must care for each other and for the land. Over time the Twins of Air had grown more powerful. They no longer feared Tarcon and the reptilian gods. They had come to understand that the confrontation between themselves and Tarcon was inevitable. And so, at last, they let down their shields. They were no longer invisible, awaiting the fateful day when Tarcon would once more seek them out.

Tarcon stood on a raised platform. The large shadow of his hunched form displayed the spiky scales on his back and enormous head.

He began, "Even now the Tarians are unsuspecting of the great terror we will bring once more. Still though, they live knowing fear, none feel completely safe, not even the Children of Light."

He laughed, amused by his own plotting. "It is true we lost control over the Twins of Fire but their efforts are useless. No matter how hard they try to change the ways of the weak-minded tribes, I will still have power when I choose to."

The crowd rose in cheers, their master was giving them permission to wreak havoc once more. He ended with, "I am still in control of what moment I will bring deception to the Children of Light!" More than a touch of doubt and frustration could be heard in his tone.

"Rise now." He commanded, clearly enjoying speaking the words in Tarian tongue again. When they rose, they grinned stupidly at Tarcon and the other reptilians. "I have a purpose for you to fulfill. Go to the tribe's people, blend in with them but begin slowly to manipulate their way of thinking. Convince them once more of the need to think independently, not believing in the fire gods. Secretly destroy their children. The tribes are to have no idea what has happened to them. Once their thoughts are changed enough once more, we will come. We have more in store for the ignorant Tarians."

With that the session closed and I was a bit relieved, not feeling I could bear more that evening. It was all so very, very much. The twins lived in my heart now, their reality was almost more real than the present moment. I wanted to rest, to be normal for a time, but also to honor the twins and to think long and well about what all this meant to me, to our world.

But gosh, the plan was not even successful, the entire beautiful continent gone, just like that but Tarcon still alive and well and evil as ever...

CHAPTER THIRTY FOUR

Liberation

O rion and I flew back to the Big Island and drove to a spot he said I needed to initiate at after Molokai.

We arrived at the oceans edge and got out of the car. We were at some massive lava cliffs that loomed majestically above the vast ocean. There were no beaches, no bays, just the wide-open blue sea.

Orion spoke of the place we were. "The kahuna say this is the place where time does not exist, where time begins and ends. It is a portal into the spiritual realm. Are you ready to hear what your initiation is?"

I nodded eagerly.

Orion explained excitedly. "You see this cliff here, it is about fifty feet up. The water below is deep and powerful. You are meant to stand at the cliff's edge and call up all your fears. You ask to purify them, and then you jump."

I gasped. "Me - jump?" Fear was already pulsing through me.

Orion seemed nearly amused. "Yes, you call up all your fears and then you leap through the barriers of time, releasing on all levels everything that prevents you from being your greatest potential."

I peered out over the cliff. "Are you going to do it first?"

He laughed, feeling my concern, excited about what this all

meant. "I suppose for your first time, I could go first and wait for you in the water. But that certainly is making it easier for you."

My eyes were wide as I looked down at the clear water. I thought I could see all the way to the bottom though it looked very deep. Large waves rolled in, crashing against the cliff. I could see though, that I would land beyond the break.

Orion asked. "Can you pay attention to what the fears are, what they really are?"

I thought for a moment. "Fear of getting hurt, I guess. Fear of death; I could die in a jump like that." Saying it sounded strange. Hadn't I learned not to fear death that day on the cliff? I had but it had arisen again.

"Do you really think so?" Orion responded quickly as if hearing my thoughts. "Fear has to be cleansed from us often. It builds up in us. You see, our world is full of fear and we pick up on that."

"Well," I paused. "I know how to jump and land straight. It should look fun. Emotionally, I feel that I could die or get hurt."

Orion offered. "Take that fear of death and see it as death of ego, death of all that keeps you in fear."

I swallowed. "Okay."

Orion took off his shirt and hair-tie. He then stood at the edge and looked with great focus upon the horizon. To my surprise, he the dove head first into the deep waters. Watching him so bravely plummet fifty-feet headfirst stirred more fear in me. I'd seen a lot of cliff diving when I was younger, but nothing topped this, it was almost supernatural. Suddenly, it was my turn!

I walked to the edge and felt like my heart jumped off the cliff first. I pulled it back with a quick breath, trembling immediately with great fear and worked to steady the dizzy feeling that filled my head. Below Orion treaded water, the powerful surf pushed and pulled him with the rise and fall of the tide.

I held my arms out to my sides and began to allow fear to surface. Some fear I could identify. There was the fear of death, fear of getting hurt, fear of sharks. I glanced at the ladder I knew we were meant to climb. The metal steps swayed in the air, with the lowest step reaching only to about three feet above sea level. As the waves rose, the ladder was closer to the water.

I looked out to the horizon. The sun was beginning to lower

in the sky. I sensed the power of the energy at this place. As I
allowed my gaze to soften, I realized I could see some sort of form
hovering in the air past Orion toward the horizon. I allowed my
vision to relax more. There was a figure! It was about fifty feet fall
tall and twenty feet wide. It shimmered with white light. I could
then see that it was the figure of a male presence, god-like, or angel-
like. I began to make out the chiseled face.

At that point I knew I had no choice, there was no way I
would back out. I worried Orion might be getting cold. I told
myself it should be fun, like the high dive back home or the cliffs
in Kentucky my cousins and I used to jump from. But no, it was
nothing like that. I truly felt that I was about to leap through
time, but instead of doing that with my spirit, this time I would be
bringing my whole body with me!

With that I lifted my arms above my head and leapt. My
heart seemed to jump out before me. Time seemed to stand still
for me then. It seemed like only a second, and yet it also seemed
eternal, as I watched the sky whiz by me, my heart in my throat.
My body plummeted below the surface with great force. I went
down and down until I thought I wouldn't rise, then the pull
reversed and I rose slowly to the surface. The water was surprisingly
welcoming, refreshing. I broke through the surface with a laugh.

Orion yelled out. "You did it!"

I wanted to yell too but in that moment I remembered the
God-like Being standing in the sky. I became quiet, reverent.
I felt the power of the water then, humbling, mysterious,
overwhelmingly energetic.

I offered a prayer. "Thank you Great Spirit, thank you angels
and Gods, thank you Pelé, ocean, rocks, thank you sun, thank you
Life!"

For a few more moments I floated in the vastness, which was
beyond time, beyond words. When I lifted my head, I knew that I
was once more, a new being, reborn.

Later, after sunset we drove to a nearby beach we were
destined to camp at. Tired, I slept the entire way.

When we arrived I was still sleepy and it was all I could do
to get into my sleeping bag and curl up. I slept long but sometime
late in the night I woke up. The sky was bright with the half moon
hovering above us. I was happy to smell the salty air, and to feel

the warm tropical air once more. Soon the Council called, and I returned to their presence.

CHAPTER THIRTY FIVE

Council of Elders Take Action

The council sat in silence. In the center sat Lady Nada, Lord Sananda, and the elders.

Lady Nada rose to her feet and swept her hands out in a gesture of love. "Luna, this session is different. Watch the screen now and be taken back to the fateful day the decision was made to aid your world. You will recall from our very first meeting how I told you we made a plan in the year 1972 based on our review of the planetary records."

I silently communicated that I remembered. "Luna you have now seen for yourself how things were in the First Time. You have learned the true potential of your kind. There is more to see, more to the records. But you are ready now to see what decision was made that will have the greatest impact upon your world."

I nodded my understanding and the council turned to watch the screen. An was there, with the council, looking just as she did in Lemuria, ageless and eternal. I looked around the room. An spoke effortlessly, calmly. "We are aware of what must occur and we feel blessed for the opportunity. We must all return to Tara, the Children of Light, all those who stand strong in the Law of the One must incarnate once more on Earth. We must stand strong for what we know to be true. If we who are of free-will consciousness do not allow darkness to rule Earth, then it shall not."

An continued, "We must raise the awareness on the planet, we must raise the energy. We will go to restore the sacred lands, and the ancient ways!"

Sananda spoke, "Will you strive with your greatest intentions to reclaim your rightful heritage? Will you do this knowing that we will all be with you?"

An stood and placed her hands in prayer at her heart, responding thus. "My lord, we have tried and tried again, but never have we found complete success. Indeed we thought we had to do it mostly alone, only calling upon Io and Ama when the greatest need was there." She paused and looked searchingly around the room. "On behalf of my siblings I will accept your generosity, we will once more return to Tara in our highest capacity to do so."

Lady Nada rose to embrace An and the crowd cheered gloriously. Then as one, they sang out in loving response to the need on Earth - "Thy Will Be Done, Thy Will Be Done."

I sensed the Council would not call me for some time. They would allow me to write the great saga of Lemuria first. My eyes were wide with anticipation of this great task. How would I find the words?

My throat ached, not wanting to leave the council, but they were already saying good-bye. I had to let go, knowing I would not forget them or the story that lived and breathed in my every cell.

CHAPTER THIRTY SIX

Honor Yourself

Iwoke to the familiar warmth of the sun on my face. I buried my face beneath my sleeping bag, wanting to relinquish all I had just seen. My heart was struck with grief.

I sat up cross-legged, my eyes closed. I felt unsettled. Images of my family and friends at home seemed to pull at me. I thought of my little brother, lost in a teenage world of drugs and alcohol. I thought of Julia who had returned from her journeys. I thought of my dog, I missed her so much, and my oak tree and the creek out back.

I knew somehow without having time to think about it, I was going home. I was going back to the place that represented human thirst for control and consumption. I would return to all those that I loved. I had gathered so much strength, so much understanding. Now I would share it with others. I supposed this somehow made sense.

I opened my eyes looking out over the sea. I was surprised at how this unexpected decision seemed to have arisen within me over night. I wasn't leaving Hawaii for good, or the teachings of Orion forever. I would return, I envisioned, after a few months. The thought of going home was almost eerie. I would be walking through a world controlled by darkness. Would I see things as I never had before?

My energies were unsettled, but I had made my choice. I rose and walked calmly into the sea

I thought about how good it was to have no material attachments. I had little money, yet trusted I would be provided for, as I needed to be. I would fly stand-by for

$100, then take the public bus system through San Francisco to Sonoma County. It was strange to think about that place while sitting in paradise. They were truly worlds apart. At least it was summer by now, and it would be hot rather then rigidly cold and gray. I lay on the beach thinking it all over.

Orion's words startled me out of my inward thoughts. "Are you asleep?"

I sat up quickly. "No, not at all, I was just enjoying the sun."

Orion smiled down at me. "Would you like to go get coconuts with me?"

I smiled back. "I would love to."

We drove in silence to a near-by resort where Orion said there were trees low enough that you could reach up and pick the nuts. Meanwhile, I contemplated how to tell him the news.

Orion chattered excitedly. "They are the best kind, Samoan dwarves. The nuts are full of perfectly sweet water, not too sour, not too sweet.

"Yeah." Orion continued enthusiastically. "Did you know coco water was used to replace blood plasma in the Vietnam War? It's that close to our blood make up. And it makes your body release toxins in a big way."

I did find it interesting. "Wow." I responded.

We arrived in the hotel parking lot, finding a spot in the corner, near the maintenance area. Orion led me down a beautiful manicured path alongside a hotel corridor.

We found the grove of trees near the hotel beach, nestled in next to a quiet cove. The hotel seemed quiet. Only a few people passed by, curious to see Orion pluck the nuts and crack them open with his machete, one by one. I sat on the lawn and blissfully drank the sweet water. I drank nut after nut until I felt I would burst.

After awhile we silently returned to the car. Just as Orion was about to start the car, I unexpectedly stopped him.

I never knew why I chose that seemingly odd moment in

time to speak. "Wait, there is something I need to tell you."

Orion looked alarmed. My voice was casual. "I have decided to go home for awhile."

I looked up at Orion blankly. His face clearly displayed displeasure, but no anguish. "What? What do you mean, home?"

I replied. "To the Bay Area, I want to try to help my friends and family to see how much they are missing in life." My eyes were filled with innocence.

Orion barked. "What! That is crazy. You agreed to let me protect you and to teach you!"

I could see he was very upset and spoke cautiously. "Yes, but first of all, I have already done so much inner-work, I need a break. Also, there has been so much that has been confusing between us. I need a break from the intensity."

Orion interrupted angrily. "The intensity? Why can't you see that it is love?"

He had said the wrong thing as far as I was concerned. My own fiery nature had been provoked. "This is exactly why I need to go. I need space to understand what this all is. Mostly, I want to see my friends, to help people."

Orion snapped. "You have no idea what you are doing or why. Can't you see that it is darkness that is pulling you?" He didn't wait for me to answer. "You have come so far. You are so important to everything that happens, can't you see that now, even just a little bit?"

I thought I heard an undermining tone there. I responded, "What are you so afraid of?"

Clearly that comment really upset Orion. His eyes were now ablaze with fire. "I am afraid because you still have no idea who you are or why you need to be protected!"

I was so very, very tired of hearing that. I put my hands over my ears. "Stop, stop!"

Orion spoke so loud my body shook. "I won't stop, it is my job to protect you and you won't even let me. You want to know why I am afraid? I am afraid because you are throwing yourself to the wolves. You have no idea what awaits you there in that God-forsaken place you call home."

My defenses were rising. "I know it isn't paradise. But it is where I came from and everyone I care about is there."

I had not meant to hurt Orion, but clearly I had. His body flinched and the look in his eyes was beginning to become wild, scaring me.

"Luna, you have no idea that you have no idea." His eyes seemed to move to some distant place. "If you go back there, something will attack you and I am not at all certain you will survive."

For a moment I thought there really was something he was seeing, and it scared me. But then I was angry all over again. "How dare you say things to scare me just because you can't stand to not control me, or possess me!"

There was a burst of wind around me and before I knew what was happening, Orion leapt across the seat grabbing me around the chest. In one quick movement it threw both of us out the open door and onto the pavement. My head and side hit the ground hard. The weight of Orion crushed me down, knocking the breath out of me. For a moment I saw purple and wondered if I was dying. Then I felt the pain in my head and down my side. I couldn't breathe. Orion was crushing me and my side ached tremendously.

I realized he was moving. He was holding me down, speaking. "You have no idea. I will keep you here and protect you even if I have to kill you and then resurrect your body."

Alarm raced through my body. It was this, this monstrous part of Orion that I had sensed and feared all along. I couldn't believe this was happening. Had he just said he would kill me? And resurrect me? Did he really think he could do that?

"Get off of me Orion, I can't breathe." I could hardly get the words out.

Orion squeezed harder. "Tell me you won't let your ego control your life, tell me you won't let it destroy you."

I would never believe that, but I needed this maniac off me! "I won't, I won't - now get off me!"

Searching my eyes, still full of rage, Orion released his hold and sat down on the pavement with his head in his hands. I struggled to sit up, gasping for breath. Each breath sent startling pain down my oblique. I looked around. No one was there, no one had seen. I could have been killed under the mad craze of this obsessed man on the concrete between two cars. I glanced at him frantically.

He was looking only at the ground, his eyes still wild.

I whispered through jabbing pain. "You really hurt me."

Orion said only. "You have no idea what you are walking into and I won't be there to save you."

I reached up for the car door and slowly pulled myself onto the seat, holding my aching side. I didn't know it yet, but Orion had probably fractured my rib. It would be over a month until I could breathe or move without pain again.

I stared numbly into the distance and said only. "Take me back to the beach, please. Leave me there."

Orion began to protest again but I turned my face and looked deep into his eyes. I had found a place of self- preservation, self-love. "Don't say another word. What you have done is wrong, so wrong. I don't care who you are, you need help."

He blinked as though hearing that he needed help, humbled him just a little. "No, you don't understand. You provoked that in me."

Even through the pain and shock I was angry. "How dare you physically abuse me and then blame me! I will not fall for that. Take me to the beach now."

Orion paused, a desperate look came over his face. "Luna, I am sorry, I had to try something. You are just so stubborn. I can't see you get hurt."

"You can't control me Orion. You will have to let me go."

Panicked, he searched my cool eyes. "You will still come back though, right."

I thought to myself, 'He is so selfish, my rib is probably broken and all he can think of is whether I will come back to him, it's crazy!' But I said, "If I have any sense, no I will never see you again."

Orion pleaded. "I am so sorry sweetie, so sorry. I just want to protect you."

I wrapped my arms around my ribcage to still the pain. "You will have to let me go to see if I will return."

Silently he drove me to the beach and watched me limp away in pain, my pack thrown over my shoulder. I felt his gaze at my back as I began to walk down the trail.

Each step was painful. The physical pain was so deep, but the emotional pain was deeper. I still felt in shock. He, who was my Teacher, had just violently attacked me. I was more alone than ever.

I slowly lifted my pack off my shoulder and sat down through piercing pain. I had enough food and water for two days, and then I would go home.

For a long time I just sat looking vacantly out to sea. I wasn't present. I wasn't anywhere but stuck between pain and fear. Somehow knowing that someone had hurt me, let alone my teacher, made me feel suddenly very unsafe in the world.

I cried myself to sleep through the pain. I must have slept really deeply. I woke on the beach with the rising sun. I looked around and saw no one.

For a moment I closed my eyes, a shudder moved through me. My vision seemed to spread out across the mainland of America, people were dying everywhere, and the rivers were clogged with thick black slime, and on the ocean's surface miles of plastic debris floated along.

Later that day I gathered my belongings and slowly, wincing through the pain, limped through the parking lot. Leaving in this way did not cause me to feel my journey was off to a good start.

I was surprised to hear Orion's voice. "Hi."

I looked up and there he was sitting on the top on his car. His blue eyes sparkled in the bright sunlight. I was very surprised to see him there, though I said nothing.

"Luna, I am so sorry. I was here all night. I didn't dare come near you. You wouldn't have wanted me to. But I knew you would need a ride, it's the least I can do."

I put my pack down, holding my side. "Given my condition, I will accept the ride." My voice was a cold whisper.

Orion forced a smile, though his face showed deep sadness. "There isn't any way I can convince you to stay. I know what I did was wrong. I just care about you so much. I feel like you're throwing yourself from the frying pan to the fire."

I couldn't imagine what he meant. Once again his intensity seemed just like melodrama. I had always been safe at home, apparently safer than here. I shook my head.

"No I need to go. I might come back, maybe, I don't know. But if I did... " I looked at my hands and backed up. "You would have to promise me nothing like that would ever happen again."

Orion leapt to his feet and sank to his knees. "If you return to me, my love, I promise to spend the rest of my life protecting you."

I had no idea if that could be true.

We drove in silence, tension filling the car. As we pulled into departures, Orion reached his hand out, but I pulled away. I got out and silently walked away, each step agonizing pain. If not to Orion, then to the dolphins, and the sound of the doves in the morning, and the warm sun on my face as it sank into the sea … to the land that had once been - Lemuria.

I was going home a new person, perhaps not knowing how different, or how all the events would catch up over time and carve me even more. I wasn't sure I would ever see the magic island again, or what the future had in store. One thing was certain, I would never forget my time, and all the people and places along the way.

I would never forget the story I'd been shown of Lemuria. I wondered if I would be shown more, that of Atlantis and the next saga of our world: once known as Tara.

About the Author

Taya Raine is a spiritual teacher, guide & healer based in The Hawaiian Islands.

Taya offers teachings that come from the origins of Lemuria, Atlantis, and Egypt. Utilizing amazing tools for awakened consciousness, Taya is a luminary whose passion it is to help guide humanity back into our ever-unfolding potential light.

Taya lives on the island of Maui, Hawaii. She offers sessions, workshops, and retreats in person and online.

Currently Taya is working on book two Tara Legend of the Earth- book two "The Immortals". In book two we journey into Atlantis, and Egypt as the Children of One continue their path on Tara; along with the continued journey of Luna where she travels back to California and eventually returns to Hawaii.

Additionally, Tara: Legend of The Earth comes with a free workbook! The workbook includes some introductory spiritual exercises and additional content relating to the Tara teachings. Found on the website.

Check out *tayaraine.com* for more or look up Taya on instagram.

Artist Aknowledgment

Kai Wilder

All art, illustrations and book design for this book, "Tara", were done by the amazing artist **Kai Wilder**. Kai is such an incredible human, one of the best I have ever known! I am deeply inspired by his artistry and the way he walks in life.

I have so much gratitude for the journey we endeavored with to co-create the vision of what this incredible art became and for Kai's stead-fast commitment to create the wonderous masterpiece paintings for the front and back cover. Kai is a visionary who has such a gift for bringing magic into artistic form this way.

I am eternally grateful for the life-long friendship, as well as deep soul connection that spans lifetimes: I bow in honor with reverence for this art; I couldn't be happier with it.

You can find his work on his website *www.kaiwilder.com* and instagram: *@kaiwilderart*

I give so many thanks to you Kai!
Mahalo Nui Loa

Tara Teachings
Publishing

Tara: Legend of The Earth
Book Two: The Immortals

Coming soon...

Mahalo Nui Aloha
God bless you and may you always walk
in the pure energy of the eternal light

Taya Raine

CPSIA information can be obtained
at www.ICGtesting.com
Printed in the USA
BVHW081804040522
635778BV00001B/3